NICOLE CLARKSTON

BESS
and the
HIGHWAYMAN

Rogues in Disguise One

PROPER ROMANCE

Ebook ISBN: 978-1-957082-19-6

Paperback ISBN: 978-1-957082-20-2

Cover Design by GetCovers.com

Cover Image Licensed by Period Images

Background image licensed by Shutterstock

Blog and Website: https://nicoleclarkston.com/

Newsletter: subscribepage.io/V5dPFd

Book Bub: https://www.bookbub.com/profile/nicole-clarkston

Facebook: https://www.facebook.com/NicoleClarkstonAuthor

Twitter: https://twitter.com/N_Clarkston

Amazon: https://www.amazon.com/Nicole-Clarkston

Austen Variations: http://austenvariations.com/

Contents

Dedication		V
Prologue		1
1.	Chapter 1	4
2.	Chapter 2	12
3.	Chapter 3	19
4.	Chapter 4	27
5.	Chapter 5	34
6.	Chapter 6	43
7.	Chapter 7	53
8.	Chapter 8	61
9.	Chapter 9	68
10.	Chapter 10	76
11.	Chapter 11	83
12.	Chapter 12	90
13.	Chapter 13	97
14.	Chapter 14	105
15.	Chapter 15	112
16.	Chapter 16	121
17.	Chapter 17	128
18.	Chapter 18	138
19.	Chapter 19	147

20.	Chapter 20	155
21.	Chapter 21	166
22.	Chapter 22	173
23.	Chapter 23	182
24.	Chapter 24	192
25.	Chapter 25	209
26.	Chapter 26	217
27.	Chapter 27	223
28.	Chapter 28	229
29.	Chapter 29	236
30.	Chapter 30	244
Epilogue		254
From Nicole Clarkston		258

To my love,
Thank you for letting me disappear into a book for months at a time, and still finding me on the other end.

Prologue

August 29, 1810
Bittern Hollow Posting Inn
Surrey

"**A**NOTHER ALE FOR THE table in the back!"

Bess Reynolds balanced the tray she had been filling with glasses and set it up on her shoulder. "I'm a-coming, Papa," she called. The man who had hired the private parlor had been a rather well-paying customer this evening, and she had discovered quickly enough to just keep her tray full.

And to stay out of reach.

He was the typical London sort—a merchant from the queues with more money than class, either on holiday in the rural districts or on his way to Brighton. A carefree, heavy-spending sort of man, the type who preferred a wench on each knee and another to fill his hands. But for now, his hands were probably still smarting from the last time he had tried to grab her.

She set down the pint and tried to whirl away before the sweating, red-faced man had even registered her presence. She was not fast enough. A tug at the knot of her apron dragged her backward until she was nearly sitting on the table.

"'Ere's a fine thing," he slurred. "I pays well for me drinks and a bit o' company. 'Ow's it I still 'ave a cold place on me lap?"

Bess shot a caustic glance at the place he indicated, between the other girls. "It's probably cold because it's rotting away, you derelict."

Mr. London, whatever his name was, roared with laughter. "I likes a lass wi' a sharp tongue! Bring another round for me and me girls 'ere!"

He released her without a struggle, but Bess did not return immediately. He was already well into his cups, and soon he would either start to sing to the entire room or fall into a drooling stupor on the table.

It was not as if she needed to invent other things to do, for the tavern was busier than usual. A group of travelers had struck up a card game, calling for plenty of spirits, and several men sat in a row at the bar, each alone with his thoughts and his drink. Some of them were regulars and would take their cares home with them in an hour, but others would stay on until morning or the next mail coach. None of them were remarkable for anything other than the coins they slid to her.

"Ale!" called one of them. Bess dropped it promptly and pocketed his coin. He turned in sharp interest as she moved away. "You must be the one they talk about." His eyes raked shamelessly over her, and he puckered his lips in a low whistle. Slowly, his hand reached into his purse and withdrew a five-pound note. He held it up with a suggestive grin as old as the world.

Bess arched her brows and smiled sweetly. "Aren't you the generous fellow?"

The man leaned forward on the bar. "I would say I'm more discerning than generous. A fellow can't have a duchess for a pittance, can he?"

She set a hand on her hip and pretended to consider. "But what good is it to take the title of a duchess, who is paid only once for her favors?" She leaned low and whispered, "Mine come somewhat more dearly."

His grin widened to a positive leer, and he found a second fiver to join the first. "How dearly?"

She slid a hand over his shoulder. "Ten pounds... a minute," she whispered.

The man bellowed in laughter. "Ten pounds a minute, indeed!"

She nodded. "And your minute is up." She plucked the notes from his hand and tucked them suggestively into her bodice as he stared gap-mouthed at her. "You are most kind, sir," she said, backing away and blowing him a kiss.

"Here, now!" he protested. With convenient timing, another customer pushed between them, shoving the first man's shoulder, and squeezing himself in at the bench. Solemn gray eyes locked on Bess's, and he held up a single finger.

She gave him the last ale on her tray, and he immediately bent over it, never looking up at her again. That suited her well enough, because the other man was still sputtering helplessly about, as if seeking remedy against her. It was time to disappear in the back.

For a moment, she paused to stretch her shoulders, roll her neck, and check her reflection in the darkened window. For pity's sake, she looked all a-beazled! Stray bits of black hair clung to her brow, her cheeks were splotched and red, and her eyes were puffy from bending over the kettle. One would have thought it would keep the likes of Mr. London's eyes and hands off her, but it never seemed to. If anything, the more harried she felt she looked, the more offers she received.

Papa never said a word, either about her appearance or the men she had to constantly rebuff. Mama would have chided her, though. "You won't make tips if you don't show the gents a bit of cheer, Bessie," she would have said. But that was not true, was it? The ten pounds were a glorious boon, but they would join the pint of coins she was keeping under her bed, all of which had come from men who wanted more than ale from her. No, she had no trouble making tips.

And Bess was weary of showing cheer. She was sick of having her rear slapped by jolly travelers, and disgusted by the leering stares that she was supposed to reward with a smile. But what was she to do? She was the landlord's daughter—a tavern wench who lived by her wits and her looks. And the good Lord had blessed her with an ample quantity of both.

She brushed impatiently at her hair. But why bother? She was happier looking a little rumpled, and it was time to fill more glasses. Papa would be calling for them at any moment.

Chapter One

One Week Earlier
Near Blackheath

CAPTAIN NICHOLAS HUNT WAS no stranger to being shot at. He took exception, however, when the balls were also flying at his men. And his best horse.

"Pin him down, lads!" he shouted to his officers, flanking him somewhere in that murky wood. "Look sharp! He has another pistol!"

He caught the reins in his teeth and called for everything his horse could give him. Brandishing his pistol in one hand and his sword in the other, man and steed charged after the villain. Round two trees they went, under a low branch, and into a narrow gulley. For an instant, Nick had a clear sight of the rogue.

He fired, and the ghostly form stumbled. A hit—but not a mortal shot, for the crimson cloak swirled about, the glittering eyes now piercing him from under a tricorn hat. The brigand's left hand braced into his wounded chest, but his right leveled a flintlock at Nick's head. He hissed to his horse and pulled him into a tight swerve around a tree. He'd veer sharply left, then run the criminal into the ground.

The pistol cracked. Nick braced himself for the ball of fire, somewhere deep in his belly, but there was nothing. That was when his horse, Roy, shuddered.

"No, no, no, Roy!"

The great gray's strides checked and faltered. Nick pulled up on the reins, trying to slow and steady the animal, but it was no good. Roy's head buckled under him, his knees folded, while his hind legs were still thrusting him forward. Horse and man drove head-first to the ground, then flipped, mere feet from a massive oak.

Roy instantly began floundering, trying to recover his feet, but Nick's boot was still in the iron. If his horse kept plunging, his leg would snap like a twig. Nick lunged over the fallen horse's neck and dragged on the rein to keep him down.

Sergent Daniels was immediately at his side, covering Roy's eye and trying to soothe the injured horse. "Did he hit you, Captain?"

"No, but my leg is pinned. Where is North?"

"I saw him jump from his horse right before I caught up to you. I think he got our man. Stay still, sir, please. Wesson! Come help the captain!"

Wesson arrived next, and the two sergeants struggled to rock poor Roy up to his chest. Nick kicked and pushed until he was free, then swayed unsteadily to his feet. His breeches were slick with blood, and his horse was groaning. What had he done? He felt down the white shoulder until his hand found the ragged wound in the darkness. "Oh, Roy. Good boy, steady. Easy, my good lad. Save your strength."

"Captain!" North called from the darkness. "Can you come?"

Nick muttered a curse. The law would not wait for wounded horses and men. "Daniels, keep him down if you can. Wesson, use my neck cloth and try to stop the blood." He spared a last pat for his horse's ghostly neck and limped toward the last place he had seen the shots fired from. North was dimly outlined in the moonlight as he stood with head lowered. The highwayman lay at his feet, silent and still.

"Did you kill him?"

"I never touched him," North answered. "Just before I reached him, he staggered and fell."

Nick set his teeth grimly and rolled the man over—none too gently. There was a faint groan. "See here, Cumberland," he commanded, "We know who you are and what your real business was. You have been apprehended by a special detachment of King George's own Light Cavalry. As your head is worth more off your shoulders than otherwise, you would do well to answer my questions straightaway."

"It's no good, sir," North murmured, pointing to a spreading dark stain on the highwayman's silk shirt. "You must have hit him in the lung."

Nick lifted Cumberland's head. The man's jaw fell slack, his eyes rolling helplessly to the sky. One last wheezing rattle pronounced his end.

Nick let the man drop and straightened. "Well, that's it, then. Six months of tracking. Blast, but I was hoping to make him talk!"

North pointed over his shoulder with a thumb. "He abandoned his horse just before he entered the wood. Probably a decoy. Mayhap there be something in the saddlebags."

"If we can catch the beast. Local legend claims he is as wily as his master was. Well, nothing for it. Have the boys collect him. I'll see to poor old Roy."

R OB ROY, HIS GALLANT gray charger, would never serve under His Majesty's colors again.

It was a shoulder wound, deep enough to tear hide and muscle, but at least the ball had passed clean through. There was a chance it might heal, and perhaps someday Roy could serve for light cart work or something of the sort. An indignity for such a noble campaigner, a horse who had stormed Boney's cannon and carried orders from the king himself.

The merciful thing would be to put the old soldier down, but Nick could not bring himself to do it. Not yet. He tended the injury himself, dressing it with spirits and his own handkerchief as a wound packing. Then he ordered Daniels to minister to the animal overnight and went to find North and Wesson.

"We caught that black brute over a mile up the road," Wesson reported. He was still short of breath and his sleeve was in ribbons.

"Good heavens, what happened to you?"

Wesson stabbed a finger into the darkness. "We were wrong, Captain. The real villain was not Cumberland, but his horse!"

"Oh, come, Wesson. It is only a horse. Let us see it. Did you tether it with the others?"

"No, sir. They're afraid of the beast. I tied him over here by the tree. Watch yourself, sir. I didn't rip my sleeve running through the brush."

Nick grunted. "Indeed." The three men approached hesitantly, stopping to study the animal from several feet away. The object of their pensive stares, a massive black horse of the Spanish type, appeared positively unruffled. Until Nick approached, and the monster nearly bit him.

Nick was quick enough to free the saddle bags and duck out of the way, and none too soon, for a hoof chased him off. He glared at the horse for a moment, then began a search through the contents of the saddlebag. A clean white silk shirt; a knot of ladies' handkerchiefs; the expected clutch of pilfered coins and jewelry, and various articles of stolen finery that would fetch a price.

Finally, in a secretive cut between the layers of leather, he found a slip of paper. It was scribbled in French, and Nick held it up to the light.

"Here it is, lads," he announced. "Absolute proof that Cumberland was in league with the Tyrant. Carrying messages, he was."

"But to whom?" North asked.

"I cannot say. It mentions a 'monk at the Old Shag,' but no names." He folded the note and tapped it against his finger. "Saddle a horse for me. I am going to London."

August 23, 1810
London

NICK WAS AT WHITEHALL by morning, with time enough to spare for cleaning up his uniform and scavenging something to eat. By the time General Richards arrived, Captain Nicholas Hunt was ready to present himself. He was not kept waiting.

"Well, you ran down the Scarlet Bandit at last," Richards grunted in satisfaction. "What have you got for me?"

"A dead body and a note. We found little else on him or his horse. Lieutenant North is investigating the area to learn where Cumberland laid his head at night, when he was not posing as a common traveler. We may yet find something of use."

Richards unfolded the paper and scrutinized it. "Mmm. So, he was indeed a message carrier. I thought you were mad, you know—a man who was already wanted, dallying in spy work? I cannot believe the French had aught to do with him. Too risky."

"But if they ever caught him, who would think he was a spy? He would be shot or hanged forthwith, for his own countrymen already had no love for him. Also, he could get to and from someone in an influential position," Nick pointed out. "No one would suspect that a robbery was truly a treasonous liaison. And is there a more convenient means of selling off stolen jewelry, items that might be recognized, than to pass them into the hands of the French? The arrangement paid well for both parties."

"Indeed, indeed. So, you have your man, but you do not have his master. What now, Hunt?"

"The trail has not yet grown cold, sir. With your permission, I mean to find this 'monk at the Old Shag' and discover what he knows."

The general shook his head. "The moment he sees your uniform riding into the parish, he will be as good as gone."

"So, I go dressed as a merchant. Do you know what he means by The Old Shag?"

Richards sat back in his chair and stroked his chin with a chuckle. "Now, there's an unfortunate name!"

"Indeed, sir. I thought perhaps it was a joke."

"Oh, it is no joke. At least, there is such a place, or was, sixty years ago. My father used to keep me awake with ghost stories as a lad. There was a legend about a beast who would drag travelers off to a particular stone in a piddling little brook to devour them. Nonsense, naturally, and some years back, the parson had enough of such foolishness and got rid of that troublesome stone. I doubt there are many who even know of that tale now."

"Where was this supposed thing?"

"Oh! Off in Surrey. Buckland."

Nick squinted thoughtfully. "Close to Reigate Heath."

"Eh?"

"I beg your pardon, sir. Our Mr. Cumberland favored the well-trod haunts of the highwaymen of old. We found him near Blackheath, but he might as easily have worked Reigate."

The brigadier general nodded slowly. "Perhaps."

"With your permission, sir, I would like to see what I turn up."

"Hunt, you know perfectly well what we are up against. This was no mere footpad you have been tracking, but a well-connected, thoroughly devious rascal with a reputation for shooting at anyone who came near. Bloody wonder he never killed anyone!"

"He was not aiming to kill. Until last night," Nick added ruefully.

"I don't believe that for a second, but no matter. The sort of men he would have dealt with know your type, even without a uniform. You practically reek of duty and command.

What, do you think you can appear on the edges of town, drop a few coins, and instantly have your questions answered? Your quarry will vanish like a hare."

"And go even further underground." Nick nodded. "You do not have to remind me, sir. We tracked Cumberland for six months, and it was a mere stroke of luck that we learned where to find him last night. A tavern wench, if you must know."

Richards arched a brow. "Ah, to be a field officer again, wooing loose maidens for stray bits of tittle-tattle."

Nick stiffened. "It was Lieutenant North, sir. He performed an exemplary service for his king."

"I'd wager he did." Richards shook his head. "No, Hunt, I cannot risk letting the enemy see you coming. Even if we were sure this 'monk' was to be found at Buckland, what is to keep them from merely slitting your throat? Best to focus your efforts on the area around Blackheath, see what else you can turn up about Cumberland's activities. We have other traitors to catch, after all."

"With all due respect, sir, I would be astonished if we found so much as a button. My men and I are of the opinion that we could draw out an informant if we..." He stopped to clear his throat. "That is, if we proceed as though Cumberland were not lying cold in a potter's field."

"You mean if we continued to send men out 'looking' for him?"

"I mean... if we had someone pose as Cumberland. Someone credible, who could act the part just convincingly enough that his contacts will carry on as if nothing is amiss."

Richards pursed his lips. "I'm listening, Hunt. Go on."

"Well, sir, we have discovered that Cumberland would disappear effectively for two or three weeks, and then hit a cluster of well-heeled travelers. Never on the same part of the road, but in a sort of pattern. Then, he would go quiet again. We believed his initial robberies were a map, after a fashion, telling his actual target where and when to find him to pass along his message."

"That would explain how one party found him, but where would he meet the Tyrant's agent?"

"We have not discovered that, sir, but we believe this note might be the clue we were searching for."

Richards sighed and pushed out of his chair to slowly pace the room. "What is your exact plan?"

"Sir, I presume you have in your ranks men of... certain skills. Men who can operate on the edge of the law, if you know what I mean."

"Criminal activity in the service of the crown?" the general scoffed. "You want someone to play the part of the highwayman, holding up civilians and running about the countryside causing fear and mayhem? Captain, you know I cannot authorize such a thing lightly."

"I know that, sir, and I would not recommend it save at the end of need. It is the only means we can think of to track down Cumberland's contacts without starting from the beginning, and as you know, every day lost here may prove critical on the Continent."

"Yes, yes, I see. Go on, Hunt."

Nick wetted his lips and forged ahead. "If you can provide me with such a man, my officers and I will operate discreetly on the outskirts, as we have done so far."

"I have no one to spare. It will have to be one of your men. Does not North speak fluent French?"

"He does," Nick answered hesitantly, "but he is too fair and his voice is too deep to pass himself off as Cumberland. Even under that ridiculous velvet coat and all. Unfortunately, I am the closest match we have, and not a good one at that. Cumberland had twenty years on me."

"How is your French?"

Nick laughed nervously. "I was not meaning to offer myself, sir. I have not the talents to—good heavens! I could never dream of holding up a coach!"

"You are all we have, Hunt. If you think this plan is worth pursuing, it must be you. Fewer mouths to whisper, and your men will follow your orders implicitly."

"It is not my own men I worry about. Highwaymen tend to attract lead balls."

Richards snorted and waved a hand. "You needn't worry about the coachmen. Half of them cannot shoot even standing on the ground, let alone atop a moving box. Watch for rich carriages carrying ladies, and their coachmen will beg you to leave without violence. As a matter of fact, did not Cumberland have something of a reputation for kissing the more cooperative among his victims?"

Nick's lip curled. "They kissed him. And still refused to describe his face afterward."

"Great gads!" the general breathed. "Perhaps I have been in the wrong line of work."

"General, it is not merely the act of impersonating the rogue that troubles me. It seems highly likely that I might be shot by my fellow soldiers. The militia are bound to take an interest, and they will only see a villain with a price on his head. How will you manage them?"

"I? My dear fellow, I do not think you understand. If you insist on the necessity of this operation, you do it alone. If I send the alert out to the Regiment, your secrecy is blown."

Nick tried to hide his scowl and was only partially successful. He cast his eyes up to the ceiling, desperate to concoct some other plan, but nothing came to him. "Is there anything you can do for my protection, should I take this assignment?"

"Again, you are mistaken, Hunt. You have convinced me that this thing must be done, so I am ordering you to do it. As for your protection, I expect a letter of assignment and identification will go some way toward keeping your neck out of the noose, in case you are caught... alive."

Chapter Two

August 29, 1810
The Bittern Hollow Inn

"B Y GAW. FLEECED BY the Duchess of Surrey." The man beside Nick at the bar nursed his drink as though he might never have another one. His eyes never left the raven-haired barmaid as she sashayed away from them and out of sight.

"What, her?" Nick wrinkled his brow in confusion. "I think you have had one too many, my friend."

The man chuckled and dragged again from his ale. "No, that's her right name, leastwise that's how the rumors all have it."

Nick grunted and shook his head.

The other put his hand out in a friendly greeting. "Name's Ostin. George Ostin. On my way to Brighton, like everyone else."

Nick took his hand. "George Cumberland."

"Pleased to know you." Ostin chucked a thumb over his shoulder. "Friend of mine, Milson, was this way a month back. Said he'd seen an angel at this hellhole. Fairest creature north of the Nile, he said, and twice as venomous."

"The girl? She looks amiable enough," Nick disagreed. "No doubt there are a score of fellows who could testify to her charms."

Ostin shook his head. "Not that one. She's a siren with a viper's tongue behind those pretty red lips. Everyone says so. Must have a decent jab, too. Had Milson eating out of her hand, poor devil, until he tried to take her back to his room. Next thing he knew, he was flat on the floor with a bleeding lip and five pounds poorer."

Nick rolled his eyes and returned to his drink. He had bigger things on his mind than a coaching inn strumpet. "Sounds like he didn't offer enough," he huffed dismissively.

"No, by gaw, he said a few lads helped him up, slapped him on the back and bought him a drink. Turns out they'd been placing wagers on how much he'd lose before she put him down. They say none has tamed her yet."

"And you thought with your ten pounds, you'd be the one to break her in?" Nick snorted. "Maid or no, she seems to have a tidy business on her hands."

"Aye, word is she makes twice what the friendlier wenches do, just because she's become something of a sight for the tourists. Everyone has to try his hand, they say. I suppose I should be put out over the ten pounds, but it was worth it. Upon my soul, she's a rare one! Have you ever seen eyes like that? I wonder she doesn't take to Covent Garden."

Nick bobbed his head idly, staring with unseeing eyes at the wall opposite them. "If you are in no hurry to reach Brighton, perhaps you might try again."

"I'm out." Ostin crossed his arms with a laugh. "The duchess claims another swain."

"Duchess," Nick scoffed into his mug. "A tavern wench. You've a fanciful turn of mind, my friend."

Ostin grinned. "Perhaps not. They say she's the natural daughter of a 'somebody,' and not the old landlord. You know how that goes."

"I do." Nick finished his drink and stood abruptly. "If you will excuse me, please."

Ostin lifted a hand in bewildered farewell, then went back to staring at the door of the kitchens, waiting for his duchess to emerge again. Nick could not help a curl of his lip at the goose-brained fool. He'd get nothing useful out of this bloke. Best to step back to his room for a few minutes, then come back and try for a seat beside someone else. And hopefully, they would have more to talk about than the tavern wench.

"**B**ESSIE!" PAPA PUSHED THROUGH the swinging door behind her. "We've another traveler to put up. Hattie's gone off lud knows where, and you be the only lass what's free. Go make up the lower room, for there be nowhere else to put him. And be quick about it! He's a cantankerous sort."

She sighed, and without a word, obeyed. A cantankerous sort, indeed. The newcomer was obvious enough, standing in the middle of the coffee room and looking as if he expected someone to come shake out his cape for him. He glanced over Bess once, as if she were of no account, then apparently changed his mind.

"Are you the house maid? I'll have an ale and a tray in my room, and be quick about it, gel. I've had a long ride with a drunken coachman."

Bess applied a thin smile. "Won't be a moment, sir."

"A hot plate!" the man added as she hurried away. "None of this cold bilge you call stew. And do not skimp on the blankets! I expect that foul room is damp and drafty by night."

Bess was nearly to the hall, but she spun back just long enough to grimace a proper, "Yes, sir." Her feet had never stopped, however, and as she turned away, she slammed into a man just coming down the stairs. She fairly bounced off his chest, but he put his hands out at once to steady her.

"Begging your pardon, sir!"

Those same cold gray eyes from the bar looked down at her from a height of over six feet. He was a striking fellow, but not in a conventional way. Bess had seen enough dandies to know at a glance that this man was not one of those, but he did not resemble a tradesman, either. Almost a gentleman... but harder. His features were even and firm, the sort of face men never looked at twice, but women would never forget.

His hands dropped smartly off her shoulders and he nodded, one eye narrowing faintly. "Think nothing of it, miss." He stepped away, never looking back at her, and went back to the bar.

Bess gazed after him for a moment, then shook herself and hurried to prepare the room. When she came back down, the impatient traveler was still standing stupidly about, fists on his hips. He threw one of them up when he saw her, as if she had kept him waiting. "Well? Is it ready?"

She thinned her lips. "If you please, sir, I will show you back." She took the lantern from the hook and held it for the gentleman. The Bittern Hollow was a smallish affair, compared to some of the better-established coaching inns on the busy London highways. Or so she was told by the travelers. Daily, it seemed.

It was built in the usual style with a courtyard and archways, a public house, and a stable yard, but the westerly side of the inn proper had been built into a slope. The main floor rooms at this end were the least popular because of their short ceilings and small windows. Too high for the servants and yet too low for the Quality, they were frequently empty.

At the end of the hall, she gestured to the door that would take him to his quarters for the night. With a look of distaste, he took the lantern from her and went his way, and Bess sighed in relief to be rid of him. "Don't forget that plate," were his final words.

As if she *would* forget. The surest way to avoid him was to keep him supplied with food and spirits in his room for the rest of the night. She was just starting toward the stairs again with his tray when he came back out and blocked her path.

"A fine thing, this! One old blanket and the sheets are damp. And I declare the window shutters are rusted shut."

She flared up at once. "That blanket is warm enough, unless a body is already half dead with old age, and I warrant the sheets are fresher than you have at whatever rubbish heap you call home."

"Now, look here, you strumpet! I paid good coin for my room, and what do I get? A servant's chamber and a mouthy house maid! I'll teach you your place, you—"

"Over-stuffed, pompous, oaf!" Bess stuck a finger toward his chest. The dishes wobbled precariously on her tray as she advanced on him. "Foul room, indeed. I'll have you know I scrubbed it top to bottom just last week. As for the shutter, I closed it myself only last month after a good airing!"

The man's face purpled. "Airing! Who needs to air it? I can feel the wind through the gap at the sash!"

Bess's mouth opened for a retort, but her father shouldered his way into the conversation. "What seems to be the trouble, sir?"

"It 'seems' that this stupid wench has put me a 'room' not even fit for a rat to curl up in," the traveler spat. "I'll just take my custom elsewhere, I will, and you can bet I won't be back to this hovel."

"Now, sir, I am sure there has been a misunderstanding," her father reasoned. "I will see to it—"

"Nay, I'll have nothing more to do with this foul den," the man said with a sniff. He raised his chin and cast an imperious gaze about, just as if he were waiting for his valet to attend him. Where he thought he would go this time of night, Bess could not say, and it looked as if he himself was not altogether certain. But he did turn to go and drew up short when a man approached him from the bar.

It was that same man again, moving with a cat-like dignity. Bess's eyes traveled slowly up from an unusually broad chest to the neatly queued dark hair and a two-day bristle shading his jaw. He favored her and her father with a slight inclination of his head, then addressed the other.

"I could not help overhearing your trouble, sir. I've a comfortable room on the first floor with a four-poster bed, fine carpet, and no bedmates. I would happily exchange with you."

The dissatisfied gentleman looked immediately suspicious. "Eh? Why's that?"

"I do not sleep," the man answered simply. "Matters little to me if there is a draft or a poor bed. You may as well have your rest, and let this good innkeeper provide you the best of his hospitality."

The newcomer pretended to consider, then after a moment conceded. "I suppose I might do worse than to stop here, if you are willing. The roads are very wet tonight."

"Indeed," agreed the dark one, with a faint hint of mockery in his tone. "If you will grant me a moment, sir, I will remove my things."

Bess heard it all in awe. Never, in all her memory, had one traveler offered to exchange rooms with another merely to appease the second person's arrogance. And no one ever took the lower room by choice.

He dipped his head once more to her father, but Bess he scarcely acknowledged. She watched him felt, to her dismay, that her hands were trembling. For the first time all night, there was a man whose attention she wouldn't mind having, and he wouldn't even look at her.

O STIN HAD BEEN RIGHT about one thing, drunk as he was. The barmaid was one of the most exquisite creatures Nick had ever set eyes on.

He stayed at the tap for the rest of the evening, hoping to catch idle bits of tittle tattle from the other travelers. The only thing he caught was glances at Ostin's "Duchess of Surrey." He doubted the real bearer of that title could have compared. Hair black as ebony, skin as fine as his mother's porcelain, and the kind of eyes that inspired poets.

As if that were not enough to fix her in every admirer's imagination, her lips were not the only part of her physique that could be described as "full." Grecian her figure was not, and a man would have to be dead not to appreciate... all of it. Nick had to keep averting his eyes when she came near, just to keep from staring. The last thing he needed was to be accounted another victim of the "duchess."

But he was not here to stare at the barmaid. It was time to call it a night. The common room was quieting down for the evening, and it was becoming too difficult to sit near enough anyone to hear their words without drawing attention to himself. The fewer people who could remark on his face and voice, the better. He had made himself notable enough with that presumptuous offer to exchange rooms with the chump from London, but he had a sound reason for it.

He inspected his new quarters and arranged his few belongings with care. His shaving tackle laid neatly in its case beside his tooth powder and pomade on the washstand, his haversack standing proudly against the latter; his cloak and hat draped on a hook. The bed was low and hard, but serviceable, if he had meant to spend any time in it. However, he would pass the greater part of the night in the upright chair. When he was in the room.

He had to duck his head through the door, and the room possessed the musty aroma of a chamber too little inhabited. It was easy to understand why the other traveler might have objected to this humble offering.

But the window made up for every other inconvenience.

He went to the casement and inspected the latch. Not entirely rusted, as the other man had claimed, but quite stiff. With some trouble and no little screeching from the rust, he worked it open and found that it would be just possible for him to pass through it to the ground above.

What luck! A ground-level window, with its exit on the side opposite the courtyard. Few seemed to use the hall but the innkeeper himself, and that would be seldom, so his presence could be overlooked more often than not. And if he could get a bit of oil, he could address the noise made by the hinge. His comings and goings could be absolutely secret.

Lieutenant North would be in position by now. Nick pulled out his pocket watch and nodded, as if he could verify the encampment with his own eyes. They would have chosen a dark bit of wood bordering the heath, banked their cooking fire, and settled quietly for the night with their horses staked nearby. Among them would be that black beast of Cumberland's, enjoying a bait in her nosebag.

Odd, all these months, they had simply assumed the Scarlet Bandit had a stallion for his fleet-footed accomplice—a crafty, hard-bitten monster of an animal that, according to local lore, could vanish in a fog and reappear in a mist. Some accounts had it that the brute would emit an eerie whistle to terrorize coach horses and freeze them in their traces, while others claimed the creature was the ghost of Dick Turpin in equine flesh.

Not that Nick had given any credence to the tales. But when, upon receiving his orders to take up the mantle of the highwayman himself, he tried to become friendly with the animal, she had showed him her heels in a decidedly mare-ish fashion. And it had gone downhill from there.

Hopefully, he could win her over before he had to trust her with his life. Tomorrow evening, he would slip out and get word to his men. For now, however, there was nothing to do but to appear the unremarkable traveler.

And try to avoid that lass with the bright, curious eyes.

Chapter Three

B ESS LEANED AS FAR as she could over the rail and gave a hard pitch of her slops bucket. The pigs scurried in, squealing and scrambling for position at the trough. As always, the bigger ones had their way, and they pushed the runt to the back. Bess pulled a rejected turnip from her pocket to toss at the little one, then collected her bucket to go back inside.

"Ah, Bessie lass!" lisped a familiar voice. "Fair morning, ain't it?"

She stopped, grimacing before she turned around. She had been hoping to reach the safety of the kitchens before the old ostler noticed her. He meant no harm, so she was always polite with him, but he had a habit of pestering her every time she stirred outdoors.

She rarely minded, but today, she had too much to do to stop and chat for half an hour. Perhaps she could keep it short. Tim was friendly, but owing to his profession, there was a constant odor about him of moldy hay and horse leavings. And rotten sweat. She took an extra step back.

"It is that, Tim. Quite a busy one, what with all the travelers taking advantage of the fine weather."

He came closer, whittling at a pipe bowl as he walked and squinting against the morning light. "What brings ye out to the yard? I suppose thou likes a bit of the outside air and the sight of folks millin' about."

She smiled thinly. "You know me."

"Aye." He looked about, then leaned low. "I've a right purty little pony in the stable. White and fat as a dumplin,' with the biggest brown eyes as would make yer wee heart break."

Bess could not help a longing glance toward the stables, but she stiffened at once. "A white pony? I wonder what he could be doing in a place like this."

Tim gestured with his half-finished pipe. "Belongs to Lord Merriweather, he does. On his way home from Brighton for the little lordship after his summer holiday. How d'ye fancy that, eh?"

"I am sure he must be a very agreeable little fellow, if he is a child's mount."

"Gave him a right good feed of oats, but he's fonder of carrots. What say, lassie? I heard tell he likes the fair ones best."

Bess pondered for half a moment. She loved the friendlier equines that passed through the stables, and children's horses were dependably spoiled by treats and petting. Her father would not object if she made quick, but Tim would want to talk to her, and before she knew it, an hour would have passed and the work would have piled up.

"I cannot, not just now," she said with a reluctant sigh. "Papa will be needing me."

"Oh, but that pony won't keep, lassie. His Lordship's coachman ordered a rest for the little bobby, but 'twon't be long."

"I suppose I will have to miss him," she lied. Perhaps she could slip out after the next mail coach left, and most of the customers were gone for the day. And if she were very lucky, Tim would be asleep in his stable chair, waiting for the evening arrivals.

She hurried back to the kitchens with renewed vigor. The pots would not scrub themselves, nor would the floors wait, but if she hurried, she would just have enough time to take a treat to that little pony before he left. The half hour after the coffee room cleared and before the dining room tables filled with midday customers would be all her own today.

When she finally tiptoed out to the stable, she paused before passing the harness room. Just as she had hoped, Tim was draped limply over a chair. His hand fell slack to the floor as if trying to retrieve the flask he had dropped, and his head sagged backward. An uneven rattle pronounced his morning slumber. He would never even know she had come.

The stable boys touched their foreheads in greeting as she passed. One of them offered a knowing smile and gestured to a box at the end of the row. This was far from the first time Bess had slipped out to visit a fine animal.

And there he was; pearly white and plump as a little cloud, his black muzzle raised just above the door. Perfectly cupped nostrils drank her in, as if he knew enough about the bearers of treats to recognize a gull when he met one. A mop of gray forelock nearly covered his eyes, and short fat ears pricked eagerly as he made a low whickering noise.

"Aren't you the little rascal?" Bess offered him the carrot and gave a fond tug to his forelock. He took it daintily, and she laughed as he twisted it about in his mouth until it hung out like an orange cigar.

"My, a regular dandy you are. And so handsome! I bet you are the first pet of the whole stable where you come from."

The gray nose bumped over the door once more, searching for another carrot or some other affection. "Sly fellow. You would have me think you haven't eaten all day, wouldn't you?" She scratched under the pony's jaw and laughed again when his eyes rolled back and he leaned into her hand with the entire weight of his neck. He shook his head, then waved it with no uncertain meaning at the stall latch.

"Oh, none of that, now," she chided. "You'll trick me into opening the door and go raid the oats bin, sure as rain."

"I see you have had dealings with ponies before."

Bess jumped and whirled around to see who had spoken. Too cultured for a coachman, too masculine for a stable lad, and too... too *something* to be forgotten.

The man who had given up his room was standing at the far side of the row. His elbow rested on a tie stall divider, and his other hand held a pail of oats. He shook it gently, pensively, then set it aside and strolled casually toward her.

Bess had forgotten to swallow, and her tongue got in her way when she tried to take a breath to speak. "Nyah—ah..." She pulled her hand from the pony and cleared her throat, her cheeks burning. "I mean, ah, what makes you say that, sir?"

He nodded toward the pony. "Cunning little rascals, they are. Fattened on treats and indulgences—one would think they had not a clever bone in their soft little bodies. And yet, when all the high-mettled blood stock are resting quietly, it will be the adorable, 'harmless' pony who plucks the door latch and gets into mischief."

"They sound clever enough to me," Bess replied. "Smarter than their unsuspecting caretakers, it sounds like."

"As is the case far too often." The man—*gentleman?*—smiled wistfully, then his expression sobered. He wore no hat, but he started to reach for one before realizing he had none, and then offered a quick bow. "Forgive me, miss. My name is George Cumberland. May I have the pleasure of yours?"

Her name? Why, everyone knew her name. Papa shouted it often enough in the inn, and all the washerwomen and laborers said it as if it were the commonest word in the world. She swallowed.

"B-Bess. Bess Reynolds." She put her hands behind her back, ticking that pony's nose again to hide how this man made her want to fidget. "Actually, everyone calls me Bessie."

"Bess," the man repeated carefully. "Like our good Queen of yore. Very fitting."

"No. Like Old Bessie the cunning woman from Barney Slough. My mother had no name for me, and one handle was as good as another."

Cumberland came closer, shaking his head, and rested his palm on the pony's neck. "Nothing could be further from the truth. A name is everything. You carry it all your life. It is who you are to the world—what there is of truth and goodness in you, what beauty and mercy you bestow. You are known by it, and you impart some bit of yourself to future bearers of that name." He ruffled the pony's mane, then looked her squarely in the eye. "Bess is a noble name, a gentle yet fierce one. You should wear it proudly."

She raised her brows and tried to keep her voice steady. How beastly unfair of the man to smile that way when he said her name, just as if she were a proper lady. Cheeky fellow!

"Well, now," she retorted, "I'm something of a queen, you say? I never saw a bit of it. Where are my attendants? Where is my heraldry, good sir?" She laughed. "Fancy notions mean aught when a body is washing the linens and putting on the coffee."

Cumberland looked away and smiled. "You would deceive me, but I am not so easily fooled, Miss. I wager most tavern girls do not sneak out to the stables to spoil other people's animals."

"Most travelers don't give up a good room on the first floor to take the lower one. They don't even do it for their friends, and certainly never for brutes like that man yesterday."

He shrugged. "If you are asking why, I shall ask the same question of you, and I suspect you would give me the same answer. A person can have their whims, can they not?"

Bess crossed her arms. "I suppose. Tell me, Mr. Cumberland, where is your horse?"

"I came by mail coach, miss."

"Then you truly are a peculiar one, out here in the stables scooping oats when you ought to be waiting for your coach."

"Ah." His face broke into an easy chuckle. "If you must know, I had a question for the ostler, but I came out to find him asleep at his duties."

"Better he should stay that way," Bess muttered.

"I am sorry to hear that. I was hoping that a man who spent his days with all manner of horseflesh might have some useful advice for me. I've something of a problem horse, you see. Back at home, I mean."

"And where is home?"

"Westborough, in Lincolnshire. My family has a small holding there."

"Then, I was right. You are a gentleman."

One side of his mouth twisted in amusement. "Just barely. My father traded in spice and tobacco until about fifteen years ago, when the king elevated him for exemplary service. There, you know what sort of clientele he kept. After that, he sold out and lived the life of a very modest gentleman."

"And let me guess—you are his only heir, with expectations of your own to build his fortune?"

"Far from it. That honor falls to my older brother. I am merely a man with his own affairs to mind."

"I wonder what you can be doing so far from home, then. What, has Tim, the world's most useless ostler, gained a reputation for horse wizardry? You have been woefully deceived, if that is the case."

Cumberland laughed again. It was a pleasant sound, soft and yet masculine, not tainted by too much beer or vice as so many she had heard.

"It was merely a convenience of the moment. I had some time to pass and thought I may as well employ myself gainfully. But I perceive that if my question was about resolving a dispute with a horse, I was seeking the wrong person," he finished with a gesture of his hand.

Bess glanced over her shoulders, then realized who he meant. "Me? What do I know of horses?"

"Perhaps more than you think. Look around you." He pointed to the stalls on either side, and indeed, four other horses were straining at their tie ropes, tossing their heads in her direction.

"They just want carrots. They must smell them."

"Unless your pockets are still full, that cannot be the entire answer. Perhaps they like the sound of your voice."

"But you are talking, too."

"That is true," he admitted. "But they brightened at your arrival, so I shall pose my question. This horse I have is a... well, I suppose she is something of a queen herself. At least, she has a very high opinion of her worth and a low view of mine. I should like to find a way to change that."

Bess scoffed. "Everyone I ever heard of would say you had to teach the horse who is master."

"Ah, yes, but I was not asking those others you have heard of. What do *you* think I must do?"

Bess blinked and gaped for half a moment. No one ever asked *her* opinion. "I have never had the management of a horse, but perhaps it is like other creatures that appreciate a bit of patience. And if it is a she-horse, you must woo her."

Cumberland's brow arched. "Perhaps you see that behavior often enough, but I am no expert in 'wooing' of any kind—woman or mare."

"From what I can see, it must be the easiest thing in the world," she said, a trace of bitterness in her voice.

Cumberland leaned closer. "Unless the female be one of dignity. I noticed it was not *you* on that rich man's knee last night, and poor Osten had to go hungry after his encounter with you."

Bess narrowed her eyes and began to protest, but Cumberland only waved away her objections, his smile still kind. "I shall not ask, but I imagine you have a remarkable stash put aside, if what I saw last night was typical."

Bess swallowed and lifted her chin, refusing to either confirm or deny his words. If anyone suspected that her treasure was now well over sixty pounds, it would not remain hers for long.

He shook his head. "Forgive me, it is not my business. Let me ask, though, as you and my mare have something in common, perhaps you might tell me the secret to winning her over."

"You seem very determined to have this particular horse's affections. Why not be rid of her and get another?"

"Because I have a sworn duty to this one. I cannot fail, miss. Will you advise me?"

What a peculiar sort this was! Who pledged himself to one horse? It was almost as unheard of as a man of means who remained faithful to his wife.

"Well," she said slowly, "you could try treats."

"And have her take my fingers instead of the carrot? No, thank you."

"Do you ever pet her and praise her?"

"I would have to get within arm's length for that. How does one earn a lady's good graces from a distance?"

"I suppose you'll have to talk to her. Tell her what a beauty she is and make much of her."

"And how well do *you* respond to that?"

Bess shrugged casually. "I wouldn't know."

"You wouldn't, eh?" he asked in disbelief.

"No, for all I ever hear is lust and flattery, not genuine compliments. Not that I would heed that, mind you," she cautioned with a finger upheld. "But I think other females might."

His lip curled. "I was afraid you might say that. I have always thought words were empty."

"And yet she will know nothing else of you until she trusts your voice. The right words have power, Mr. Cumberland."

He drew in a breath and nodded decisively. "Indeed, you are right. I shall try it, Miss Bess."

She made a playful curtsey at his formal address and was about to say something rather impertinent in reply, but an angry shout stopped her.

"You, there! What are you doing with that pony?"

Cumberland turned, and they both faced a portly coachman. He was waving a riding whip as if to chase away naughty boys, and his teeth were bared like a pit dog. "Spoiling that little beast, are you? I'll have to answer to His Lordship when that brute nips the children. Off with you, now!"

Bess's temper rose. Mr. Cumberland could do whatever he wanted, but it would be a dark day before she took such an insult without an argument. "If this pony bites anyone, it is because he is provoked to it. Have you been such a poor coachman before that you permit him to be ill-used? Or do you do the mishandling yourself?"

Mr. Cumberland's hand caught at her elbow, but Bess refused to step back. Her fists were balled, and she stared down the puffy-faced fellow as his color brightened.

"Hussy! Do not presume to tell me my business, you cheap whore!"

Mr. Cumberland made a thunderous noise in his chest and started to step in the way, but Bess ducked around him to lash back, "Not cheap enough for the likes of you!"

The coachman's mouth dropped, and so did his whip. "What the devil! Where is the landlord? I'll have words with him!"

Mr. Cumberland pulled her back by main strength and stepped in front of her. "See here, sir! You have no cause to address the lady in such a tone."

The coachman spat on the ground. "Lady! I don't know what you've been drinking, my man. She's naught but a tavern wench, and you are meddling with affairs that are not your business."

"The conduct of a churl toward a woman is every man's business."

"Then take your 'woman' out of the stables before I call a constable! Indecent tart, she is!"

Mr. Cumberland was biting his lips together, his countenance suffused with sudden wrath, but he turned to her with a visible effort not to explode. "Come, Miss Bess. Let us live to fight another day."

Tim chose that moment to stumble toward them, bent at the shoulder and tugging up the waist of his trousers. "What be the trouble?"

Cumberland cast a quick, experienced eye over the ostler, and apparently decided not to enlist him in the defense of Bess's honor. "No trouble," he replied easily. "Miss Bess, I expect you are wanted indoors."

From anyone else, that would have been a shaming comment—an accusation that she was shirking her duties or did not deserve to go about as she wished. That her place, the only place she was worth anything, was in the scullery. But there it was again—the slight twitch about his gray eyes, and she recognized Cumberland's words for what they were. A graceful escape, with which no one could argue.

She thinned her lips and nodded slightly. "I expect so. I have spoiled enough ponies for one day." She dipped a teasing curtsey to Cumberland, but from the corner of her eye, she enjoyed watching the ostler scratch his head and the coachman's chest swell for another outraged bellow. Mr. Cumberland took her hand like she was a proper lady and bowed in return, and Bess raced away.

And spent the rest of the afternoon wondering what kind of man this was, who poeticized names and spoiled ponies and treated tavern wenches like ladies.

Chapter Four

TALKING TO THE GIRL had been a mistake.

Not that he regretted it... not much. But he had given her another reason to remember him—a girl who saw fifty new travelers every day, who probably talked to everyone, and who would be sure to say an inconvenient something to the wrong someone about the odd stranger she met in the stables.

Nick spent the rest of the afternoon in his room, trying to make little of his presence. A day's work lost! He felt it in his bones. He had been close to *something*. *W*as it not strange that the head ostler was asleep in the harness room while a dozen traveling coachmen had the management of the horses?

Then there was the way the stable lad had looked him up and down, evaluating him. The furtive movements and the second, significant look from the lad after he had come out of the feed room. He thought it was a tip, a cue, so he had gone to investigate.

And then the girl had wandered into the shed row and ruined the entire scene. At least she seemed to have bought that nonsense about trying to learn how to gentle a horse. As if he, Captain Nicholas Hunt of the Light Cavalry, needed advice about an obstreperous horse from a barmaid!

He would just have to try again on the morrow. North's latest informant, a negligible rodent of a man who traded shady intelligence for ale, had been so adamant that the real Cumberland had some connection to this inn. Yet, he had been equally insistent that Cumberland never stayed there himself. No one knew his face. It had been a desperate decision to use the villain's name, a wild hope that it would draw out the contact he sought. So far, however, the only person to really take note of him was the black-eyed goddess who masqueraded as the landlord's daughter. And she had certainly taken note of him.

It was not impossible... indeed, the Tyrant had crafty agents, and not all of them were roughened soldiers. Some wore lace instead of swords. Eyes and whispers they were—watching and waiting, using their charms as a weapon. Soft and warm until their cold black hearts were revealed.

But that seemed unlikely, did it not? She was more stunning than any tavern girl had a right to be, but she was too frank, too quick, and too hot-tempered to be one of the enemy's enchantresses. Besides, it would be the work of a moment to learn if she really was the daughter of the old landlord. Too many people would have known her as a child.

No, it could not be the girl he sought. Nor her father, he did not think, though it was too early to discount the harried old man. The most likely connection was one of the lower servants, who could move easily without attracting notice. He would have to risk staying another day, gather what he could, and then move on.

A gallant full moon was cresting the trees when Nick slipped out of his window that night. The hour was late, and the noises of merriment from the dining room had quieted. The last mail coach was long gone, and not a soul ought to be stirring. He held his breath as he eased himself through the casement and up to the rise of ground outside.

Nothing. Not even a neigh from the stables or a...

But there *was* something. A creaking sound, just overhead. Nick flattened himself against the brick of the building and looked up. The window from the room above his was ajar, the shutter rocking faintly with the breeze. He slid away from that open window, and silent as a cat, dashed for the moon's darkness of a nearby oak.

He slipped behind the tree and looked back, to be certain he had not been seen. With any luck, whoever was in that room above him was blinded by their own lantern and utterly ignorant to his presence. His heart gave a guilty lurch when he saw the woman's figure, shadowed in that window. She was burning a single candle, and a humble linen curtain fluttered gently in the casement.

And she was undressing.

The effect was ghostly seduction; dream-like and hazy, like a languorous evening with sweet wine. No details of her form did she reveal to her enraptured observer, but her beauty was as real and rich to Nick as if she stood before him. She raised a delicate arm to pull the pins from her hair, and his breath caught when a silken cascade fell around the silhouette of her shoulders and tumbled well past her waist.

His mouth ran dry. This must be why women kept their hair so sacrosanct, if it held this kind of power over a man, even from a distance. He did not even know who she was, but he would have traded his pistols, his duty, his very place in the world for just once chance to taste the dewy softness of that woman's hair.

He shivered and forced his gaze back to the dappled twilight sky. He had been too long away from society, that was all. Six years of war, and the last two leading a roving detachment with no set location, no direction or permanent situation for even his family to write to him when they wished. It played havoc with a man's heart and his head. When this was all over... He clenched a fist as he walked...

When this was all over, and the spies locked away, he would go home. Embrace his mother and sisters, reconcile with his father, and perhaps even think of settling down and taking a fixed post with the War office. And maybe then, he could even think about finding a woman of his own—one who would let him kiss her hair.

For now, he had his duty.

It was not far to the encampment, but he purposely took a more meandering route, walking on the harder packed earth, so his initial footsteps away from the inn would not be noticed. Half an hour later, he brushed through the trees ringing the camp. Daniels, on watch duty, saluted him at once.

"Captain in the camp," he announced to the others.

His men assembled in a moment, all smartly to attention and looking exactly as a squadron ought, though they were only three. "Sir," North said, stepping forward. "Everything is in order."

"At ease, Lieutenant. Have you learned anything?"

"Yes, sir. I investigated the lowlands around Reigate myself to learn the prospect of the land, and I have one or two promising locations marked for you. Sergeants Wesson and Daniels explored Buckland the last two days, particularly the brook you spoke of."

"And what news of that?"

Wesson spoke up. "The brook itself is of no account. Hardly any secret, sir, and barely more than a trickle of irrigation water flowing into the River Mole. We saw nowhere along its banks where someone could hide for long. Nor did we hear anything of anyone calling himself a 'monk.' There was once a priory at Reigate, but it is now a private mansion."

"No ruins where a hermit might dwell? That was my first notion."

"No, sir. The old buildings were demolished over two hundred years ago. I had thought it might be a whimsical code for the parish priest, though. I invented a chance to happen across him as he was about his duties."

"And what was your impression?"

Wesson frowned. "He is a doddering old fool, no doubt secure in his incumbency. Daniels spoke with some tenants at Reigate, and they all thought the vicar to be quite worthless in his post."

"Which might mean he has other employment," Nick mused.

Wesson gave a curt nod. "My thoughts exactly, sir."

"Very well. Keep a close watch on him. North, have you a map of the road and the heath for me?"

"Yes, sir, in my tent." North was back a moment later, unrolling a sheaf of paper from his saddlebag. Daniels raised a lantern as North held up the map.

"The Brighton Road crosses the lowland here," he said, sliding his finger along a diagonal path. "Here, here, and here are places where you could view the road without being seen yourself. And here—" he pointed— "a wide-open area, perfect for attack."

"Perfect for me to 'attack' a carriage, or for someone to attack me?" Nick asked wryly.

"Both, I should guess. I marked a few other areas as well. You can see them here and here."

Nick scanned the map again, then rolled it up. "Very good. I will examine this more closely in the daylight."

"What of the inn, sir?" North asked. "Have you located the informant yet?"

"If I had, he would not be much of an informant." Nick sighed. "No, I imagine Cumberland's contact must be a cautious sort, probably waiting for the right moment to reveal himself."

"Does he even know the name?" North wondered.

"No way of telling. I wish I knew Cumberland's methods. All we have as a lead is that he struck his marks in rapid sequence, and he tumbled tavern wenches for sport."

North raised a brow at Daniels. "Are there any pretty maidens worth your notice?"

Nick scoffed. "Was Cumberland terribly choosy in his pursuits?"

"Actually, he was. He was said to favor the dark-haired wenches, the sassier the better, and he especially liked those with generous... ah..." North made a vague gesture with his hands near his chest, then dropped them guiltily when his captain pierced him with a hard look.

"I do not mean to stop at the Bittern long enough to dally with the tavern girls," Nick snapped. "We have a duty to perform. Good soldiers have died because of that ring of spies, and I intend to put an end to it."

North stiffened and his eyes lost focus. "Yes, sir."

"Good. Now, where is that equine monster I must ride? Has she bitten anyone lately?"

"She got Daniels in the shoulder this morning."

Nick had already turned away, starting toward the picketed horses, but turned back in surprise. "I was in jest."

"But I am not," North said. "Got a nasty bruise, he did. Watch her, Captain, and do not turn your back on her."

"Indeed." Nick fumbled in his pocket for the carrot he had stowed there. It would behoove him to keep that put away for now—no need to give the old witch more reasons to greet people with her teeth. "Perhaps I will need to learn how to woo a lady."

T HE MARE PINNED HER ears as soon as he stepped around the tree securing the picket line. The black tail swished, and she tossed her savage little head with malicious warning. Nick paused, letting her get his scent.

The mare was unimpressed. She snorted and stamped one foot, then flung her head again.

"Yes, shake your mane at me, you old beast," he murmured. "Look, I am not come to harass you. Shall we be friendly?"

He might as well heed at least some of the tavern girl's advice. The trick seemed to work for her, after all. This demon of the heaths might not comprehend his words, but his soft, easy tone, she would surely understand.

He paused, watching the tense form for any signs of movement. "Oh, I see how you feel, old girl. Quite the black-hearted lady you are. How many men have you devoured in your day, eh?"

One ear swiveled to him, but her eyes still glittered, and the sharp nostrils curled in distaste.

Nick held out a hand, palm down, and cautiously approached her shoulder. "Easy, my dear. Yes, you are a true villainess, are you not? I should not be surprised to see fangs in your—Hallo, there!"

Nick jumped back as white teeth flashed in the moonlight. Like a snake she was, head slung low and wrathful as the rest of her body slithered quick as lighting. He pulled his hand to his chest and stared at her for a moment, his heart still pounding. He had known some valiant animals in his day—creatures that could fight as nobly as their riders, striking blows against the enemy before the eye had even seen the beginnings of their attack. But this viper, coiled and silent, could out-streak them all.

Still, he was fairly certain those teeth were not fanged. Almost certain, anyway.

"See what I mean, sir?" North said from a safe distance behind him. "Oh, stay out of range of her hooves as well as her teeth. Wesson found that out, did you not, lad?"

A grunt from Wesson seconded this caution. "And she can untie herself. Almost did it twice yesterday. That's why we got the chain on her halter. I won't try to catch her again," he said, rubbing what must have been a bruise on his chest for emphasis.

Nick turned to look at his men. "Good heavens," he whispered. "The mare is a devil's spawn!"

"She just needs a name," North laughed. "You know what they say about a ship that has not been christened."

Nick scowled at the mare. "I think it would be bad luck to christen a ship Hellion or Jezebel."

"What about calling her after that Buckland Shag phantom we are chasing? I heard it was a monster of a horse that devoured travelers."

"I thought it was a gorilla," Wesson countered.

North shrugged. "She's almost as friendly as a gorilla. Seems a right fitting name."

"Not helpful." To the mare, he spoke low and soothingly. "There, there, my lass, I won't harm you. Handsome girl! Aye, you old cobra, you—look, nothing to fear." He kept his hands low this time, and slowly moved into the mare's space. Her lip twitched and her head lifted, but she remained still.

"Oh, I do not think she is afraid, sir," Daniels offered.

"It is the only thing that makes sense," Nick answered softly, keeping his voice to a low singsong. "Perhaps she has been misused somewhere. No horse is born this vicious, are they?"

"Mares are," North grumbled.

Nick ignored him. "Easy, there. Come, now, my girl, nothing to worry about. Great gads, but you are a lovely old gel, when you aren't trying to behead a man."

The flesh over her withers shivered and the black hips bunched, but the mare did not move to strike. Nick decided to test his luck. He slid his right hand lightly over the sleek shoulder.

This time, he was ready with his left hand to fend off her teeth as they slashed toward him. Surprised and angered that she had been thwarted, the mare peeled back her lips and threw her head high, up and down in a furious display of frustration.

Nick continued petting her shoulder until her temper had subsided. She stomped and pawed, not precisely aiming at his boots, but not avoiding them, either. Nick danced to escape the black iron hooves but stuck beside her shoulder. The instant she dropped her muzzle with an unhappy snort, he stepped away. The great ebony head swung about; ears pricked in bewildered interest.

"There you are, my beauty. See, it was not so dreadful." He waited a moment, and noted how the longer he stared at her, the more the heavy black tail would swish in agitation. One more time, he stepped close.

Her hip sliced toward him, but rather than to recoil into the striking range of her hind feet, Nick darted up to her shoulder again. The dark head tossed, the wicked hooves stamped, then, all at once, she went still.

"There, there is a fine lady," Nick crooned. He stroked her glossy coat, a stream of silly nonsense pouring from him as he kept talking.

It seemed to be working. The high-crested neck was no longer rock hard, and her ears remained cocked toward him rather than flattened against her skull. At last, Nick nodded in satisfaction when the hateful crinkle disappeared from the mare's nostrils and the hardened jaw slackened. They were the first signs that she was at least grudgingly accepting his presence. After a few more seconds, he moved away.

"By Jove," North whispered. "You lived."

"I may not know much about wooing ladies," Nick muttered, "but I do know one thing about trespassing in their territory. Pay your compliments well, and do not overstay your welcome."

Chapter Five

B ESS WAS POURING COFFEE the next morning when Mr. Cumberland came in. His eye fell on her at once, but rather than to approach, he turned silently away to a small table in the corner. Bess watched him go.

"Have a care, girl!" cried the man whose cup she was filling. "Blimey if you haven't burned my hand."

Bess jumped and righted her attention. It was only a few drips, but he was shaking one hand as if thoroughly scalded, and jiggling his cup and saucer so much that he was burning his other hand far more than she had done. "Oh, excuse me, sir," she apologized. She snagged a napkin from the nearest table. "Here."

He gaped indignantly at the cloth. "And what am I to do with that? I hardly need a bandage, you clumsy girl."

She patted it against his arm and left it there. "I am so very glad to hear it. Do wipe up after you have finished, please."

He sputtered, but Bess was already walking away. She had just enough hot coffee in her pot for one more serving, and Mr. Cumberland looked like a man in need of a cup.

He slanted an amused half-smile up to her as she drew near, his left eye squinting as he had a habit of doing. "Ungallant fellow, that," he observed.

She shrugged airily. "And a miserable tipper, too. I shouldn't wonder if it was not the first time he wore a bit of his drink."

Mr. Cumberland chuckled and pulled a few coins from his pocket. "As I am neither, perhaps you will be so good as to let me have a bit of that in a cup, rather than on my sleeve."

"Oh, but it would compliment your coat so well!" she teased as she poured his coffee. He accepted it with a grateful inclination of his head, and Bess studied him while he drank.

"If I may be so bold, Mr. Cumberland, you look as though a second cup would not go amiss."

His brows arched as he set his cup down. "How is that?"

"I supposed that when you said you did not sleep, you were speaking carelessly, but you were in earnest, were you not?"

"I am afraid so."

"And what do you do instead?"

A smile crept across his face. "You ask very frank questions, Miss Bess. Perhaps it would be indelicate of me to answer them."

"If you are meaning to spare my sensibilities, there is no need. I may not be the one sitting on the men's knees, but I know how the other girls spent their evening. I also know how they did not spend it, or rather, with *whom* they did not spend it."

He sat back and crossed his arms, laughing. "I must take care to never let you discover anything shocking about me. I cannot decide if you are scandalously informed for a young lady, or blunt and bold enough that even the finest dames of Mayfair would titter and fawn over you."

"Well, that hardly seems to be a dilemma worth pondering, Mr. Cumberland. I am no lady myself, and it appears unlikely that I should ever move among such creatures."

Some of the humor behind his eyes cooled. He gave a short huff and nodded. "I suppose not." He took a slow, pensive sip of his coffee. "In answer to your question, yes, a second cup would be most welcome."

Bess dipped him a brief curtsey. "Then, I need a fresh pot. Won't be a moment."

She twirled away, but he called her back. "You forgot your tip money."

A daring smile formed on her lips. "I didn't forget it, Mr. Cumberland. And now, you may ponder whether I am angling for more, or if I simply consider my time adequately compensated by good conversation."

He grinned, and Bess could not help but like how his smile was wider on that side where his eye always narrowed. "In that case, Miss Bess, I shall try to procure more of both."

T HERE WAS NO MORE effective way for a man to learn what he most desired, than for him to pretend he did not care. Nick dawdled in the coffee room, listening to idle chatter, and ostensibly watching nothing more interesting than the cream swirling in his cup. That was what he persuaded himself that others might see, and he fooled himself into thinking they would not notice him watching the landlord's daughter.

How could they notice when most of them were doing the same thing?

It was impossible not to. She moved lightly among the morning crowd, easing away groggy stares with a smile and a hot cup of motivation. Even those few who seemed immune to her exotic beauty could not ignore her ready charm. She teased those who could be made merry and soothed those who could not.

This early in the day, there were no drunken boors to harass her, and she was less wary, less ready to snap at an offense. She was friendly, as anyone serving at an inn ought to be, but there was a slice of dignity atop her morning cheer. She drew near, but still held herself aloof, as if she were a fine lady serving tea to her honored guests, rather than a buxom bar maid working for tips.

He could watch her all day without growing weary of it.

For a moment, it passed through his mind to truly take on the mantle of the highwayman. If anyone was watching him to be certain that he *was* Cumberland, pursuing a girl after his supposed type might settle it. Not that it would not be a pleasure, either. The notion was worth considering, for his eye and his imagination had seemed to fix on her. And he thought she liked him at least a little in return—at least, it seemed that she was more friendly with him than with others in the room. Surely, even a watchful and sassy creature such as she had her weaknesses.

But the thought died as quickly as it had come. He might be masquerading as a rascal and a villain, but he was still Captain Nicholas Hunt, and Nicholas Hunt did not fight his battles at the expense of women.

Almost the very moment he had dismissed the idea, the object of his musings came round. She tilted her head, letting a soft ringlet of black hair drop tantalizingly over her brow, and pursed her lips. "You must be the slowest drinker in the entire county, Mr. Cumberland."

He lifted his empty cup. "No, I managed the task well enough. It just seemed a pleasant place to sit and think through some... some business."

"Are you leaving us today, then?"

He shook his head. "I am waiting on word from another before I determine my plans. It may be another day or two before I hear from him."

She nodded vaguely, her charcoal eyebrows gently arched. "I see. Will you be seeking to improve yourself again today by asking others how to do their jobs? If so, there is a very fine blacksmith, half a mile up the road. How do you like swinging a hammer?" She puckered her lips, and those black eyes twinkled.

"Actually, I thought I'd try my hand at barkeeping next," he replied. "What do you think? Could I hold my own on a busy night?"

She tilted her head, and her smile widened. "I think you should not give up your present employment, Mr. Cumberland."

He lifted his empty cup in salute and set it on her tray. "Wise advice, Miss—"

"Bessie!" The innkeeper strode in from the hall and pushed to his daughter's side. He cast a curious, somewhat unhappy glance at Nick, then spoke to her. "Go and help Sarah with the linens. I will close up the coffee room."

"But, Papa, I was just finishing—"

"At once. There is extra washing today, and it needs to be aired while the sun is out. Go now."

A helpless sort of sadness appeared around her eyes. Humiliation, no doubt, at being ordered to the menial task of washing when she had been doing so well at hostessing. Her cherry lips thinned, and she slid one last look to Nick before bobbing a subdued, "Yes, Papa."

Nick watched her as she walked away, but looked up again when he realized the landlord had not departed. He cleared his throat and got to his feet. "Well, I suppose I ought to be about my business. Good morning."

"Will you be staying another night, Mr. Cumberland?"

"At least, yes. I am happy to settle my bill in advance."

The innkeeper was peering hard into his face, in a manner rather invasive and unprofessional for a man who let rooms to strangers for a living. He seemed to brush off his curiosity, though, and his expression returned to the accustomed neutral look he had worn before. "No, that will not be necessary. Cumberland, is it? I wonder, have you any family? Begging your pardon, but the name strikes me as familiar."

A guilty throb made Nicks' heart surge in his chest, but he congratulated himself on the even tone of his voice when he replied. "None, sir. Not for many years."

The innkeeper's mouth worked strangely, but he sighed and broke eye contact. "My condolences, and my apologies for asking. Do, please, speak if there is anything I can do to make your stay more comfortable. Would you wish to change rooms? A bigger suite, perhaps. What about this evening, shall you be returning late? I will have Hattie serve your supper in the private parlor, or Jenny, if you prefer."

He swallowed. If he were of a disposition to ask for female companionship, it would not be one of the other girls. And he had a feeling that Bess answered to no man's pleasure. "No, no, thank you. Good day, sir."

Nick left without another word, but he felt the innkeeper's eyes on him all the way out the door. Perhaps there was more than one reason the bewitching daughter of the house did not engage in the same sport as the others. Her father put a stop to it before it ever got started.

But that could not be true, because how many young bulls taunted and flirted with her regularly? Enough that she had apparently risen to folklore status in the county, and her father had not intervened there. Perhaps it was Nick himself the father objected to... or just "his" name.

He went to his room and scribbled a note to be left for North at their agreed upon drop location. He would have his men sniff around a bit and see what they could turn up on old Reynolds, the landlord of the Bittern.

HER EARS STILL BURNED from the shame of being sent away.

Bess scrubbed at the washboard until her shoulders ached. She stretched, cast her face to the sun as the life tingled back in her arms, and set to work again. There was still a pile behind her that was not even started, and now she was doing it alone.

Sarah, the girl from the village they had hired in the spring, had taken one look at Bess's sullen manner, and slipped away when she went to hang the sheets to dry. She was probably cavorting in the hayloft by now, but Papa would not send her away, no matter how unreliable she was. Papa never even reprimanded anyone unless they offended a customer.

And he had never spoken a harsh word to Bess. Never.

Perhaps he was worried about money again. They still owed the stonemason for the chimney repair, but the debt ought to be nearly paid by now. It had been a good season, but that season was coming to a close soon. In another month, they would shutter half the rooms and dismiss the help from the village, and the Bittern would survive on the meager fare of winter travelers and post riders.

Yes, surely it was worry that had made her father speak to her so. Or it could be fear for her brother. They had expected to hear something from Samuel weeks ago, and still, nothing had come. Letters from the Continent were always slow—everyone said so. But when it was someone dear out there, someone who faced death constantly, each day without word split a deeper ache in the hearts of those back at home.

Bess hung the linens one by one, pinning them on the line and looking occasionally up into the sky, hoping it would not rain on the washing. It was hot and overcast, a perfect recipe for an autumn thunderstorm. There were patches of blue sky here and there, but a dense pack of silvery clouds clung to the horizon. Just the color of Mr. Cumberland's eyes.

The man was a puzzle. There was something about him that made even his idle moments seem terribly purposeful, as though at every minute, he was going about serious business. She supposed he was the sort of man who would forever turn over his troubles in his head, even when nothing else was to be done. Yet, he was not so self-indulgent that he could not spare a smile and a kind word.

In a way, he reminded her of Samuel. Bess chewed thoughtfully at her lip as she pinned the last sheet on the line. Yes, that was probably why George Cumberland fascinated her. He had an easy charisma and a steady turn of mind. He was no lush, at least not that she had seen. He was intelligent and considerate, which was more than could be said for most of the travelers who passed through the Bittern. And whatever this business was that had brought him to her inn, he took it with deep seriousness and no small measure of privacy, despite his playful banter.

A smile touched her lips. Perhaps she should ask him more frankly about it. After all, he was staying another day, was he not? He had already said he liked the conversation. Even if he could not or would not talk of his business, he had a clever way of turning the subject from his affairs to hers, and she would not mind... studying how it was done. That was all.

"Bessie lass, there ye be." Tim the ostler's face appeared above the wash line, grinning and lifting his hat like he was a fine gentleman.

She sighed. "Yes, here I am."

"Thought ye'd be comin' to the yard when ye've done. I feared I'd miss ye."

She bent to pick up the empty wash basket and walked back to the basin to start on another pile. "No time for that today, Tim. Besides, I thought the pony left yesterday."

"Oi, he did, he did, but there be a handsome team of bays. Never a finer stepping pair, says I."

"I am sure they are, and I am sure they have an equally fine coachman who is no doubt particular about his charges."

"Made me strip out the stalls and put out all new bedding, he did," was Tim's resentful reply. "Without so much as a by-yer-leave, as if he were the King 'imself."

Bess thinned her lips and doubled over into the basin with another sheet. Tim was rumored to leave soiled bedding down, sprinkling a fresh layer of straw on top and swearing that the smell was only from bad drains. Occasionally, he was found out by coachmen who knew their business, but all too often, nothing was done. And her father would never dismiss him, either.

"I say, lassie, 'tis an uncommon fine day."

Bess paused and squinted dismally up to the heavens again. "It promises to be a hot, sticky sort of day, if it does not rain."

"Aye, but... a day like today be good for a bit of... fresh air."

Bess dropped her gaze from the oppressive clouds down to the ostler. There was an odd tone in his voice, and an almost hungry gleam in his eye. He licked his lips and grinned. It was then that she realized his purpose. Kneeling and bent over the washbasin as she was, she was unwittingly offering a full view of whatever bosom showed above her dress. Especially when she raised her head. Drenched in sweat and wash water, she must have presented a scandalous scene.

Bess leaped to her feet. "You're no better than a rutting old swine!" she hissed. She reached into her wash basin for the entire arm load of soggy sheets and threw them over his head. Then, she marched back indoors, leaving the ostler to stumble blindly about.

She never went back to finish the washing.

NICK SETTLED THE NOTE for his men in notch of the tree at their secret location, about three hundred paces into the wood surrounding the southeastern side of the inn. They would find it by early afternoon. In return, there was a message from North waiting for him. It was short, only two lines, but it made Nick's blood freeze.

Informant found dead from a musket shot.
Searching for murderer.

He crumpled it at once and shoved it into his pocket. North's informant was dead? Nick never knew who it was—had not wished to know—but from what he understood, the fellow did not keep savory company. He could have been killed by anyone, for any number of reasons.

But a musket, not a blade had been his end. This had not been some scuffle over cards. Someone wanted him silenced, and that meant that Nick could be next.

He needed information, and he needed it now. The time for eavesdropping in the pub was past. Where the bloody hell did one dig up a French spy? He needed ears in places he could not go.

The stable boys. He would start with one of them. The smallest, least important of them, the one he had seen outside the grain room. A few shillings, well-placed, might give him just enough warning to escape the same fate that had befallen the informant.

Nick found an old trail through the trees, well-worn by others, and made his way back to the inn. He shoved his hands in his pockets and hummed to himself, as if he were only a careless man out for a stroll and daydreaming of his sweetheart. It was not a difficult manner to copy, for he could easily think of one face worth meditating on. And, so, meditate he did.

There was something about the prim little point of her chin that made her face look almost like a heart. London circles spoke in praise of an aristocratic nose and noble cheekbones, but Nick had always been partial to a softer look. Voluptuous was probably a better word for it, and he would apply that to more than just a woman's figure. Never had he seen a more perfect example of the lavish relief of colors and curves than Bess Reynolds' face.

He had conducted a pleasurable reminiscence of her creamy brow and the fine, ebony sweep of hair at her temples, and was then moving on to the rather exquisite turn of black eyes fringed with heavy, dark lashes, when a mild commotion caught his notice. He was within sight of the inn now and approaching the vegetable gardens and a well house from the south. Several sheets hung dripping and dead in the still air beyond, but it was the voices that caught his notice.

Egad, it was *her*. Even from this distance, he could not help but recognize Bess, nor keep from hearing the fire in her voice. Some poor sod must have been a bit too cheeky, and Nick watched as she nearly drowned the man in a bundle of wet washing. Whoever he was, he almost fell over as he swayed and clawed for air. Serve the blackguard right if she smothered him, Nick thought with satisfaction.

He was not near enough to identify the man. Instead, he put his head down and chuckled all the way to the stable. He found the boy he sought, taking out a load from the stalls. It was the work of a moment to coax the lad away, ask him a few questions, and engage him to listen for anything useful. The boy seemed clever enough. Judging by the fading black eye he had received from one of the older boys, he was probably also one who tendered little fealty to his betters and knew how to hold his tongue.

Nick let the lad return to his duties, counted several minutes, then followed. He was almost to the courtyard when he passed the ostler, who was drenched from head to toe. The older man gave him a seedy glare as he walked away but said nothing.

Nick could not help a grin as he solved the puzzle. So, Bess held her own both with the travelers and the scum her father employed. He felt an unaccountable swell of pride in her—unaccountable, for he had no part in the making of her. He could not look on her in the joy and honor of a husband or even a lover. And he certainly could not regard her with paternal delight, but somehow, his heart still longed to applaud her.

His thoughts darkened again. Paternal delight, indeed! Her father was quick enough to send her away from Nick, who meant her no harm, but he seemed to do little to protect her from the other dastards who would importune her. Perhaps, Nick mused, if he found an opportunity during his stay, he himself could do something to make her existence more bearable. Or at least, safer.

But first, he had to stay alive.

Chapter Six

"**B**ESS, WHERE HAVE YOU been? The coffee is run out!"

Bess nearly dropped her tray as she raced for the pot and kettle. Her father had hardly spoken to her since the day before, when he had sent her so ignominiously away from the serving area. Now, it all seemed forgotten in light of the busy coffee room. She sent a quick glance around... no Mr. Cumberland this morning, to her exquisite disappointment. But she had no time to care about where her favorite customer had gone, when her father was tapping his foot.

"What kept you?" he demanded. "Oh, never mind, just see to the tables. Put yourself a bit straight, girl."

Bess cleared her throat and swept a hand through her hair. She blushed in mortification when she found a twig still stuck there from her morning ramble. She snatched it from her hair and went to fill her pot.

It was well that her father was more interested in putting her to work than asking where she had been, for she would rather not tell him the truth. She returned quickly with the full pot and gave him a contrite smile. Her father merely shook his head, with one hand on his hip and an indignant huff as he turned away.

Bess watched after him. *Poor Papa!* A year ago, he would have returned her smile with a playful smirk, a wag of his finger, and a secret amusement shared. He would have known precisely where she had gone—behind the inn, away from the busyness of the road and the coaches and the bustle of The Bittern. Somewhere to be alone for a few moments—down to her little nook in the trees, where she had read many a book as a girl. And it was where her mother had planted that one old rose bush with the dark red petals.

That was the real reason her father had stopped smiling. She should have thought of it sooner.

Her mother had been gone a year ago last May, and not a day had passed that did not see her father grow a little darker, a little older. A little wearier of this world. Bess's great terror was that one day, he, too, would simply fade away, and all she would be left with was this huge old place. An anchor, really, tying her to a future that would only sting of the past.

She was quiet as she went about her duties. Filling mugs, bringing trays, trying to keep everyone happy. The other serving girls could have done some of the meaner duties, but staying busy was the best way to prevent the drear and dread from stealing over her again. When the coffee room closed for the day, it was Bess who armed herself with a hot pail to wipe down the tables.

She polished until she could see her reflection in the gloss of the wood, then moved to the next table and did it all again. Her face gleamed up at her from that old mahogany—a vague outline of a furrowed brow, thinned lips, and a dark ring of hair working loose from its pins. And then, another face was peering over her shoulder.

She froze, but this time she did not squeak like a ninny. Instead, she turned around with almost a credible degree of dignity as the man behind her stepped back. "Good morning, Mr. Cumberland. I did not know you were still with us."

His expression flickered, then smoothed into a pleasant smile. "Yes, my business is not yet finished. I expect I will go tomorrow."

"If you are to stay another day, I think we could supply you with a better room. That one you took is by far the worst of the entire inn."

He lifted his shoulders, and a bashful grin appeared, almost boyish. "I do not mind. You may as well let the finer rooms out to more particular guests. Besides, that is one less set of linens you would have to wash." He followed this with a coy smile and a suggestive lifting of his brow.

Bess bit her lip uncomfortably. Could Mr. Cumberland have found out what she did to Tim? She hoped not. She would not like him to think she treated everyone like that... just those who deserved it. "The linens are no bother," she said hastily, "but the ceiling in that room is very low. And did not the noise trouble you?"

He frowned. "Noise? What noise?"

"Well, it is only that the window on that side faces the chicken coop. I like to hear the rooster crowing in the morning, but many do not."

His smile widened, growing crooked, and even more interesting than before. "Indeed, he certainly had me rubbing my eyes early. I wonder *you* do not take that room, if you enjoy his morning posturing."

"Oh, I hear my share of his theatrics, for I have the room just above yours."

His cheek flinched and his expression sobered as he squinted carefully at her. "You do?"

"It is not one of our finer rooms, either," she rushed to explain. "You know, it is not as if any guest would like that west-facing room better than most others. Hot in the summer, dark mornings in the winter."

"And you have to sleep somewhere, I suppose," he reasoned, but there was an odd note in his voice.

"It is very small," she added hurriedly, eager that he should not think her a vain creature, like one of the primped and pampered "kept" women from Town who came through the inn. "It's little more than a closet, really. My papa let me have that room after Mama... that is, we each took smaller rooms, and now we let our old suite out to the wealthy gents."

Mr. Cumberland blinked and swallowed, then he nodded. "Of course. And it is just the two of you?"

She nodded. "My brother Samuel went into the army two years ago."

"I see. Army or no, it must be a great comfort to you to have an older brother."

"He is my twin, actually." Her ears tingled with heat. Why was she telling him this? But he was so patient and attentive, and it was so rare that anyone actually wanted to just *talk* to her. What harm could there be? "Anyway, yes, it was a great comfort to have a... a champion, you could say. I am afraid I worshiped him as a hero."

"I did the same of my older brother," he replied. A pained twinge passed through his eyes, and he forced a smile. "That was, until he fell ill, and then it was I who had to be his protector."

Bess brushed one hand over the other and steadily met his gaze. "I understand something of that. My mother was very weak when we were born. She almost died, and so did I, but Samuel was strong from the beginning. I think my mother drew her strength from him," she finished with a soft smile.

Mr. Cumberland said nothing, but his open face and steady gaze encouraged her to continue.

She brushed a hair from her cheek. "We-we seldom hear from him. He is not an officer, you know, so pen and paper are harder to come by. His last letter said he was somewhere in Spain, with General Crauford."

"That is very fine. A brave and noble fellow, no doubt."

Bess surveyed him with a tilted head. "Were you ever in the army, Mr. Cumberland?"

He started. "What, I? No, no! Whatever would make you think so?"

"Oh, it is only the way you carry yourself, perfectly straight and all. And I saw the day you arrived, how you would seem to disappear in the crowd. You said very little to anyone, but you were always aware of everything. Then there was that bit with the horse and the way you are always watching... But forgive me," she apologized when she saw how pale and offended he looked. "Surely, it is none of my business."

He cleared his throat and waved a hand. "Nothing to forgive. You are a very observant, Miss Bess, and I ought to be flattered by your study of such a boring chap as myself. I am merely a solicitor. Nothing nearly so dashing or honorable as a soldier, I am afraid."

"But there is honor in that, too."

"Oh, indeed! I have the great honor of writing up documents for wealthier men, advising them when they are not in actuality so wealthy as they believed, and trying to keep them solvent when they finally accept how truly un-wealthy they are."

Bess laughed. "Perhaps it is not so glamorous an occupation as I thought."

"I am by no means ashamed, Miss Bess. But forgive me, I have quite forgotten why I came to see you. I am seeking someone—on business for my employer, of course—and my time is running short. I wondered if you might be able to direct me. As you say, I observe people, and of all the people here at the Bittern, I suspect you might be the best person to ask."

"Then, it is I who am flattered. What is this person's name?"

"That is just the trouble. I do not know his name, but he is said to be employed in some manner of curacy. Or perhaps he is only a lay person."

She looked up as she searched her memory. Her hands fumbled with her rag until she realized that she still held it, then she hid it behind her back. "Aside from our local parson, Mr. Crandle, the only cleric I know of is Mr. Sanders, over in Goose Hollow."

"Sanders? Goose Hollow?" He was all interest and looked as if he would step away the instant she confirmed it for him.

"But he is very old," she added quickly. "They say his eyesight is so bad, he has to have his housekeeper read the post, and she makes up half what she reads because she never learnt properly."

Mr. Cumberland's face sagged. "Then it sounds as if he is not the man I seek. I will take no more of your time, then. Thank you most kindly, Miss Bess."

He bowed and swept away, leaving Bess standing gap-mouthed in his wake. She had hoped he would ask about someone else, or that he might like something to drink, or... well, that he would do anything but leave her standing there with a word on her tongue he would never hear.

It was pleasant, the way they so easily smiled and bantered together, as if they were old friends rather than bare acquaintances. She was good at talking to strangers—she had to be, for heaven's sake—but there was something different about talking to Mr. Cumberland. It was as if all the appetizers of a usual conversation had been skipped, leaving them free to enjoy the main course. She smiled at the droll thought and wondered what "dessert" with such a man might be like.

But even if such a silly thing existed, she would never know it. He would go away on the morrow, just like every other person with whom she had ever thought to be friendly.

Bess sighed and returned to her tables, and the reflection that shone through her labors bore a strong resemblance to resentment.

G OOD HEAVENS, WHAT HAD come over him?

The innkeeper's daughter was becoming a problematic fascination. He watched her almost constantly, even when she was not aware of it. He had been watching her last evening, from the darkest corner of the room when another young cock had tried to lure her upstairs. She came away two pounds richer, and the man went upstairs alone.

He had been watching her again this morning when she walked out. Indeed, he had to, because she almost found him out on his return from the message drop site. He hid behind a tree and waited, admiring the way she bowed her head over that lone rose bush, cupping its fracturing petals in her hand and drinking in its fragrance. He followed her back at a distance, but dared not approach her when her father was about.

After the old innkeeper left, though, he could not make himself turn back. It seemed he could not pass by her without claiming some reason to talk to her. And every time he talked to her, he said something he should not. A fine spy he made!

But it had been impossible to walk away. Not when he saw her leaning over the table, her white apron strings marking the perfect curve of her waist and swaying gently with her work. Not a moment later, when he noticed a shining black ringlet dropping from her soft ebony crown and brushing that ivory neck. And certainly not when she turned slightly, and he could see the gloomy, lonesome heartache set in her cheeks and brow. Aye, fool that he was, he simply had to stop and talk to her, did he not? And probably spill enough to get himself killed.

To make it all even more embarrassing, she was the woman he had spied undressing in the room above his! Of course, it *had* to be her. Who else in this miserable inn could pass as Venus herself in the shadows? But some part of him had hoped never to learn that woman's identity. The moment of watching her in secret, being privy to something that only a lover would know, was too ethereal and dream-like to attach it to a flesh-and-blood woman.

No longer was she a nameless beauty upon who he could hang his fantasies. The woman with the waist-long tresses and sumptuous form had a face, a voice, and a character. And now, he felt not only a fool but a cad, because that image was forever seared into his memory as his first taste of sensual perfection.

Nick paced his room, pounding his forehead with his fist as if he could rid himself of that midnight vision. Even if he did not have his present duty—say he was at liberty again, a young man in his prime, ready and willing to let some pretty lass catch his heart—she would still be outside his sphere.

She was a tavern girl, for pity's sake! Just another one of a thousand such maids from a hundred other inns all over England, plying a dozen travelers a day with their mugs of ale and their calloused hands and their practiced charm.

But he was willing to bet that few of them could boast lips so red or hair so black or eyes so bewitching. Not to mention a temper so sharp, or a mind and spirit that seemed formed along the same paths as his own.

He sighed, grabbed his satchel, and sank down on the bed. Station and class mattered not anyway, because he *did* have a duty, and it did not include losing his head over the landlord's daughter. Even if she was easy to look at, and even easier to talk to.

He pulled out the map that North had drawn for him and rolled it out to study it. Over and again, he tested himself, closing his eyes and recalling every scratch, every note and hill and bend of the road. Perhaps it was unnecessary, but it was better than other things that could be flashing in his mind.

An hour later, reasonably sure that he knew the map by heart, he tucked it away and went out for a walk. It was too far to traipse the Brighton Road on foot, at least if he wished to avoid drawing attention. He would have to trust North to survey the road in the daylight and follow the map in the darkness. For now, he wandered into the village, meaning to look the part of a casual traveler waiting for his coach, or a solicitor about his master's business.

The first shop along the way was a barber surgeon's that shared space with a tobacconist. As he needed neither a shave nor a good leeching, he pretended to inspect the pipe tobacco offerings before wandering out again.

There was a blacksmith across the street. Probably the one Bess had told him about. Nick dawdled long enough to be noticed, admiring the various pokers, tongs, nails, and horseshoes displayed in the blacksmith's window. When he was certain that he had been seen, he strolled casually on. A meat-seller, a baker, and a small stand where fresh fish were sold... Nick took them all in with the air of a man who had nothing but time and a bit of spare money on his hands. Provided North's informant had been correct, God rest his soul, someone around here ought to be looking for the man who answered to the name Cumberland.

As he passed a draper's shop at the opposite end of town, he finally saw someone bold enough to stare back at him. The woman was dressing the window, and she pressed a hand to the glass to peer suspiciously out. She was well past her prime, if she had ever had one, and she cocked a weathered eye at him as he turned at the top of the street and wandered back.

Finally, she stepped out and confronted him. "I have what ye're looking for."

Nick stopped and glanced around. "I beg your pardon, madam?"

"Why ye come ter town." She nodded knowingly. "I have just what ye're wantin'."

"And pray tell, what is that?"

The woman only turned away, beckoning him with a single wrinkled finger.

Nick watched her warily. A quick glance about assured him that no one else was paying them any notice, and the woman was obviously insistent that he follow her for a private word. His palms started to sweat, and he went after her. Perhaps he had found his informant, after all. She never looked back at him until she had reached the door of her shop again, and then paused only long enough to see that he closed it behind himself.

"Well, now," he addressed her, "what is this you say you have for me?"

The hair on the back of his neck prickled when she squinted one eye at him and raised a finger to her lips. "Not 'ere. Lord ter goodness! He thinks to stop me right 'ere, 's if I'd have it on the shelf! Ain't 'e a smart one, Captain Bennick?"

Nick scanned the room. Nothing but shelves of fabric, rows of ribbon, and the odd hat or two, festooned with whatever was in fashion last season. "I believe there has been some mistake. My name is not Bennick, madam."

She snorted and waddled to a darkened corner of the shop. "I weren't talking ter *ye.*" The woman bent over, and when she straightened again, she held a scrappy old cat in her arms. Half his ear was missing, and mangy tufts of hair stuck out from his head at odd angles, but his eyes were perfectly round orbs of green gold. He was the eeriest looking cat Nick had ever seen, but the woman stroked his angular cheek and the cat responded with a purr that sounded like rusty carriage wheels.

"Captain Bennick, I presume?" he asked.

"Jest as ye please," the woman replied. "What d'ye think, Captain Bennick? 'E'll do, won't 'e?"

Nick smiled tightly, wondering exactly what he would "do" for. "I am glad to have Captain Bennick's approval, but was there something in particular you had to tell me?"

The woman scrunched her face into a cunning smirk and carefully lowered the ancient cat. "Back 'ere. Watch yer step," she cautioned, as she led him from the main room of the shop and into a darkened chamber behind.

Nick's senses were firing in alarm now. Perhaps the cat was merely a delay, while others got into position. Perhaps he was to be ambushed, silenced, like the informant. Was it to be a swift death, or kidnapping and torture? Were these friends or foes of the deceased Cumberland, and which would he rather encounter?

Silently cursing his general for assigning this drafted affair, and himself for insisting on its necessity in the first place, he carefully entered the back room. It was nearly dark, illuminated only by the light from the front windows that cut around his figure through the doorway.

"This," the old woman whispered reverently.

Nick could see that she was holding something for him to take, but he could not tell at first what it was. A letter? Map? It was folded into a square shape, and she pressed it into his hands.

Definitely not a letter or a map, or any kind of paper at all. He turned it over, tracing the edges with his finger. "I do not understand, madam. Is... is it a handkerchief?"

The woman roared with laughter. "Is it a... Why, any man worth 'is brass ought ter know the finest ribbon from the Orient when 'e touches it!"

"Any man, indeed. It is very fine, quite like silk, madam, but I fail to see what this has to do with me."

She threw her arms out in indignation, and fairly pushed him into the light of the front room. "Only see!" she cried as she reclaimed the ribbon from his hands.

Nick watched in confusion as she stretched out the length of folded ribbon, and then startled in shock when she boldly reached up to brush his cheek with it. "There, now, soft as a wee one's bott, it is."

"Have a care, madam!" he protested, pushing her away. "Now, let us have enough of this rubbish and come to the point. What is your business with me?"

"Business?" she cackled. "Laws, but 'ow can I 'ave business when the gent is too thick ter do for 'is lady? This be the finest ribbon from 'ere to the Far East!"

Bewildered, he permitted her to shove the satiny shimmering thing into his hands once more. "That is all? You just mean for me to buy the ribbon?"

"The lad's a slow one, Captain Bennick," the woman lamented. "Ee, don't ye 'ave a fair lass a waitin' in Brighton? Ye won't find this sort there." She leaned close with a loud whisper. "Me lad smuggled this straight from India, 'e did. Brought all the way from the czar's palace, that's what."

Nick raised a brow. "The czar, eh?" He sighed and stroked the rich, watery length of it. He was no expert, but he had two sisters, and he was fairly certain they had never owned anything like this. It was the deepest, richest shade of claret, and about an inch wide. The weave of it was so tight and soft that it felt like it would never wear or snag, but it was light as air.

Whether it had been smuggled from the "czar of India's palace" was doubtful, but it did look like a quality item. If he had a sweetheart, this would make for her a lavish courtship gift. And buying something like this would make him look like a regular traveler, instead of a redcoat posing as a highwayman/spy in hiding.

"Very well, madam. How much do you want for it?"

"Five bob," she answered confidently.

"Five! I do not want it that badly."

"Aye, then, six," the woman returned.

"Six? I just said—"

"For seven, I'll make a 'at just for yer lady fair. What color does she favor with the red?"

"Madam, that is not... oh, hang it all." He drew out his coin purse and dropped the money into her outstretched palm. "No, just the ribbon, thank you," he protested when she offered to take it back to weave into a bonnet. "Thank you, and good day, madam."

She wrapped the ribbon for him in a square of cotton, then collected her cat and walked him to the door. She opened it and began to wave him off. Nick, grateful to have completed his purchase and made his escape, was barely half out the door when it banged shut behind him. He looked back through the window, but the woman was nowhere to be seen.

"Peculiar!" he huffed to himself. "And now, old boy, what are you to do with four feet of blood-red ribbon?"

It was not until later, when he was back in his room and unwrapping his strange purchase, that he understood. He pulled it from the cotton and unfurled the entire length of it once more, admiring its sheen and softness, when a scribbled note fell to the floor.

He was half a moment in realizing what it was, but in an instant, everything became clear.

"Tonight," he muttered. "So be it."

Chapter Seven

I T WOULD BE A bright moon tonight.

Bess was in her dressing gown, curled up in the window seat of her room. She had long since blown out her candle for the night, and ought well to be in bed, fast asleep. Heaven knew she would have to wake up with that infernal rooster and would not sit down again until the next evening. But tonight, her mind was wandering a drowsy path through the day's end and peering hesitantly into the morrow.

Her father's words over their brief supper had put her in a nervous kind of melancholy. "Bess," he had said, "I've been thinking. It's not decent, you being unmarried. You need a man around."

"Whatever for?" she had asked, more in surprise than disagreement. They had never spoken anything of the kind before.

"Well, for... you know, you are quite a handsome girl."

Bess merely stared back at him with narrowed eyes.

Her father refused to look at her. He merely scraped his plate with the last of his bread and kept talking. "You know how it is for the other girls. Not being attached, well... people will make assumptions. *Men* will make assumptions."

She blinked. Her mouth opened, but she had nothing to say. Apparently, her father did not either, for he gathered his plate and cup and rose. "Best see to the tap," was all he said.

Hours later, that brief conversation, if it could be called such, was still all she could think about. A long sigh lifted her shoulders, and she let her head drop against the casement.

What would her father take it into his head to do? Find a husband for her? Send her to the cousins she had never met, who supposedly lived in London? She knew nothing about them, except that her mother used to talk about some shadowy relation of some sort. Papa had never joined in that sort of talk, and no letters ever passed between them that Bess knew of, so it could not be much of a connection.

Perhaps it would not be so distasteful to be married. To have someone of her own, someone to talk with and dream with—oh, that she could be so fortunate! More likely, she would end up with someone like Will Waters, the blacksmith. Conveniently single, able to support a wife, and not vicious, but hardly good company. Not like...

Oh, for mercy's sake, why was she thinking about Mr. Cumberland? If there was one thing every tavern girl learned quickly, it was not to fall in love with the customers. They moved on soon enough, and the girls unlucky enough to lose their hearts were always left behind.

Always.

But Mr. Cumberland *was* pleasant company. He was a different sort than they usually got, which spoke in his favor. It was true, he seemed to seek her out, but not like other men did. He talked to her, and what was better, he listened to her. No one else did so much. She liked the way he smiled, and the way he spoke so fondly of a troublesome horse that most would have sold. Such a man could not be bad, could he?

Bess traced her finger through the fog on the glass and let her gaze drift. The worn oak tree outside her window breathed gently in the night air, and in the distance, a mail coach rambled away from the inn, headed west toward the Brighton Road. It would be clear and cool for their drive tonight; a pleasant change after the sweltering August. The leaves would be tinged with red and gold in a few more weeks, and not long after that, the inn would go into hibernation for the winter. That would probably be when her father did something more than talk about seeing her married off.

Bess lingered a moment more, toying with the end of her plait and trying to imagine how or why she should object to her father's wishes. What sort of man would he find for her? Or would he permit her the choosing of her own husband? Papa might. He had loved her mother to distraction, had he not? Surely, he would be sympathetic toward his daughter. With a sigh, she stretched until her feet brushed the floor. It did little good to fret about it now, did it? She might as well try to sleep.

Just as she was easing from her seat, a flash of something below caught her attention. The rooster, probably... but no, it was outside the bounds of the coop. She leaned against the glass, squinting into the darkness.

It was Mr. Cumberland.

He must have climbed out of his window, though how he did so silently, she did not understand. Why would he not have used the door? And why slip into the trees, fleet and furtive like a fox?

She watched as the shadowy figure paused once at the edge of the wood for a glance back at the inn. Surely, he could not have seen her, hidden at the edge of her darkened window, but she drew back all the same. For an instant, she was certain that he looked directly at her, and her heart stopped. But then, he was gone, just as silently as if he had never been.

Bess stared for a long time into the line of blackness at the trees, but he did not return. Questions simmered in her mind, banishing any hope of sleep. The only thing she did understand was that Mr. Cumberland had some reason, after all, for taking the lower room.

NICK STEPPED OUT OF the tent, his arms held up, and surveyed himself. He had to look the whole bit tonight, and that meant the French cocked hat, the thigh-high boots that were soft as butter, and the deer-skin breeches that molded to him like his own flesh.

North cocked his head and nodded. "You look good. Very smart, I should say."

"I look like a popinjay. A red velvet coat? Next, I shall be taking a thimble of snuff and driveling 'Odd's fish!' And what is this?" Nick fluffed the lace cravat in distaste. "How shall I even see around this monstrous thing?"

"You only need to tie it proper. Have Wesson do it. He's as good as a batman when you cannot get one."

The sergeant came to attend him at once, and in a moment, the offending cravat was tucked softly under his chin. Nick stretched his neck side to side and found that the silk of the shirt really did feel... quite nice.

Wesson came behind him and tied the scarf for his face next. It took a few tries before they had a knot that would hold the vexing thing in place over his eyes, with the holes lined up so he could see anything at all, and yet not tangle in his hair or get in the way of his hat. Nick cocked his head and worked his mouth and nose this way and that, to see if it would slip. He couldn't see the lower half of his body, and he was sure it would slip sideways and blind him at the most inopportune moment. But for now, it was holding.

Two flintlocks were strapped at the front of his belt, with a sword dangling down his left leg. This was the only part of the get up that felt familiar. He experimented with the coat and the pistols, sweeping the heavy velvet away until his hand could descend on polished brass and steel. The lace cuffs bungled him almost every time.

"Egad," he muttered. "How the devil did this man ever manage to get his pistol out and see what he was shooting at, let alone make himself the scourge of the highway for three years?"

"Just wait till you have to do it horseback," North said with a grin. "Black Bess is waiting for you."

Nick froze, still clutching the hilt of the rapier at his hip. "What did you say?"

"Well, we thought it fitting, you know. That was old Dick Turpin's horse."

"No, that's a myth," Daniels interrupted. "Black Bess was Swift Nick's horse. You know, the one what galloped two hundred thirty miles in a single day and tricked Bonny Prince Charles."

"I still say it was Dick Turpin," North argued, "but Swift Nick works, too, I guess. Anyway, that horse was supposed to be a daring beast like this one."

"I thought of it," Daniels bragged.

"Aye, so he did, and we've all been calling her Bonny Black Bess, after the old one. Fine handle for the fancy she-devil, don't you think?"

Nick closed his eyes and blew out a sigh. Could they have chosen a more inconvenient name? "Just bring her over."

Wesson trotted up with the mare, then tossed the reins to Nick and retreated behind North. "I almost lost a finger when I bridled her, sir," he complained.

"Before or after you got the bit in her mouth?" North asked.

"Both!"

They carried on thus, with North and Daniels teasing Wesson for not knowing how to handle a horse, and poor Wesson protesting that the mare was "fit only for the grim reaper to ride." Nick blocked it all out. Pacing his breathing, he swept a careful hand down the mare's shimmering neck, over the satiny leather of the saddle, stopping to caress a spot just at the mare's loin.

She swung her head into him, but this time, it was not with savage intent. Wide nostrils pushed into the crimson coat and she huffed three sharp, deep breaths. Her head came up and she stamped a hoof, as if impatient to be off, then stood stock still with muscles aquiver.

"Gadsbudlikins," Daniels breathed. "She must smell the old boy on your coat."

Nick grunted in reply and gathered the reins at her withers. Boot met iron and he was in the saddle, aboard a keg of gunpowder. She trembled and surged against the bit, but stilled when she found his hand.

Nick held her for an instant—as long as he dared. He cast one last glance over his men as they saluted him, then he let the black demon have her head.

T HE MAN WHO MET him was no monk.

    Whatever else he was, none could say, but there was nothing holy about the stooped and swaggering figure in the black cape. Nick drew rein on the far side of the brook when the man held up a hand in warning.

"*N'approchez pas*," he commanded. This order was followed by a ghostly leer from under the hood of his cowl, from a face barely outlined by the brilliant moon. Unlike Nick, the man wore no disguise for his face, but neither did he need one with that heavy hood.

Nick lowered his rein hand and held the other aloft to show that he held no weapon. "*J'attends*."

The man moved up the length of the brook, putting the moon more behind his back. There was a faint limp to his steps in the soft loam, but it was impossible to know whether the man was a cripple or simply walking on uneven ground. At length he stopped, perched on a rock that jutted into the water.

"*Qu'est-ce que vous voulez?*" Nick demanded.

There was no answer for nearly a minute. The mare must have sensed the tension in his thigh, for she shifted her hip and gave a low snort. He dropped his hand again and stroked the tight flesh near her mane with his thumb to settle her, just as he used to do with Roy before they would charge the cannon.

"*Une semaine à partir de demain,*" came the reply. *A week from tomorrow.*

That would be a Thursday. Then what? Nick squinted into the darkness, wondering if the spy had companions surrounding him. His own men would be scattered in a loose perimeter, but out of caution, none of them would be close enough to do anything, if matters went awry. He steadied his breath, and his right hand slowly found the edge of his coat. "*Où ça?*" he asked.

The man chuckled—a sound less menacing than it was revolting, for his lungs rasped and heaved until the "monk" gagged and spat upon the ground. He whirled and disappeared, fading behind a tree. Not a noise did he make this time, lame or sound, and Nick wondered if he had simply slipped into a nearby hole.

What was he to do now? If he was to meet his mark in just over a week, how was he to know where to find him? Or was it he who chose the site of the "attack?" Yes, certainly, that was for him to do. But was there a message?

Nick looked about for a few moments, turning the mare this way and that to examine his side of the brook for clues. Finding none, he stopped once more and glared at the spot where the "monk" had stood...

At the round rock, poised just at the tip of the larger stone that jutted out into the brook. From this new angle, he could see a sliver of white, pinned under the rock.

Mare and man splashed through the slow-moving waters of Shag Brook, and a moment later, the note was in his hand. He held it up in the moonlight just long enough to see a coded scribble. Then, he tucked it into his coat and put his heel to the mare's black sides. The less time he spent at this murky hollow, the better.

"HERE," NORTH ANNOUNCED, TAPPING his finger on the map. "It lines up with that stand of trees opposite the moor. And look—there's a dip in the landscape, about fifty yards from the road. It is hardly worth noting by day, but Daniels and I tested it. The grass is high just now, and if you lay along your horse's neck, no one from the road can see you until you are almost upon them."

Nick tied his own cravat once more, happy to be back in familiar clothes, and leaned over North's map. "Yes, I see. That settles the time and place of my real target. Now to lay down a trail of robberies beforehand. Cumberland seems to have struck four times, with the fourth, we assume, being his contact."

North nodded and trailed his quill down the length of the road. "So, three decoy strikes. I found just the right fellow for the first run. He is coachman to a London merchant, with a fine, expensive-looking carriage, and he will be traveling without his master. He does, however, have his master's man of business, and swears him for a chattery, easily frightened sort, sure to spread reports of the terrifying villain on the road."

Nick stared at his lieutenant. "You hired a decoy? How do you know he will not say the wrong thing? We cannot afford for anyone to think these attacks less than genuine."

North looked over at Wesson, who could not hide a faint grin. "He's my cousin. We happened across him yesterday when we were coming back from Reigate. Not to worry, sir. Barney's as true as they come. Well, I suppose he did prevaricate a little, because when I asked for his help, he said he would tell the solicitor that the carriage wheel needed to be mended so they could stop for a day or so. But apart from that, I would trust my life to him."

Nick blew out a sigh, then shook his head. "I wish to heaven they could all be so easy. Very well. We shall plan for... here, in the grove." He pointed to a bend in the road on the map. "The first 'attack' must be about half a mile north of where we intend to meet our mark. The second a mile and a half south, and the third on another road, as directly west as possible."

"When do you mean to begin?"

Nick swallowed. "Tomorrow night. Say, eleven thirty. And the following morning, you or Daniels can carry that message from the French spy directly to Richards, so he can set his team about decoding it."

"Right, then. We'll tell Barney to be ready tomorrow. Have you got what you need from the inn?"

"For now," he said slowly. "I made it known that I would be departing in the morning. However, do you recall how we learned that Cumberland would move around? That was why it took us so long to learn it was actually him. He would come and go from the coaching inns, sometimes disappear altogether. His robberies seemed to overlap here and there, but not consistently."

"What do you mean, sir?"

"I mean that I might do well to 'go away' for a few days, then come back. Make myself something of a regular. The dates when I show my face will neither match nor completely diverge from the dates of the robberies."

"I see. Where shall I have the men, sir?"

Nick took the quill and studied the map, making marks at certain points. "Daniels will be my outrider. You and Wesson will be in uniform... here. The militia should not be a problem the first night, and possibly not the second. By the third outing, for certain, you will need to be a diversion to keep the troops from shooting me. Colonel Stanwick commands the regiment at Crawley. Do you know him?"

"Only by reputation. He is said to be a just man, for good or ill."

"And I imagine he takes a low view of highwaymen," Nick muttered grimly.

"No fear, sir. It won't be the colonel out chasing villains at night. He would send one of his junior officers out, and if I know most of them, a mug of ale is far more interesting than a cold highway. We can outwit the best of them."

"Let us hope, because I am rather fond of my neck."

Chapter Eight

"ARE YOU READY, SIR?"

Nick shook his head and sucked in a cleansing breath. He had no business ruminating on dancing black eyes or hair that shone like a rook's wing... not now. His hands smoothed down the front of the claret velvet coat and caught the edges near his belt, testing its weight and feel. He nodded to Daniels. "As ready as I will ever be. Do you understand everything you are to do?"

The tall, ruddy youth's face was nearly blue, so pale was he, but he jerked his head smartly. "Yes, sir."

"Good lad. Take up your position, then. I will wait for the signal."

Daniels clucked to his horse and was off, leaving Nick alone in the copse of trees. The night air grew still around him, save for the soft breathing of his horse and the cricket song in the tall grass. He closed his eyes and tried to focus on the task before him.

He could do this. It was for King and Country, after all. He only had to *look* menacing. Cumberland had ranged relatively free for so long because he had never actually killed anyone. The militia had searched for him, to be sure, but they had never been out to avenge blood. Fear of inconvenience and harm made the coaches cooperative victims. The reputation of the ruthless highwaymen of yore had worked for George Cumberland, and it would work for Nicholas Hunt.

He checked his first flintlock once more, to be certain it was loaded with a blank wad. If he had to fire it for a bit of intimidation, he could not harm anyone. But that was probably an unnecessary precaution. Tonight's target would be an especially easy one for him to practice his technique on, thanks to North.

The black mare's neck stiffened, and she gave a low snort. Nick's eyes followed the swiveling ears, but he neither saw nor heard anything. "What is it, old girl?" he asked.

She tossed her head and her skin shivered under his hand as if she were trying to shake off his touch. "Very well, then. I see where I stand," he grumbled. "Just promise not to bite me tonight, will you?"

The mare dropped her head and rooted against the bit, then her feet began to fidget. Nick had his hands full trying to keep her quiet. It would not do for a restless horse to send birds fluttering or crack twigs under her hooves and send up the alarm. She resisted his best efforts and danced in place, champing her teeth, threatening to rear, and twisting her hip away whenever he would try to redirect her. Then, all at once, she went dead still.

Nick was more unnerved now than when she was fighting him. He was slow to drop his hand, cautious in relaxing his seat, and his stomach quivered with dread and anticipation. And there it was—the call of a tawny owl. The signal from Daniels!

He never knew which of them made the decision to gallop. They were off in a rush, tearing through the wood and up the rise to the road. Black hooves sliced through the crackling autumn grass—too much noise! But it mattered not, for the coach loomed before them, and there was nowhere for it to go.

"STAND AND DELIVER!" NICK aimed his empty flintlock at the driver and prayed his horse would cooperate for just a half minute.

She did better than cooperate. She dropped her hindquarters and slid on the last of the grass until her feet hit the dirt road. Then she shot her head into the sky and snorted like a savage at the terrified carriage horses. Had Nick been prepared for her to rear, it would have been the thrill of a lifetime, mounted on Fury itself.

As it was, he had to grab her mane at the last second to keep from falling off. He was very nearly toppled on his head, but just as he was losing his irons, the mare crashed to the ground and lunged with bared teeth at the wheel horse's head. She sprang back at once, thank goodness, or the driver might have got a shot at him. But she had done her deed faithfully and well—the carriage horses locked their heels and refused to move forward.

Nick finally recovered his reins and aimed his pistol again. It was a bloody good thing this was a set-up, or the coachman would have taken advantage of his distraction to get out a...

Oh.

He swallowed as he looked down the barrel of a blunderbuss.

"Try to rob me, will you?" the driver snarled. "I'll teach you not to meddle with Terrence Jackson!"

Terrence... Jackson? Oh, heavens! This was the wrong coach!

But it was too late to retreat now. He tightened his aim, worthless though his pistol was at the moment, and bellowed back in defiance. "Drop that dragon, or I'll have your teeth!"

The driver was silent, as if deliberating. Jackson's weapon never wavered, but neither did Nick's. The driver had him outmatched, and they both knew it. So why did he hesitate?

Nick nudged his horse, and she edged closer to the heads of the carriage horses, her ears flat and her teeth bared. A little distance between them now, and the half-moon was behind Nick's back, but more importantly, the horses and anyone behind the driver in the carriage were now technically in the line of fire. If his pistol had actually been loaded.

"Blast you, you vermin," the coachman spat. The blunderbuss dipped faintly.

Nick stiffened his arm. He would have liked to switch the flintlock to his left hand and draw out his rapier as a double show of force, but he could not dare let the driver take advantage of the instant his finger left the trigger. "Throw down your valuables, and you and your passengers will go unmolested."

The driver hurled another curse at Nick's head—something to do with his parentage and exactly how hot Hell ought to be for those of his ilk. Then there was another sound.

"Papa?" squeaked a small voice. "Is the bad man going to shoot us?"

Horror filled Nick's heart. He had just threatened a man and his child! No... *children*, for at least one more voice joined the first. Sickened, he straightened his trigger finger and started to cast his own hands up in surrender.

The driver buckled first. He hurled the blunderbuss down by his feet with an oath, then spoke to his children. "'Twill be all right, Thomas. Toss out my purse. Millie, and keep your head down, doll."

A small, heavy object sailed from the carriage window. Nick had no intention of checking its contents or demanding more. He pointed his pistol up and backed his horse out of the way of the team. Cumberland was rumored to sweep his victims a gallant bow and thank them most graciously for their contribution to his hedonistic existence, and Nick had practiced such a speech to keep up appearances.

But no words would come. Bile simmered in his stomach, and he only wanted to run and never touch that cursed purse.

Jackson wasted no time, nor did he spare the whipcord. The coach thundered on, with its master glaring darkly and muttering well-deserved curses. Nick let it pass. Bad enough that he had terrified and inconvenienced them, but the final blow came when two small faces stared back at him through the rear window of the coach.

He hung his head and stowed his pistol. "A fine work we have done tonight, old girl," he groaned. The mare sighed and shook her heavy mane, as if she agreed and was now ready for her oats. She chewed contentedly at her bit and fanned her tail, perfectly happy with herself.

She was the only one who felt that way.

A moment later, Daniels galloped up. "Sir! The other carriage is coming now! Do you wish to stop them?"

"No... Wait, the other carriage? Why did you give the signal for this one?"

The sergeant looked baffled. "I did not, sir. Oh, but I did hear an owl some ways off."

Nick closed his eyes and shook his head. "We need a different signal. Collect that purse there and let us retreat to the trees."

"What of Wesson's cousin, sir?"

"He can drive all the way to India tonight, for all I care. I will not be stopping anyone else."

THE MORNING DAWNED CRISP and silvery, with the first hint of frost nipping the air. Nick stretched out his legs near the camp's cook fire and swirled the hot tin of coffee Daniels had just brought him. He needed it, for he could not recall his last proper night of sleep. He propped his cheek on his fist and closed his eyes for just a blink or two.

Some time later, he awoke with a jerk. Hoofbeats were approaching. He stood and saw Lieutenant North saluting as he returned to camp.

"It is done, Captain. I found Jackson at the Iron Cross, five miles on."

"I imagine he was happy to see his purse again," Nick sighed. "What did you tell him?"

"That we had run down a no-account robber and that he had given up the name of his victims after a bit of old-fashioned 'persuasion'."

"And he bought it?"

"I think was just happy to have his purse back. He seemed to care little about the means. It was a good job we found him when we did, Captain. He just lost his wife, and he has a chance to make a fresh go of it in Brighton, provided he can be there by Friday."

"And that purse was probably all he had in the world." Nick rubbed his eyes. "North, I am for London today. I'll take that message we gathered from the French spy at the brook, and I'll tell Richards to go hang before I hold up another innocent person!"

"Come, sir, you could not have known. People have gotten bolder taking to the roads at night with the militia stationed nearby, but even so, no one in their senses travels at night with children."

"So, who would you have me prey on instead? Richards told me straight to my face to target wealthy ladies."

"That would be the safest, yes," North replied, stroking his chin as he thought.

"I will not do it."

North sent a sideways glance to Wesson, who was collecting the horses to tend them, then cleared his throat. "Yes, sir."

"Do you want me to saddle Bess for you, Captain?" Wesson asked.

He cringed. Did they *have* to call that battle axe of a horse such a sweet name? "No. Best not to let her be seen. I will slip back to my room at the inn and take the post. I expect to be back day after tomorrow."

A NYONE WATCHING BESS WOULD never know she was thinking of anything besides serving coffee and talking to the customers. She always made the best tips when she was animated and cheerful, and this morning, her pockets jingled most satisfactorily. But the moment Mr. Cumberland drifted by the entrance to the coffee room, her spine tingled and he owned all her senses.

He did not come in directly. Rather, he seemed to be deliberating, standing around without an object for a moment. Bess pretended to ignore him, until her father's voice from the hall gave her an excuse to look that way.

"Well, Mr. Cumberland! I see you are leaving us. Fare thee well, sir."

Mr. Cumberland looked slightly flustered, for the first time in Bess's memory. "Thank you, sir. I believe I shall be returning in a few days."

"You will, then? Will you have a coffee while you wait for the mail coach? My Bessie, she makes the finest cup south of London. And we just got a fresh crate of tea—no thrice-steeped skimmings no better than bath water at the Bittern, if I do say so. Bessie," he called, "go and make a fresh pot. I'll have Hattie come pour."

Mr. Cumberland finally raised his eyes to Bess, then looked quickly back to her father. "That will not be necessary. I do not intend to remain long."

Bess's father grinned proudly. "Very good, very good. Well, Mr. Cumberland, until we meet again."

The gentleman bade her father a very civil farewell, then stepped slowly into the coffee room. Bess's father lingered a moment, watching Mr. Cumberland, then shook his head oddly and went away.

To her everlasting embarrassment, Bess had not stirred through the whole exchange, and now the man was facing her directly. And smiling in that bashful way of his.

"Good morning, Miss Bess."

She lifted a brow. "You are highly favored, Mr. Cumberland."

"Oh? How so?"

"My father is an excellent innkeeper, but he rarely shows special interest in travelers who have never stayed here before. He must like you."

Mr. Cumberland glanced over his shoulder. "Odd, for until just now, I would have thought the opposite. Perhaps he is simply glad to see me leaving."

She shrugged with a smile. "Or perhaps he is recalling that rather notable incident when you first arrived and offered to trade rooms with that odious man. I expect it saved a deal of face for us. Very noble of you, sir, to take into account the feelings of a poor innkeeper and his daughter."

His forehead creased, but his eyes locked on to hers. "You have mentioned this a few times, but truly, it was nothing."

She smiled, a purposeful, tight expression her mother used to use when she knew Bess was being untruthful. "I suppose not. Coffee, Mr. Cumberland?"

He drew a slow breath, and Bess could almost swear that he looked crestfallen when he finally answered. "I am afraid I must be going. There was... someone I was to meet."

Bess tilted her head and affected an innocent look. "Indeed? Why, if you are meeting someone from the village, you would do better to wait for them here and take the coach together. Going into the village now, how very strange! You will be sure to miss the post, sir. You might just as well traipse off into the woods."

His eyes narrowed instantly, but Bess refused to give him the satisfaction of either calling him out or letting him off. She merely smiled and waited. His voice, when he answered, was lower than before.

"I suppose I will have to take my chances, for the arrangement is already made. I did wish to bid you a proper farewell, Miss Bess."

"Why do you call me that?"

The earnest look on his face changed to one of confusion. "Call you what? Miss Bess?"

"Yes, that. I mean, everyone calls me Bessie, or if they are strangers and particularly respectful, they might call me Miss Reynolds once or twice before they have had a few drinks."

"Have I offended you?"

"Not at all. To be truthful, I rather like it. I was just wondering, that is all."

The side of his mouth tugged upward. "I like it, too. I hope to see you again... Miss Bess."

Chapter Nine

Bess squinted one eye, took aim, and fired her small stone into the stream. It dashed against a rock before dropping into the water. She frowned and picked up another. Some day, perhaps she could set it to skim over the surface, the way her brother used to do.

Three more stones sank with disappointing promptness. Oh, if she had only paid better attention! There was something in the way Samuel held it, between his thumb and middle finger...

"Ah, now there's a pretty sight!"

Bess froze and her stomach coiled when she recognized the ostler's voice. How careless of her to come in sight of the stables at this time of day! She clenched her teeth, then turned and forced a smile.

"It is a pretty stream," she agreed, as lightly as she could.

"I dinna' mean the stream, Bessie lass." Tim grinned and gestured with his pipe as he came closer. "Puts me in mind o' yer fair dam, it does. How she'd twinkle and shine when she'd go about!"

Bess took an uncomfortable step backward, but the stream was at her heels, and she could hardly wade to her ankles just because the ostler came to talk to her. How people would laugh! "I am not half so beautiful as Mama was."

One of Tim's eyes narrowed, and his throat rumbled in a low chuckle. He wagged a finger at her and shook his head. "They that be the handsomest oft think the least of theyselves. Be it not time the pretty lass found a man?"

Bess's face flamed, and her hands were suddenly clammy. She would have to be blind and stupid not to notice how the ostler stared at her, sought her out, followed her around these last few months. She had grown up waiting tables at the inn, and she knew a lecherous look when she saw it. Men were always eyeing her, trying to touch what they had no right to, and dropping comments designed to make her blush.

But no one had ever pressed her. Not like this, so close, and all alone.

"I... I suppose, someday, I ought to marry," she stammered. "But..."

"Oh, but a lassie wants a man what can do for 'er. A strong man, is it? Aye, no sapling'll serve!" He stepped nearer still, and she could feel the heat of his breath on her cheeks. "Beautiful Bessie lass likes the horses, aye? Coming to the stables? Were it only the horses she were coming ter see?"

Bess swallowed the rock that had formed in her throat and gasped a little when she tried to speak. "You are quite mistaken! I only came to pet the animals. I have no... no aims toward... toward anyone in that way!"

"Have ye not! Nay, I see wha's in the lass's eye. A thousand miles is that look, i'n't it? There be only one thing on 'er mind when she sets 'er eyes yonder and sighs to break 'er poor heart."

She cleared her throat and stepped sideways, wetting the heel of her shoe a little. Tim followed her. "I really cannot know what you mean. Oh, but look, there is Papa!"

It was true, to her eternal relief. Her father was trotting down the slope from the stable yard, looking even more urgent than he usually did. Bess neatly sidestepped the ostler. Surely, he would not dare pursue her with her father at hand. "I am sure he must be wanting me in the scullery," she said.

Tim backed away, and Bess met her father halfway up the little rise. He was fanning a letter in his hand, with an eagerness in his face that she had not seen in far too long.

"Bess! Come and see. It is from Samuel!"

"From Samuel!" She caught her father's arm and hurried with him to the back rooms of the inn. She never knew if Tim lingered and stared after her, for she refused to look back, but she could have sworn that she felt his eyes burning into her shoulders.

M R. REYNOLDS SPREAD HIS son's letter on a round table and drew a lantern
nearby. Bess sat close to his shoulder and tried to keep herself from peering
eagerly over. "What does he say? Where is he?"

"The River Coa, he says. This letter is a month old already." He clamped his teeth and
read grimly. No exclamations of fear or dismay did the father utter over his son's safety,
and Bess was left to discover the contents of the letter by watching the deepening lines
around her father's mouth.

"It is a bad business!" he sighed at last. "A fearfully bad business."

"What has happened? Was he in a battle?"

"So it seems. And he speaks rather poorly—quite impertinently, I daresay, about
General Crauford." He shook his head and passed the letter to Bess. "I can read no more.
Tell me the rest, my dear."

She was less eager than she had been a moment ago. Dread coiled round her heart, and
she scarcely dared to breathe. What had frightened her father so? Her brother's words
blurred on the page, and she was obliged to sniff faintly and blink several times.

When she finally was able to read, she discovered that her father must have scanned it
to the end. At least, there was no more report of Samuel's doings. The rest of the letter
was all inquiries about them, and his regrets at being so long away from home.

"Tell Bessie," he said, *"not to grow any older until I get back, for I do not wish to miss the
fun of frightening off the dozen men who must be taking note of her."*

Bess hid a giggle at that bit. Oh, Samuel! He had always been her champion. *"You may
be assured that my entire regiment plans to race each other to Surrey when we come home, just
to see if the tales of my sister's beauty have been exaggerated. But they will be sadly thwarted,
because I mean to take her to London as soon as may be, so she can see how well she outshines
the pedigreed ladies."*

She smiled fondly at her brother's teases. He was putting her on, of course, but what
sort of brother would he be if he did not try to pamper a sister's vanity somewhat?

"What more of the battle, Bessie?" her father prodded.

Her brow pinched, and she frowned as she went back to read the more painful details
her father had skimmed over. "He says there was some great row between Crauford and
Wellington, and many men died because of one general's ambition... oh, dear. And later
on, he says that the French seem to have poor informants most of the time. Their maps
were bad... oh, and they were quite indolent about besieging Cuidad Rodrigo, as if they
were waiting for something that had not happened. The French took a poor position at

Coa, but... but at one point of the battle, our troops' flank was overwhelmed... almost as if the French knew what they would do before they did it."

"Spies," her father spat. "Faithless mongrels! I'd like to see their own children on the line of fire. Their own daughters... Bah!" He got up from his chair in a rush and began to pace by the fire.

Bess was swift to join him, resting an imploring hand on his arm. "Papa?"

He pinched the bridge of his nose and grimaced, then offered her a soothing smile. "It is nothing. Only that there is so little I can do to protect my children."

"Surely, you are not fearful for me, are you?"

"In truth, I am more frightened for you than for Samuel."

She sobered in thought, and her eyes fell to the floor. "Is it what you were talking about the other day? About how I should marry?"

"Bess, tell me quite honestly. I see how the men stare at you. There is... talk. Has anyone ever harassed you beyond that?"

She hesitated. "Not... precisely."

"But you have been made uncomfortable? Has anyone been too free with his hands?"

Bess shook her head and chewed her lower lip. Tim had never touched her, had he? "A bit, but nothing terribly serious. Just... excessive compliments."

Her father sighed, as if that were the end of it. "I am glad to hear it. I had not thought anyone to be too bold, but... well, I am somewhat relieved. And... is there... or, rather, has there been anyone you favored?"

A conscious tingle shot down the back of her neck, and she could scarcely meet his eyes. Papa would not understand or approve of her fascination with Mr. Cumberland. She stared at her toes and shook her head.

What hope there was in her father's eyes faded, but he also looked relieved. "I see. Well, perhaps this winter," he decided. "Yes, there will be more time... come winter."

Bess swallowed at this ominous promise, and her gaze wandered to the window. Distantly, she heard her father's flustered pacing, his oddly punctuated sighs. She toyed with the fringe of her skirts, lost to a thousand of her own thoughts, when her father interrupted her. "Bess, is something the matter?"

She denied it at once, then tilted a curious glance up at him. "Papa... why do you keep Tim on as ostler?"

He looked surprised. "Tim? He has been here more than twenty years. I could not dismiss him. Why do you ask?"

"It is only that he is scarcely about his duties. The stable hands do all the work, and most of the coachmen think ill of him."

"You have heard complaints?"

She lifted her shoulders. "No one talks about it because everyone knows."

Mr. Reynolds blew out a weary sigh. "Aye, I know it, too. He never was much use, even before his accident. I suppose it is for the sake of old days."

"What do you mean?"

He stopped his pacing, hooked his thumbs in his trousers and gave her a wistful smile. "Your mother, it was. He wished to marry her, but she chose an innkeeper over a farmer."

"A... a farmer?" Bess shook her head uncomprehendingly.

"As was. His landlord accused him of shorting the rents and threw him out. He protested that he had been served unfairly, but the master was decided. About the same time, he had a bad fall, and could hardly have done the farm work, anyway. Your mother, generous creature that she was, begged me to take pity on him. I never could refuse her," he finished softly.

"I did not know," Bess replied in a raw voice. "He loved Mama—how strange!"

Her father's dewy eyes sharpened. "He *wanted* her. I *loved* her. They are not the same thing, Bess. Don't ever think they could be the same."

Her jaw dropped, and she fumbled for some kind of answer. But her father only shook his head and went out, leaving Bess with a hundred questions.

"I AM SORRY, CAPTAIN, but General Richards is away." The general's secretary, a young lieutenant named Saunders, looked wretchedly apologetic as he twisted his quill between nervous fingers.

Nick restrained a sigh. He would have to come back in the afternoon, which wrecked all hope of catching the coach back out of London by evening. "When is he expected to return?"

"A fortnight or more, sir. He went to Portsmouth on some business with Admiral Hawley."

"Portsmouth? Has the navy conscripted him now?"

"I do not know the nature of the business that took him there, sir. But he said to forward any messages to General Clay."

General Clay? A rheumatic earl's brother whose only true usefulness was to be trotted out to appease some nobleman. He was not in Intelligence and could be privy to nothing of Nick's assignment. He bit down on his lip to keep from blasting his frustration at Saunders. It was not the lieutenant's fault, but bloody bollocks! How was he to beg off this outrageous assignment without actually speaking to the general?

His jaw worked in frustration. There was nothing for it. He would have to return to Surrey and carry on. "Thank you, Lieutenant, but my business will keep."

"Shall I tell the general you will come again?"

He frowned. Indeed, he would *like* to come again the very day Richards returned, but he was already technically violating orders by marching back to London once. He could not leave his men a second time. "No. Tell him my assignment is proceeding as planned and give him this message." He held up a copy of the note he had collected from the "monk." "Give it only to Richards, do you understand?"

The secretary nodded. "Yes, sir. I will put it in his safe right now."

"Good man. Are there any messages for my men or for me?"

The lieutenant brightened as if he had just remembered. "Yes, sir. There is a bundle here, and I believe the general even left a note, in case you came before he returned." The secretary went to a locked cabinet behind his desk and sorted through his files until he found a clutch of letters. "Nothing for Lieutenant North, sir, but I believe there is something for everyone else. And here is that note from General Richards."

Nick thumbed through, ignoring for now Richards' thin missive. There was one for him from home, with his father's bold script over the front. He would break that open later. Three for Daniels—there were rumors of a sweetheart in Sussex—and one fat one from Wesson's mother. North never had any mail.

He tucked the stack into his breast pocket. "Thank you, Lieutenant." He went out, only dimly conscious of the curious glances as he trod the corridors of Whitehall. He was out of uniform and unshaven, but he would just dare someone to speak to him over it. He hailed a hackney and asked to be taken to an oyster house. Anywhere he could sit down and sup for a quiet minute, and maybe even read his father's letter. The moment he seated himself, however, a voice cried out his name.

"Hunt? Nick the fox, it *is* you!"

Oh, how tiresome. He knew that voice, and it brought back no fond memories. Nick rolled his eyes, but pasted on a smile before he looked up. "Chesterfield? What the devil brings you to London?"

"I should be asking the same of you." Captain Chesterfield, wearing his militia uniform, plopped into the seat opposite and gestured for a round of drinks. "Last I heard, you were making waves in Spain. I'd no idea you were back in jolly old England."

"I'm on leave," Nick lied. That was the bothersome thing about his assignment—he could never tell anyone the bald-faced truth, even if they were someone he trusted. Which Chesterfield was not.

"Well, fancy that. I imagine you blokes must be taking all the worst of it, eh? Yes, rather quiet here back home, for the most part."

"Oh?" The drinks arrived, and Nick lifted one briefly in the other's direction. "Where are you posted these days?"

Chesterfield swallowed, and a lazy smirk appeared. "The quietest little village you can imagine. Little more than a stop on the way to London. We spend more time managing stray dogs and putting down disputes over broken fences than subduing any insurrections."

"I envy you."

"No, you don't. Blasted bore, it is! I tell you, Hunt, if I had half a chance, I'd hang myself on the next sheet to Portugal."

Nick smiled tightly. Chesterfield was still in the militia because he could not afford the commission for his desired rank and would not settle for a lower one. "Perhaps your commanding officer can give you a letter. Surely, a man of your experience could be useful in the Regulars."

Chesterfield banged his glass down and sighed. He frowned, as if a thought had annoyed him, then shook his head. "Well, it is not *all* quiet. You asked why I had come to London."

Nick lifted a shoulder. "I supposed you were on leave, as well."

"Oh, ho! Someone may wish I was. No, I rode up to deliver an urgent report. Just came from Whitehall."

The self-importance on Chesterfield's face was almost nauseating. Could he not simply go away? But Nick could ill afford to be short with anyone. Polite and forgettable was his aim, so much as it was within his power to be so. "Urgent, eh? Then, you must be doing more than requesting munitions and supplies."

Chesterfield snorted, then leaned forward and whispered. "The Scarlet Bandit."

A pit of dread opened in Nick's stomach. "I beg your pardon?"

"Oh, I forgot. You boys on the Continent probably never heard of the beggar. Been holding up the night highways for a few years now, but he's like a ghost. No one has ever seen him."

"A ghost?" Nick repeated, a trifle numbly.

"He's a coward, that's what. He's come to Surrey, and I mean to bag him."

Nick's pulse was galloping, but he swallowed and fingered his glass. "You've come all the way to London just to deliver a report about a single robber?"

"Aye, I have. Colonel Stanwick sent me to gather information from the uppity-ups. There's a rumor that a special squadron was after him some months ago. I expect they gave up," he said with a shrug, "or got reassigned. Anyroad, no one's caught him yet, but that's about to change."

Nick lifted his eyebrows, pretending to be impressed. He was, in fact, horrified. If Chesterfield was the man who would be hunting him, his problems just multiplied.

Then again, perhaps they were a deal simpler than he had ever imagined.

"You say you are looking for intelligence on the matter?" he asked.

Chesterfield nodded. "I was told to come back tomorrow to see Colonel Bradley. He wanted a full report."

Nick nodded. "Well, I hope you learn what you need to catch your man."

"Oh, I will, make no mistake. And where are you off to from here, Hunt?"

He finished his glass. "Home, I suppose. Good afternoon, Chesterfield."

Chapter Ten

M^{Y SON,}

We had the most curious surprise yesterday. A young man came to the house, leading a crippled gray horse and asking for me. He would say nothing of whence he had come or what business he had with the poor brute. He only told us the horse's name was Rob Roy, and that he had been left to me by his former owner.

You must know what a state that put your mother in, fancying you had been killed in action. Imagine her relief when old Tom was grooming the horse and found that twist of paper knotted in his tail, informing us that you were well. I know not what business resulted in your horse being shot, and I daresay I may never do, but we will tend Roy the best we can. Theresa has already taken quite a shine to him, and the old boy has ribbons in his mane and an apple twice a day.

I cannot know when or if this letter will be put into your hands. I trust that the business keeping you from us just now is of great importance to the Kingdom, and not a product of your own unwillingness to come home. You were a fool to go, and a fool to stay away, but I am not so unreasonable that I would throw you from the doorstep. Despite what passed between us when you last left home, I can think of nothing finer than to see you again.

I know you have your duty. But you will find I care almost nothing for the king's business for there is another matter which, I fear, bears much weightier import to me. It concerns your brother. The old illness is upon him again. We have even had the surgeon from Town, and no one seems to know what to do for him.

No one can say what may come, but if Alexander does not recover, your family will need you as we have never done before. It pains me to put such words to paper, but the truth of it is that he looks worse each day, and the surgeon told me privately that it was only a matter of time. Nick, you must come home.

I will close now. Your mother and sisters have included their notes for you. Brace yourself for memoirs of dashing beaux from Isabelle and a sermon on the newest fashion in lace from Theresa.

May God keep you until we see you again.

Nick's hands were shaking as he finished his father's letter. The last he had heard, Alex was doing well! Better than well—he had been courting the daughter of one of their neighbors. No mention of her, so nothing must have come of it. If Alex was now so ill that their father was now asking for *him*, things must be bad, indeed. Alexander might never marry anyone at all. Never produce an heir to carry on their father's good name, never live long enough to secure the futures of their mother and sisters.

And that meant it was all up to Nick.

He ran a hand through his hair and closed his eyes for a moment. Exactly how was he to race home now? Give up his commission and settle with his father once and for all?

Even if he *had* managed to see Richards in London, he knew perfectly well that the general would pull every string to keep him on assignment. And such an assignment! He growled in frustration and turned over Richards' note once or twice before breaking the seal.

Hunt,

If indeed you are reading this, as I believe you will, then you have come to London in an attempt to change my mind about your current assignment. I suspect you might, as the first time you have to terrify some poor citizen will be too much for an honest chap like you to stomach.

I wish I could agree to such an alteration. A day ago, I might have, but there has been a development on the Continent and even more here. You understand I can write no more. I can only impress upon you the urgency of the matter. Many good officers have been deceived of late, myself included. Hunt, I depend on you to cut the head off this snake.

Gen. M.T. Richards

Well, that capped it. He sat back and stared at the floor, his mind spinning. Richards must have learned something, and if Nick had to guess, it was that the spy network threaded its treacherous way into Whitehall itself. All this time, he thought he was chasing intercepted messages, corrupt lower officers. But if it was worse than that... if the very orders to His Majesty's troops were being sniffed out before they even left London, before they were ever dispatched to Wellington, then the roots went deeper than they had all feared.

He was trapped playing the highwayman until someone hanged for it... and hopefully it would not be him.

B ESS NO LONGER WANDERED into the stable yard.

When she had to stir outdoors, it was never without first peeking through the windows to see if she could do her tasks quickly, without being noticed by anyone. Even when she heard that a horse van had stopped for the night, carrying a prized racing stallion on his way to Hampshire from Newmarket, Bess did not join the curious onlookers. She stayed safely indoors, preferring even the ruder customers at the inn to the company she might keep elsewhere.

She ought to speak to her father about the ostler, but what could she say? If her only complaint was that Tim looked at her, then nearly every traveler to pass through the Bittern ought to be thrown out. She could not condemn a man for that, particularly not one her father admitted to taking in on pity. Truly, if she spoke too strongly and convinced her father to turn the man out, what would become of him? Starved to death this winter, most likely, and it would be on her head if her accusations were petty.

And perhaps they were, for the worst she could convict him of was being too friendly. No, that was not the right word. There was something in the old ostler's manner that she could not place, could not describe. So, until she could find the proper words, she would simply avoid him.

Three days passed, with little more excitement than the cream turning earlier than it should have. Then, one afternoon she happened to be passing by the window when the mail coach arrived. Ordinarily, she paid them little notice, but something snagged her eye—a figure she would know even in the dark, though she had seen it only a handful of times. *Mr. Cumberland.*

He was dismounting the coach among a swell of fellow passengers, replacing his hat, and pulling it low over his brow before he swept a gaze over the inn. She stepped closer to the window, pressing her hand to the glass. Oh, for mercy's sake, she was staring like a ninny! And what was this odd warmth forcing its way to her cheeks?

Mr. Cumberland's face had been hidden from her after that first glimpse, but she could not be mistaken. He glanced to the right and left, nodding to this passenger and that, and then he stopped and looked toward the door of the inn. He paused, shook his head, and started to turn away, toward the coach.

Bess almost cried out in protest. He was not leaving, was he? Without staying overnight? He could not go!

But that was precisely what he seemed to be doing. He lifted a hand to the driver, spoke something to him, and waited for someone to permit him to step back into the coach. That was when he rounded one last time, and his eyes fell on her at the window. He froze, his jaw visibly flexing as he stared back at her. Then, he said something else to the driver and started toward the door of the inn.

She waited for him in the coffee room. He paused in the hall, greeting a couple others as they passed, then he looked at her. The hand holding his hat dipped when their eyes met.

"Good afternoon, Miss Bess."

She dipped a fancy curtsey. "Good afternoon, Mr. Cumberland. What brings you back to us so soon?"

He walked slowly toward her. "Business, of course, but I was not planning to stay."

Her disappointment must have been plain, for he added, "I should be coming back through in a few days. A week... a fortnight, at most."

She twitched a smile and nodded, hoping she looked more cheerful than she felt. "Brighton, of course. I hope your business concludes to your satisfaction."

He studied her, mist-colored eyes taking in every inch of her face as if cataloging it. "A fortnight will not see it all done, but it will bring me back here, even if only briefly."

"Shall I keep your favorite room for you, then?" she asked with a hint of a grin.

A crinkle formed around his eyes. "Please, do. I have grown fond of that rooster."

Bess arched a brow. The rooster was apparently not the only thing about that room that Mr. Cumberland liked. When he came back, she would try to learn the whole of it—his sleeplessness, his midnight outings, all of it. Even if the truth was unpleasant to hear. "Then we will see you upon your return, I suppose, and not a moment sooner."

His chest swelled in a deep breath, and he came a step closer. "Forgive me for saying so, Miss Bess, but I daresay I will be seeing you long before I return."

Before she could ask what he meant by that, he held out his hand, like a gentleman would do for a lady. Bess gawked at his fingers in confusion until embarrassment crept over his features. His hand began to drop, but without thinking, she reached out and caught it before it could fall. The smile that lit his face then was one she would carry with her all her waking hours, and probably even in her dreams.

He brought her hand to his lips, and Bess's eyes widened when she realized what he was doing. His caress on her work-hardened fingers was gentle—soft in a way she had no right to experience, and every reason to doubt.

This was how it began, was it not? This was how maidens surrendered their virtue to men who had no intention of honoring their promises. And she was giving her hand in friendship, and possibly more, freely to a man she knew almost nothing of. What an unrepentant fool she was!

But when he looked up at her again, it was with so much tenderness and honest admiration that her misgivings were forgotten. Heaven help her, he might be just as much a wretch as the worst of them, but there was something in those smoky eyes that begged for her trust. And she was powerless to withhold it.

"Until I see you again, my bonny Miss Bess," he whispered. And then, he was gone.

She raced back to the window to watch the mail coach ramble out of sight. Her breath fogged the glass until she leaned back on flat feet once more, then she turned around. And to her mortification, there stood her father.

He looked... she could not describe it. Heartbroken and angry at the same time, and covering it all with a mask of quiet doom. He regarded her with a long sigh, then shook his head. "Don't set your heart where it don't belong, Bessie."

"Y OU WANT ME TO go to London, sir?"

Lieutenant North was trying to mask his surprise but failing utterly. Nick handed Daniels his letters, feeling a pang of jealousy when the younger man's face changed hues. At least one of his men had something to look forward to. He turned back to North.

"Yes, and I need you to leave this very afternoon. You are to see that a report reaches Colonel Bradley about the doings of the Scarlet Bandit." He followed this with a quirk of his brow and a meaningful jerk of his head.

North nodded slowly. "Ah. What specifics shall I report, sir?"

"Tell him the truth, or what the truth was, as of a fortnight ago; that you are part of a special detachment tasked with following the Bandit and bringing him to justice. We dare not try to report that the highwayman has moved on from Surrey, for the next week's activity will prove your claims false. But if Bradley is given to understand that someone higher up has authorized your assignment, perhaps he will call off the militia dogs."

"I understand, sir. Shall I say that you sent me?"

Nick shook his head. "No. Tell him you are under Richards' command. Hopefully, my name will not be mentioned." Seeing his lieutenant's confused expression, he elaborated. "I ran into an old acquaintance, Captain Chesterfield, in London. He is stationed with the local militia, and he has made it his personal mission to bring in the Scarlet Bandit. I made no mention of any involvement in the matter."

"I see. Then, it might be awkward if he later learns differently."

"Indeed, but if he is ordered to keep his men at bay for now, I have a better chance of avoiding lead balls."

North's wide grin split his face. "A fine notion, sir. By the time they trouble themselves to ask again, we will have completed our mission and left the area. I wager they would just as well wash their hands of the matter, anyway."

Nick snorted and walked toward his tent. "Perhaps Colonel Stanwick will be convinced, and even pleased with the order, but not Captain Chesterfield. He is clever. What is more, he is ambitious. He used to say he meant to make Colonel by thirty-five. His father has a modest estate, enough to qualify him for his rank, but the coffers are empty."

"So, he needs to make a name for himself. Well, then, he might be more of a problem. How well do you know him?"

"We were stationed in Plymouth for the winter when I was a lieutenant in the militia. He was always trying to show me up and, I daresay, rarely succeeding."

"But he is still in uniform, like we are. I suppose if he does make trouble, you can always identify yourself. If he hears your voice and sees your face, he will hesitate before pulling the trigger."

"Not likely."

"Sir?"

Nick gave a rueful laugh. "I got the promotion he wanted."

Chapter Eleven

"A RE YOU CERTAIN YOU wish to go out tonight, Captain?" Daniels protested. "Lieutenant North will not return from London until tomorrow."

Nick fumbled with the black mare's reins, his palms aching with nervous tension. He flexed his gloved fingers and drew a ragged breath. "I am certain. The militia are still flat-footed. They hardly know where to look, or even if they should be looking for anything at all. If you and Wesson make a suitable show of force, it will back up North's report in London that the militia needn't get involved."

Daniels and Wesson shared dubious looks. "Yes, sir," they agreed together.

Nick tugged at the scarf over his eyes, repositioned his hat, then swung into the saddle. Truth be told, he felt quite the dandy in the highwayman's rich apparel and mounted on a horse that probably cost more than all his annual soldier's pay. Were it not for present circumstances, he could almost fancy turning out in Hyde Park or perhaps even Rotten Row... assuming Black Bess did not try to maim the other horses.

"Good luck, Captain," Daniels wished him.

Nick nodded crisply, then bent over his horse. "Well, old girl," he said, stroking the sleek arch of her neck, "shall we?"

He felt her shoulders lift in reply, and that thick tail swished eagerly. She was almost docile tonight, save for the sparks of energy he could feel surging from her mouth to his hands. He spared an admiring glance over her crest before giving her the signal. Even in his finest hour, old Roy had never felt so alive and eloquent beneath him.

Yes, tonight would be different than the last outing. Tonight, the black nightmare was his partner, his right hand, and even his courage. Tonight, they were invincible.

"**B**ESSIE, SIT DOWN."

It was past eleven, and Bess was wiping down the last table in the dining room when her father found her. He had not spoken to her all day, and now, his tone was as grave as she had ever heard it. She swallowed and carefully lowered herself to the nearest bench.

"I know what this is about," she mumbled, her eyes downcast.

"I doubt that." Her father sighed and scrubbed his weary features with his hands. "Bess, there are things I... God forgive me, I never told you."

She blinked and looked up at him but did not dare to speak.

"Bessie... do you recall..." he stopped to bite his lips together, then forged ahead. "When your mother was dying, do you remember anything of what she said?"

She shrugged vaguely. "Yes, a bit. I couldn't understand much that last day. She asked for Samuel, then for me, though I was holding her hand."

"It wasn't you she was asking for. It was her sister."

Bess narrowed her eyes. "The one in London she used to talk of? I always wondered if it was even true."

Her father nodded. "Oh, it was true. Your mother named you after her. She was called Elizabeth, or so I was told."

"I was?" Bess's brow furrowed. She had always been told her name was nearly plucked from thin air. "You never met her—my aunt?"

He leaned his mouth into his fist and cut loose a bitter chuckle. "No, I never met her. Your mother never even saw her after she was eighteen. I heard a rumor she married well... too well for the likes of us."

She shook her head. "Papa, what are you saying? Does this have to do with... with what you said a few days ago? That I should marry?"

"Not in the way you think, but yes. Bessie, I..." He drew a breath to blurt out whatever burden was on his heart, but he stopped himself and stared blankly at her. He blinked then and seemed to change his mind.

"No, before you ask, I have not had some word from this long-lost aunt of yours. I doubt I ever shall. There are... well, there are things that I would rather not speak of things long in the past. I should like to keep them there, but the past seems to have a way of festering."

She glanced uncomfortably at her shoes. "Papa, I do not understand any of what you are saying."

"I know you do not, and I hope you never do. I can only ask you to trust me in one thing—one thing only."

"Anything, Papa," she answered softly.

He leaned forward and took her hand. "I know the men fancy you. How could they not? I daresay one or two of them might even have caught your eye in return. Bessie, I would not see your heart broken. There is someone, isn't there?"

She felt her cheeks heating, and a guilty tingle surged in her stomach. She could not meet his gaze.

"I thought as much. Of all the men to walk in here and turn your head..." He sighed and kneaded his eyes again. "I will ask you... no, I will warn you only this once. Have nothing to do with that Cumberland fellow if he ever comes back."

She huffed, then laughed in denial and hurt. "Mr. Cumberland? That is what this is all about? He has been nothing but a gentleman! I can name a dozen who have been more offensive."

"It is not his manner to which I object. I wish he had been a beast that you had given one of your set-downs! But the whelp had to be quite a likable fellow, after all, and there lies the rub. He's not for you, Bessie. That's the end of it."

He stood abruptly, avoiding her gaze. His hand traced her cheek fondly, but he spoke no more and left the room before she could protest.

Bess sat in open-mouthed shock. She did not even know how she felt about Mr. Cumberland. Heavens, she did not even know if she *should* bother sorting her feelings about him! But to think that her father had seen something between them, enough that he felt it necessary to warn her off before she even confessed her own interest... why, that was more than humiliating. It was outrageous.

She had done nothing wrong! It was not as if she was making plans to escape into the night with him. What could be so terrible about such a kind man as Mr. Cumberland seemed to be, that her father forbade her to associate with him?

It was with a sulking and bitter heart that she finished her tasks for the night, then went to her room. As she stood in her window, unpinning her hair, she pushed the shutters open and leaned down to peer at the window of the room below hers. Many things about

Mr. Cumberland were still a mystery to her. Before her father's warning, he was a matter of curiosity. A diversion; intriguing, but not to be taken seriously.

Now, a defiant urge compelled her to search out the answers to every question. She *must* know; where did Mr. Cumberland go at night? What history did her father have with him? And what of those odd things he would say, the strange questions he would ask? Bess sat down at the window seat and peered out into the darkened wood.

One thing, she was sure of. She would have no rest until she discovered some answers.

N ICK JERKED HIS PISTOL skyward and backed his snorting mount off the road. There had been no cowering passengers this time. No terrified women or children, no one harmed. Just an outraged merchant who had taken a risk, driving at night, and a bag of coins cast directly into his hand. The merchant was obviously wealthy, and a proper highwayman would probably have shaken the coach down for more valuables, but Nick was not after money.

"I hope you rot!" cried the driver as he whipped his horses into motion. "You'll hang for this!"

Nick's lips thinned as he watched the man depart. He had been lucky this time, picking just the right sort. A man comfortable enough not to be too injured by the temporary theft, clever enough not to fight back, and indignant enough to report the whole encounter at the next bell. And the robbery was not the only thing he hoped would be reported.

"You, there! Stop, thief, by order of His Majesty!"

There it was. Wesson's voice rang out like the peal of a bell in the still darkness, and Nick hesitated just long enough to see them charging round the bend. They shouted the expected questions and directions at the retreating carriage, then they were in "pursuit." Nick held Black Bess in for another second and fired a blank shot in the air. Just enough to sound like he was putting up a fight.

He gave the mare her head and then held on. One wringing twist of her neck, a celebratory hop that might have unseated him if he did not know her better, and the black dragon swooped over the dike beside the road and down to the heath.

Hooves tore up the soft turf as she flung herself out like a seabird, drinking in the night air and snorting for sheer joy. Little wonder the Scarlet Bandit had been so difficult to capture! He had saddled Poseidon's monster, a beast with wings on her heels that reveled in wrongdoing and defiant fugues.

And she was exhilarating to ride. Devil take it, but when this was all over, if he lived, he might just have to find a way to keep her.

Nick bent low to avoid a branch and glanced over his shoulder. There were his men, right where they should be. One, two... three, four, five, six...

The militia! Terror gripped him for the first time, and he hissed to his mare. She flattened her ears in answer and bolted, but not before a shot whizzed by his head. That was no blank wad, but a real lead ball.

Shouts rang out behind him—Daniels in the lead, he thought, but he could not stay to enjoy a conversation. His best hope was to dash for cover, and hope his own men led the others on a vain chase. Nick risked one glance over his shoulder, and just caught Wesson's quick signal to him to go right.

Thank heaven he knew the land by heart. There was a stone piling up ahead, beside a low rail fence, and just beyond them a hidden stream bed that twisted away to the right. To the left was a stand of cottonwoods, where the militia riders could quickly lose their line of sight. It might work.

He held his breath as Black Bess gathered herself for the leap and shifted his weight mid-air to strike the right lead when she landed. Then they were up, over the rail and down the other side. A quick snatch of the rein, and they were in the wash, around a bend, and running freely.

The shouts and pounding hooves that had been so close now faded. Wesson's feint had worked, but the militia riders would not be fooled for long. Nick pulled up his horse and looked back at the deep hoof prints gouged into the sandy stream bed. Someone was bound to notice them. He wheeled the mare about and pointed her toward the rise of the hill. There, among the rocks and trees, he would pass the night.

B

ESS DID NOT USUALLY have trouble sleeping. Typically, she fell into her bed late,
in a dead stupor, and caught just enough of the sweet abyss to stumble forth again
in the morning. But tonight, she was a hopeless case.

She paced to the casement and stood watch there, communing with a waning moon.
She lit her candle again to work on her mending, but her eyes were too bleary to focus on
it. Eventually, she bundled back in her bed and tried blocking out the creak of the old inn,
the distant song of the owls, and the clamor of her thoughts.

What was it about Mr. Cumberland that her father disapproved? It had to be that he
was a gentleman. Was that not her own whispered caution? Gentlemen did not let their
feelings carry them into inconvenient alliances. Even if Mr. Cumberland did admire her,
he would never make someone like her an honorable offer.

But why would she expect him to make an offer of *any* kind? He had been friendly.
Chivalrous. But nothing he had said or done seemed to indicate that he was looking for
either a short diversion or a long-term mistress. So why did he alarm her father so?

Bess twisted and fretted until more of her blankets were covering the floor than her
body. She was making herself wearier in bed than she would out of it. It was well before
her usual waking time, but there was no help for it. Shivering in the darkness, she pulled
on her wool stockings, her chemise and stays, her dress and her shawl. It would be too
early to light the fires, but perhaps she could slip out beyond the garden gate for a brisk
walk before her day started.

The sky was a watery silver when she stepped out, with the moon's parting glare still
sulking above the tree line, and the early promise of the sun just beginning to claw its way
over the rooftops of the inn. Bess tightened her shawl around her and watched puffs of
her breath condense and rise. Even the stable was quiet this early in the morning, and no
one was about to trouble her. She was free to do whatever she wished.

A mischievous thought tickled her mind. How long had it been since she plucked any
of the roses from her mother's hedge? Perhaps her father would be cheered out of his
recent melancholy by one of those velvet blooms with his morning egg. She wove into
the skirting of the hickory wood until she reached the bush and crouched down before it.
Black were the heavy rose heads in the dim light, and she put out her hand to stroke the
nearest one. How her mother had loved coming here to prune and care for this old thing!

Bess had never known why it was planted in the shade of the wood, rather than
adorning the gates of the inn in the sunshine, but this place must have held some special
meaning. So many times in her childhood, she would search for her mother and would

find her here, knelt in the mossy earth by her roses. Sometimes it seemed that Mama had been weeping, but she always smiled and welcomed her daughter with a tender kiss when she was discovered.

She caressed a few of the fuller blossoms before choosing one for her father. Her sewing scissors were still in her pocket, and she drew them out and angled them for her cut. The waxen petals fell into her hand, and she buried her nose in the rose's perfume. How she missed her mother!

It was time to be going back. The girls would be lighting the kitchen stove, and before long, the inn would come to life. Bess tucked her scissors back into her pocket, but the rose, she kept close to her face as she straightened and turned around.

Several seconds passed before she saw *him*. At first, she was not certain she had seen anything at all, for he was quite still. Little more than a shapely shadow he was, but a quiet wisp of steam rose from the fore.

Bess squinted. Was it a horseman? A phantom? With as little sleep as she had had, it could be a simple figment of her imagination.

Then, a hoof sliced the air, and an inhuman snort split the night. Bess's rose fell from nerveless fingers, and slowly, numbly, she backed away. Was there a rider? She saw no face—only a billowing form and the dim silhouette of a cocked hat.

A chill raced down her spine, and every ghost story she had ever heard echoed hard upon her. Horsemen with no heads or souls, reapers who came to steal the hearts of the living. Masked savages who stole women right from their beds.

Had she a few seconds to collect herself, a bit more light to see better, or even some rest to put away the delusions of exhaustion, she might not have panicked. But just then, the demon horse let out a shrill whistle, a sound unlike any living creature she had ever known, followed by another feral snort. The rider lifted the brim of his hat... and she saw only blackness below it.

That was all Bess's poor heart could withstand. Her legs wobbled, then a dread feeling of nausea and trembling washed over her. Then, the void was all she knew.

Chapter Twelve

"MISS BESS!"

Nick caught her hand and pressed it to his cheek to test its warmth, but his confounded mask got in the way. "Oh, blast," he swore under his breath, and stripped his gloves off. Her fingers were icy, but possibly just from being outdoors. He would never forgive himself if he had done her an injury. Why, oh why, did she have to turn around when she did, before he could slip back into the shadows without alarming her?

"Wake up, my girl. What are you doing out so early, hmm?" he muttered. "I might have known you would be the one to discover me. Here, what's this?" He pressed the heel of his hand to her forehead and found it quite warm. She moaned softly, and her lashes fluttered.

He sighed in relief when her eyes groggily opened. She was blinking slowly and her gaze was unfocused like someone just rousing after a long sleep, but after a few seconds, her eyes sharpened and seemed to snap. Her mouth flew open, and her body jerked in fear, and it was then that Nick realized he had been cradling her limp form like a lover.

"I mean you no harm!" he cried, just as she was trying to scramble away. "You took a fall. I was only making sure—"

"Stay away from me!" She bolted to her feet; hands spread out in a warding gesture.

Nick put his own hands up to show his goodwill and took a step back. "I am sorry if I frightened you. I was only passing through. I did not know I might happen upon anyone."

She remained frozen, only her eyes moving over him as she panted in terror. It was stupid of him, but he could not resist trying to inch closer again. It tore his soul to think she was afraid of him, but he could not exactly set her at ease the way he would have liked.

"Pray, madam," he said, careful this time to avoid using her name, "be comforted. I shall not harm you. You only swooned."

Her teeth bared in the dim light. "What do you take me for, some pampered lap dog? A parlor princess? I do not swoon!"

He opened his mouth, then closed it rapidly, unable to wholly prevent the smile from creeping into his face and voice. "I beg your pardon, but I believe you did. There is no shame in it, Miss—"

"Who do you think you are, flouncing about the woods dressed like a goblin? Wearing a scarf over your face and lurking in the shadows. How very ridiculous!"

His hands lowered, and he was smiling in earnest now. "Maybe I am a thief, come to steal your valuables."

She crossed her arms and threw back her head with a sniff. "I'd like to know what you think I have."

"The smile of a goddess, for a start."

Her chin dipped fractionally, and her eyes narrowed. "If you mean to violate me, sir, I have but to scream."

"I already told you. I mean you no harm. A thief may lay hold of whatever he pleases, and it pleases me very much to admire a bewitching woman without marring her beauty or giving her cause to despise me."

One of her brows lifted. "You are a very peculiar kind of thief."

Nick risked another step closer to her. "You may find it difficult to believe, but I do not take what I do not mean to replace, and my motive is honor, not avarice."

"How very strange. Are you a sort of Robin Hood, then? I'm afraid you are wearing the wrong color."

Nick glanced down at his red coat and grinned. "My tailor was fresh out of green. But to prove my goodwill, I shall leave you a gift, rather than taking one."

He walked a few paces away and collected the rose she had dropped. When he returned to her, he paused. "It is very fitting, you know."

"What is?"

He fingered the stem of the rose, then held it up. "This deep crimson. It is not the flower of a child, nor even a... what was it you said? A parlor princess? Such a creature could merit a dusky pink at best, but a woman of your vivid passion deserves the richest red." Boldly, he tucked the rose behind her ear and stood back to admire the complete picture.

She had tilted her head, her eyes now slitted in suspicion. "Who *are* you?"

Nick grinned. "Just a thief, madam." He caught the mare's reins and stepped into the saddle. "One who knows better than to try to steal a real prize when he sees it. Adieu."

Lieutenant North slapped his hat down on the makeshift table outside Nick's tent and entered with a broad grin and very little ceremony. "Mission successful, Captain. You oughtn't to have any trouble for a while with the militia."

"It's a little late for that, Lieutenant." Nick turned to face him, his finger poking through the hole he had just discovered in his tricorn. The bullet had sliced through the braid at the edge, and he had not even known how near he was to meeting his end on that moonlit road.

North's face turned white. "Buggar," he whispered. "How did they get so close? They could not have known where you were!"

"Luck, I suppose." Nick tossed the hat on his sleeping mat. "Whatever good you might have done in London is now officially undone. The militia saw only two officers on my tail, and unless Bradley issues them a direct order not to interfere—which I doubt—they will act as their colonel sees fit."

"So, what now, sir? You have to go out twice more, and the mission will certainly fail if they get mixed up in it. Someone might even get killed. What did Wesson and Daniels say to them?"

"That may be my only saving grace. Wesson said they had been tracking suspected patterns in 'the bandit's' attacks, and he told the militia to be on watch on the south road for the next several nights."

"Clever fellow," North mused. "You should recommend him for promotion."

"If I survive long enough, I will. What of Bradley? Did he at least welcome your information? He may yet be of some help, even if only to throw them off my scent for a few days."

North shrugged. "He seemed doubtful at first, especially when I told him I was under Richards' command. 'What does Army Intelligence want with a common criminal?' he asked, but I played it off as a special interest of His Royal Highness, which explained our involvement."

"That much is true. The Scarlet Bandit is said to have accosted one of Prince George's mistresses on the London Road last year."

"Aye, and rumor has it she found old Cumberland a better kisser than Prinny."

Nick snorted and rubbed his forehead. "I doubt that was much of a contest."

"Of course, sir." North drummed his fingers on his breeches, his eyes roving uncomfortably about the tent. "I hear you and Bess are getting on famously."

"What?" Nick's gaze sharpened on his lieutenant.

"The horse, sir. Big, black, hairy. Mean as Satan?"

"Oh. Yes, the horse."

North was regarding him quizzically. "Who else would I be talking about?"

Nick blew out a sigh. "Nothing, never mind. She certainly relishes her job, I will say that for her. If she were any less capable, I would not be standing here this morning."

"Yes, sir. So, what next?"

"We wait two days, then I want you to ride into Crawley to have a conversation with the colonel. Tell him your captain is spreading his men around the county and that we are requesting support near Haywards Heath, if they can provide it. That evening, I will strike south of Buckland, near the Reigate Mill."

"And what of our 'monk'?"

"What about him?"

"You don't expect any complications from that quarter?"

"Why should I? It is in his best interest to have nothing to do with me, once I have received his message."

North nodded. "Very well, sir. Do you plan to put in another appearance at the inn, or do you think it too much of a risk?"

"I think my credibility as the Scarlet Bandit is well enough established for my purposes. Besides..." he squinted over the lieutenant's shoulder, at no particular object. "I worry about appearing too often. There may be those who could trace an unfortunate connection."

"What, are you suspected? Did someone see you last night?"

Nick's thoughts drifted and his gaze become more unfocused, then he shook his head. "Certainly not, but I do not care to test my luck. Now, go on back to your tent. You probably need sleep as badly as I do."

"Yes, sir." North saluted, then ducked out of the tent, leaving Nick alone.

He dropped down to his pallet, then stared up at the canvas with his hands folded over his chest. *Had* he been recognized in the thin morning light? If anyone in the entire south of England could recognize him under the highwayman's mask, it would be Bess Reynolds. He had taken too much of a chance in lingering and talking to her. Swoon or no, he ought to have turned his horse and slipped away, but he had to rush down to her like some besotted fool!

Still, he was probably safe. For now, at least. If he showed his face again too soon, she would surely make sense of it, but if he stayed away until it was all over... yes, that was what he must do. She could not have known him in the darkness with his face covered. Much as it pained him, he had to let her go on wondering who the "stranger" in the woods was.

No, surely, she had not guessed. She had been too fearful when she came around and found herself in his arms. And the way she had demanded his identity—no, she could not know who he was. He would remain to her a mystery.

NOT AN HOUR HAD passed before curiosity had become clarity, and then clarity developed into conviction. Now, as the full light of day shone upon her, and her drowsy thoughts were revived by two black mugs of coffee, Bess was certain beyond a doubt.

The masked man *had* to be Mr. Cumberland.

His voice, and the way he had jested and flirted with her in the face of her fear and shock... yes, that was very much like the man she knew. And his shape, too—his height, the exact slope of his shoulder and cut of his chin. Had she not already discovered how familiar was his figure? Confessed to herself that she would know him even in the dark? And had she not once witnessed him walking into the woods for some strange purpose?

More than these, it was his eyes that gave him away. The smoky gray of them, even in the weakling light, it was impossible to miss. But then he had narrowed that right eye when he smiled. The instant she had seen that look, a shiver lanced through her and her heart nearly stopped. It could be no other.

Who are you?

She had asked him, and he had not answered. Not to her satisfaction, anyway. A thief, he had said. What sort of thief lurked in the woods, nowhere near anyone who could be robbed? He ought to be out on the highway, oughtn't he? Unless... She chewed her lip as she went about her morning tasks until it was raw and swollen.

Unless he was planning on robbing the Bittern.

But if that were his design, why would he treat her so kindly? Why cradle her in his arms and speak gently and then let her go back where she might report his presence? It made no sense.

"Bessie, what ails you?" Her father stopped her midway from the still room, his brow furrowed in concern. "Did you not sleep?"

Sleep? Oh, that she could know such a luxury! "No... That is..." she cleared her throat and looked uncomfortably at her feet. "I went for a walk, early this morning."

His eyes narrowed. "I saw the rose in the kitchen. You are lucky no one threw it in the stove."

"That was for you," she blurted. "I... I forgot to bring it to you when you awoke."

He drew a slow breath. "Bessie, I would just as soon you did not. Let that dratted bush go wild or let the shadow of the wood kill it off."

"But Papa—"

He held up a hand. "If it pleases you to look at the wretched thing, go ahead and do so, but do not trouble me with it. There be naught but sorrow there." He set his teeth grimly and walked away.

Bess gaped after him. When did her father's bitterness overcome his love for her mother? Perhaps the pain was too raw still, but it had been over a year. For mercy's sake, if she could not even talk to her father about her mother's roses, she could certainly not bring up the enigmatic Mr. Cumberland again.

Her father knew something of the man's secrets. She was more sure of it now than ever before, and equal to that knowledge was the understanding that he would never tell her what she most wanted to know. She ought to leave it alone, and trust that her father meant to protect her from... something. But Bess had never surrendered easily, and she was unlikely to do so now, when she knew perfectly well that the truth was being kept from her.

Was Mr. Cumberland dangerous? Her father seemed to think he was, but that was not what Bess had seen of the man. After so many years working at the inn, seeing some of the most vulgar of their kind, she felt she could read men's characters better than most. No, whoever he was and whatever his business, if he had meant to do her harm of any kind, he would have already done so.

She would simply have to keep her eyes open and hope she had a chance to answer her own questions. For now, her heart whispered, best to keep her knowledge a secret.

Chapter Thirteen

Nick's third assault on all that was moral and decent went off appallingly well. At least, no shots were fired, but he left the encounter more shaken than if they had been.

A significant part of the night's success was due to Daniels and Wesson, dressed in plain clothes, taking supper at two different post inns, and reporting back with intelligence about anyone planning to travel the Buckland Road by night. A Mr. Winters, with a respectably sized purse and only one footman riding on the back of the coach, seemed to provide the perfect target.

What Daniels had failed to report was that Mr. Winters had a wife.

Nick had discovered this crucial bit of information only when he stood at the window of the coach, with his empty pistol pointed at Mr. Winters, and the flax-en-haired creature began beating her husband over the head with her fur muff. At first, Nick took her to be his daughter, so much younger was she, but the truth was readily apparent.

"You see, you fool, I said this would happen!" she cried. "You simply *had* to take to the roads at night, even after the reports of ruffians on the way. And now I suppose he will make us get down and molest me while he makes off with your purse!"

Poor Mr. Winters could only mutter oaths and put his hands over his head to fend off his wife. Nick felt some sympathy for the fellow as she rained blows upon him.

"Pray, madam, fear not that I mean you any harm," Nick objected, but it did no good. The wife was well and truly in command of the situation, though it was he who held them all at gunpoint.

"Nay, nay, it is all my foolish husband's fault!" she huffed, as she left off pummeling her spouse and pushed out past him to disembark the coach. "It was he who said we simply *had* to make Southampton before Sunday. Off to see his fancy bit, I shouldn't wonder," she sniffed.

"Sir, madam, there is no need for you to get down," Nick said, but the couple appeared not to hear him. Down they came, bickering all the way.

"Esmeralda, for the last time, it is business! I will lose the deal with Carruthers if I am tardy by so much as a day. Preposterous woman! There was no reason for you to have come, save to make me go bald with exasperation."

"And I ought to just let you stray, with no by-your-leave, no one to keep you on the straight and narrow? Take Thomas as your footman, I said, not Jeffrey, but you absolutely insisted—"

"You only wanted me to take Thomas because he's your maid's brother. I'll not have my wife spying on me," Mr. Winters snapped. Then he looked up at Nick and reluctantly raised his hands again. "Here, are you going to search the coach or not?"

Nick cleared his throat and kept his pistol trained carefully on the couple as he got down from the saddle. "I am much obliged for your cooperation," he replied as gallantly as he could. "I'll not be a moment."

"Oh, take your time," Mr. Winters grumbled. "I am in no hurry to get back into the carriage with this witch. See that you take this monstrous muff so she will stop hitting me with it. I'll be hanged if she hasn't got the dratted thing full of bricks."

This prompted a fresh wave of spousal insults and mild violence, in the face of which Nick could only grimace and back away. He performed a cursory glance around the inside of the carriage, enough to satisfy appearances, then offered a courtly bow like he imagined Cumberland might have done. "Nothing more. Thank you, kind sir and—"

"Look under his seat!" Mrs. Winters cried. "He keeps an emergency purse and a pistol under the cushion!"

"Esmeralda, you fool!" her husband hissed between his teeth. "Keep quiet, for once in your confounded life. Do you want to get me shot?"

Nick glanced at the seat, then back at the couple. He could hardly avoid at least searching there after such an outburst, but it was a bit troubling to see a deep look of contemplation on the wife's face. She seemed to be weighing her prospects and appeared not at all horrified at the notion of her husband being mortally wounded.

"I'll just take the pistol," he said after a few seconds. "Far be it from me to leave a gentleman and his lady wife with no resources whatever to hire a comfortable bed for their travels."

"Lady! There be no such creature here!" Mr. Winters scoffed aloud, and Mrs. Winters sniped some complaint that the money would not be spent on her, but on some other female.

"Enough!" Nick interrupted. "Mr. Winters, do be so good as to assist your wife into the carriage, and let us all be on our way." He backed up to catch his horse by the bridle, permitting them to mount the box again, but Mrs. Winters was having none of it.

"I declare, you must be the poorest highwayman ever to grace the roads! No proper search for our valuables, no shots fired, and you never even tried to ravish me. And I not yet eight and twenty! What manner of thief are you?"

He offered a thin, pained smile. "One with no taste for terrifying ladies, madam. Now, please—"

He got no further with his objections. Mrs. Winters apparently had her own ideas about how a proper highwayman ought to conduct himself, and she undertook to educate him most enthusiastically. Before he could even draw a breath, she fairly lunged for him, clubbing him in the back of the head with something heavy inside her fur muff, and dragging his face down to hers for a thorough, if not pleasurable, kiss. It was at least ten seconds before she let him go, but when she did, he could only stand there and quake.

"Now see what you've done, Esmeralda! Assaulted the poor man just like you did to me ten years ago! Only he will not let you off with a tin wedding band."

Mrs. Winters drew back, licking her lips suggestively as she patted Nick on the cheek. "Oh, be quiet, my dear. Can you think of the disgrace if Charlotte Smithers found out our carriage had been accosted and your wife was never even pinched inappropriately? I should never hear the end of it! Who is on the shelf now, I ask? Now I will have a tale to beat her account of the impertinent sailor."

"Esmeralda, let the poor man go! Bad enough I have had to suffer you all these years. Robbing our carriage is not a sufficient crime that he should have to endure your vanity. Sir," he said to Nick, glaring occasionally at his lady, "I beg pardon for my wife. Pray, try not to strangle her as she deserves."

Nick coughed and blinked. "Madam, he said hoarsely, "I think you had better leave with me whatever that heavy thing is in your muff. For your husband's sake."

She sighed, gave him a prim shrug, and withdrew a rather large whiskey flask. "I suppose the pleasure was all mine. For a certainty, that was better than I've got out of Bernard here these five years together. To your very good health, sir."

The couple never ceased heckling one another as they mounted the coach. A terrified footman closed the door, the jaded driver cracked his whip, and Nick never even bothered training his pistol on them as they lumbered away. Unconsciously, he kept wiping out his mouth as he heard his men around the bend set up their hue and cry.

The carriage was out of sight, and Nick was still leaning unsteadily against his horse when North galloped up to him. "Are you all right, sir? I never heard a shot, but you look frightfully pale. Are you injured?"

Nick shook his head and pulled the stopper on Mrs. Winters' flask for a long, deep draught. "Shot, no. But I think this business will yet be the death of me."

"SARAH!" BESS HISSED TO the maid, "who is that?"

They were peering around the edge of the doorway from the kitchen. Six red-coated men sat around one round table, lounging easily, and talking louder than anyone in the rest of the room.

"What does it matter who they are?" Sarah asked with a wicked grin. "They're officers! Come, Bessie, don't be a prude."

Bess caught the girl's arm. "They won't have had their pay yet this month, Sarah. Best not pay them too much mind."

"And what if I want a bit of fun? I can pour the drinks, can't I?" Sarah shook off Bess's grip and within a minute, she was leaning on the shoulder of the tallest officer, with his arm around her middle. Bess sighed. It seemed that fetching the ale would be her job.

When she approached with the mugs, she sent a casual eye around the group. Three ensigns, two lieutenants—one of whom Sarah was canoodling—and a captain. She was used to seeing a handful of officers arrive together for an evening of drinks, but not typically of such varied ranks. This was not a social outing.

Bess set down the drinks, then nodded toward the captain. "What'll you have?"

He was a fair-haired, clean-shaven fellow, perhaps seven or eight and twenty, with piercing blue eyes that lifted and settled on her with unnerving familiarity. Even white teeth flashed as he replied, "Just some good conversation for now, and maybe something else later."

Bess lifted a brow with dry civility. "We've a cold ham in the back, or perhaps you'd like the lamb stew. Fresh yesterday."

He laughed. "I see I'll have to work a bit harder. Captain Chesterfield, at your service."

She inclined her head. "Bess Reynolds, and that silly bit of fluff is Sarah. Will your men be needing another round, Captain?"

"Soon enough, I should think." He reached into his pocket and offered her a few coins, and his men followed his example. "We don't mean to ask for credit."

She counted the money in front of him and frowned at the lieutenants. "I haven't seen them here before. Thought I knew all the troops quartered nearby."

The captain leaned back easily in his chair. "We are just up from training camp at Brighton, posted to Crawley for the winter."

"Crawley, is it? A fair piece off, then. What brings you and your men up this way?"

"Oh, nothing but a trifle. Some report of trouble, but I'm sure we will put it down soon enough."

Bess dropped the coins in her pocket and collected the mugs that were already empty. "There's no trouble here, Captain, and I'll thank you not to start any." She walked away, but his next words stopped her.

"And if word gets round that there is a highwayman plundering travelers? That would dry up your customers pretty fast." He grinned again when she turned around to face him. "Wouldn't it?"

"A highwayman?" she whispered.

"Robbed three people this week alone. One of them had a coach full of children. The poor dears, frightened out of their wits, they were! And word is, he misused another man's wife right in front of him. Laid hold of her, bold as you please!"

"Misused..." She cleared her throat. "Excuse me?"

"Oh, forgive me. That must be distressing to a..." He let his eyes rove over her body in a way that made her feel sullied. "Lady. I assure you, you've nothing to fear, so long as you stay indoors at night."

A burning surged up her spine, and Bess drew herself up straight. "There's no need to be insulting. I'm no kind of lady, but neither do I need such a caution from the likes of you."

He chuckled and held up a hand. "I meant no offense, madam. I would ask, however, if anyone among your recent visitors stands out as suspicious."

Bess narrowed her eyes. "It's my father you'll be wanting to ask. I'll fetch him."

"Yes, please do that. You won't be long, I hope?"

She shot him a curious glance over her shoulder. His eyes were somewhat lazy in drifting back up to meet hers, but when they did, he offered another cheerful grin and lifted his mug. "For another round, of course."

"Hmm." She marched briskly away, but once out of sight, she scurried like a hare. *A highwayman!* Here, in her little village! Who would believe it? Such villains were supposed to be legends of the past, were they not? Bess hastened to the stillroom to find her father, bent over one of his casks.

"Papa, you won't believe it. There are some soldiers here looking for a robber!"

Her father straightened. "Robber, what robber?"

"A highwayman, he says."

"A what? Oh, he must be exaggerating the exploits of a common thief. We haven't heard anything like the old tales since I was a boy."

She shrugged helplessly. "He wants to talk to you—the captain does, I mean."

His expression became unfocused, and he rubbed his chin. "Yes, I imagine he does. See to this, will you?"

Bess took the glass flask and finished pouring the refined spirit into it, then set it aside and filled six mugs of ale for the officers. It gave her a better excuse to hear what was being said, but she needn't have hurried. The entire common room knew it all within a few moments.

"The Scarlet Bandit?" her father repeated. "Yes, as a matter of fact, I had heard something of that. Near London, was he not? I thought it was no more than a stunt. Some fool out to fill the gossip rags or other such nonsense."

The captain accepted his mug from Bess and lifted it toward her father. "No stunt, I assure you. The blackguard is quite real, and he has been making a terror of himself in these parts of late. You haven't seen anything peculiar, have you, sir?"

Bess did not miss the way her father flexed his fingers and wiped his palm on the leg of his trousers. "Ah, no, nothing I can think of, Captain. What does this devil look like?"

"Well, that is just the trouble. None has seen his face, for he wears a mask. They say he is a tall fellow, though some claim he is quite thick in the chest while others say he is cut more sparingly. Athletic, either way, for I suppose he would have to be. Nothing remarkable about his voice or person that I am aware of, but he always wears a red velvet coat. Quite the dandy, they say. Oh, and he rides a beastly black creature. Trying to make after old Dick Turpin, I shouldn't wonder."

The shivers down Bess's neck grew more intense, and her breath became short. *Dear heavens...*

"Are we in danger?" her father asked.

"Oh! No, I think not. He's a coward he is, preying upon the helpless in the dark. Wouldn't dare show his face among decent folk."

Bess's father grimaced. "From what you say, he does not show his face at all. How are we to know whether we have sheltered a criminal? I hope you do not think I run that sort of establishment."

The captain scoffed. "Not at all, of course. But I do ask you to keep a sharp eye out for anything suspicious. Odd comings and goings, men what keep to themselves, that sort of thing. And I heard a rumor—mind you, only a rumor—that he had a taste for sporting with the fairer sex." The captain's eyes had begun to drift toward Bess during this last bit, but he snapped them back to her father.

"Half the men who pass through here would match that description."

"Aye!" the captain laughed, "but if the rumors be true, this bounder has rather... discriminating taste." Again, his gaze flitted over Bess, and this time, her father shot her a conscious glare. The captain shrugged away his interest, however, and merely added, "Mind if I have a word with your ostler? I should like to enquire after that horse. Rather distinctive creature, I should think it would have been noticed."

"Hmm? Oh! Yes, yes, of course."

Bess hid a snort of contempt. She put no faith in Tim to notice any of the horses, unless he thought he could tempt her to the stable to see them. But a horse as magnificent as the one she had seen in the woods that night... Yes, he probably would have brought *that* one to her attention, if it had ever been here.

If it *was* the same horse. But how could it not be? Black, with a masked rider who haunted the twinkling hours and wore a coat of deepest red velvet... A pit of horror had sunk into her belly with each point of the captain's description. Her Mr. Cumberland was not only a mystery. He was a cold, black, villain. And she had been in his clutches.

"Captain," she heard herself ask in a shaken voice, "what exactly is this man wanted for? Has he... has he murdered anyone?"

"Not yet, but I am sure that is only by sheer chance. Soon enough, he will carry his infamy to its natural conclusion."

"But he has not done so yet? You are sure?"

The captain tilted his head to look her more fully in the face. "I report only what I hear, madam, but I do not believe so. Are his other crimes not sufficient to brand him a loathsome devil?"

She swallowed. "I expect they must be."

"Gone are the days when these highway rogues were accounted heroes for the broadsheets and flirtatious fantasies for wealthy ladies," the captain added. "And it is my duty to see that it stays that way."

"Hear, hear!" her father echoed. "I'll have no truck with such a villain. You've no need to fear that, Captain. Decent folk ought to be able to go about as they please without fearing violence on the road."

"But if it is as you say," Bess interjected, "then he is not guilty of violence, is he? He has taken no one's life. Surely, you would not hang a man over stolen jewelry."

The captain settled a long, searching look on her. "I will caution you, if I may, madam. If the rumors are *all* true, it is not only money he loves. He is said to be favored among your sex, and I doubt not that he possesses ample charm. Should you encounter this rogue, do not credit his lies or give heed to his smooth tongue."

Her father stepped slightly forward, shaking his head, and speaking in a voice that quavered faintly. "My Bessie is as pure as they come."

The captain's lip turned up in what nearly passed for a smile. "Really."

"It's true, sir. She's a sharp one, misses nothing, and what's more, she wouldn't hesitate to turn the rascal in. No fancy words ever turned her head, I can vouch for that."

The captain offered them a crisp bow. "In that case, my fears are allayed. Lieutenant Beasley here will tell you how to contact me, should you notice anyone suspicious. I believe I will have a chat with your ostler now."

Bess never took her eyes off the captain as he went out, though she felt her father's nervous glances darting off her cheeks. She refused to meet his look. What was she to say? That she already knew, almost with certainty, who this masked mystery was? Did her father, who seemed to comprehend something of Mr. Cumberland's past, also know? And if he did, why was he protecting the man instead of turning him in?

"Bessie," he murmured unevenly, "see to the drinks. I'm going out with the captain."

She finally turned to face him, but he was already walking away. "Yes, Papa."

Chapter Fourteen

"**I** NEED MORE INFORMATION. There are simply too many unknowns here."

North leaned over Nick's shoulder and nodded as he examined the map laid out before them. "What if you dropped a note with that old hag in town? The one that sold you the ribbon?"

Nick shook his head and squeezed the bridge of his nose. "I don't think she knows anything of value. All I have of this supposed spy I am to meet is a date, two days from now. No information to convey, no notion of who it is. I don't like it."

"But you knew this before," North pointed out. "It is hardly new information. The entire endeavour was a risk."

"Are you saying I should not have taken the assignment? I was not given the choice."

"No, I only meant to say that now is hardly the time to be losing your courage. You have known for a while that you only had the barest of information to lead with."

"I am not losing my courage! I suppose you might say the frustration is growing. I know how to operate without specific directives, but this is something completely different. I do not know whether I am to meet magistrate or miscreant. Shall I find myself confronted with a peer of the realm or a pirate? I simply wish I had eyes in places where Cumberland might have had them."

"What do you mean by that?"

"It occurred to me that his infrequent and rather salacious visits to his favorite posting inns were not without their purpose. Beyond the obvious, I mean."

"You think he was doing more than indulging himself?"

"Perhaps. It was one of his doxies who turned him in at last, was it not? He must have revealed something to her."

North grunted. "You can hardly blame the wench. After the way he left her..."

"Yes, I can imagine. But there had to have been others, aside from the usual criminal network. Sources that were uniquely his own, and one wonders what they knew. What secrets they kept, and more importantly, what secrets they told. No one accounts such girls of any importance, yet they see everything. It would be a brilliant scheme for him to have enlisted his paramours to keep watch for him where he could not show his face."

North scratched his chin thoughtfully. "You may have something there, Captain. So, have you found any such girl?"

Nick frowned and tapped his quill on the map. "Perhaps. I know one clever enough, that is for certain. Whether she will help me is another matter."

"How did Cumberland persuade his beauties? Stolen baubles and well-placed kisses would probably suffice."

"Naturally. But the lady I have in mind would not be swayed by such inducements."

"Then perhaps you need another 'lady'."

Nick smiled vaguely. "No, I need the noblest, fiercest girl to be had, and I know just where to find her."

"OCH, BESSIE LASS, IT be a bad business! Yes, a bad business."

Bess hefted her water pail and walked on as if she had not heard the ostler, but he followed her doggedly from the well to the back door. "What a terr'ble thing 'tis. A ruffian haunting the roads? Liftin' the Quality's finery? Be'nt my concern, though, less'n 'e takes to foot with some'at else." He finished with a vicious giggle and then a hacking cough. "Be thou not afeared?"

"Whatever and whoever this rogue is, I do not see how it concerns me," she answered flatly. She refused to stop and spend an unnecessary moment with him.

"Now, hold a minute," Tim implored. "Had a notion, I did. 'Twould see into your protection and all."

Bess sighed and lowered her bucket. "And what is that?"

He cocked his head and gave her a twinkling grin. "I've a fair bit put by. Enough to see a handsome lassie through the cold winter. I'd make for ye a fair bloke, and no mistake."

She recoiled, shuddering and backing away even as her stomach rebelled, and she was almost sick. "I've no interest in marrying you!"

"Oh why, to be sure, the lassie is balky for she's a wantin' a younger man," he lamented. "A handsome face, I never had that, curse me! But I'd make a right stout man for thee, and I ain't so very old that the lassie couldn'a cradle a wee one in time."

She stumbled slightly on a stone and wheeled about, sloshing half the water out of her bucket. "No! Pray, do not even think of it!"

"Gad's teeth, but ye'r a fine piece!" he groaned as he scurried in front of her. "Did I say as the master gave leave? I didn't, did I? Had words with thy sire, I did. 'Hasten,' says he, 'afore disgrace claim my lassie.'"

Bess's vision swam, and she staggered back. "My father would never have given you his blessing."

"He gave more than that." Tim grinned. "He says if I keep thee safe from harm, then, says he, I becomes the master and landlord when he passes on."

"But you're as old as he is!"

"Nay, nay, 'tis not the coat nor the mane what tells the age. 'Ave a look at 'is teeth, I allus say. I've not a day more than six and forty years, but thy sire is two or three lustrums farther on. I know an old carthorse like meself holds no fancy for a handsome filly, but ye'll come ter lean on old Tim, ye will, ye will. 'Tis only a matter of time."

Rage overcame her revulsion and horror, and her cheeks burned. "No. It is not a matter of time. It is a matter of opinion, and mine is not favorable. Now, leave me be, and should you dare invoke my father's name again with such lies, I will empty a chamber pot on your boots!" She hefted her bucket once more and stomped through the back door of the inn.

"Papa!" she cried. "Papa, where are you?" The only answer was Hattie, poking her head bug-eyed around the corner, then disappearing when she saw the look on Bess's face. Three more times she called for him, her voice growing more insistent and angry.

Finally, he appeared, wiping his hands on an apron and looking about as if searching for a fire. "What ails you, Bessie?"

"Did you know that Tim has this notion of marrying me? He even said you gave him your blessing! He has become a fearful nuisance, and now he is spreading lies!"

Her father's face turned white. "I did not... explicitly grant my blessing."

"What! Why would you not turn him down with a vengeance? I can barely stand him! He is a vulgar, ignorant, useless old lecher. The way he is always staring, he makes me uncomfortable. I wanted to ask you to dismiss him altogether, but I knew you kept him on out of human charity. I'll not see a man starve if I can help it, but I will not marry him!"

"That is quite enough, lass! There be no cause for you to act the shrew."

"A shrew! I am outraged, and justly so. Why, even to consider the thing is indecent, and you, my own father—"

His face hardened and he roared to silence her—the first time in her memory he had ever done so. "You talk of indecent! What of flirting with a bounder and a cad who would ruin you and leave you destitute?"

She was panting, her ribs aching against her stays, and she shook her head in bewilderment. "What are you talking about?"

"You know bloody well. That Cumberland blackguard—the bastard! Dancing in here after all this time and trying to tug at your heartstrings. Aye, he was not content with merely ogling you or smacking your rear as the others do. He had to make you care for him, the rogue!"

Bess shook her head as frustrated tears stung. "I don't understand, Papa. You said yourself he seemed like a decent enough man, and I have no attachment to him."

"Not yet, but I saw how you were eying each other. Looks can be deceiving. He'll shame you, and you're naught but a blind fool." He nodded, sucking air between his teeth. "That is my fault. I have left you a fool, because I wished to keep you ignorant and safe, rather than seeing the worst come to pass."

"Papa!" She stomped her foot and braced her fists at her sides. "What is this about? I've done nothing wrong, but what do you know about Mr. Cumberland?"

His face closed like a shutter. "Nothing you need know of, Bessie. Fool you may be, but you're still mine, and that's the end of it. Cumberland can go hang."

"Ah! You'd like nothing better, wouldn't you? Why do you hate him so?" She narrowed her eyes and leaned close. "Who is he to you?"

She was waiting for a confession. An admission that her father knew the same truth as she herself had discovered—that Mr. Cumberland was the mysterious man hunted by the militia. And once he owned that truth, she would demand to know why her father had not turned him in out of hand. One of them must have some power over the other, and she meant to know what it was.

But her father never buckled. He screwed his mouth into a scowl and turned away. "Leave it alone, Bessie. Nothing but trouble and shame there."

"You speak of trouble and shame! We must have different understandings of the words. What about that proposition I just entertained from the most repulsive character in all the kingdom? I'd rather be take up with a philanderer and be left to shift for myself than be forced to marry Tim."

Her father's teeth clenched. "You don't mean that."

"Try me." She crossed her arms and glared back at him.

"See here, Bessie, I never encouraged Tim, but I was quite serious about seeing you wed. There be no two ways about it. If you don't marry, you'll fall just like the other girls. I'll not see you used up and worn out like a whore."

"But I'm not—"

"I've had enquiries," he interrupted.

She blanched. "From more than Tim?"

Her father resumed wiping his hands, and Bess noticed for the first time how they trembled. "Silas the butcher. Waters, the blacksmith. And Tompkins, His Lordship's steward. There was even an apothecary, came through here a se'nnight back. One look at you, and he called me to his table to ask after your hand."

"But that is just talk!" she protested. "I remember most of them, and they were foxed, that's all."

"Stone sober, to a man. I'd swear my life on it."

She sucked in a long sigh. "Anyway, it's all foolishness. I suppose you told them all no."

He thinned his lips and looked away uncomfortably. "I have refused no one out of hand. My answer has always been they must first court you and see how they fared. You shot each of them full of arrows, I'm afraid. But of late, I've been thinking you may not have the luxury of choice. You need stability. Respectability. And... I have been entertaining more ambitious notions."

Bess squinted. "Ambitious how?"

"You need a man, Bessie. The sooner, the better. I'm not in favor of any man who would take you far off or into society unknown to us, but others..."

"I will not marry Tim," she warned.

"He is better set up than others," her father objected weakly. "He has some savings..."

"I cannot stand the sight of him, the old pervert! You said yourself he was not fit to love Mama, but you would ask *me* to take him?"

"Only because he would not take you from the home you know. He could help you carry on here, after—"

"No, Papa, stop there. What's this about, you talking of being gone all of a sudden? I won't have it! I'd sell or give away the whole lot before I let Tim share my bed, or even lay a finger on me."

He looked deflated, and his eyes fell to the floor. "Well, be that as it may, you must marry soon. I've been meaning to speak to you on it even before this whole highwayman business came up."

"What has that to do with anything?"

"Nothing, nothing, save that I have been a bit distracted, you know. Always a redcoat hanging about now, and never a moment to think. Bessie, you cannot go on as you are, we both know that. With ruffians dashing about the countryside, snatching up loose affections where they may find them, it is all the more reason to have you safely accounted for."

"I won't marry the closest man to hand."

Her father shrugged. "Perhaps I'll drop a note to Thompkins, inviting him to renew his addresses. He was rather keen, and he's a young fellow, decent looking. You'd be leaving the inn, I suppose, but you'd be near the manor house, and that's a fair step for an innkeeper's daughter."

"I hardly know him!"

"You'll get to know him, I imagine."

Bess sighed and pressed the heel of her hand to her forehead. "Papa, I do not see why this needs to be so urgent."

He set his jaw and held up a hand in the way that he had always done when he meant to settle the matter. "It is no longer open for discussion, and I'll have none of your objections. I hope to see you settled within the month, if possible, but certainly before winter."

Within the month! Her mouth fell open as she stared at her father as he walked away, but he would entertain none of her objections. *So soon!* Of course, he had been making comments, but she had not expected him to press her to make a choice.

Simmering with indignation, she raced past Hattie, who was just coming back in with the eggs. "Bessie? Bess!" called Hattie, but Bess only slammed the door and ran. There was only one place where she might find solace.

Dappled sunlight kissed the petals of the boldest rose on her mother's bush. By the time Bess reached it, righteous fury had melted into bewildered grief. Her father had rarely taken her in hand, but the few times he had, his will was irrevocable. There would be no swaying him. He had determined that she was to marry, had decided it was in her best interest, and he would hear no objections.

And so, without ceremony, her life was to be forever altered because something in the wind had made her father nervous for her virtue. It was ghastly unfair—inhumane, even! What was she to do?

She had never cared to follow the ways of the other girls, even if she thought her father might have turned a blind eye to her doings. Hattie, Sarah, Jenny... they seemed to enjoy themselves, and even had ample spending money due to their exploits, but Bess had no interest in giving her body without giving her heart. The two seemed one and the same, and unfortunately, neither seemed inclined to obey her bidding anymore.

She had been very near to falling for the rascal Cumberland. So near that the memory of waking in his arms, feeling his sweet kiss on her fingers wooed her to sleep at night with impossible fantasies. It was a troublesome fascination; one she could not rid herself of nearly by the application of common sense. By all she could tell, he was born a gentleman of means, and now he made his way as a nefarious villain. He was as firmly out of her reach as she was Tim's.

But that did not stop her heart from fluttering when she had entered the wood where she had last seen him. It did nothing for the restless, willful hope that she would discover a secret missive from him, lowering her and dragging her, willingly or no, into the forbidden. Dash it all, but if he should appear before her, even now, with that crooked smile and something of a plausible explanation for everything, she would not have the strength to resist.

And so, when at last she dropped to her knees to stroke the velvet rose petals against her cheek, she was not nearly so alarmed as she ought to have been when a twig cracked under a boot. Bess lifted her head...

And there *he* was.

He stood under a hickory tree, tricorn in hand, his expression remorseful. His was a face she could trace in her sleep, that expression one she could read as if it were printed on a broadsheet. He had come for her, unaccountably, and against all better judgment.

And he was wearing His Majesty's colors.

Chapter Fifteen

"I WAS HOPING I might find you here."

Bess rose to her feet. She said not a word, but locked eyes with him as she walked slowly, carefully toward him.

"I hope you will forgive me for waiting for you," he apologized. "It was the only way I knew to speak with you on the quiet."

Bess walked closer, still silent, and his look grew hesitant.

"I say, no doubt this must come as something of a shock to you—"

Bess closed the distance in a rush, bracing a fist like men did, and delivering a blow to his jaw that left her wringing her hand. "You lied to me!"

He staggered back, holding his face, but there was no anger in his voice. "Yes, I did."

"Why? Why would you lead me on and use me? You made the veriest fool of me!"

"I never used you, madam."

"Did you not? What was all that about then, that foolishness about some rogue horse, all that nonsense about names. Was *anything* you told me true?"

"What I said about my family. That was true. And I thought our friendship was true. The rest, about my business—"

"A lie!"

"A secret," he corrected.

She tossed a loose ringlet of hair behind her shoulder, and his eyes followed it for a second, then snapped back to her face. "What is a secret but a truth untold? How is that different to a lie?"

"When it is designed for convenience, that, undoubtedly, is a lie." He slapped his hat on his leg and glanced uncomfortably away. "I have tried to persuade myself that it is a forgivable offense when it is done out of necessity, in the service of a greater good. Miss Bess—"

"No! You have no right to address me so." She could hardly keep the hurt from wavering in her voice. Her brow crumpled, and the tears burned. "I'm no 'miss,' and I never was, but you, you tried to tickle my fancy with yet another lie, and it was so much worse, because you lied to me about myself."

He put out a hand as if he meant to comfort her, but she drew back her shoulders, though her chest felt like it might burst.

"I know who and what I am! I don't need the likes of you feeding me sugar and honey, talking like I was a proper lady and all. You're just like all the others, except you thought you found another way to lift my skirts."

His face grayed and his chest rose and fell sharply. "If that is what you think of me, madam, I will trouble you no further." He turned, his expression broken, and slowly, he walked away.

The sobs came in earnest now. She covered her mouth to keep from crying out, but she could do nothing about the salt tears blinding her. One last retort—she could not help herself. "Do you even have a respectable name? I'd wager it is not Mr. Cumberland... *Captain*," she finished with a pointed look at the epaulets on his collar. "Where did you steal that uniform?"

He stopped. "Spain," he bit out without turning around. "At the front. I was with the Regulars, just like your brother."

Bess sobered. It made sense, much as she felt she ought to doubt his word. Had she not taken him for a soldier that first evening? "What was your assignment there?" she asked cautiously.

He faced her. "With Wellington. I had a lieutenant's commission, though not by my father's leave. He would not forward a farthing, because he did not wish for his son to march off to war. But I was determined, and I suppose you could say I earned my commission through distinguished service in the militia. I..."

Here, he colored slightly. "I apprehended a house burglar, quite by accident, but I later learned it was not money or jewels that had the criminal crawling through a second-floor window. The... ahem. The father of the lady in question was exceedingly grateful for my... tactful management of the affair."

Bess arched a brow. "You must have a lot of 'secrets' to keep."

He shrugged lightly. "A few. This gentleman took an interest in me, saw to it that I got a commission. Perhaps he really just wanted me somewhere I couldn't spread talk, but it suited me well enough."

"So, what brought you back here?"

"I was injured in Spain. Caught several bomb fragments when it shattered the stone wall we were defending. After the battle, they sent me home to recover, because there was some doubt at first whether I might lose my eye."

Bess tilted her head and approached softly. "The right one?"

"Yes. Dashed near impossible to shoot straight without it. But I was lucky, for the largest wound was just below my eye rather than in it. How did you know?"

Carefully, she lifted her hand toward his cheek, but drew back. "You always squint on that side when you smile. That was all the proof I needed to know it was you in the mask."

"Egad," he breathed. "You already saw through me! I would not last a week in this business, if my men did not watch my back at every turn."

"You have men under your command?"

"Three. They are waiting for me at our encampment."

"But you still have not told me, what are you doing here? Why were you dressed like that, why all the hiding and moving about?"

He fingered his hat and looked down. "My apologies. My men and I are on a special assignment that requires much secrecy."

"And, ah, *Captain*, do you have a name?"

"Good Lord! I am quite the thing, am I not? You see why I need all the help I can get." He smiled winningly and bowed. "Captain Nicolas Hunt, at your service."

"Stop there." Bess held up a hand. "The last captain who placed himself at my service did not take my fancy, and I am still undecided about you."

His smile faded. "I am very sorry to hear that. I was hoping to ask for your help."

"What, have you misplaced another name? Am I to learn next that you are also a pirate? A nobleman?"

"I am quite serious, madam."

Bess sighed. "Very well, I surrender. Tell me what you want, and I shall consider it. By the way, does your commander know that you masquerade about as a highwayman, plundering innocent travelers?"

"He was the one who ordered me to do it. Miss Bess, I do not expect to win your trust after having once deceived you. Please know that it was done unwillingly and accept my humblest apologies. The only thing I do not regret so far about this... this foolhardy errand, is meeting you."

She crossed her arms against a sudden rush of warmth in her belly. Why was she such a fool over him? He was just a man, with honeyed words and no character, just like all the others. Wasn't he? When she trusted herself to speak again, her voice was tight and hoarse. "What do you want from me?"

"Your eyes, if you will lend them. Your ears, too, if they can be spared. I need to know who is who, and I can think of no one better to ask."

She swallowed, then lifted her chin. "Go on."

He looked at the ground and paced a few steps to the side. "I think it best if I start from the beginning. After I returned home, I was reassigned. Some gold-braided hero determined that I was not fit to return to the Continent when I was due to go, because an incompetent surgeon claimed I might not recover my full sight after the swelling had gone. But fortunately for me, I did."

Bess stepped to the side to see his cheek better. "It must have been serious, but I see no scar."

"Just here." He indicated the place with his fingertip, parting the short hairs of his beard under his cheekbone. If one looked carefully, there was a slight dip, and a faint palsy on that side of his face.

"The surgeon probably did more damage than the shrapnel. By the time it finally healed, I learned that I had been promoted to Captain, and my services had been requested at the War office. In Intelligence."

"Intelligence?"

"Sometimes I think the name of the department is the only intelligence to be had, but yes. We gather information vital to the war effort, and we see that Wellington knows what he needs to know."

"Meaning?"

"You have probably guessed it. I hunt spies. Until a fortnight ago, I was hunting a notorious one, suspected of intercepting messages between Whitehall and Wellington himself. The middle link in a long chain, he was, and he had adopted the highway robbery bit to throw suspicion off whomever was at the other end of that chain. We caught our man, but we did not find his accomplices, and so I have been obliged to assume his identity until all the villains are found."

"So, it really was you, those last robberies we heard of?"

He nodded. "I think it's taken a year or two off my life, but yes. I do take precautions, so if anyone gets hurt, it will probably be me. My men see that the money goes back to its rightful owners. It's all for show, until two days from now, anyway. That's when it will all become very, very, real, and I should like all the information I can come by before riding in with nothing but a brace of pistols."

She puckered her mouth. "Supposing I believe you, how did you find out what you know already? I mean, the highwayman, Cumberland. How did you find out who he was?"

"We were tracking the leak for months and it led to him. He was deliberately set up as the most obvious target, to take the fall for everyone, but we wanted to catch his masters." He cleared his throat. "We, ah, got an anonymous tip that paid off. When we learned his real name, the threads of deception started to unravel, and we found a second informant to confirm it. He's also dead now." He frowned.

"Good heavens!"

"You see why we must keep our circles close. We could not involve the local constables or the militia, because we needed him to carry on unhindered so we could draw out his associates. The law wanted him, it is true, but his worst crime as far as they were concerned was pillaging baubles and dallying with the local women. A menace, to be sure, but the real danger was the men he associated with. Crafty devils, to a man, and no greenhorns at their business. And it is for that reason that I come to you now."

"If they are so expert, what can I possibly do? What am I to look for?"

"Loose threads. People who know things—a stranger who talks to too many people... or too few. Someone from town who disappears on occasion. People loitering where they should not. Anything out of the ordinary."

"That is odd, for that is exactly what Captain Chesterfield asked me to report."

He stiffened. "Chesterfield? Do you know him?"

"He came to the inn today looking for a highwayman."

He swallowed visibly, and his chest rose in a deep breath. "I suppose it is to be expected. Did you tell him anything?"

"I was debating on it, but he walked away with my father before I had the chance."

"And would your father have had anything to say?"

"I... I am not certain. They went to the stables together." She darted a quick glance over his shoulder. "They were looking for *him*."

He followed her gaze to the black horse behind him and then smiled. "*Her*, actually. They won't find her."

"She is the one? The horse you were talking about?"

He held out his hand for her to take. "She is. Permit me to introduce you. Bess... This is..." He coughed. "Bess."

She was putting out her hand to touch the mare's muzzle, but she froze. "The horse is named after me?"

He chuckled. "Not exactly. We never knew what Cumberland called her, but my men decided she must be called Black Bess after John Nevison's horse. You might remember him as Swift Nick. They were so determined about it that there was nothing to be done to dissuade them. It has caused me a few moments of confusion, I will say that!"

She laughed and then raised her knuckles. Black nostrils flared and quivered as the mare extended a cautious touch to the back of her hand.

"Be careful," he warned. "She and I have got something of an understanding now. Leastwise, it's been a few days since she offered to slice me to ribbons, but I wouldn't trust her too easily."

Bess lowered her hand and began to step back, but the mare gave a low whicker and stepped into her. Bess dared to comb her fingers through the horse's satin mane and the horse responded by arching her neck and wriggling her upper lip in a show of pleasure.

"Well..." he laughed nervously. "The old girl does have her moments."

"She is magnificent!"

"She is," he agreed, with a note of pride in his voice. "But it is not this Bess whose good opinion I am most interested in winning."

He rounded and looked down at her with an intensity that made her breath catch. "Please, Miss Bess, I know I do not deserve your trust after everything that has happened. Were I a brother, someone in a position to advise you, I would encourage you to have nothing to do with me. But matters are coming to a head soon, and I am in need of a friend."

Bess had progressed to scratching under the mare's chin, evoking a sneeze and then a snort, and she laughed. "Is this how highwaymen carry on, then? Leaning on poor tavern wenches for information?"

He lifted his shoulders and in a humble tone she could not help but like, he said, "I wouldn't know."

"I thought you said you were in 'intelligence.' Is it not your business to know these things?"

A cautious grin passed over his face. "I see there is no fooling you. Yes, in that case, I do know. Cumberland had such sources, for we discovered enough of them to lead us to him. But they will not serve me now, and I need to find my own."

"And what will happen if you find the man you're looking for?"

"I wish I knew. All I know is that two nights from now, I am to stop a carriage on the Brighton Road and its occupant will be the man I seek, or someone in his employ."

Bess let her fingers tangle in the thick black forelock as she gave the mare one last caress, then she deliberately stepped back. If she was not careful, she would be caught up in this madness before ever thinking a rational thought. She would let Captain Nicholas Hunt, or whoever he was, throw her over his saddle and ride off into the night with her, and she would probably thrill to every moment of her own undoing. "Do you mean to kill him?"

"Not if I can help it. I am a soldier, not a cold-blooded killer. I mean to let him think his message has been conveyed until we find a way to cut his legs out from under him. I would see him answer to justice, but I am no executioner. Does that set your mind at ease?"

She nodded slowly, her eyes traveling over his horse before daring to meet his again. "And after that?"

"After that? I suppose I wait to learn what Whitehall would have of me. I'd like my own life back and to have done with lies and shadows forever, but the time for that is not come. What do you say, Miss Bess? Will you help me?"

She shook her head. "There you are again, talking to me like some fine creature. Why should I help you?"

His face went blank. "Men at the front are in danger because of these scoundrels. Men like your own brother! I thought I expressed that."

"Oh, yes, you did, quite well. Because of that, I can forgive deception, and I think I can even forgive the robberies you have carried out in the course of your duty. But why do you keep filling my head with fancies, addressing me like a lady of quality? I cannot trust such treatment. Why not just ensure my cooperation by offering me money, like everyone else?"

He bit into his lower lip and turned so his profile faced her. "Because," he gritted out, "I have never used a woman ill, and I do not mean to start with you. What I ask is no trifling matter, and you deserve fair treatment. And because in my eyes, you *are* a lady of quality."

Her heart gave one great thud, and then she could have sworn that it went dead still. She gaped at him, tilting her head in wonder, until her throat swelled.

He stepped forward in concern. "Miss Bess? Are you well?"

"Well..." she whispered. "A simple word with such a difficult meaning."

"Miss Bess, if I ask too much of you, then I beg you would forgive me and forget my face."

She shook her head. "It is not that. It is only that no one has ever..." She knotted her fingers before her and stared down at them. And then, he was gently prying one hand away from the other and cradling it in his own.

"Pray, what is it?" he asked gently.

A tear started in the corner of her eye, and she blinked it away. "Girls like me... we don't get much choice in life. No one asks leave to treat us as they do. The best that can come of us is to marry someone who will provide for and not use us too roughly."

She felt the muscles of his fingers harden, but his grip did not tighten on her hand. He still held it gently, but there was an iron at work in him. His right eye twitched ever so slightly, and his nostrils fluttered in anger. "I am sorry for that," was his quiet answer.

"It is the way of the world," she said with a shrug. "My father is insisting that I marry very soon, so that I can avoid falling in with the other girls."

This time, his fingers did tighten. "Are you in any danger of that?"

"For myself, no. But I am not always in control of what happens to me, am I?"

His jaw flexed, and she saw him swallow before he spoke. "In the end, none of us are. Whom are you to marry?"

"It is not decided, so far as I know. My fear is that now my father has made his wishes known, I will have little choice in the matter. And if I get myself mixed up with you, he will push me even harder, perhaps even make me marry somebody I despise just to see me settled and out of trouble."

His Adam's apple bobbed, and his gray eyes widened. "You're worried that I could ruin your reputation?"

"Reputation! I'm a tavern girl. I don't have a reputation. I can either cause trouble or not, that is the extent of it, and if I cause trouble..."

"I will see to it that you do not," he said quickly.

Bess raised her brows. "How do you mean to do that?"

"I will have words with your father myself, if I need to."

"I do not think that would be wise."

"Why not? Would he blow my concealment?"

She shook her head. "He told me to stay away from you."

His eyes narrowed to slits. "Me? Whatever for?"

"He would not say. Just said that you were not for me and that I should forget about you."

His chest rose and fell, and he reached up to trace her cheek with one of his fingers. "You should, but I hope you do not. I know I will never forget you, no matter what happens, my bonny Miss Bess."

Her breath stilled, and there was only one answer she could give. "I will help you, Captain Hunt, in any way I possibly can."

A warmth lit those stony gray eyes, and his smile was all the beauty she ever hoped to see in this world. "Thank you."

Chapter Sixteen

N ICK'S GOOD SENSE WARNED him to let go her hand, but it was the last thing he
could do. Instead, he caught her second hand and kissed it, stopping just short of
turning it over to brush his lips on the inside of her wrist. One gesture could be interpreted
as gratitude from a man whose life she held in her hands. The second, unquestionably the
actions of a rake, and he was no such thing.

Black eyes widened; the lashes heavy with what remained of her frustrated tears of a
moment ago. Her lips parted in a soft gasp, and she allowed her fingers to curl lightly over
his. Every instinct compelled him to heed the demands of nature, to lay his hand at the
dip of her vivid curves, to pull her close until his nostrils filled with the scent of her.

He ached to draw her head to his shoulder, rest his cheek on her crown of black satin,
and kiss the wayward curls that fell at her brow and temple. His body yearned to make
her his own in blood and fire, but his heart would settle for nothing less than having such
a woman in truth and honor. He fought down a savage quiver in his being and repeated
to himself what he had told her earlier. The time for his own wishes had not yet come.

Instead, he forced his touch to remain light, his voice gentle. "You have... allow me,"
he murmured.

She blinked in confusion, but remained still, almost trembling as she visibly battled
with her instincts to trust him. "What?"

He drew out his pocket handkerchief and gingerly dabbed the cold tears that still
streaked down her cheek. Her lips opened in a startled sigh that warmed his hand and
made him shiver anew. "There. I may return you without looking as though I had made
you cry."

She stiffened and swallowed. "It was not only you."

"I bore my share." He released a long breath and braced his hands on her shoulders. "Bess, I am sorry. I never meant to hurt you."

She shrugged and shook her head. "It was my fault as much as anyone's. My father would never have warned me to avoid you, and he would not be pressing me so now if I had not let my fancy wander. I am afraid I was quite too obvious even for my own comfort in my admiration of you."

He blinked. "You... admired me?"

"How could I not? You were so different to what I had ever known, and the way you treated me... I suppose I craved the feeling that I mattered to someone for more than just my looks. I let myself see something I wanted to see, and damn if it didn't hurt to learn I was wrong!"

"Bess..." he wetted his lips. No help for it—he blundered ahead. "You were not wrong. I saw... or rather felt something too."

Liquid black pools turned up to him. "You did?" she whispered.

He traced her chin lightly with his thumb. "My life on it."

She lowered her face with a bitter laugh. "Do not be ridiculous, Captain."

"Nick. My name is Nick."

"But it does not matter, does it? You said it yourself. You're a gentleman born, and I'm a... well, I *won't* be a mistress. I'll scrub floors until my knees break before I let any man make me his whore." She lifted her chin and those black eyes flashed.

"And why do you think I would try to make you one?"

"You could hardly make me aught else. Wouldn't your family disown you?"

"They have already done so!" At her look of confusion, he sighed and took her hand tenderly between his. "It is a long and sorry tale, and not worth repeating now. Someday, I hope, I will tell you all of it, but if one day I am so blessed to marry, it will not be done to please my family. I am an Army captain, and someday, I hope to be respectably settled down with a desk job and an officer's quarters. I've quite had my fill of being shot at and bivouacking under the stars."

The flesh around her eyes creased, and she studied him in hesitant wonder. "I would like to trust you."

"Don't do it," he replied with a rakish grin. "I'm probably after your fifty pounds."

She pinched her lips and slapped him lightly in the chest. "I knew it!"

"Ho, there!" he laughed. "You are a cruel woman, Bess."

She grinned up at him, but the look caught and held, and grew rapidly into something a vast deal warmer. Her mouth softened, and her eyes scanned his face, but then she cleared her throat and looked away.

"You have not told me what you want me to look for. I am not, after all, a trained spy, like you are."

He straightened and dropped his hands. "Ah, yes. Well, perhaps I ought to tell you what I know so far. We were brought here to find someone called a 'monk at the old shag.'"

"That explains why you were looking for a parson."

"Indeed. I did locate him to receive a message, but I've no notion of where he is now or his real name. My men have been searching where they can, but so far, they have turned up nothing. I should like very much to know what he knows, and if appropriate, bring him to justice for his part in the scheme."

She nodded. "Anyone else?"

"How well do you know the old woman at the milliner's shop?"

"Mrs. Riley? Why, she is not old at all. Not more than five and thirty, and her husband is not much older."

"Husband? No, the old crow I saw had to have been sixty if she was a day. She appeared to be quite alone, save for a ragged cat she called Captain Bennick."

"That... does not sound right. Are you certain it was the milliner's shop?"

"I thought you might ask that." He slipped a hand inside his coat. "She sold me this. Well, sold! Robbed me blind, more like. There was a message folded up inside, so she was certainly an agent of some sort."

She accepted the crimson ribbon and stroked its shimmering length with reverence. "It is exquisite," she breathed.

"It is yours."

She looked up swiftly, an objection on her lips, but he stayed her hand when she tried to give it back to him. "What earthly use have I for such an item, save to give it to the fairest, bonniest lass I know?"

She stretched it out and a pang of longing shone in her eyes. "I've never had anything so fine." A smile touched her lips, growing in mischief when she held it alongside her cheek. "What do you think, shall I look the part of the lady now?"

He pretended to consider. "No more than before. It does nothing to make you more beautiful. I do not think anything could."

Her eyes flashed up to him with a look of doubt. "Fine words."

"But true words. I've seen many a maid turned out in all her finery, but it is all a sham. I've never seen anyone to compare to you. This—" he gestured to the ribbon—"it is almost fine enough to be worthy of you."

Her cheeks reddened to match the ribbon. "I thought you said you were not much one for flattery. I'll not be able to pass a mirror without stopping to stare at it now!"

He laughed, admiring the way those black eyes danced. "Do you not know what they call you? The first night I set eyes on you, they said you were called the Duchess of Surrey. I scoffed at it until I actually looked at you."

She ducked her head; her lashes beating furiously. "Captain, please. I'm no such creature. It's not even right to say such things."

"You think I speak of your beauty still? Others might stop there, but I saw your boldness and spirit. If there ever were a duchess in these parts, I've no doubt you would rival her. And that is why, Miss Bess, I trust none but you with my life."

Her shoulders lifted, and she raised her eyes to his once more. "I won't let you down, Captain."

N ICK SLIPPED DOWN FROM the saddle and hesitated, his gaze unseeing on his horse's flank. Had he done the right thing in dragging Bess into his troubles? It was too late to turn back now, but had he to do it over again, he would not have asked. It was one thing to approach a sharp-eyed woman who would invest nothing and could lose nothing by helping him. But Bess had as much as confessed feelings for him, and he had blurted out a similar admiration for her.

Now, it was personal. Now, she would take risks she should never have taken. Moreover, if anything went wrong, she would pay for helping him with her freedom and her future. And that was a thing he could not bear to see.

"Something wrong, Captain?"

Nick flinched and turned around as North approached. "No, nothing wrong. Report?"

North gestured. "I sent Wesson to the village for supplies. Daniels is on watch tonight, so he's in his tent now. Any luck with the wench?"

Nick pushed away from his horse with a sigh. "She's not a wench. And yes, she has agreed to help. I'll give you a map of where to exchange messages, should I be detained. For now, I'm going to follow Daniels' example."

North saluted. "Very good, sir. Shall I unsaddle Black Bess for you?"

"Aren't you afraid she'll bite you?"

"Yes, sir," North answered crisply. "But after this assignment, I think I wouldn't mind losing an arm in the line of duty. A retirement in London sounds mighty fine about now."

Nick chuckled and passed the reins to his lieutenant, letting his gaze trail over the magnificent creature once more. She looked like he and North both felt. Tired, frustrated, and ready for all of this to be over. He gave her an affectionate pat on the hip as North led her away. "Extra oats in her feed bag, if you please. She and I have a deal of work in the next few days."

He trudged into his tent and pulled his boots off. The first thing he had learned as a young scout on the Continent was to look to his horse, his boots, and his weapons. If any of them failed, he was as good as dead. Every soldier knew how to keep his equipment clean and in good repair, and his horse's needs came before his own. But no one had ever taught him how to look after an innocent woman on the battlefield.

He never should have gotten her involved. How plain it had been only a few hours ago! Bess Reynolds had seemed so perfect—clever and honest, fearless and loyal. Able to eavesdrop without being noticed or lure information out of any man with eyes, and well-positioned to see and hear everything that happened in the area. If only he hadn't gone and ruined it by falling for her first.

What if her father caught wind of it all and forced her to marry? Nick lay back on his cot and laced his fingers over his chest as he stared at the canvas overhead.

She'd said her father disapproved of him, but why? As far as the old innkeeper knew, Nick was just a common traveler who smiled at his daughter. That hardly made him unique. How much worse if her father learned the truth! Poor Bess would be dragged to the altar and wed to the nearest man with a pulse. And he would bear the responsibility for ruining her chances of happiness.

Unless... unless *he* could be the one to marry her.

Nick snorted to himself and rolled over. As long as he was dreaming, he might as well imagine running down the entire spy ring, helping win the war, then retiring from the army for good—reconciled to his father and maybe even knighted by the king to boot.

No, much as he might fancy Bess Reynolds, he had less than nothing to offer her. She would be better off married to a man of her father's choosing than tangled with him.

"CAPTAIN, THERE IS NEWS!"

Nick snorted awake and blinked into the darkness at the opening of his tent. "Wesson? What time is it?"

"Half-past nine, sir. The lieutenant said to let you sleep, but I've just come from the village and there's something you should hear."

Nick shook his head to clear it and bent to find his boots. "One moment." He tugged his suspenders over his shoulders and went out, squinting at the small cook fire that provided the only light in the camp. "What is it?"

Wesson stepped forward. "It's the militia, sir. They've arrested someone on suspicion of being the highwayman."

Nick snapped completely awake. "What? Who?"

"I didn't see him myself, sir. I'm told he was a drifter who appeared around Reigate about a month ago. No one seems to know his proper name or where he came from, but they say he was fifty if he was a day, and had a Cockney accent."

Nick crossed his arms and tapped a finger against his sleeve. "What evidence did they have to arrest him?"

"He was spotted loitering about town at odd hours. When the officers questioned him, they found he had a little satchel of jewelry. I spoke with a woman at the inn who had dealings with him. Apparently, he told this woman the jewelry had belonged to his mother, and it was all he had left in the world to live on, but of course, no one believed that story."

"She was the only person you spoke with?"

"And a man at the pub. I was trying not to draw too much attention to myself, sir, so I thought it would not be right if I were to ask through official channels—"

"No, no, of course. You did right." Nick sighed, chewing his lip. "Any chance he could have been connected to Cumberland?"

"I'd wager on it, sir. Leastwise, I'd wonder what a fellow like him was doing with all that jewelry."

"It is a pity we did not find him first. I would have liked to question him."

"Yes, sir. He'll be taken to London, though. Would General Richards take charge of him? Mayhap he'll get some information from him."

"Possibly. If so, he might not be hanged all at once. But if he is innocent, he will have a dashed monstrous time proving it. Poor devil!"

"He could not be hanged until the next Assizes, sir. Besides, it might throw the militia off your trail, just long enough for us to carry out the mission," Wesson suggested.

"It might. Then again..." Nick squinted and began to pace, scratching his chin in thought. "It might be a ruse by Chesterfield."

"Sir?"

"An old trick of his, I'm afraid. Catch one thief and let your real quarry think he is no longer under suspicion. Then, you have but to wait for him to become careless."

Wesson nodded slowly. "Ah," he breathed. "Then, sir, let us not become careless."

Chapter Seventeen

"Miss Reynolds! What a pleasure to see you out walking this morning."

A bolt shot through Bess's stomach and she stopped as if guilty. "Captain Chesterfield. I did not know you were still in town."

He dropped his hat and bowed. "I am a man of duty, Miss Reynolds, and at present, my duty seems to lie near Reigate."

"Then I take it you are still searching for that ruffian of the highways?"

He replaced his hat and fell into step easily beside her. "Oh, had you not heard? We made an arrest yesterday."

Her neck prickled in fear. It could not be Captain Hunt...

"Why, Miss Reynolds, you've no cause to look so alarmed!" Chesterfield laughed. "Fear not, he was neither young nor handsome. Long in the tooth and stinking of old spirits he was, and an unprepossessing figure he cut, I must say."

Bess forced a calmer expression upon her face. How could she have given her fears away so easily? "Well, then, Captain, I congratulate you," she said in the steadiest voice she could manage. "You have rid the county of a menace, to be sure."

"Do you think so? It is a pity I cannot. Such a rascal as we arrested could not possibly carry on alone. I am in town today seeking information on his accomplices."

"Ac—" She cleared her throat. "Accomplices?"

"Ah, you are afraid, is it Miss Reynolds? You've nothing to worry about, for it is not more violent men I seek. No, no, quite the opposite. Such men always have their sources of information; those who protect them from the law."

"They do?" Her ears felt hot, and she only hoped her cheeks were not flaming.

"But of course. Even a thief must have someplace to buy his food and lay his head at night, mustn't he? Do you think they are all ignorant of his doings? Yet, the local shopkeepers seal their lips when anything about him is mentioned. A folklore hero, I shouldn't wonder. They say the highwaymen of old were like Robin Hood, stealing from the rich and giving to the poor, and the common man holds him as his own son. Don't believe a word of it, Miss Reynolds. Rubbish!"

"I would never trust any man who steals for a living, no matter what he does with his money."

"Wise words, Miss Reynolds." He gave her a quizzical look. "By the by, I was asking among the locals about a few of the travelers that passed through the Bittern in the last two weeks, and a few questions arose. There was a stable boy who had suddenly come into possession of half a crown, and I believe he is lying to me about their source. I wonder if you might be able to help shed some light on the matter."

A conscious tingle raced down her spine. "I can try."

"Do you recall a Mr. George Ostin who came through last week?"

Bess cast up her eyes vaguely, trying to recollect. "Should I?"

"He was seen in the area just before all the robberies began happening. Then, two days ago, he was picked up by a London constable for embezzling funds from his employer. You are certain you don't remember him?"

Bess shrugged. "I don't see what he has to do with me. I don't remember the man."

Chesterfield turned to face her, drawing her purposefully to a halt. "He was seen giving you a rather substantial tip when last he was here."

"Lots of men give me tips."

The captain's eyes wandered down for just an instant, but long enough to make her stomach squirm. "I imagine they do, but this was more than tuppence, so they say. Ten pounds is quite a generous tip."

"Captain, are you saying that now you suspect *me* of something? If so, I cannot know what or why. A crooked man tries to entice me to be his entertainment for the evening, and the best conclusion you can draw is that he must be your highwayman and I must be his mistress? If that's the limit of your nugget, then you belong in Parliament and not the militia."

The captain laughed and held up a hand. "I've no intention of riling your temper, Miss Reynolds. I understand it is legendary enough already. I only wanted to ask if you recalled anything of import. Pray, let me buy you something by way of an apology."

"No, really, Captain, I could not permit that. I'll let you return to your business. There is no need—"

"I insist. Please. Something for the lady's pleasure? Just a gift from a friend," he assured her.

"Well... I was on my way to the milliner's," she relented.

"Capital! I shall buy you some ribbon for your bonnet."

Bess smiled tightly and allowed him to escort her. When they stepped into the shop, Mrs. Riley came forward with a cheerful smile. "Well! It is about time you came in, Miss Reynolds. We haven't seen you in more than six months."

Bess thanked her for the welcome and performed the introductions. The captain bowed most disarmingly, then took her lightly by the elbow to tour the shop. Bess stiffened but did not pull away. He seemed proud to have her on his arm, and all too familiar with the offerings on the shelves. With the air of a man who often made such purchases, he pointed out shades of pale rose, soft yellow, and even a spring green.

To each, Bess politely shook her head, but if she'd had her wits about her, she should just let him choose the first one that came to hand and leave her be. Except he would insist on escorting her back to the inn, and she had a purpose of her own in coming here today.

Mrs. Riley stood back enough to let them shop, but kept a wary eye in case they should ask to see more of a certain color. Bess was chafing, biting her lip, and sending imploring glances to the woman. If only the captain had not happened upon her! She could not very well learn what she wanted to know when she was stuck to his arm.

"Ah! Here is a fancy one. Let me see," Chesterfield said. He pulled out a length of lavender and held it beside Bess's face. "What do you think, my fair lady?"

Bess smiled wanly. "I don't feel the shade suits me, but it is lovely."

"Well! We must see what we can do to change your mind. I always thought a gentler color more fitting to a fine maid. Mrs. Riley, do you not agree?"

Mrs. Riley came forward, saw the grimace Bess wore, and settled on diplomacy. "Most of the young girls prefer the softer colors, but I've a fine, rich violet in the back that I think would please everyone. Bess, will you come and look?"

Thus uninvited, the captain lingered alone in the shop while Bess followed Mrs. Riley to the back. She heaved a tremendous sigh. "Oh, thank you! I was coming today to talk to you, but he insisted on following me."

Mrs. Riley cast a suspicious look over Bess's shoulder. "You're not with him?"

"Only because we were on the street at the same time. Why?"

"I've seen him around. He came in with that lot from Crawley. You be careful, Bess. Naught good comes when a town be crawling with redcoats."

"I'll do that," she promised, thinking with a mixture of chagrin and amusement about another red coat.

"Well, what brought you to town? I know it's not wanting ribbons. I was saying to my Robert only the other day how Bess Reynolds seems to keep her light under a basket, and as how I'd like to set her up. What's it to be? A new bonnet? Something to trim your dress? You're not just another serving girl, Bess, and it's time you started dressing like a landlady."

She shook her head. "I am sorry, Mrs. Riley, but I did not come to buy anything at all. Another time, I promise. I came to ask if you sold someone this ribbon." She slipped the blood-red ribbon from her reticule and let it fall to its full length.

Mrs. Riley squinted and ran her fingers expertly along it. "Gracious me! Where did you get this?"

"It was a gift. I was told it came from here."

"Indeed, not! Why, I've been after my Robert for years to stock this kind of quality, but it won't fetch a price in this town, so he says."

"And you've not had anyone else here, someone who might have brought it and sold it for you?"

"Och! What would make you ask that? It's only the two of us, since our Billy took off to the Army with your Samuel. Now, let me see, I had a mind to show you that violet ribbon…" Mrs. Riley tapped her chin thoughtfully as she surveyed the shelves. "Ah, there it is! I found this in London last week, and is it not everything dashing? Of course, not as fine as your red ribbon, but if you mean to let that captain out there buy you something…"

"Did you say you were in London?"

"Aye. Closed up shop and gone three days, we were. My Robert even took me to an oyster house," she giggled. "So fancy and fine! I expect those gentry knew we were not of their class, but I wore my best dress, I did, and no one ever said as how we didn't belong. Now, Bess, what do you think of the violet?"

Bess was still blinking, her mind a whirlwind. "You were not here which days?"

"We set out early Monday morning. The weather was quite agreeable, though Robert did complain somewhat of his rheumatism."

"And no one kept shop for you when you were away?"

Mrs. Riley's brow dimpled. "Why, no. The only thing to come in here would have been that impossible rat we've been trying to catch. Went through the pantry and put a hole in the flour sack, but it looked like a cat might have got in after it. Tufts of fur all over the floor. I only hope it ate the sorry beast and it won't be back to trouble us."

"I see. Well, Mrs. Riley, I suppose we oughtn't to keep Captain Chesterfield so long from his duties."

The woman beamed. "Shall I wrap up the violet for you, then? Though, if I were you, I'd put it away somewhere after you get home, and wear that crimson ribbon instead."

Bess smiled. "I think I might do just that."

NORTH GAVE A LOW whistle. "It seems you were right, sir."

Nick folded the note from Bess and held it over the cook fire. "And I've never been sorrier to be so, but this settles it. Chesterfield is still on the trail. Thank heaven we've but one more night of this madness. I'm looking forward to being back in my proper uniform."

"Yes, sir. Shall the men and I set up a diversion again? We could lead the captain's men astray."

Nick watched as the last of Bess's note withered into black ash. "No. Tonight is no sham. I need you posted nearby, in case something goes wrong. One of us, at least, must be able to carry word to Richards of what we discover."

North gave a quick salute. "Sir. I'll go make ready to break up camp."

Nick's eyes were still on the fire, but he stirred himself to return his lieutenant's salute. "Very good."

It would be a relief to be back to a proper bed and board. Many times, he and his men had bivouacked in search of their quarry. Heat of summer, dead of winter, they did as duty demanded, but his taste for it was waning. He was far from an old man; most of his commanding officers on the Continent had been at least a decade his senior and had stared down far more sabers and bullets than he. But no one ever doubted their authority or questioned who they were. Nick was weary of having to hide his face.

It was more than this current assignment. Posing as a criminal was a new low for him, but searching for spies for His Majesty was a dirty, harsh, usually thankless, and oftentimes dishonorable task. But the trouble was, he had been very good at his job, and his general knew it. He was fooling himself with thoughts of a desk job. Nick's only hopes of getting out were to be crippled in the line of duty or sell his commission so he might have something to live on, and... well, after that, he could not know. Perhaps he would heed his father's letter and return home.

Or perhaps he could find a wife and a place to start over and begin a new life with her. He smiled to himself as he doused the cook fire. A bonny lass with raven hair and a stubborn streak to match his own... that was sounding more and more appealing.

But first, he had a traitor to catch. He pulled out his pocket watch—it was just after mid-day. Chesterfield might still be lurking around town. Would it be unwise to show his face there, where everyone else knew him as Cumberland? Probably.

But he had an idea, and it might just be crazy enough to work. If fortune smiled upon him, he might be able to twist Chesterfield's jealous ambitions for his own purpose. He could even send the man on a goose chase, just long enough to carry out tonight's mission.

Indeed, it seemed worth a try.

T HE BITTERN LOOKED BUSY. It was the height of the afternoon, with coaches jostling for space at the gates and a steady flood of unknown faces filing through the doors. And posted conspicuously out at the street were two militiamen.

Good.

Nick loitered in the shade of the trees as he watched yet another mail coach rattle up to the gates. Passengers were piled inside and high on the roof, with two or three even hanging off the back. With any luck, he could blend in with them as they all disembarked, and no one would be the wiser. All he had to do was avoid the regulars inside the Bittern, and somehow attract the attention of the officers. He drew close and waited for an opportunity.

A peasant woman was struggling down from the top with a small parcel in one hand and a babe lashed to her chest, but her plight seemed little to trouble the male passengers who rushed before her. One brash young fellow even stepped on her hand, and another pushed her from the side at that exact same moment. She yelped in pain and alarm, but the youth who pushed past her only laughed as he hopped to the ground. Nick ground his teeth and put out a hand to steady the woman. Then he turned on the thoughtless boy who had stepped on her.

"Have a care, my man!" he barked, catching the lad by the collar, and giving him a good shake. "You nearly toppled this poor woman! Stop there and be so good as to help her down."

The boy—for he could have been no more than seven and ten—gaped blankly at Nick, as if trying to decide if her were in earnest. "She's only a washerwoman," he mumbled.

"And you're only a witless mongrel. Turn about, and look sharp, boy."

The woman was, by this time, stepping down on her own, but at a stern look from Nick, the lad doffed his cap to her and shuffled his feet. "Carry your parcel, ma'am?" He received a surly glare and a sniff for his trouble, but the woman did permit him to carry her sack of belongings into the inn.

"Ah, very good. Another wrong put to rights," a familiar voice said behind him.

This could be better than he had hoped for. He turned. "Chesterfield? I was not expecting to see you here."

The captain sauntered close and put out his hand. "I might say the same, Hunt, old boy. You were bound for the country last we bumped into one another."

"The country?" Nick feigned a moment of confusion. "Oh, yes. As it happened, I never left London until just this morning. Emergency orders, you see. I am afraid I am not at liberty to discuss them."

Chesterfield's brow clouded. "Something serious? You know, Hunt, it is my duty to keep the peace in the area. I hope you're not here to put down some secret sedition!" he finished with a laugh.

"Hardly. I am for Brighton on the fastest coach I could catch. A matter of the greatest urgency." He cast an annoyed glance around and tugged at his pocket watch. "Bloody driver had better not be at the tap," he grumbled. "How long does it take to change out those horses?"

"Greatest urgency, eh?" Chesterfield mused casually. "Yes, well, we have something rather pressing here, ourselves. I don't suppose you recall that bit about the highway-man—"

"And there is another coach blocking the road," Nick growled, ignoring Chesterfield. "We shan't be on our way for another quarter hour! I knew I ought to have taken the General's private coach."

"General, did you say?"

"I'd have been there in half the time, and not been packed with a dozen drunken rascals to boot," Nick continued, starting to pace. "Dash it all!"

"Come now, Hunt!" The captain laughed. "You will be on your way soon enough. What can be so confounded urgent?"

Nick stopped pacing and gave his old companion a hard look. "You know very well I cannot disclose the contents of my orders. I ought not to have even told you my destination. You see I am traveling out of uniform."

"Indeed. Well, I am sorry for the delay, and far be it from me to make light of the urgency of your assignment, but perhaps I may offer a bit of diversion while you wait. We've had a bit of excitement here, you see."

Nick put his pocket watch away with a sigh. "Forgive me, Chesterfield. Yes, do go on. You said you were still after some highwayman?"

"I should say!" Chesterfield drew his shoulders back. "You cannot imagine the mischief he's caused, but I'm a step ahead of the bounder. He's no idea with whom he has to deal."

"And how can you be so certain of success? What was your last report of him?"

The captain offered a little smile. "Ah, well, Hunt, you have your secrets and I have mine, but you'll see. I'll see the villain arrested or dead before a se'nnight is out."

Nick shrugged and turned away. "Ah, well, the very best of luck to you. I've more pressing matters on my mind than a local thief, so I shall leave you to your business."

"Well, hang on," Chesterfield said, stopping him. "What's this all about? Surely you can spare a bit of information for an old friend."

Nick glanced about, then drew the captain aside and spoke in a low voice. "I probably oughtn't say as much, but there is a matter of interest to persons in the very highest places, if you take my meaning. I'm to locate an informant, and word is, he was on his way to Brighton to flee the country."

Chesterfield's eyes narrowed. "Informant, you say?"

"I pray I may beat him there, so I may lie in wait as he arrives," Nick murmured, as if to himself.

"You mean he's not even there yet? You travel ahead of him?"

"I can only hope. He has the advantage of me, but it is rumored that he favors the lowlands, far from the main roads. I say!" Nick brightened as if struck by inspiration. "Indeed, old fellow, you can be of some help to me. I should think we could even split the purse if you should help me track him."

A glint brightened the captain's eyes. "Purse?"

"Oh, aye. Now the fellow I'm looking for is an older chap, I should say fifty or so. He sounds like a London rat, but don't be fooled! He's a Frog, sure as I draw breath, and he's like to be traveling with a satchel of jewelry, for that is how he was last paid for his services. What General Richards wouldn't give to have the rogue delivered on his doorstep, without the bother of any 'official' paperwork! But I suppose it is all for naught, as he cannot be still in the area. Oh, where is that bloody driver?"

"And you say there's a reward for this rascal, eh?" Chesterfield mused, rubbing his chin.

"And a promotion, if I can deliver him as ordered," Nick confirmed. "If you or your men should see anything, you'll think of me and help out an old friend, won't you?"

"Oh! We could do no less. Peace and order in the county, that is my duty, is it not? And there, is that not your driver come back? You shall be on your way in a moment."

Nick glanced over his shoulder. "Sloshed, I shouldn't wonder. I only hope he is fit to hold the ribbons."

But when he looked, it was not the mail coach driver who caught his eye. Weaving among the passengers all making their way back to the coach was a raven-haired beauty with ruby lips softly parted in a smile. And her eyes were all for him.

His instincts pulled him toward her, but his better sense stayed him. He gave a subtle shake of his head, and his heart squeezed at the flash of disappointment in her eyes. But she understood him, at least, and came no closer.

"There's a picture and no mistake," Chesterfield whistled.

"Sorry?" Nick tore his eyes from Bess, but too late, for the captain was regarding him with a knowing smile.

"They call her the Duchess of Surrey, and you can see for yourself why. Untried and wild as a hare, or so I'm told, but I've nearly got her eating from my hand."

An unfamiliar stab struck Nick in the heart. He had never been jealous of any man, nor had he ever lost sleep over a woman's affections. But having Chesterfield so close to Bess and having to leave her unprotected from the captain and his leering men, sent sick waves through his stomach. He narrowed his eyes and glared. "I hope you've done nothing unbecoming to a man in uniform."

Chesterfield snorted a laugh. "What are you, a captain or a parson? But I daresay... she's taken some note of you, lucky bastard. She hardly gives most of us a second glance. A pity you're leaving in the next moment, or you might discover the lady's charms for yourself."

Nick looked at Bess again and could not help the little pang in his soul as he drank in the sight of her. She was turning back to the inn, blushing shyly and frequently glancing his way as she walked. "A pity," he sighed.

"Indeed. Are you sure you cannot stay, Hunt? I'd buy you a drink, and we could see if that vixen will stay and pour them for us."

"Some other time, Chesterfield." The coach was nearly full already, so Nick caught the handrail at the back and stepped up. "Good day," he called. "You'll not forget what I said, will you?"

Chesterfield rested a hand on the hilt of his sword and lifted a brow. "Never fear. If I should catch your man, you'll be the first to hear of it." He glanced back over his shoulder as Bess disappeared inside the inn. "Who knows what reward may lie in store for us, eh?"

Nick gave a jerk of his head, not caring to salute when he was out of uniform, and waited for the driver to crack his whip. But his eyes were locked on the red door of the inn, so long as it remained in sight. Would Chesterfield give the shout, rally his men and race to London with his prisoner, leaving the highways unpatrolled this night?

Or was the captain more diverted by Bess's beauty than his own ambition? Nick watched with a thumping heart as Chesterfield wandered back into the inn. And once again, he feared that he had left her vulnerable.

Chapter Eighteen

B ESS WATCHED CAPTAIN HUNT as the coach lumbered out of the courtyard. He made a sort of salute to Captain Chesterfield, which was returned, and then turned his attention forward. Chesterfield was already engrossed in conversation with one of his men when the carriage disappeared round a bend in the road.

Why had he come to town? It must have been a matter of urgency. She found an excuse to pass by the window outside of which the militia officers were talking, and through the glass, she distinctly heard the captain utter the name "Hunt."

Of course, Chesterfield knew her captain by his proper name, but she had been under the impression that they were not friends. Were they now in one another's confidence? That seemed odd, for had Hunt not told her that he could not involve the militia? What, then, could have brought him here? Whatever it was, he didn't seem to want her involved, either to protect her or himself.

The men stepped away from the window a moment later, and Bess was left to simmer in her own curiosity. Captain Hunt's mission was tonight—*Nick*—for he was more to her than just another army officer. Just how dangerous was it? That worry had preoccupied her thoughts since his confession, and there was no relief for her. Certainly, there was none in whom *she* could confide. She bore the curse of her sex, only able to watch and wait in fear for the man she...

Did she love him?

Bess bit her lip as she scrubbed at a stubborn stain on the kitchen kettle. The work kept her hands busy and kept others from bothering her as she let her thoughts roam. Surely, it was silly! She cared for him. He was kind and gentle, dashingly handsome in his own way, and there was a certain weakness in her for a man who would invite her into his adventures.

But love? She had seen enough broken hearts pass through the coaching inn that she could never confess such a thing after so short an acquaintance.

But what if something happened tonight, and he never came back? Would the void in her soul inform her only too late that she had given her heart away? Or could she just admit it? Captain Hunt: soldier, gentleman, and occasional highwayman, mattered deeply to her.

Perhaps it was the little things she admired about him—the way his entire being seemed to soften when he spoke to her, or the way he fretted over that monstrous horse of his as if it were a child. How he never sought attention for himself, but he always seemed to be the one to step up when he saw an injustice.

Or maybe it was just the way it had felt when he held her in his arms.

"Bess?" Her father's voice broke into her musings, and she jerked to attention.

"Yes, Papa?"

He was looking at her oddly. "You're flushed. You've not fallen ill?"

Bess shook her head. "No, sir."

"That's well, then. It would not do to meet your suitor with a fever."

The kettle dropped from her hand with a clatter. "S-suitor?"

"He's in the private drawing room, waiting for you. Take him a mug when you go, and put yourself a bit straight, lass. You don't want to disappoint the man."

"Disappoint *him*! What about me? Papa, who is this person? Do I even know him?"

Her father shook his head tiredly. "Bess, I've not the patience for this now. It's Thompkins, the steward at the manor house, and you'll get to know him."

Bess crossed her arms and lifted a defiant glare to her father for the first time in her memory. "No."

His eyes widened, and his brow creased in confusion and anger. "*No?* How dare you refuse me?"

"How dare you simply order me to marry a man I do not know?" she shot back. "Have my feelings nothing to do with the matter?"

"I *am* considering your feelings. Would you rather marry Tim the ostler?"

Bess clenched a fist. "I was not aware he was truly an option."

"Neither is falling into disrepute," her father snapped. "Bess, I am not asking. I am ordering you, take a drink to Mr. Thompkins!"

Bess trembled. Never had her father spoken to her in anger, and never had she considered refusing him. Until now. She lifted her chin, her eyes flashing fire. "No."

And in the next instant, she fled out of doors.

T HERE WAS NO NOTE from Captain Hunt at their tree. Bess poked her fingers into the knot hole a second time, just to be sure, but unless a squirrel had carried it off, he had left her no word.

What was that all about with Captain Chesterfield? She had not heard what they said to one another, but when she ran from the house, she'd had to dodge two militiamen running for their horses. They were gone in a flurry of shouts and hoofbeats, back toward Crawley. Perhaps Captain Hunt had said something to them to keep them away for the night. She hoped so. It was bad enough that he had to face spies and risk everything. How much worse if he were mistaken by the law for a criminal himself?

Bess dropped to sit on a stump, her hands clasped at her stomach. She hadn't eaten all day, but it wasn't hunger that gnawed at her. Her captain—*Nick* was marching into terrible danger, and she was powerless to do anything about it. All she had was worry, and she clung to it as if it could help him somehow—as if God could take whatever suffering was given a soldier and share the burden with the woman he left behind.

What if he were shot? Stabbed out on the road tonight, and left to die? She had seen a man stabbed to death. It was years ago, when a drunken pair of travelers started fighting about a game of cards. Others had tried to separate them, but the man who believed himself cheated snapped out a blade and attacked his fellow before he could be stopped. The fatal rasp as the dying man choked on his own blood was a sound that still haunted her nightmares.

That could not be Nick! He *had* to come back from this one last mission. Had he not said himself that after tonight, it would be over? He would find the answers he needed, report back to his superiors, and bring an end to this.

But what would that mean for her? Even if he meant all the things he had said, a man who hunted spies could ill afford a wife to tie him down. She would be a liability, a chain to ensnare him, so long as he remained in the king's service. Did he really mean to resign his commission? Oh, if he could! He would be safe... but even farther out of her reach. If he went back to his family, he would be expected to marry and settle with a woman of his class.

Not a tavern wench.

Her fingers worked into the fabric of her serving apron, twisting and bunching it until her knuckles ached. There just wasn't a way around it. Captain Hunt would leave, even if he didn't want to. She would be alone again—worse off than before, because now, she knew the sort of man she could love. And her father would force her to choose another.

Hot tears dashed down her cheeks. Her father would be livid with her when she returned. How could she even face him? He might thunder and rage at her in front of the other serving girls. Force her to wash linens or cook, where she made no tips and could speak to no one. Or worse, he might ignore her completely. Either way, humiliation and hard decisions awaited her.

But she had no choice. She had to go back, and delaying would only make it worse.

She sniffed and pulled out a handkerchief to dry her eyes. There wasn't much she could do about how puffy they would be, but Bess Reynolds was not the girl to cry before others. She sucked in a shuddering breath and pushed to her feet, her gaze drifting through the trees toward the river.

That was the spot, under the sprawling oak. The first place she had seen Hunt in his highwayman disguise. If she squinted just right, she could still recall how he had looked in the morning gloom, with that rich velvety cape and his face shadowed. Proud and strong and mysterious—but not dangerous. Not to her. He was the safest person in the world for her. Even if he ended up shattering her heart.

Bess's feet dragged all the way back to the inn. Her eyes fastened to the ground and she worried her apron between knotted hands. If she apologized to her father, told him every-thing, perhaps he would not press her so hard to marry. He might give her time—time for what, though? She only postponed the inevitable. Her life stretched before her, and Captain Nicholas Hunt was not a part of it. She had to let him go.

But not until she knew he had survived the night.

"ONE LAST NIGHT, OLD girl," Nick promised as he swung into the saddle. He paused half a moment to stroke the black mane, twining silken locks between his fingers. The mare arched her neck, then surged against the bit as she felt him gathering the reins. "Always ready to charge into the fray, are you not?" he chided. "Patience, my girl. We shall be away soon enough."

Nick gave a self-conscious tug at the mask covering his face, then a swirl of his hand to straighten the lace of his cuffs. He had grown mostly accustomed to the highwayman's finery, and if need be, could probably fight in the luxurious velvet coat nearly as well as his stout English broadcloth. But hopefully it would not come to that.

It would not be long now. Nick rested one hand on the hilt of his sword and stretched out with his senses for the faintest warning that his quarry was nigh. A silence had fallen over the moor—the dead still just after midnight, broken only by a distant owl and his own heartbeat. Even Black Bess, her skin shivering with excitement, stood quiet as the grave.

And then, he heard it. From far up the road came the faint clatter of shod hooves and carriage wheels. A driver called out something to his horses, and as they drew closer, Nick heard the jingle of harness bells normally reserved for busy city streets. Whoever was coming up the dark country road was not trying to do so quietly. They would be ready for him, and most certainly armed. He could only pray his disguise was convincing enough for the spy in the carriage.

He glanced to the rise on his left, where he could just make out North's silhouette in the moonlight. The lieutenant raised his hand, and Nick lifted his in reply. Then North drew back into the shadows, well out of sight.

"Easy, now, old girl," he murmured as his horse shifted beneath him and began to paw. "Steady, steady... now!"

The mare's great muscles bunched and her hooves ripped up the sod as she catapulted herself into the battle. They tore down the gentle slope and up to the crown of the road, skidding to a halt just before the astonished head horses. The carriage pulled up sharply and even the coachman, who must have been expecting an "attack," cried out in alarm. Black Bess made a gleeful terror of herself, snorting and whistling to the skies as her hooves sliced the air.

Nick took advantage of her antics and had his pistol trained on the driver's heart before the man had followed all her storming and raving to aim his own weapon. "Stand and deliver!"

The driver said nothing. His jaw set like a bulldog and his hand strayed cautiously to the blunderbuss at his side, but at a flick of Nick's pistol, he raised both hands.

"Toss down your valuables!" Nick demanded. Best to keep up the ruse until he was certain of what the driver knew of tonight's rendezvous.

The driver's only response was a tilt of his head toward the carriage. Nick felt his eye twitching under the silken mask. There had been no noise or movement from the inside of the carriage—no indicator other than the driver's gesture that he even had a passenger. Nick's pistol never wavered. "I'll not step back there until you surrender that blunderbuss or hop down yourself," he ordered.

"Oh, come, Duncan," a woman's voice called from within the coach. "Do as he says and keep your hands up. You do not want our old friend to shoot you again, do you?"

The driver gave a visible snarl and raised both hands in the air. "Ah dinnae ken how a'body's a'feared o' this auld blunt. 'E canny aim for keich."

"And what makes you think he was not aiming for your hat last time?" the voice purred as a hand drew the curtain from over the coach window.

Nick had been prepared for almost anything. A hardened criminal from London's darkest corners, a nobleman in a dinner jacket, or even a French general. But a ravishing blonde who looked like she belonged at the queen's court by day and in a man's fantasies by night... He swallowed and instinctively lowered his weapon.

"Madam," he greeted her.

Her rich ruby lips curled into a coy pout. "So formal, George? Very well, I suppose after our last encounter..." She slipped a gloved hand out the open window of the carriage to lift the latch, and then stepped down in a swirl of golden umber taffeta. She wore neither shawl nor spencer, but a diamond-studded pin at her shoulder caught the moonlight and a long black ostrich plume crested a wave of her hair.

"Will you not come closer? How shall I know 'tis really you?" She held one hand aloft and waited beside the carriage.

Nick hesitated. He had chosen this spot on this road because the waning moon would be at his back. From where he stood, she could only see a shadow, and he must have managed to mimic Cumberland's voice adequately enough. But if he stepped nearer, into the dim glow of the carriage's lanterns, the game was up.

"What have you dragged me out here for?" he growled. "Let us have it."

She sighed and shook her head. "Oh, very well. No kiss for me tonight, I see. Are you still angry with me, George?"

Nick thought quickly. "I do not trust you, madam."

She laughed. "You never did, but when did that ever stop you from taking your tuppence? To think I wore my best brooch to donate to your cause."

His mouth ran dry. He could almost stomach holding a woman at gunpoint and behaving violently. Intimidating. Dangerous. But this woman expected something different from him, and he would not get what he needed unless he complied. Could he carry it off?

He was the same height as Cumberland. With the mask on, and in poor light, his face was nearly indistinguishable. But Cumberland had two stone on him. If she got her arms around him, there was no hope of disguise.

Well, His Majesty did not employ him to be safe. He was a spy catcher. He had killed in the king's service, had "stolen" from the innocent, had held terrified citizens at gunpoint. He could kiss a spy in the line of duty.

Nick nudged his mare closer to the carriage, watching the woman's expression warm in approval. He was near enough now that he could see her eyes scanning his horse, then him. If she did notice anything amiss, she was too masterful at her craft to reveal it.

"I see you still ride that Spanish demon. Will you not take his lordship's advice and mount one of his swiftest thoroughbreds? Only think how much more easily you could blend in, disappear. And perhaps poor Duncan would not be cowering behind the box if you rode something more docile."

Nick pulled his hat down and kept his voice to a hoarse rasp. "I've no use for docile."

The woman laughed. "I suppose not. How very fitting that the man who swears no loyalties saddles a beast who knows no master."

"You are wrong." Nick turned his horse slightly so he could dismount out of view. He gave a final jerk of his hat and face mask, then stepped around Black Bess and stalked toward the woman, letting his cloak billow and snap in the light autumn breeze to help disguise his form.

Duncan on the box reached for his blunderbuss, but the woman shook her head. Nick's gaze never wavered from her face, and she waited for him with a knowing leer. "I am wrong, am I? Tell me."

He advanced with long, heavy steps, taking a few extra seconds to memorize every detail of her appearance for his report. "I answer to one, and one only." Without breaking stride, he pushed her up against the door of her carriage, pinning her forearms up to her shoulders and making it impossible for her to reach for him. Or stab him.

The daring vixen only smiled more—no fear, no dismay. This was what she wanted. This was what Cumberland had taught her to expect.

This was probably how Cumberland proved his identity to his fellow villains. Who better than a seductress to get close enough to a man to either test him or slip a blade between his ribs?

Nick was no Cumberland, but that would not stop him from trying. Bracing himself, he leaned down and crushed her mouth with his. Swift and a little rough, so she would not have time to look at him closely in the lantern's light and he had no opportunity to admire her deceitful charms.

He did not mean to linger. Sumptuous, ravishing as she was, she held no appeal for him. But pulling back meant that she would have a chance to see him, and he still needed to extract the message from her. How the devil was he to do that? He was making this up as he went.

Somewhere, this woman had been well instructed in the art. She nipped his lower lip and let her own lips graze the stubble he'd grown at his chin to match Cumberland. It was all he could do not to shudder. For an instant, he toyed with the notion of pretending this willing, brazen woman was Bess, cradled in his arms and offering her love. But that would be an insult to Bess—and would probably get him killed.

He was about to pull away when the blonde woman's right hand shifted under his. She managed to turn his wrist just enough that he felt the sharp edges of the diamond brooch at her shoulder. And he understood.

Before he released her from the kiss, he slipped his hand against her bodice, then snatched the pin. There was the sharp sound of seams tearing and a laugh rippled in her throat. "Do you mean to ravish me now, George?" she purred against his mouth.

One last thing to do—Nick tucked his own message, the original one he'd obtained at Shag Brook, into the ruin of her gown. Then he broke free, and pushed her back as he turned his face and let his cape sweep between them. An instant later, his boot was in the iron and he was aboard Black Bess, shadowed in the darkness.

The woman had yet to mount her coach. She stood, chin high and shoulders thrown back as the torn neckline of her gown drooped wickedly low on her bosom. "You have nothing else for me? I am disappointed, George."

He spat the taste of her from his mouth with a snarl. "Have so many men caressed you that you do not notice another?"

She glanced down and with two dainty fingers, withdrew the slip of paper he'd tucked against her breast. "Clever fellow. I am looking forward to next time, my love." She blew him a kiss, then turned to mount her carriage.

Nick backed his horse into the tall grass of the heath, disappearing under the shadow of the slope. As the carriage rattled away, he pulled off his glove and held up the brooch to the moonlight. And there, tucked under a silver hasp, was a tightly folded wad of paper.

Mission accomplished.

Chapter Nineteen

I T WAS WORSE THAN Bess had feared.

Her father did not meet her at the door, boiling with rage and ordering her to the kitchens. And he did not punish her with stony silence, glaring at her then brushing past without a word. He did not even force her to carry drinks and sit at table with some man she cared nothing for. In fact, he never showed his face the rest of the evening. If he meant to punish her for insolence, he had succeeded. Bess was sick and preoccupied all night. She tried knocking on his door before she turned into her own room for bed, but he never answered. Already fearful for Nick's safety, now she was guaranteed a night of sleepless heartache.

How hard would it have been just to take the mug of ale to Mr. Thompkins? She could smile, couldn't she? Sitting at the man's table wasn't an acceptance of a marriage proposal, and if it kept her on better terms with her father, would it not have been worth it?

But even as she tried to convince herself of it, she knew it was a lie. Share a drink with Mr. Thompkins when his very presence there rankled and stung? No one cared what she wanted or thought. She had stated her wishes, and they'd been bluntly ignored. She would have spent the evening fretting about Captain Hunt, wanting *him*, not this stranger, Mr. Thompkins.

The whole thing was insulting. Still, her father had always been good to her, even if she didn't understand him lately. Perhaps she could reason with him, try to discover why he was suddenly so afraid for her that he would push her into an unwanted marriage. She ought to try to make things right with him. And she would—just as soon as she saw him in the morning. But she had to see Captain Hunt first.

Bess arose early the next day and slipped out to the rose bush at the edge of the wood. If he was safe, he had promised to meet her there at dawn, to let her know all was well. But when she stumbled into the little clearing, just before the morning sun shattered through the bare trees, all was silence.

She paced for a moment, then leaned against a tree to wait. A quarter of an hour passed, with nothing more than a rabbit dashing into the thicket. Bess shivered and wrapped her cloak more tightly around her shoulders. What if he'd been shot? Captured by the very criminals he'd set out to apprehend? Would she ever even learn the truth?

The sun had fully broken over the distant heaths when a twig snapped somewhere in the woods. Leaves rustled, and a few seconds later, a horse snorted. Bess's heart flooded with relief and she ran toward the sound. "Captain! Are you well?"

He did not answer at once. Caped and hooded, he stepped from his horse and came toward her with long strides, the brim of his hat concealing his eyes.

She hesitated. Was it really him? "Captain?"

He looked up, and that smile flashed. "Miss Bess. Oh, you are a bonny sight this morning."

She rushed to him, and could not stop herself from touching his chest, his shoulders, inspecting for gunshot wounds. He was warm and solid, and she felt his muscles bunch under her fingers. That was more than she had accounted for, and she pulled back, her cheeks flooding with heat. "Captain, are you really well? I was so afraid for you! You are not a ghost, come to torment me?"

"I am real. See?" He pulled off his hat and tugged away the scarf over his face. "Truly, everything went as planned."

She gasped. "Oh, I am *that* relieved! I felt sure you might be shot or, or captured, or worse. All I could think was if you were tricked and tortured by the enemy, or hunted by the militia, or—"

"Bess!" He laughed and caught her hands, bringing each by turn to his lips for a gentle kiss. "Feel—I am quite real, I am here, and no blood has leaked from my body. See?" He brushed a hand over the front of his red coat, then pulled it back to reveal the pure white silk of his undershirt.

She sagged with a weary smile and let him keep holding her hands. "Then, is that all? Tell me it is over and you will be in no more danger."

"I am afraid I will always be in danger, so long as I serve under the king's colors. But as to this mission, I hope it is at an end. My men are breaking camp even now, and we are bound for London within the hour to make our report."

She nodded slowly, her joy at finding him unharmed now dampened with the realization that it was all over. He was leaving. "And... what of *her*?"

He glanced over his shoulder at the black mare behind him, whose very breath seemed to thicken the morning fog in the woods. "I have not decided yet. I daren't take her with me to London until my general calls me off the mission. She is too distinctive, you see."

"And for that reason, you also could not risk leaving her here at the stables," Bess mused. Her heart sank. She would have liked to be able to visit that magnificent creature each day, even if only to remind herself of the horse's master.

"Indeed, that would be the worst of all places. Even if the enemy is no longer about, the militia would probably seize her as 'evidence' of a crime. No, I might have to bring her as far as Thornton Heath and leave Wesson bivouacked with the horses while North and I take a mail coach into the city. He will not think much of that plan, though."

Bess nibbled her bottom lip. "Is she much bother?"

"That depends on whether she likes you." He chuckled and dropped one of her hands, only to tuck the other under his arm, escorting her as if she were a real lady. "Come. She deserves a kind word or two after her hard work last night. I could not have carried out half my orders were it not for her..." he cleared his throat. "Flair, I suppose you could say."

Bess reached cautiously toward the mare with her free hand and allowed her fingers to tangle in the long black mane. The mare arched her neck, then tossed her head up and down and stepped closer. Wide, curious nostrils searched Bess's skirts, then her hands. Bess stroked the velvety nose, and the mare gave a low chuckle in her throat, as if she'd just rediscovered an old friend.

"There. She is quite taken with you," the captain declared.

Indeed, she appeared to be. For such a terrifying beast, the enormous black was gentle as a kitten and seemed to want nothing more than a kindly word and some petting. "Hello, old girl," Bess whispered.

The mare shook her head, sneezing in Bess's face. She flinched, laughing, and Captain Hunt pulled out his handkerchief.

"Sorry about that," he apologized. "I think she objects to being called 'old.' Here, let me help." He dabbed the silk against her cheek, his touch so light it was almost a caress. But she wasn't paying attention to the handkerchief. It was his gray eyes that locked on her own, the faint tick of his right cheek that betrayed some feeling beyond words. His throat bobbed and his chin dipped as his gaze wandered from her eyes to her lips.

She couldn't blink. Why even breathe? Her heart was fluttering erratically, and she let herself drift forward. What would it be like to kiss a man *she* chose, whose touch could trace fire over her skin and leave her wanting more? Just once…

The captain leaned down, his lips inches from hers as he brushed a strand of hair back from her face. Bess closed her eyes, waiting for that first touch. A warm breath, a hesitant stroke of his fingers at her throat, and she leaned into him. "Oh, Bess," he whispered, then sweet rapture claimed her.

She slid her hands up that velvet coat, then threading her fingers into his hair. This, *this* was what she'd been aching to feel since she'd first set eyes on him. He was gentle—so patiently and tenderly he captured her mouth again and again as his hands slid down her waist, pulling her closer as their lips moved together in a dance as old as time itself.

More. She wanted, *needed* to feel more, to feel everything. For so long had she held herself aloof, kept herself apart, but in Nicholas Hunt's arms, she was finally free to feel, to explore, to *be*. Could she hold him more tightly, become more his? Her fingers dug into the fabric of his coat as she clung to him. If only he could be hers for more than an hour!

The captain's hands roamed over her back, caressing and comforting as he deepened the kiss. His heart pounded against her own. What would he say when he pulled back? Would he tip his hat and ride away? She knew that was how it had to be, but for a moment, it felt like she was all he wanted in this world. If she just held him a little longer, he need never go.

But that dream was not for her, and she knew it as well as he did. He pressed one last kiss to her lower lip, then the tip of her nose and then her forehead and pulled back. His chest was heaving and his eyes were black with longing. "I should not have done that."

She shook her head, her fingers already locking into the velvet of his coat to pull him to her again. "Neither should I, but…"

He let himself fall toward her, more easily this time. He was not so gentle as he had been; his touch was almost hungry, his kiss like that of a desperate man. But when the time came, it was she who was the more unwilling to let go.

"Bess, I cannot stay." His thumb gently wiped away a tear that had escaped down her cheek.

She sniffed and ducked her face to hide the next tear. "I know. You'll never come back, will you?"

His jaw clenched, but his eyes were still soft with sorrow. "I don't know. Someday... yes, someday, I hope. Perhaps when I have earned some leave."

She swallowed and gave a bitter laugh. "Aye, in five or ten years. No doubt you'll take the Brighton Road one day with your wife and wee ones, and you'll try to remember why the old inn looks familiar."

His hands still cupped her cheeks, and his gaze never flickered. "Then I will make you a promise. I *will* come back, and I will come back for you, Bess. Just as soon as I can. I will even leave you proof of my sincerity." He stepped back and caught the mare's rein, then passed it to Bess. "Would you look after her for me?"

Bess's eyes widened. "You would leave her with me?"

"If I may. There is a stream and a little grassy clearing just a few minutes' walk from here. She would be quite safe there, and you need only look in on her to see that she is well. As soon as I have made my report to my general, I will be back for her... and for you."

"And then what? You cannot truly mean to..." She sighed. "I'm but a tavern girl, and you are—"

"A man of my word."

Bess fell silent. He was holding her with a steady gaze, his gray eyes intense with feeling. "Will you wait for me, my bonny sweetheart?"

Could she? Would her father allow her to wait long enough for him to return? And what would he say when he found out the man she was waiting for was the very man he had attempted to keep her from?

But she found herself nodding, despite all her doubts. If there was even the slimmest chance that she could be his, she would choose Captain Hunt.

The dawn broke over his face—light splintering through the barren trees just as his smile brightened. "Then, my fair and noble Miss Bess, let us make our plans. I ride for London within the hour, and you may look for me by nightfall, two days hence."

H E WAS A FOOL to promise such a thing.

A soldier's life was not his own. There could be no surety that his next assignment would permit him the liberty of coming back, as he had said. But there was also a great deal about Nick's activities that his general did not know—of necessity, for his duty was more often than not a secret burden. Even if he were sent elsewhere, he would find a way to slip back to the Bittern Hollow Inn.

One way or another, he would keep his promise to Bess.

But to what end? Could he marry her? He cared less than nothing for what his father would say. If his parent disapproved of Bess's humble origins, it would trouble him not a whit.

But his duty—that presented another problem. A man who tracked spies and operated in the shadows could not risk taking a wife who could be discovered used as leverage for the enemy. He would *have* to resign his commission and retire to civilian life, assuming that the general would let him, and that he would find a means to support himself and a family if it ever came to that.

And since the only skills he could boast belonged to the Army, that left him going back to his family... and hoping they would accept Bess as his wife.

But that was a problem for another day. Nick uncurled his gloved fist and stared at the note he'd captured from the female spy. It was encoded, so he could not know what it said. What he would give to learn who she was! One of Bonaparte's trained seductresses? The mistress of a powerful British nobleman, someone close to the king who made no objection to selling secrets?

More importantly, he needed to know if he had carried off the ruse. She had tested him before offering her message. Had he intercepted a genuine message to Napoleon? Or could he be giving his general information that would lead good soldiers to their deaths?

There was no way to be sure of any of it. All he could do was to make his report in London, including all the pertinent facts. Then he would receive his next orders and come back to talk over the future with Bess.

"EXCELLENT WORK, HUNT." GENERAL Richards slapped a stack of paperwork on his desk as he dropped into his chair. "Truly a marvelous bit of fieldwork. I shall be recommending you for a promotion."

Nick stood with his back rigid, his eyes on the wall behind the general's head. "Thank you, sir."

"And you are certain you were never made out?"

He filled his chest with air and let it out slowly. "No, sir. I cannot be certain of that, but there were no indications of suspicion."

Richards lifted his eyes from the papers, studied Nick, then grunted. "Well, the lads are deciphering the message. Perhaps we will know more when they have it all transcribed. And now, Hunt, I suppose you and your men could do with a bit of leave?"

Nick's heart picked up rhythm. "If I may be so bold, General, I would like to request a month for each of them. They've scarcely seen home and hearth these two years or better."

The general nodded, stroking his chin. "We shall see, Hunt. First, I must know that you have put us on the right trail. But here, tell me more about this blonde vixen in the carriage. It may be that we can identify her and trace this leak back to the source."

"She had a Scottish driver named Duncan. Well, at least, that was what she called him. The brogue could have been faked."

"Anything else?"

Nick did not hesitate. Years of training made recalling faces as natural as breathing. "She had a mole under her left eye. Her teeth were even and her features fashionable. Figure: trim but voluptuous. It was too dark to discern exact eye colour, but they were some shade of blue. Her speech was almost certainly the product of one of the finer finishing schools. Her gown was of expensive make and she referred to her benefactor as 'his lordship.' She was well educated and is generously supported by someone."

The general nodded. "Yes, yes, that was all in your report. Can you think of anything more? What of the carriage?"

"It was a plain coach, nothing remarkable about it, save that it was of top quality and pulled by a matching pair of chestnuts wearing bells as if they were in town. But that could describe a hundred teams in London alone. If I may, sir, I believe we ought to be investigating the diamond brooch. Surely, we can discover something by that. Is it of French origin?"

"I have men looking into it. Come back tomorrow, Hunt. I ought to have something more for you by then."

Nick suppressed the sigh of impatience that would have given him away. He remained, still stiff and staring at the wall.

"Something else, Hunt?"

He blinked and released a slow breath. "Sir, is there anything else I ought to know?"

A cautious smile grew on Richards' face. "Should there be?"

Nick's arm flexed over the tricorn hat he held to his side. "Respectfully, sir... I believe a prisoner was captured under suspicion of being the Scarlet Bandit. Obviously, the man was innocent. When I heard of it, I did what I could to see that he would be heard and released. Was he brought to your attention?"

"Leave that to the militia. You have bigger problems to worry about than a petty criminal."

Nick's brow furrowed. "But sir, I am responsible. It was because of my activities the man was arrested. I cannot permit—"

"I ordered you to leave it, Hunt." The general's tone brooked no argument.

He swallowed and straightened. "Yes, sir. And your recent travels—I presume there was nothing connected to this case that would assist in the completion of my orders?"

Richards shook his head. "I recommend against asking too many questions, Hunt. You ought to know better than that by now."

Nick stiffened and offered a salute. "Yes, sir."

The general gathered the papers on his desk, tapped them together once more, then stood. "Report tomorrow morning. I will either have new orders for you and your men, or I will be able to authorize that leave you requested."

"Thank you, General."

Chapter Twenty

B ESS MADE HER WAY through the dense woods, her breath visible in the chilly early fall air. The rustling of leaves and the occasional snap of twigs underfoot were the only sounds accompanying her as she walked towards the secluded clearing where Nick had left his horse. As she approached the clearing, she could see the burly mare, pulling nervously at her tether. The horse's ears were twitching and her nostrils flared as she caught Bess's scent.

Of course, she was nervous. Nick had gone away, and the horse counted herself almost as his right hand. She'd known dogs like that—content and brave and everything noble, but let their master pass from their sight, and they became snappish and uneasy. The horse might not be so docile to approach, without Nick here.

Bess walked forward slowly, speaking softly and offering a piece of carrot from her pocket. The white ring of the horse's eye flashed as she lipped the carrot cautiously, and Bess stood still, letting the horse sniff her hand. The mare snorted, the thrust quivering nostrils into Bess's palm as she crunched the carrot. At last, she dragged in a long sigh that sounded a little like a snort. She licked her lips, then reached toward Bess's pocket to beg for more.

"Nay, that'll be all for you, lass," Bess scolded. "I'll catch it for raiding the larder if I bring enough to satisfy the likes of you. Here, how's a bit of grass?"

The mare sneezed and shook her head, then continued sniffing her skirts. Bess slowly ran her hand down the horse's muscular neck, feeling the warmth of the animal's skin through her gloves. She spoke softly, as she had heard Nick do, and gradually worked her way towards the mare's withers.

The horse stood still, with her head cocked, her lips flopping playfully, and an ear drooped to one side—she enjoyed the attention. Little wonder Nick was so fond of this monstrous creature. She might look like a demon, but once she decided to trust someone, she was gentle as a pup.

Bess lingered above half an hour with the horse—letting her to the stream for a long drink, twining wisps of autumn flowers into her mane, and generally making a great fuss over her. The mare relished every moment, even nuzzling Bess's hand to ask for more attention. And she gave it, wholeheartedly. It was easy to bask in the great mare's shadow for her own charisma, but Bess lingered long after she should have, because her thoughts dwelt on the horse's master. How long would he be away? And what news would he bring on his return?

But the morning shadows were now in crisp relief, and she would be missed in the kitchen. "Well, I suppose that's enough now, you rogue. I best be getting back, but do you fancy a little exercise?" Bess took a step back and tugged at the rope tethering her halter, then led the horse in a great circle to stretch her legs. She had watched the grooms do this in the courtyard, and it seemed like a simple way to let her move.

The enormous black mare flung her mane and struck out in a joyous trot, kicking up her heels every few strides. She made several loops around Bess before she suddenly stopped and lowered herself to the grassy earth with a groan. Bess laughed when all four legs began to thrash the air as the horse wriggled about on the ground. Then she lurched to her feet, shook herself off, and came to Bess as if to say she had had her play and was ready to get back to business.

"I'm afraid that's all for now, lass. I've got to get back to the inn or my papa will skin me." She led the mare to a fresh part of the clearing, where the grass was plentiful and the water from the creek was within reach. That would have to do, but she didn't like leaving such a fine creature to shift for herself until she could look in on her again.

But Nick would be back soon. And the horse had to be accustomed to being hidden in the woods—after all, was that not how it had been with her first master? With one final pat, Bess turned and started back towards the inn. She walked quickly, eager to check in on her father and make sure he was safe. She had much to do, and she couldn't afford to waste any time.

The kitchen fires glowed through the windows as she approached the inn. That meant Sarah and Hattie were already up, tending the fire and cooking breakfast, and probably wondering where she was. It had probably been nigh an hour since she had set out. She walked quickly and quietly, hoping to slip back inside unnoticed. Just as she was about to make it to the door, she heard a voice behind her.

"Good morning, Bessie lass." She turned to see Tim removing a worn pipe from between his teeth. "The lassie wanders back into the woods, I see. Where be ye goin' this cold, frosty morn?"

Bess shivered and forced herself to meet Tim's gaze. "It is not that cold."

"Aye, not that cold, the lassie says!" he laughed. "When the fire in the stables won't warm the hair on a flea, she says it isn't cold! What might there be in the woods, asks I?"

She swallowed and drew her shoulders back. "I did not sleep well. That is all. Good morning, Tim."

He only winked, giving a sly nod and a tip of his pipe as he turned away. Bess trembled, then yanked open the door of the inn and closed it swiftly behind her. Had Tim been watching for her this morning? He seemed to know that she had not simply stepped outside for a moment. Was it her cheeks? They were cold as ice, and probably bright red. But it seemed like he had been waiting for her. Almost like he had watched her leave.

She pushed the thoughts from her mind and plunged into her work. There would be time later to think about Tim. Perhaps she could ask her father, if he would still speak to her after yesterday.

But she couldn't shake the feeling that Tim was watching her every move.

"WE ARE UNABLE TO identify your contact."

Nick blinked. "But, sir, she was very distinctive. How many blonde goddesses can be masquerading about in a nobleman's carriage? And with a Scottish driver! Surely, someone must know who she is."

"Patience, Captain." The general made a quelling gesture with his hand. "We will discover her soon enough. I have a man on the case, but so far, we have only managed to decode the message."

"And?"

The general folded his hands on his desk and leveled a serious look at him. "It confirms our suspicions. Tell me—what have you heard of the Battle of Buçaco?"

Nick shifted in his chair. "Sir, in my position, recall that I frequently hear things that no one else does, while I often know nothing of the news that is general knowledge."

"Quite right. Well, no matter. A week ago, Masséna tried to drive Wellington from his stronghold in the mountains. Our forces fell back to fortified positions and then held the line. The French were humiliated, but we've just received word that Masséna's troops are gathering at Sobral, seeking to break through."

"Forgive me, sir, but what has that to do with the spy network?"

"Come, now Hunt! You were a soldier before you were in Intelligence. What lies just beyond Sobral, scarcely out of Napoleon's reach?"

Nick searched his memory. "The Port of Lisbon."

The general grunted. "With a dozen warships and uncounted supply ships passing through the channel."

"But surely, Wellington has taken all possible measures to defend the port. That would have been almost his first consideration."

"Naturally. But if Masséna thought he could exploit a weakness and overplayed his hand..."

Nick narrowed his eyes. "You're going to lure him in. And then what?"

"We break him. Send him back north to lick his wounds for the winter. But Masséna is no fool—he won't commit himself unless he believes there is a chance of victory. And that, Hunt, is where you come in."

His stomach sank. "You want me to feed false information back the French."

"My men are encoding a letter even now. You will carry it back to your contact—that monk or whatever he was—and then, pfft." He waved his hand.

"I beg your pardon, sir?"

"Vanish! You will disappear, gone, *in absentia*."

"So, the highwayman will be no more?"

The general withdrew a tin of cigars and tapped out two of them. "Yes, that will suffice. No more. Are we understood, Hunt?"

Nick sighed, his eyes downcast, and shook his head when the general offered him a cigar. "Sir, are you certain you can in good conscience authorize me to—"

"My conscience will be quite clear because you will not be telling me the details, Hunt. Carry out your duty. That is an order."

"But it means putting innocent people in harm's way!"

The general rapped a fist on his desk. "And what about Wellington's troops, every man jack of them? What about our Spaniards and Portuguese, trying to fight back the Tyrant from their very homes and gardens? Would you rather Napoleon caught us off our guard and broke through? Crushed our navy and waged an attack on our own soil? Wellington's men are exhausted. They need to resupply the whole bloody line, but he scorched the ground on his march south. There be no better chance to cripple the enemy upon his retreat, but our soldiers are starving in their tents until we can turn back the French. We stop Masséna *now*, Hunt."

Always for a good cause. No matter how dark, how wrong it all was, there always seemed to be an overriding moral imperative forcing him to commit the unthinkable in the service of the greater good.

Nick closed his eyes and silently swore, once again, to find a way out of uniform. "Yes, sir," he said, his voice heavy with resignation.

T HE MORNING ARRIVED WITH a sense of unease hanging over Bess. She had not seen her father since she had refused to take a drink to Mr. Thompkins. Yesterday, she had been avoiding him, for fear and shame and anguish at having her hand forced by the man who had never been unkind to her.

But today, he was not there to avoid.

By early afternoon, she was starting to worry. Her father had a routine, diligently attending to his ledger and mingling with the departing guests in the coffee room. But no one had seen him all day, and Bess's fears were mounting by the minute. He had never been angry enough to avoid her for two days together.

She assembled a tray for him and tapped on the door to his room, her mind conjuring up grim possibilities. What if he, anxious for her and worried about Samuel, had suffered a heart seizure in the night? What if he had taken a simple tumble, and could not answer the door? She knocked again, more urgently this time.

Silence greeted her. A surge of fear crawled through her as she hesitated for a moment, her hand trembling as she reached for the master key. With a deep breath, she turned the lock and pushed open the door. Would she find him crumpled on the floor, his heart given out at last?

But the room was empty. At least he was not dead, but her worry deepened. A wild notion struck her—if her father could not make her do as he bade, could he dare go to her wealthy aunt in London to ask for her help? Even as her neck stiffened in refusal, her better sense swept away the ridiculous idea. Papa would not have gone to a woman who shunned her mother to beg help.

But he might have gone to the manor, to try to make arrangements with Mr. Thomkins, or the parson. Panic choked her throat, and she rushed back down the stairs, her footsteps echoing in the dimly lit inn.

"Sarah?" Bess called out when she reached the coffee room. "Have you seen my father? He is not in his room."

"Don' know where he is," Sarah shrugged when Bess asked where he had gone. "Last I saw, he were talkin' to that handsome Captain. The one with the gold braid and all."

"Chesterfield?"

"That's the chap. He were here yesterday afternoon."

"But that was a day ago. Where did he go after the captain left?"

Sarah set her tray down to pull off the empty mugs. "Well, he went with him. What did you think I meant?"

Bess's neck prickled in dread. "What, back to Crawley? With the captain! Surely not."

"That's all I saw. He were right put out when you flew out the back door, but then he got real quiet-like. Next I knew, he left with the captain when he were here. That were... oh, right after the London coach arrived, so I had me hands full."

She shook her head. "Were they on foot? Did they take a coach?"

Sarah snorted and stacked the fresh mugs on her tray. "What do I know? I were busy. Give us a hand here, Bess. Those gents be a'wantin their ale."

Nick had arranged to meet his men in an hour to share their orders and plan their next course of action. North would be eager to plunge back into the fray. Wesson would feel much like Nick himself, and there was no telling what Daniels' reaction would be. But they were soldiers, and they had a duty, and that was that.

He had chosen a tavern near the docks, where they would blend in with the sea of old sailors, traveling merchants, and soldiers on leave. There was no better way to remain unseen than to mingle with a crowd. As he walked, his mind turned back to Bess. Had he caused trouble for her, leaving his horse for her to tend? And what of the next phase of his assignment? Things were going to become even more dangerous for him and for his men. He couldn't risk letting her be involved any longer.

He arrived at the tavern and ordered a drink, then proceeded to consume it as slowly as possible. No one would think twice about him, lingering at a dark table and demanding nothing of the barmaid. He sat with his back to a corner, the better to survey the room, and though he adopted an air of bored fatigue, his senses remained alert.

And still, the stranger managed to surprise him.

"Captain Hunt, I presume?" a voice said.

His hand moved under the table to rest on the grip of his pistol. "I'm afraid you have the advantage of me, sir. Who are you?"

The man chuckled. "My apologies, I should have introduced myself. I am Lord Durham, a member of the Foreign Office. I have heard a great deal about your mission, and I must say, I am impressed."

Nick was silent as Lord Durham drew up a chair and sat down. His Lordship—if that was truly his name—was not attired as a nobleman. He was at least three days unshaven and he wore plain linen and soiled breeches, and his cravat was sloppily tied. He looked precisely as Nick himself did. "My orders are top secret. May I ask, sir, who is your informant?"

Lord Durham smiled again. "Let us say that I have my sources."

"I am afraid that will not suffice. I am under orders to speak with no one, so unless you come from the King himself—"

"In fact, that is precisely why I am here," Lord Durham interrupted. He reached into his breast pocket and withdrew a note, sealed with the king's own signet. "Satisfy yourself."

Nick narrowed his eyes. Durham bore a scar on his left hand that looked like a defensive sword wound. So, the man knew something of weapons, but in what capacity? He cautiously took the note and broke the seal. It was brief and vague, stating little but that Lord Durham was acting on behalf of his king.

"How do I know to what matter this letter pertains? You could be purchasing tea for the palace, for all I know."

Lord Durham shrugged and took the note back. "I carry out many errands for His Highness. This is but one of them. I only ask for a moment of your time."

Nick studied him for a second, then gestured to a passing bar maid. "Two ales, please," he said.

His lordship smiled. "Thank you."

"Do not thank me yet. I have yet to hear what you want from me, and how you obtained your information."

"Of course." Durham settled more deeply in his chair and lifted the mug of ale that had dropped before him. "I've been tasked with a mission of my own, and I believe that our paths may cross. I presume you recall a Lord Aston?"

Nick's hand stilled on his mug and he gazed long and hard at Durham. "Lord Aston was responsible for helping to secure my commission."

"Yes, he said that, but declined to tell me how you came to his notice. Something to do with that daughter of his, I shouldn't wonder."

Nick gritted his teeth and stared at his mug.

"Ah, I see it. The lovely Carmella and her little 'indiscretions.' Oh, you needn't play the noble soldier, Captain. 'Tis far from a secret, though I know Lord Aston was grateful for your efforts at shielding his daughter's honor."

He lifted his gaze. "You were testing me."

His lordship saluted with his mug. "And you passed, Captain. Congratulations. Now, then. I believe we both know how you have been carrying on of late, and if what Lord Aston says of your character is true, I imagine you like it as little as I liked hearing of it. But look here, Hunt, I need your help to complete a little mission of my own."

Nick narrowed his eyes. "What kind of mission?"

Lord Durham leaned in closer, his voice lowering. "I have reason to believe that there is a traitor in our midst, someone who is passing information to the enemy."

Nick snorted. "If that is not the most puerile statement. What the devil do you think I'm doing? Trying to keep our local militia entertained? Of course, there's a traitor!"

"But not where Whitehall thinks, and that, my friend, is the trouble."

Nick fixed his gaze on the man while he downed a slow, thoughtful draft of ale. He set his mug down. "And just where does Whitehall think this traitor is?"

"Why, they believe it's someone along the chain of command. Someone with access to Wellington's correspondence to Viscount Castlereigh—perhaps even Castlereigh himself."

"And who do you say it is?"

Durham spun his mug about to grip the handle, almost as like a weapon. Nick's neck prickled as Durham smiled and looked him in the eye. "Me."

Nick's pistol whipped out, inches from Durham's nose, but the other man hardly blinked. "By the authority of the crown, I place you under arrest!"

Durham shook his head as if in boredom. "I see you do not understand. Put that thing away, Hunt, and listen." He sat back and withdrew a jeweled snuff box from one of the many pockets within his greatcoat. If Nick had any doubts of Durham's wealth and position, they were quickly put to rest, for the box bore the royal crest.

"Now, then. I understand you've met my Adelaide." Durham took a dip, then tucked the snuff box into his chest pocket.

"I meet a lot of people," Nick said with a shrug. "Who is this Adelaide, and why should I remember her?"

Lord Durham snorted. "Egad, lad, but you have a short memory! Is she not the reason you just had general Richardson's men shaking down every rat in the streets of London for information? But you won't find her."

Nick sat back, narrowing his eyes. "The blonde in the carriage. She works for you?"

Durham shrugged. "Something like that. She's a piece, isn't she? Found her down by the queues when she was but a wee thing, selling posies to anyone who passed."

"What does she sell now?"

"Whatever she pleases. She was impressed by your disguise, captain. She said you almost had her fooled into thinking you really were that old reprobate."

Nick curled his lip and pinched the bridge of his nose. "I knew I should never have kissed her."

Durham scoffed. "Oh, she had you pegged as a soldier long before you touched her. Old Cumberland slouched and smelled of ale."

"So, this whole thing has been a ruse? You were playing cat and mouse with me all along? You even knew who Cumberland was! Why did you not stop him yourself?"

"Because Cumberland was useful to me, just as I hope you will be. I could always count on Cumberland to do what he was paid to do, even if I was not the one pulling his strings. But I suspect you will be more difficult to convince."

Nick crossed his arms. "What makes you think so?"

Durham leaned forward and poured some ale from the decanter. "Soldier, man of duty and honor, never swayed by a bribe. No wife or lover, no scandalous past. Second son of a Knight of Bath with a pleasant little country estate, but your elder brother's health is failing and you stand to inherit the property before a twelve-month is out. And yet, here you are." He gestured at Nick's uniform. "Still in the game, doing your best to soak up lead balls, when you could be living comfortably at the manor, with a pretty wife at your side and children playing at your feet."

Nick lurched in his seat, his fingers grasping his pistol again as he bared his teeth. "Who are you, Durham? Really?"

"I am someone who knows people. That is enough for you. Stop snarling like a cur, Hunt, or people will stare."

"I want to know how you know all this!" Nick hissed. "What game are you playing?"

Durham sipped from his glass, then set it on the table and leveled a long stare at Nick. "General Richards ordered you to carry another message, did he not?"

"Do you truly believe I would tell you one way or the other?"

"You do not need to. I already know what the message said."

Nick drummed his fingers on the table. "It's encoded. Even I do not know what it says."

"Then, I suppose you have no choice but to take my word on the matter. Now, then. Richards intends to provoke Massena into overplaying his hand, correct? But is he certain that he is not instead setting Wellington's men up to be butchered? Cornered at the port of Lisbon with no means of standing their ground?"

Nick blanched. "I... I do not know. I am not always privy to..."

"Of course, you are not. Your duty is to follow orders, not question them," Durham sniffed.

"Are you saying I should not? That Richards could be working against Wellington?"

"Of course not, lad. Wellington is no fool. He has most certainly taken steps to protect the port, but Richards's actions are too bold. He knows something that he ought not know."

Nick squinted and shook his head. "He is a general in His Majesty's Army. Are you saying that you, a private gentleman who never picked up a musket or commanded a battalion, ought to know more than he?"

"I am saying that the *king* knows more than a lowly general. *Captain*. And something is amiss."

"I will not betray my orders, sir. General Richards has ordered me to carry a message, so I will carry a message. And that will be the end of the highwayman."

"And to whom are you supposed to give this message? Let me guess! He calls himself a monk."

Nick studied the nobleman seated across from him. "How did you know?"

"He was one of Cumberland's connections. They had a history, those two. I may not know the whole of it—I certainly do not—but they hated each other as much as they depended on each other. Cumberland made him an intermediary years ago, and paid him well for it."

Nick nodded. This matched what he and North had discovered. "Cumberland used different networks as the need suited him."

"And in Surrey, he was most often in contact with the man at the Buckland Ferry. The monk at the Old Shag, he called himself." Durham winked. "Adelaide is terribly clever at her craft."

Nick sighed and rapped his fist on the table. "So, you want to use me to trap him? Find out who he is and what he knows?"

"Waste of my time. You are missing the point, Hunt. I need to know what Richards knows, and how he knows it. And I need you to carry on as if nothing were amiss."

"Then why go to the bother of coming here and revealing yourself to me? Do you expect me to doubt my commanding officers, to give you information? What do you want of me?"

"To caution you, that is all. Indeed, carry out your orders, and trust no one, not even me. But keep your wits about you, Hunt. I would not see Lord Aston's pet—a good and useful soldier to His Majesty—shot down like a dog merely for want of a fair warning." Durham uncurled his long legs and glanced over his shoulder. "And I see your men have arrived. Best of luck to you, Captain."

Nick glanced over Durham's shoulder to see North and Daniels at the door. They were dressed as traveling merchants—nothing remarkable about their appearance to the common eye. But Durham had recognized them for the soldiers they were.

North caught Nick's eye at once and his hand slipped inside his coat, but Nick shook his head. Durham smiled grimly and reached for his hat. "I will contact you as needed, Captain. Take care of that scarlet coat and see that it gets no holes in it."

Chapter Twenty-One

NICK SAID HE WOULD return today. This very afternoon, she might look on his face again—if all had gone as he hoped in London.

Bess darted through the inn, her steps quick and purposeful as she dropped fresh mugs and tidied up dirty tables. If she could slip away after the London mail coach departed, and before the Brighton travelers arrived in the evening, she would be in time to meet him. The inn was abuzz with activity, patrons clamoring for attention, plates clattering, and laughter echoing through the air. Slipping away would be a matter of discretion and timing.

She wove her way to the back entrance, and relief washed over her when no heads turned her way to summon her back. The door creaked open, revealing the serene expanse of the woods beyond. The rustling leaves and the gentle whisper of the wind muffled her footsteps, and she pulled the hood of her cloak over her head to hurry into the trees.

Bess's heart pounded in her chest as she ventured deeper into the woods, her eyes searching eagerly for the tethered horse. Had Nick come, as he'd promised? Each step brought her closer to the answer—to *him*, and to losing herself once more in the only place she had ever felt at home. Anticipation and hope swirled within her, intertwining with the slight tremor in her limbs.

And then, there he was. Captain Hunt stood beneath the canopy of trees, leaning against that great black beast of his and idly flipping a small stone through his fingers as he waited. The afternoon light cut through the canopy and played upon his features, casting a glow upon his bristled jaw, and silhouetting those broad shoulders she knew so well. Bess's breath caught in her throat as she took in the sight of him, her heart skipping a beat.

He dropped the stone when she broke into the clearing, and his outstretched hand beckoned to her. Without hesitation, she closed the remaining distance, her heart pounding like a captive bird yearning for freedom.

"Bess." His gray eyes were shadowed under his tricorn, but his voice, low and welcoming, was all she needed. "You've come."

"I said I would. *She* gets right put out when I'm tardy," she said, tipping her head toward the horse at his back.

His laugh was everything she had learned to treasure. "I see she has *you* trained, too." He reached out to caress her cheek. "My sweet Miss Bess. Aye, but you're a sight to my poor heart today!"

The weight of the world melted away, and she turned her face to press a gentle kiss to his gloved palm. The tremor in his throat as he exhaled was barely audible, but it reverberated through her entire being. It was a sound that spoke volumes, a mixture of relief, longing, and quaking emotion.

Unable to hold back any longer, he crushed her to him in one swift motion. Bess let her body melt into his—the heart that thundered in time with hers and the strong arms that felt like her natural place in the world.

"Is it finished, then?" she murmured into his coat. "Are you free?"

A groan rumbled deep in his chest, and his arms tightened around her. He buried his face in her hair for one last caress, then loosened his embrace and held her back to look into her eyes. "Bess, I..."

She shook her head. "What is it?"

His throat bobbed, and he glared at the ground. "It's not over."

A spear of jealous indignation shot fire through her core. It was not fair! "But Nick, I thought... what more can they ask of you? You've done everything! Can you not refuse?"

He gave a rueful chuckle. "Refuse my king? Even if I could, you know I would not."

Her breath left her. There was that sense of duty again. The thing she first admired about him was very the thing that pulled him away. "No. You would not. But when will it end? Will you ever have peace?"

Nick's voice softened. "Bess, you know I want that more than anything. I'd cut off my sword arm if it could see me clear of this. But I want to know I've the right to take off my uniform and come for you with honor."

She swallowed the sob of awe that swelled in her throat, her voice barely above a whisper. "Come for me? You really mean what you said before? But what am I for the likes of you?"

He reached out and gently brushed a tear from her cheekbone. "You're the reason I hope. The one thing I mean to ask for, for myself. If I am found worthy when this business is over, I will make you my own, and live an honest life, with you."

She closed her eyes and leaned into his hand. "Then I'll be waiting for you. But how long, Nick?"

"I wish I knew." His gaze lingered on her face, as if etching her features into his memory. "I won't have you mixed up in this anymore. Bad enough that I have to carry on like a brigand. It's not right that you should have to live a lie, too."

She stiffened. "I'm not afraid. You'll need me, Nick. I can see things, I hear things—"

"Out of the question. I have reason to believe the mission is more dangerous than I'd imagined, and I cannot risk bringing that danger to your door."

Bess blinked, the cold reality settling into her bones. "Then you're leaving again?"

He studied her, then looked away, unable to confess the truth while looking into her eyes. "For a time. But not until I can be sure you are well. Your father has not pressed you yet?"

"My father... He went away with Captain Chesterfield."

His teeth flashed. "Chesterfield? Do you know why?"

She lifted her shoulders. "I don't, but I'm afraid he knows something. He won't speak to me of it, but I'm sure it has to do with you—or who he thinks you are. Nick, can we not tell him the truth?"

Nick drew a breath, his gaze settling somewhere beyond her—back toward the inn. "Would that we could. Too many know the truth already. Look, Chesterfield is only doing his duty, and no doubt your father thinks he is doing his."

"But they could track you down, shoot you on the road for a criminal, and I'd know nothing of it!"

He squeezed her shoulders. "Fear not, my Bess. I'll have North look to the militia. The man is a wizard at distracting them until I am safely away. All will be well, I promise."

Nick leaned in, meeting her with a bittersweet kiss. One final caress and their lips parted, but he whispered against her skin, his voice filled with determination. "I *will* come back for you, my bonny sweetheart. No matter what happens, I will find my way back to your side." With one final, lingering gaze, he tugged at the horse's lead shank and disappeared with her into the long afternoon shadows.

Bess watched him go, her heart filled with a panging ache. Could he really complete his mission without being caught? And what if he did? It seemed the more successful he was, the more was asked of him... and the less he could offer of himself.

She clutched her fist to her chest and closed her eyes. Nick was a man of his word, and he had sworn a faithful oath. He would find his way back to her. And she would be waiting.

THAT AFTERNOON, NICK DONNED the clothing of a field laborer and slipped into town on foot, timing his arrival to blend in with the passengers who disembarked from three mail coaches that arrived in quick succession. With any luck, no one would know he had not been a passenger on board one of them. Feigning a cough and holding a handkerchief to his mouth, he kept his gaze down, studying the faces around him as he maneuvered through the crowded streets.

The old woman from the ribbon shop occupied his mind. She knew something about this "monk" he was supposed to meet, and if he could find her, induce her to talk, she might lead him straight to the old vagabond. Perhaps he could even avoid the whole highwayman charade and escape the need to rob more innocent travelers.

As he passed familiar shops, his eyes darted from face to face, searching for any sign of recognition. He strained to catch whispers of passersby, hoping none of them saw in him anything remarkable. No one seemed to. When anyone looked his way, he covered his mouth with his handkerchief and coughed like a consumptive until they spun on their heels to scurry away.

He drew close enough to the ribbon shop to look through the window, and saw Mrs. Riley, the owner, talking to a pair of ladies at the counter. Could she truly be unaware of the woman who had first lured him in there? How could the old hag have let herself into Mrs. Riley's shop without the shopkeeper herself discovering the break-in?

It seemed improbable, but Bess swore Mrs. Riley was an innocent. He would leave her be, for now. But that did not mean there was nothing there to be learned here. He continued past the shop, his mind tumbling with possibilities. Was the old woman hiding somewhere nearby, observing his every move? Or had she slipped away, back to the mists whence she seemed to have come?

Taking a moment to collect himself, Nick found a secluded bench where he could watch the ribbon shop discreetly. Minutes seemed more like hours as he waited, his patience wearing thin. He calculated various scenarios, weighing the risks and potential outcomes of his next move. Should he confront Mrs. Riley directly or continue his search elsewhere?

Bess said Mrs. Riley had been kind to her. Perhaps he would do well to approach the woman gently, ask her a few frank questions. But if she knew nothing, all he would accomplish would be to frighten her. No, there had to be another option. As he prepared to rise from the bench, a flicker of movement caught his attention—a hidden corner, a pair of guarded eyes. His heart quickened, hope mingling with caution. Could it be? Was the old woman watching him from the shadows? He held his breath, studying the figure, searching for familiarity.

But as quickly as the figure appeared, it vanished. He swore silently and darted after her. He couldn't afford to lose her now, not when he was so close to unraveling this nightmare. But even as he raced after the apparition, bursting through doorways and peering down empty alleys, he knew how fruitless it would prove to be.

Doubtless someone *was* watching him, but they had no intention of revealing themselves. He knew only one way to reach the French agents—the way old Cumberland had always done.

He would have to take to the highways again.

PAPA HAD COME BACK while she was away—his mood foul and his manners brusque. Hattie and Sarah were scampering like frightened hares when Bess walked into the kitchen, and everyone was avoiding the master. Bess did the same, and when she hung up her apron for the night, she made her way stealthily toward the stairs, hoping to slip to her own bedroom unnoticed. But just as she passed the door to the stillroom, her father's voice cut through the air like a sharp gust of wind.

"Bess! Where were you tonight?"

Her grip tightened on the fabric of her skirt, her mind racing for a plausible explanation. She turned to face her father, her eyes meeting his gaze defiantly.

"I just went for a walk. Sarah was minding the tables, and—"

Her father tore the work cloth from around his waist and threw it on the counter. "You were in the woods again. Tell me the truth."

Her jaw clenched. "And where have *you* been, Father? We looked for you all day! I was only out for an hour."

His expression darkened. "Don't play games, Bess. I know you've been up to something. Who are you meeting? Sneaking off into the woods like that, it's not proper."

A surge of anger coursed through Bess's veins. "*Proper?* Father, I am not a child anymore. I've done nothing wrong, and I can look out for myself. You've no right to accuse me like this."

Her father's face softened, a hint of sorrow in his eyes. "Bess, it's not that I don't trust you. I worry about your future, about the dangers that lurk beyond these walls. I want what's best for you, and I'll see you married to someone respectable, someone who can do for you—keep you right."

Bess's frustration turned to outrage. "Someone who can 'do' for me? Father, I never agreed to such a thing! I'll have the choosing of my own husband, just as Mama had when she chose you."

His cheek flinched. "That's what you think, is it?" He sucked in a breath and turned away, his feet scuffling heavily on the floor.

"That's what you and Mama always told me," she shot back. "Was that a lie?"

He stopped, still with his back turned, his gaze wandering and distant. "It was almost true."

Bess stepped closer and rested her hand on his shoulder. "Papa?"

He looked up and clasped her hand tightly to him. "'Tis a hard world, lass. A hard world. I can't bear to see you waste yourself on men like that bastard they call Cumberland."

Her mouth dropped, and her breath stilled. "It's not like that."

"Oh, don't tell me how it is. I have eyes and ears, haven't I? You've had stars in your eyes since your first sight of the blackguard. You don't know what he is, lass. He'll break you and leave you a shell of yourself."

Bess's voice quivered with a blend of anger and hurt. "But he won't! You don't know him as I do. He's a good man."

"Good! There were never a good man born under that name. Don't you know who he is? What he's done?"

She narrowed her eyes. "Do you?"

"I know enough." He pointed toward the door. "I may not know *this* Cumberland, but if he is like his sire... Bess, you've no idea what you've got yourself into. Why, it's not just the lies, the deceit. It's... heavens, lass, it's abominable! You cannot know what he is! I won't allow it, and that's the end of it."

The room fell silent, the tension thickening between them. The weight of her father's expectations pressed sharply upon her, suffocating the one flame she had ever carried for herself. She clenched her fists with a mutinous glare. "Try to stop me, then." She turned on her heel and stormed the stairs.

Her mind swirled as she fled to the sanctuary of her bedroom. How dare he speak to her that way? He knew nothing! She slammed the door hard enough to make the mirror rattle on the wall and flung herself onto her bed to scream into her pillow.

"Why, Papa? Why do you hate him so?" She closed her eyes, memories of her stolen moments with Nick flooding her mind. Their sweet kisses, the warmth of his touch, the promises of a future together. It all seemed so impossible in the face of her father's scorn and Nick's new assignment.

How could she make her father see Captain Nicholas Hunt for who he really was? What matter if the real Cumberland was a blighter? Nick was not that man! If only her father could know that! But the risk to the man she loved was too great—she dared not speak the truth until he was safe, his mission complete. The frustration of it all tore another sob from deep in her belly, and she wept into her pillow until she was too exhausted to make another sound.

But, after a long while, some of the indignation faded. Bess sat up and dried her eyes. As Nick had told her earlier, her father surely thought he was doing right. She ought not to have spoken to him as she had. Silly and petulant! And what better way to force his hand than to make him think she was set on ruining herself?

She'd have to pacify him somehow, try to make him understand that she was not in the danger he seemed to fear. If only he would let her wait, but a little longer, perhaps she could reveal the truth.

Chapter Twenty-Two

"I SWORE I WAS finished with this. Aye, but look at you, my lass!" Nick stroked his mare's crested black neck, the ringlets of mane cascading to her shoulders. He crooned gentle nothings, attempting to soothe her stamping impatience. She twisted her pert ears to listen to him, but Black Bess, the terror of the night highways, was having none of his affection just now. Her ears swept forward once more, she played nervously with the bit, and her heavy tail swished in eagerness.

At least one of them was ready.

Nick had positioned himself near a dipping turn in the road, hidden amidst the dense foliage. Sergeant Wesson had scouted a trio of tradesmen traveling from London to Brighton and deemed them to be an easy target. The tradesmen were unarmed and slightly inebriated, making them vulnerable to a staged attack. Hunt adjusted his mask, ensuring his face was concealed, and tightened his grip on the rein as he waited for their carriage to approach.

Daniels' fake owl call reached his ears first, followed by the sound of approaching hooves and rattling wheels. The carriage came into view, a lantern flickering dimly at its side. Black Bess sensed his anticipation and shot over the rim like a cannonball, snorting to the skies with the fire of the very devil.

As ever, the carriage horses wheeled back in terror, and the driver was helpless to force them on. Hunt leveled his flintlock at the passengers, with those lace cuffs swirling at his wrists, and raised his voice. "Halt! Stand and deliver!"

The three men inside exchanged bewildered glances. "Go!" one of them cried their driver. "Get us away from here!"

But Hunt, his heart pounding with adrenaline, had flung the rein on Bess's neck and aimed his second flintlock at the driver. "Your purses and valuables, gents! I'll not ask again!"

The tradesmen scrambled to gather their belongings. "Have a care, sir!" one of them protested. "I've a wife and three little ones!"

Nick closed his eyes and growled to himself, then readjusted his grip on the pistol. "Then do as I ask, and you shall return to them unharmed. Quickly!"

Three bags of coins flew out of the carriage window in quick succession. Nick gave a twitch of his leg and his horse danced backward as he kept the driver in line with his pistols. "I thank you kindly, gentlemen," he called as the carriage lumbered into motion once more. Once it was out of sight, he stowed his pistols and signaled his men.

North was on the scene first, and he swept the purses into his saddlebag before the others could even halt and dismount. "You'll see that returned to them by tomorrow morning," Nick ordered.

"Aye, sir," North answered as he mounted again. "Right, lads, let's put on a fine showing for our newly impoverished tradesmen."

Nick saluted his men, and they galloped into the night with cries of "After him, men!" and, "Stop, thief, in the name of His Majesty!" All in all, a fair display.

Hopefully, a convincing one.

T HE INN HUMMED WITH activity as Bess weaved through the crowded tables. Weary travelers and boisterous locals filled the room, seeking respite or companionship. Bess moved with purpose—avoiding further confrontations with her father being her chief concern. But anyone with a mind to look see plain as day that her mind was miles away, under the shade of an oak arbor. Papa would only excite himself again if she paused long enough for him to see the dreamy haze clouding her face.

"Bess," Molly said with a breathless swipe across her brow, "I'm knackered. Would you be a doll and help me with the gents in the back?"

Bess glanced over her shoulder. Three men had arrived with the London post and had promptly set to drinking hard enough to miss the coach when it left. She sighed. "One minute."

She filled her tray with fresh ale mugs and followed Molly to the table. The loudest of the men, a burly fellow with grizzled three-day whiskers and a permanent leer, caught sight of Bess and called out, "Well, 'ello there, Duchess! Why don't you set down that tray and keep me company. I could do with somethin' to keep me lap warm." His companions joined in with crude gestures and guffaws.

Bess drew up short. "If I set down this tray, it'll be to douse you with five mugs of ale. And if you're wearing them, you'll pay for them."

The man roared with laughter. "Told you, lads! She's a feisty filly if you ever did see one. Come on, lassie, let us have a pinch, love."

Her lip curled and her hand twitched under her tray. She ought to upend the whole lot in his filthy lap. But she could not afford to make a scene just now—not when her father was already suspicious of her judgment. She simply lifted her chin. "Did you want another round or not? I've no time to bother with your nonsense. Molly? Settle their bill."

The man's face flushed with anger as he pushed his chair back from the table. "Who d'ye think ye are, lass? Too good for the likes of us? What, is our coin not as shiny as someone else's? Ye're a barmaid, and nothin' more. Might as well play the bit."

Bess's temper flared. "I'm no fancy lady, nor am I a plaything for drunken fools like you!"

Molly gasped, hands clasping together in alarm. "Bess, mind yer tongue," she whispered, glancing around nervously.

"Now there's a lass what knows what's what," the man grunted. "Ye need someone to teach ye a lesson. Come here, wench." He made a grab for Bess's waist, tugging at her apron strings with one hand while the other reached for her breast.

Her vision flashed red, and her resolve to maintain her composure snapped. Bess grabbed the mug of ale and doused his foul mouth, drenching him from head to toe, then clubbed him across the cheek with the empty tin mug. The man was so astonished that he stumbled back, releasing her, as the room erupted into raucous laughter and applause.

But Molly's face had drained of all color. "Bess," she whispered. "The master..."

She whirled, and there, indeed, was her father. He was watching the whole scene from the door to his still room, his eyes hooded and dark, and his jaw set. He met Bess's gaze for an instant. Then, he turned back to his still and let the door swing closed behind him.

Bess dropped the rest of her serving tray on the table with a bang and a clatter of sloshing mugs, ripped off her apron and tossed it to Molly, and fled the room.

S HE COULDN'T THINK OF anywhere else to go. Tim was lurking in the barnyard, so she did not dare sneak out to her rose bush, lest he follow her. And she might endanger Nick if she went traipsing through the woods to find him, just to weep her frustrations out on his shoulder. And so, she found herself staring up at the swinging sign above Mrs. Riley's ribbon shop, her heart sick with questions and her stomach burning with worry. Sucking in her breath in resolve, she swung open the door.

Mrs. Riley was behind the counter, stocking a roll up on one of the higher shelves when the bell jingled. She stopped and turned carefully on her step stool. "Why, Bess! Wha' brings ye 'ere today?"

Approaching the counter, Bess tried to smile, but failed. "Mrs. Riley, I'm in a right state. I'm sorry to bother you, but…"

The woman swept down from her stool to lean over the counter and cup Bess's cheek. "Well, lass, either you've run all the way from the inn, or you're flushed with fever. Either way, a cuppa tea cannot go amiss."

Bess closed her eyes and sighed in gratitude. "That would be just the thing."

"Let me just put the kettle on. Go bolt the door and come to the back, will ye?"

Bess did as Mrs. Riley asked, sliding the bolt on the door to prevent interruptions. Mrs. Riley kept a sign in the window, and Bess turned it around to say that the shop was closed. As she did so, she caught a flash of red, and drew aside the lace of the curtains to see better. It was a pair of Captain Chesterfield's men, loitering by the nearest tavern and trying to look casual. Bess narrowed her eyes and let the curtain fall again.

A few moments later, she was settled in Mrs. Riley's kitchen, with the tea steeping and a scone set before her. "Now, then," Mrs. Riley said as she seated herself. "What be the trouble, lass?"

Bess dipped the tea leaves from her cup and sought the words. "It's Papa. I have this awful feeling there's something he's not telling me. Something… dodgy, you know?"

Mrs. Riley furrowed her brows. "Dodgy, ye say? What kind o' mischief do ye suspect 'im of, Bess?"

Bess sighed, frustration mingling with fear. "It's hard to put my finger on it. He's always put out with me these days. There's a…" She chewed her lip. "A man. A *gentleman.* I'm fond of him, but Papa won't hear of it, and he won't tell me why. He keeps wanting to bundle me off to wed some steward I do not know, and he's been terribly short with me about it all. It's just not like him not to talk to me!"

Mrs. Riley studied Bess's face. "A man, you say? Not that Captain Chesterfield, is it?"

"No. He's... well, he was a traveler from London. That was how I first met him."

"'First met him,' you say?" Mrs. Riley fluffed her apron and shook her head with a clucking sound. "Ye've not been sneaking round, have ye, Bess? I'd have thought better of ye."

"No! I've done nothing immoral, and neither has he. Not truly, anyway. But Papa is convinced that he's a scoundrel. I know he's not, but I cannot tell Papa that. There are things I cannot say—they are not mine to say, do you understand?"

The woman thinned her lips. "Aye. But is your papa so much in the wrong to be stoppin' ye?"

"He would not be, if he were right about things, but he is not. Still, it is more than that." She took a breath. "I've this terrible feeling that Papa's involved in something. Something dangerous. But he keeps it all close to his chest, and I can't make heads or tails of it. To make it worse, I feel like it has something to do with me, and I'm afraid he's told Captain Chesterfield something about it."

Mrs. Riley sipped from her cup, then set it aside with care, her eyes never meeting Bess's. Then her hands fell to smoothing her apron over her skirts, and her tone was reluctant when she spoke. "Bess, ye must understand, what I'm 'bout t' tell ye ain't common knowledge. 'Tis a secret kept tight."

Bess leaned forward. "Please, Mrs. Riley, tell me what you know."

Mrs. Riley hesitated for a moment. "Well, I shouldn'a say. Lord knows, 'tis water under the bridge by now, but yer papa is right to be frettin' about yer virtue. Ye and yer brother were born only three months after yer folks were wed."

Bess straightened, her head tilted. "I... we were? No, I am sure you must be mistaken. I've seen the marriage license. Papa keeps it in his room. He takes it out and looks at it now and again."

"A fake, my dear. Yer mother's sire were a powerful man. Not a good man, but a rich one. Rich enough to pay the right folks to keep their mouths quiet."

She shook her head. "No, you must be mistaken. That's an old rumor that got passed around once in a while, but there's nothing to it. Mama was a gentleman farmer's daughter. Her sister married above her station, and mama married a little below, so they rarely spoke, but..."

Mrs. Riley scoffed. "I know that's what ye were told, Bess, but my memory's not so short that I can't recall the day that fine carriage first pulled up to the inn, with the black-haired lass inside carefully robed to hide her condition."

Bess swallowed, her heart pounding in her ears. "I don't..." She sniffed and scrambled to her feet, almost upsetting the teacups. "I'm sorry, Mrs. Riley. I have to go."

NICK COULD SEE THE puff of his breath in the moonlit night, mists and shadows dancing around him as he drew back among the tall grasses beside the road. Two nights had passed since his last hold-up, and the thrill mixed with trepidation coursed through his veins once more. He still hated robbing innocent people, but hang it all, if it was the only way to gain the spy's trust and achieve his mission, was it wrong to relish the shot of thrill that sent fire through his sinews and seemed to blend him and his horse into one fearsome beast?

Tonight's target would not be so easy as the three inebriated tradesmen, but he expected little difficulty. He'd scouted this one himself—a minor gentleman on his way to London after a holiday. Traveling alone—a wife or child with him would have made him more cooperative, but Nick had never grown accustomed to frightening women and children. This one would do.

The lumbering shape of the man's carriage loomed larger on the road, and he gave Black Bess her head. Puffing and pawing with exuberance, the horse vaulted over the rise of the road and bore down on the carriage. This would be over quickly.

But Nick's heart sank when the silhouette of a blunderbuss shot out from the carriage's window and whipped round to train on him. Another crawled out of the window on the far side. *Blast!* The gentleman must have hired these blokes since the last coaching inn. This was not the soft target he had hoped for. Panic clawed at him, but he had to think fast.

"Stand down!" he called out, trying to project a confidence he didn't entirely feel. "No one needs to get hurt."

The guards hesitated, their eyes locked on him with a mix of uncertainty and suspicion.

"Heed my words!" Nick bellowed, the adrenaline coursing through him and making his palms sweat. It would be easier to threaten them if he had a clear shot at the gentleman who held the purse strings. But he *did* have a clear shot at the horses... Nick adjusted the aim of his right hand. "Hand over your valuables, or I will cripple your carriage and leave you here for every other ruffian traveling the roads!"

Not that he could bring himself to kill an innocent beast, but they didn't know that. The threat seemed to carry some weight with the guards, for they glanced back at their employer.

Then one of them leaned farther out of the window, and Nick heard the lever drawing back on a flintlock. "We'll not be tossin' out any valuables," snarled a gravely voice. Decidedly not the voice of the gentleman. "I've as clear a shot at *ye* as ye have at us. And we're better armed."

Nick clamped his jaw, his eyes darting for the best path of escape. The road was clearly not an option. The only way out of there was a whirl and a dash back whence he had come, but he had both hands full of his pistols. If he lowered either of them, for even an instant, he was as good as dead. He'd have to depend on Black Bess to save his hide again, but could she even read his signals, with the rein hanging freely about her neck? It was the only idea he had.

"Lower your weapons!" he shouted for one last diversion. Then his heel moved, he shifted his weight, and prayed.

And his horse knew. With a grunt, she spun about and leaped into the darkness, leaving nothing but flying clods of mud in her wake.

"Shoot him!" one of the guards shouted. Fire exploded in the air to his left.

Nick shoved one of the pistols in his coat and groped for the flapping rein, urging Black Bess into top flight. Another shot whizzed past, and her mane snapped as the ball passed through it. "Oh, God," he breathed, lowering his head, and begging her for just a little more speed. "I can't lose you, too!"

Bullets splintered the tree to their left, and Nick ripped the reins to the right. His only hope was to put the thick of the wood between them and their pursuers, but he, of all people, knew how a tiny bullet could lance through the gap between the trees.

But Black Bess seemed to hold lead balls in no awe. Her nostrils were drinking in great scoops of wind, her churning strides catapulting them away from the road. Great lashes of autumn air whipped at his face, and the puffs of his breath were growing heavier in the evening frost. Anyone with a mind to chase them down would have no trouble following the trail of broken tree branches or tracking the sounds of their strained breathing. But they'd have to catch up to him, first, and that would be no easy feat.

Another shot rang out somewhere behind them. Nick cursed himself for getting into this mess. Stupid, how stupid he had been to let them take him by surprise! At least the guards had no saddle horses with which to pursue him, and that was the only thing keeping them at bay. A little farther on, and he'd be entirely out of range of their bullets.

Black Bess spotted the narrow deer trail before he did, and he trusted her enough to give the mare her head as she veered off the main road and onto the hidden path. The branches of the trees scraped against him, the forest closing in around him. He urged Black Bess on, pushing her to her limits. Her muscles strained beneath him, her breaths coming in heavy bursts. By now, he wasn't even sure where they were. They could be stumbling into the militia patrol North had spotted on the far side of the wood, for all he knew.

And then he saw it—the river. It was rushing past, its waters dark and treacherous. Round, heavy stones rolled within its depths, and no horse could keep its footing at speed in there. But if he was right, and he *was* closing in on that patrol, crossing the river would see him clear of them. And it got deeper and swifter the farther he went, so this would be his only chance to cross.

Without a second thought, Nicholas pointed his horse towards it. As they plunged into the icy waters, the shock of the cold took his breath away. Black Bess scrambled for her footing until the bottom fell away from her feet and she had to swim. Nick slid off her back, letting her drag him along behind as her powerful strokes carried them across.

They stumbled out of the water side by side, dripping and gasping, and Nick leaned a quaking hand on the saddle as he caught his breath. "Well done, my beauty," he whispered. "You did it. Saved my fool neck yet again."

Black Bess dropped her head and shook like a dog, then rubbed her dripping face on his shoulder.

He chuckled and pushed her away. "Enough of that now, you rogue. I'll fetch you a carrot when... Shh..." A branch snapped nearby, and he held his breath to listen more closely.

His senses tingled, and he drew his flintlock—dripping and useless now, save as a bluff. "Show yourself!"

A pair of hands shot into a ray of moonlight filtering through the thick canopy of the forest. "It's only me, sir! Don't shoot!"

Nick sighed and stowed his pistol. "Good lad, Wesson. Have no fear. Though, if we have come across you, we must be even farther out of the way than I thought."

Wesson's horse appeared through the brush. "Aye, sir. I was keeping an eye on the militia to the west. I thought you were two miles to the east!"

Nick snorted and pulled off his boot to dump the water out of it. "I was, until I wasn't. Let's rejoin the others and get back to camp."

Chapter Twenty-Three

BESS HOVERED BY THE window; her eyes fixed on the archway outside the inn's entrance. Where was Papa now?

Worry gnawed at her, because Captain Chesterfield's men had been in the coffee room earlier, and she had not seen her father for two hours. He *had* to be coming back soon. The Brighton coach was due any minute, and he never missed meeting the incoming guests.

She'd tried to speak with him after racing home from the ribbon shop yesterday evening, but he had kept busy with travelers and sent her out to help Sarah with the washing. And then, this morning, he'd been up and about before the cock crowed, even before Bess and Molly had stirred to light the kitchen fires.

What on earth could he be about? He simply refused to permit her a spare moment to speak with him. That was not like Papa! As long as she could remember, he had taken endless pains with her, and with Samuel—teaching, counseling, or even just listening to whatever they might want to say. Indeed, he had changed when Mama died, but this was different. It was as if he could not even bear the sight of her.

Bess tried to look busy, wiping down a table that already shone like a mirror. There was the Brighton coach, with its passengers starting to trickle in the door, but where was...?

Ah. There he was, at last. Her father was walking towards the inn, accompanied by a tall and imposing figure in a red uniform. Bess's shoulders sank with a sigh. Captain Chesterfield. Her hopes flagged, and she couldn't help the scowl that crept onto her face. She was in no mood to entertain the captain just now, and she did not like to think about what he and her father might have been speaking of.

As her father came through the door, he caught sight of Bess and drew up short. His face—the conscious look, the sudden formality he assumed—told her everything. Even if she did manage to corner him now, he wouldn't tell her anything.

"Ah. Bess. There you are. Would you get the captain an ale, please?" He gestured apologetically to Captain Chesterfield, suggesting that he make himself comfortable at a table. Then he held the door to attend to some travelers who were just arriving off the coach, requesting a room for the night.

Bess huffed with frustration. How long would he keep this up? Until she just gave up and married Mr. Thompkins? Out of the corner of her eye, she noticed Captain Chesterfield's gaze fixed on her. A shiver ran down her spine as she felt the weight of his stare. He wasn't even trying to hide it—he was watching her intently, as if waiting for her to make a move.

Bess glanced away, pretending to be occupied with polishing the table for him, but she could still feel his eyes on her. "I'll be right back with that ale," she mumbled.

Captain Chesterfield lowered himself into the chair. "Take your time."

She grabbed her polishing rag and slipped away without looking at him. Papa was behind his registration book, dipping his quill and recording a guest's name. He blotted the ink and called for Hattie to show the travelers to their room. Then he closed his book and his eyes accidentally collided with Bess's.

Now was her chance. Summoning her courage and forcing an easy smile, she walked over with as mild a manner as she could manage. "Prosperous-looking fellows. Where are they from?" she asked disinterestedly.

He removed his spectacles and set them on the counter. "Northampton. And the other was from Scarborough. Did Captain Chesterfield get his ale?"

"I suppose he might have. Sarah should be waiting tables."

"I meant for *you* to be the one to fetch it for him."

She squinted. "Whatever for?"

He sighed and slid his registration book under the counter. "Just do it, Bess."

"But Papa, I need to talk to you. It's important. Can't we go to the back room for a minute?"

"Later." He gestured to the taproom and slid into his overcoat. "I must have a word with the ostler. See to the captain."

Bess scowled as he walked away. But what was she to do? She couldn't force him to turn around, make a scene. She couldn't make him talk if he was determined not to. There was nothing to do but to fill an ale mug and carry it to the captain's table.

Chesterfield's eyes were still fixed on her as she came back into the room, with a look every tavern girl knew. Not the longing of a parched man waiting for his drink—no, it was an altogether different kind of thirst that made his eyes grow dark and the corner of his mouth turn up when she approached.

Bess dropped his drink on the table with a curt bob of her head and turned to whisk herself away when a hand caught at her elbow. "What, not even a friendly by-your-leave?"

She glanced down at his hand, then swept her gaze to him. "Something amiss, Captain?"

"Why, no," he laughed. "Except a bit of company. Come, please. Join me."

Bess turned back slowly, her head tilted. "I've work to do."

"But you can spare a moment, can you not?" He took a sip of his ale and smiled up at her. "You keep glancing at the door. Are you expecting someone?"

She took a breath and shook her head. "Only my father."

"Oh." He sipped from his mug again. "I thought it might be someone else."

Bess fisted a hand at her waist. "And who might that be?"

"I am sure I do not know. But I do hear things, you know." He filled his chest with a long sigh, then leaned back in his chair, sweeping her with a penetrating look. "Rumors. Tittle-tattle. You know the sort."

"I'm afraid I don't."

"Well! No matter, then." He shrugged, setting his mug down, and his tone altered. "Your father speaks very highly of you, did you know?"

Bess drew back, a new notion tingling her senses. "Does he, now?"

"Oh, come, you sound downright suspicious! What father would not be proud to claim such a daughter? I say, you could boil water with the look in your eye right now. Have I offended you, Miss Reynolds?"

"No." She tugged at the corner of her apron to swipe a few drops of ale that he'd spilled. "Beg your pardon, Captain. The tap wants seeing to."

Captain Chesterfield shot out of his chair and caught her hand. "Let it wait. You have not yet heard me out."

Bess snatched her hand away. "And just what do you have to say? Is something wrong with your drink? Care for something to eat? Blurt it out, why don't you, and let me get back to my work."

The captain shook his head, his teeth flashing an admiring grin. "I have never known you to mince your words. Very well, then. Your father *did* just spend an hour warming my ears with your praise. And then he also mentioned something I found rather interesting—the possibility of us becoming better acquainted."

Her heart gave a little hiccough, and she resisted the urge to frown. His words were carefully chosen... *too* carefully. She continued to meet his gaze, her expression polite but guarded. "Oh, did he now? What a kind, thoughtful father I have."

"Quite right," he replied smoothly. "He seemed to think you were unsatisfied with your present options, so he made the suggestion after we finished discussing something else. And I must say, I find the idea rather appealing. You're a remarkable woman, Bess, and I have plans for my career. I'll have my commission before the year is out. A captain in the Continental Army, Bess! Think on it. I mean to request transfer to the 95th."

Her eyes narrowed, and her pulse throbbed. "Samuel's regiment," she whispered.

"Yes, your father said as much. And do you know..." He brushed the edge of her apron with the back of his fingers. "Officers' wives often accompany them. I've heard nothing but they have the merriest parties and the finest gowns. Warm Mediterranean winters instead of the freezing drear of England. What do you say, Bess? You are as fine a lass as I've ever seen, and I'd certainly be proud to have you on my arm when I don my new uniform."

Her grip on the tray tightened, and her eyes flickered for a moment. She forced a composed smile. "I appreciate your interest, Captain Chesterfield, but I'm not currently seeking a match. My father is mistaken regarding my wishes."

Captain Chesterfield took another sip of his ale, his eyes narrowing slightly as he studied her. A faint trace of impatience flashed across his face before he masked it with a smile. "I quite understand. Your affections must be engaged elsewhere, eh?"

She clenched her teeth. "What makes you say that?"

"Oh." He shrugged. "Like I say. I hear rumors."

"Just what are you implying, Captain? Are you trying to say that I'm a light-skirt? A doxy? Who says such things about me?"

He finished his glass and set it aside with a lazy grin. "I'll keep my own counsel on that, thank you. But do consider what I've said. Opportunities like this don't come knocking every day. At least keep my offer in mind."

"I will do no such thing," she shot back, the hairs on her neck prickling with anger. "And I'm not a piece of baggage to be passed about. I'll make up my own mind on whom to wed, and it won't be some lippy militia captain who's suddenly got chummy with my father."

He stood up, pushing his chair back with a little too much force. This time, when he spoke, his voice had lost its courtliness, and his eyes had grown hard. "Very well, then. I'll leave you to your duties."

As he made his way to the door, she watched him carefully, her mind racing with questions and concerns. She had angered him. Wounded his pride, surely. She swallowed and kept well out of his path to the door. She would be content never to set eyes on the man again, but would he let the matter drop so easily as that?

She darted her gaze to her father as he passed through the room, deep in conversation with some travelers. The longer he put off talking to her, the more questions she had... and the more frustrated she became.

"AND YOU ARE SURE of the man who gave you this message?" Nick turned over the folded note that North had pulled from his inner pocket. "Tall, with black hair and a scar on his left hand?"

"The very man. The one we saw in London. I don't know how he found me, but he slipped up behind me when I was tying my horse at the last tavern and directed me to give you this."

Nick studied the note, with the plain, unembellished seal. "The man concerns me. He knows far too much."

"Aye, he does, Captain. Can we trust him?"

Nick swallowed. "I don't trust anyone. He even said I should not trust him. But let us see what he says, eh?" He broke it open and scanned the two spare lines Durham had penned with a frown.

"What is it, sir?"

"He wants me to meet him in public. In Westcott."

North shook his head. "No. You can't sir. He'll draw you out, get you surrounded somehow."

"By whom? For what crime?"

"Whatever he wants. You said yourself he's got all the wrong sort in his very pockets. You cannot risk it, sir."

Nick tapped the note on his open palm. "We've been nowhere near Westcott. He choses a place where he knows I'll feel less exposed."

"Exactly. He's setting you up."

"I don't think so. I have to go, North. Follow me if you like, but Durham knows something. I mean to find out what it is."

Nick waited in the dimly lit back room of the inn, staring meditatively down into the bottom of a whiskey glass. Lord Durham was late... but Nick would have expected no less. Surely, he was keeping his distance to see that Nick had come alone, and to not appear that theirs was a coordinated meeting. It was over an hour after the appointed time when an unkempt, limping bulk slid into the opposite chair.

"Two ales," Durham growled to the tavern girl, without looking up at Nick. "Or should I ask for a third, for your friend outside?" he added as the girl walked away.

Nick snorted and pushed away his empty whiskey glass. "I wondered if you would notice him. North is top notch. You are keener than I had realized."

"Not keen enough, I am sorry to say."

"Are any of us? So, what was so important that you demanded to meet face-to-face?"

Durham lifted a finger and kept his silence until after the bar maid had dropped their ales. "Ugh," he complained after his first taste. "Abominable stuff. You can always tell a skinflint innkeeper. He waters down his ale."

"Most of them do," Nick sniffed dryly. "You were expecting Brooks' of London?"

Durham grunted and casually let his gaze drift around the room. Then he lifted his glass to casually nurse it—or to appear to do so—as he muttered, "They've decoded that letter you got from the French spy."

Nick leaned back with a nonchalant stare. "I'd expect they would have by now."

"And I've intercepted a reply. What, surprised, Hunt? Yours is not the only channel employed for the relaying of illicit information."

"I didn't imagine it was. What is this reply, and why should it concern me, if I am not designated to carry it?"

Durham swilled from his ale. "Because it comes directly from General Richards and is addressed to a high-ranking naval officer in France."

Nick sat up. "Richards is in Intelligence. It is his duty to play behind the screen, as it were."

"But not to convey top secret information to French officials. He probably told you that we were sending false intelligence, 'leaking' the word that Wellington meant to leave the British ships at Lisbon unprotected and cut off."

Nick nodded. "That is what he told me. He wants to lure the French army into an engagement they cannot win, thus securing the victory and a winter's reprieve for our men."

"But that is not what we intercepted. In fact, he was warning them of the true nature of our defenses and telling them where our forces were the weakest. Richards means to set Wellington up to be cornered at Sobral."

Nick was too seasoned to let his expression alter, but a yawning pit opened in his stomach. The implications were staggering. If true, Richards's treachery would endanger countless English lives and jeopardize the entire war effort. "How can we be sure the letter is authentic?"

Durham reached into his coat pocket and pulled out a folded letter. "See for yourself."

Nick unfolded the letter, his eyes scanning the contents with growing alarm. "This... this is treason. Are you sure of its origins?"

"Look at the handwriting. Particularly the shape of his 'W's' and 'L's.'" It matches your orders from General Richards."

Nick's eyes narrowed as he examined the writing. The similarity was undeniable. "By Jove," he breathed. "It's him."

Durham lowered his glass, his expression softening somewhat. "I know it stretches credulity, Captain, but we have evidence that Richards meant to cut *you* loose, as well."

He produced another document, and Nick's hand trembled as he read. It was a signed order to capture him—*him*, by name—sent to the local militia by Richards himself. "Bloody devil," he swore under his breath. "The traitorous bastard! He set me up!"

"Oh, come off it. Richards is nothing but a well-placed pawn. His orders come from someone even higher up the chain. Now listen, Hunt. I need you to carry on as if you knew none of this, because we've not yet worked out all the names responsible. But understand what you're marching into. You know too much already, and you're a marked man. They won't want to leave any loose ends."

"So, that's why Richards kept sending me back out in the guise of a criminal. He hoped I'd catch a stray bullet."

"That, and he really does need you to plug the hole you opened up when you killed Cumberland. Someone has to keep the attention of the French contacts, whoever they are. But ultimately, he wants you out of the picture, and Captain Chesterfield will be more than happy to oblige."

Hunt's jaw tightened, and his eyes flashed to Durham. "You know Chesterfield?"

"I know he is ambitious. And I know he has been chasing you like a dog with a bone—in *both* your capacities. Yes, I should think he would be only too happy to receive such an order."

Nick thinned his lips and pushed the orders back to Durham. "Then you tell me. What do I do? I've no intention of engaging in hostilities with my fellow officers. But if I stand aside, am I failing to warn Wellington?"

Durham leaned back, and his voice dropped to barely audible. "Continue with the plan, Captain. I've had another letter encoded—the one you *thought* you were carrying. Play along with Richards's ruse for now but pass on the *right* message. What the French do not yet know is that Wellington has built strong fortifications at Sobral. Our troops will be secure and able to withstand attack. We need but wait for them."

The hair on the back of Nick's neck prickled. "What is this?"

"One of the things Whitehall does not know. One of many, I should say. Wellington kept this secret to avoid letting it trickle out to the French. His Highness knows, but we thought that was almost the extent of it. Clearly Richards has learned of it, and we must not let him caution the enemy."

Nick shook his head. "How do I know it is not *you* who are truly passing on the wrong information? The messages are encoded. I could just as easily be telling the French where Wellington lays his head at night."

"I thought of that. You still have Cumberland's saddle, yes?"

"What about it?"

Durham shrugged. "It bears a closer inspection."

Nick narrowed his eyes. "He had a key to the code?"

"It might still be there. It might not be. One of the things he got from Adelaide. But if it is found on your person, know that both of us are likely to stretch. Even His Highness would not spare me if he thought I was so loose with his secrets."

"Understood." Nick drummed his fingers on the table surface. "If you need me to carry on, you must need to know whatever I discover. I assume you've already worked out a way for me to contact you."

A ghost of a smile touched Durham's lips, and he tugged the snuffbox from his pocket. "You look too much like a soldier. Try cultivating a vice or two." He cracked the lid open and offered it to Nick. Except it was not white powder in the gold leaf well... it was a tight ball of notepaper.

Nick's eye twitched, but he dipped his finger in the snuffbox. "Only the finest, I assume?"

"Naturally. Stay alive, Hunt."

Nick swallowed. "As you wish, my lord."

"Good man." Lord Durham collected his hat, deposited several coins on the table, and limped away like an old cripple.

"AND DO YOU BELIEVE him, sir?" Nick doused their cooking fire with what was left of his coffee and got up to kick dirt over it. "I pulled out all the flocking on Black Bess's saddle, and the key to the code was written on the leather underneath. Just as Durham said."

"And?"

"He was correct that the message I carried was not what I thought it was. And the orders to the militia that he showed me looked dashed convincing. I know Richards' handwriting like it was my own, and it would be difficult for anyone to make such a fair copy."

Wesson was standing as if in a trance, his arms crossed, and his eyes fixed on the ground. "What do we do, sir?"

Nick tugged at his cravat and loosed the buttons of his coat. "Just what we have been. You gentlemen take your ease. Daniels shall have first watch."

"Where are you going, sir?" North asked.

Nick stopped just before ducking his head into his tent. "I'm going to get out of these clothes and go see a girl."

Chapter Twenty-Four

BESS PRESSED HER PALMS against the windowpane, her gaze fixed on the moonlit woods. It had been a discouraging sort of day, with no answers and no peace anywhere she turned. Papa was still brushing her off, and Captain Chesterfield's advances had rankled all afternoon. What she would give to see Nick's figure emerge from the shadows outside her window! It had been days since she'd seen him, and she ached with worry for his safety. But it seemed her only companion would be the velvety darkness of night.

And then, as if the moon answered her silent plea, a glimmer caught her eye. She gasped, her breath hitching in anticipation. There, amidst the inky blackness, she spotted him. Captain Hunt, a mere shadow among the trees, but for the white silk of his cravat catching the moon's glow.

He had come! He must have news. Perhaps it was over, and he was free at last! Bess grasped her skirts and peered into the hallway, to see if anyone was about. The common room was still occupied for the evening, but if she slipped into the lower hall, she could climb out the window in the room below, the one that Nick himself had used. It was rusty, and Bess jumped when it squeaked hideously as she pushed on the hinge. But it did give way, just enough for her to squeeze out.

As she slipped through the window, her dress rustling softly, a thrill coursed through her veins. The night air was cool against her flushed skin, and the leaves that blew across the courtyard crackled beneath her feet. But she almost didn't care if anyone heard her. Nick had seen her coming, and moved to a darker part of the wood surrounding the yard so they might meet in privacy. Her heart thumped as she darted around stacks of hay and litter that had not been cleaned away. She could hardly see a thing, but she did not need to see Nick now, to know how to find him.

And there he was, slipping from the cover of the trees to reach for her hands. "Bess," he murmured as he pulled her close. "I was wondering if you would see me. I didn't dare come closer."

She let him press a kiss to her temple, reveling in the tickle of his breath against her scalp. "I look for you every night."

Nick tightened his arms around her, caressing the back of her head and drinking in a deep sigh. "I wish I could always be here. Some day, I promise. You won't have to look for me."

"I'll take you at your word, Captain."

A chuckle rumbled in his chest, but he said nothing for a few moments—only held her, as if memorizing the sound of her heart beating against his. At length, his fingers strayed to her hair that brushed well past her waist, and he gently twined and tugged at the black waves as if they were a meditation for him. "You have the most glorious hair, you know," he whispered against her cheek. "I shall never forget the first time I saw it like this."

She drew back enough to nuzzle his chin with a laugh. "And when was that? Were you spying on me?"

"You do like to stand at your window at night." He tilted his head and swept a stray lock behind her ear, then kissed it into place. "Have you ever worn that ribbon I gave you?"

Bess shook her head. "I've been afraid someone would see me wearing it and ask questions that I didn't care to answer."

"Just wear it for me sometime. Braided into your hair, a crimson love knot against the black silk of your hair and your alabaster skin."

Bess touched the backs of her knuckles to his bristled cheek. "You are very poetic tonight, Captain."

He drank in a long breath and let his arms drop. "I suppose I am. I was just longing to see you. I know I shouldn't have, but after today... I couldn't stay away."

"Has something happened?"

He turned away for a moment, his jaw working. "I learned something today that... if it were known, it would topple some very powerful people. And knowing something like that can be dangerous."

She caught his sleeve. "Nick, what is it?"

He shook his head. "I can't endanger you, too, Bess. I shouldn't have come, but..." On a sudden impulse, he wrapped one arm around her waist and pulled her into an urgent embrace, with a kiss that spoke less of love and tenderness than of parting and sorrow. When his mouth broke from hers, his breath was ragged, and he was staring into her eyes.

"Stay close to the inn. Don't go to your roses and stay off the streets. And whatever you do, don't leave the inn at night again, not even if you think you see me." He cupped his hand to the side of her face and dragged a lock of her hair to his lips to drink in her perfume. "I will come for you, Bess, but promise me, you will stay safe."

"Nick, don't go," she pleaded. "Not yet."

He hesitated, his breathing gone quiet, then suddenly crushed her to him. "My bonny lass!" he whispered into her ear. "I can't stay."

"When will I see you again?"

His chest filled with a quaking breath. "I don't know. There's someone I need to reach, and I have to wait for him to make contact. He won't do that unless he is sure of me—that's why I've had to keep on with the 'robberies.' But 'tis a nasty business. I almost washed my hands of the whole affair today." He tangled his fingers in the hair and smiled down into her eyes. "I wish to heaven I could have."

"Why can't you?"

He let his hand drop. "It's got more complicated now, Bess. I'm not following orders anymore... well, not orders from Whitehall, anyway. There's someone else—someone above and outside the army, and he's got the kind of connections that even we spy-catchers only whisper about in rumors."

Bess's eyes widened. "Nick, what does that mean?"

He thinned his lips. "It means this will all be over soon, love. Very soon."

She studied his expression. There was something new there tonight—something she had not seen before. "You're worried," she accused softly.

He nodded. "But not for me. For my men. For you." He lifted one shoulder. "Even my family, because they'll soon be needing me like they never did before."

Bess slipped her fingers over his hand and turned up his palm to kiss his warm skin. "Come back to me, Nick. Promise me."

His smile did not touch his eyes, but he offered a small chuckle and inclined his head. "I promise, love. Kiss me once more, and I will watch you inside."

His lips were warm and gentle, and lacking the urgency of a few moments ago. It was like he was savoring her one last time, as if he could carry that kiss to the grave and beyond, if that were where he was bound. It struck a terror into Bess's heart, for she had never seen him this way. Resigned. Regretful. And resolute.

She wanted to ask for another kiss, and another after that, but he would not hear of it. Gently, he tugged her arms from around him and clasped them against his chest, holding her gaze.

"Promise me, Bess. Whatever happens, you will stay close to the inn."

She nodded. "I promise."

"Then go now, and don't look back."

THE LATE AFTERNOON SUN cast long shadows across the cobblestone courtyard of the inn, where the rhythmic sounds of horses being exercised and harnessed filled the air. Bess dipped her kitchen pail into the well—a thing she had done every day since girlhood. But today, it did not feel like such a rote task. After Nick's pleas last night that she would stay close to the inn, even the ten steps out her door to the well felt like a dangerous venture.

And also, there was Tim. He'd spotted her the moment she stepped outside, and had been loitering near the door, waiting for her to walk back in. Bess dallied as long as she could, pretending that her bucket had a leak or the knot on her rope was loose, but it was all too obvious that he meant to wait her out.

She'd been able to avoid him for days, but apparently, not today. Bess blew out a sigh and rolled her neck, then hefted her bucket to carry it back inside.

"Bess, I've been tryin' to talk to ye," Tim said as she approached.

"And I've not been listening. Don't bother," she tossed over her shoulder as she reached for the door handle.

His fist pounded into the door, blocking her from opening it, and he pushed his way in front of her. "Bess, why won't ye listen? I need to know why ye won't marry me."

Bess heaved in exasperation and lowered her bucket to put one hand on her hip. "You're in my way."

"Is that all ye have to say? I've asked ye to marry me, lass!"

She shrugged disinterestedly. "And I've been as polite as I can be. My mother taught me when I cannot be kind, I must simply be silent."

"Ye despise me?" Tim's voice dripped with sarcasm, his lips curling into a mocking smirk. "Careful with yer words, Bess. Ye may look like a goddess, but looks fade, and after all, ye're naught but a tavern wench."

She closed her eyes and loosed a long-suffering sigh. "So, I've been told."

"'Tis not every day a lass like ye receives an offer from a fine fellow like meself." He jabbed his thumb into his chest and jerked his head for emphasis. "I've got more put by than ye think, and I'd feather yer nest right fine."

"Tim, I've told you no. My heart has been spoken for, and nothing will change my mind. Now, leave me be and go tend to the stables for once."

Tim's face flushed, and he rapped on the door once more in anger. "Spoken for, ye say? Who's this lucky bloke ye fancy? That dandy from the village? Or perhaps ye're settled on some lord with more coin than sense?"

Bess's fists clenched around her bucket handle. Through gritted teeth, her voice trembled with all the suppressed frustration of the past weeks. "You know full well it's no one of the kind. And it's no one you can threaten or mock or even try to impress. He's above you, Tim."

His smirk faded. "Above me, ye say? What's this? Ye think yerself too good for me, don't ye? So, that be where ye go after dark. I see it—when the world sleeps, the lassie slips out to see her lover, is it? She's naught but a whore."

Bess felt the blood draining from her face and pooling somewhere in her stomach. "How dare you?" she whispered. Her breath came hot and fast; fury colored her vision and spiked her voice. "How *dare* you! You follow me and call me a whore? You're a blackguard and a whelp, you creeping spy!"

"Spy? Spy, she says!" Tim laughed, then his laughter crumbled into a wheezing cough. "I only look after what's mine by right."

Wrath took hold, and before she quite knew she had done it, Bess swung her bucket and doused him from head to toe. "Mongrel! You're a brute and a fiend, you lousy, lazy good-for-nothing monster!" Her voice quaked in rage. "I will *never* be yours, not if you live a thousand years! Don't you *ever* come near me again! I'll see to it that you're turned out by morning. You're nothing but a burden on this inn, and you believe you're entitled to *me*? Papa should have sacked you years ago! Don't know why he kept you on."

Tim shook the water off his coat, malice dancing in his blackened eyes. His voice turned colder, his words cutting through the air like a blade. "Don't ye? There be a deal what thee don't know about thy sire."

Bess's heart skipped a beat. "Leave me be, Tim," she hissed. "And don't ever speak to me again."

"Ye won't have me, ye say? Fine, then. The lassie says she don't want one such as I. Let her please herself, I say. But I'll see to it none other has *her*."

His final, ominous words hung in the air as he turned away, his brisk strides carrying him toward the stables. Bess stood there, her heart pounding, a mix of anger, confusion, and unanswered questions swirling within her.

"**H**ERE IT IS, LADS. The word we've been waiting for. And two days earlier than I anticipated."

Daniels's and Wesson's heads came up as Nick galloped back into the camp and swept off his mount. They were preparing powder wads and cleaning their weapons, while North had gone out to scout the present location of the militia. Daniels got to his feet. "What is it, Captain?"

Nick drew a red ribbon out of his pocket. "Recognize this?"

The men glanced at each other, then shook their heads. "Should we, sir?" Wesson asked.

"Probably not. This is the same stock that the old hag sold me a few weeks ago out of the ribbon shop in town. I was making my rounds earlier, and I found this tied to a tree limb, where it could not be missed. And look here." He slipped the ribbon through his fingers to point out an ink mark scrawled into the end. "*Demain.*"

"Tomorrow," Wesson translated. "What does it mean, though?"

"I suppose it means that I have an appointment at Buckland tomorrow night. After how that last 'robbery' came off, I am surprised the contact did not turn tail for the next available ship across the Channel."

"It could be a trap, sir," Daniels warned.

"It could be. But have we any choice?" Nick wound the ribbon around his fist, then shoved the loops back into his pocket. "We break camp tomorrow morning."

N ICK SWEPT A RAG over Black Bess's neck and shoulders, as his thoughts wandered many miles away. He should have written back to his father, that last time he was in London. He should have made his amends the best he could, before plunging back into the fray. What if he were shot during tomorrow's mission? His family would never even learn what had happened to him. And they would never have a chance to hear the name Bess Reynolds or know what she meant to him.

His hand had gone still, and his horse snorted and stamped her feet, as if reminding him of his duty. Nick shook himself and smiled. "There, there, you queen, behave yourself." He got back to work, scrubbing the dirt from her coat and making it shine once more. Her winter hair was starting to come in, thick and glossy, and another wave of nostalgia broke over him.

He'd been acting the highwayman for nearly two months. It had been two years since he'd last seen his home. And his men would be breaking ice in the streams for their cooking water before long. He heaved a sigh and crouched to clean his horse's feet. It wouldn't matter if they captured the French agents tomorrow, because there were always more lurking in the shadows. Always more to do. This bloody business would never be over.

"Captain? Is it safe?"

Nick dropped Bess's hoof and straightened. North was standing hesitantly by their cook fire, eying Black Bess as if he expected her to slither and snap his head off at any instant. He never had settled in his mind that the mare was not a she-devil sent straight from the pits of hell. Nick laughed softly to himself and walked away from the horse. "I'll come to you."

North offered him a steaming mug, and together they squatted by the fire. "I have an updated map of militia postings for you," North said.

Nick nodded. "Good. I'd like to give them a wide berth—particularly now."

"Chesterton and his men are near the Heath. But not all of them. I was not able to learn where the colonel has sent the rest, but I did *not* encounter them anywhere near Buckland."

"That will have to suffice," Nick mused.

They were silent some minutes, but North kept glancing up, then looking away. Nick set his mug down and braced his forearms on his knees. "Out with it, Lieutenant. What's on your mind?"

"I was just wondering, sir... Just curious, of course... You said you went to see that girl at the inn last night."

"I did."

"Ah. Yes. Sir, I was wondering—did she know anything? About anything? We need all the information we can get, and you said she was sharp."

Captain Hunt's gaze flickered to Lieutenant North before returning to the crackling fire. "That wasn't why I went to see her."

"Oh." North sipped from his mug. "Oh, I see."

"I'm not sure you do. I asked her to stay close to the inn and not put herself in harm's way. I don't want her endangered. She has already risked enough by helping us."

North straightened and gave him a peculiar look. "I thought you were just... amusing yourself. You sound rather serious."

Nick held his gaze, his words measured. "I mean to marry her. If I survive. And if I don't..." He heaved a sigh. "I wish I knew how to better protect her. She is vulnerable, and I have made her more so. I could never forgive myself if harm came to her that I did not prevent. But I don't have the luxury of being able to put my duty aside to protect her."

North grunted thoughtfully and sipped from his mug. Nick watched him for a moment—the flickering of North's jaw, the taut lines around his eyes as he stared at the fire. "You know something of it, don't you, North? The weight of duty, the fear of losing something—some*one* precious?"

Lieutenant North met his captain's gaze, his features tight with hidden emotions. "What makes you think that?"

"There's a heaviness in your eyes. I've watched you carry it since I first met you. Regrets, Lieutenant? Every man has them."

North's jaw clenched; his gaze hardened. "Some things are best left buried, Captain. The past can haunt a man more than any foe."

Nick studied him for a few seconds longer, then let go a sigh. "Aye, that's true. Well, then. Once more unto the breach, and all that nonsense. Are you ready?"

A flicker of relief passed over North's face, his mood visibly altered by talk of duty once more. "I am always ready, Captain. The maps are precise, our routes studied, and we know the militia's habits. I cannot imagine there is anything we have left undone, apart from the doing of it."

"You should earn a promotion after this assignment, North. You are too good to be stuck with a lieutenant's commission forever."

North grunted softly. "With all due respect, Captain, you're the one who deserves the promotion. Every success we have had these many months has been solely because of you."

"I appreciate your words, much as I vehemently disagree with the sentiment. But when this is over, I'm selling my commission. I'm tired, North. Ready to put down some roots."

North tossed a jaunty salute. "You would make an excellent farmer, sir."

"I am serious," Nick laughed. "I've turned it over in my head a deal of late. Should I be truly welcome there, I can think of nothing I would rather do, than to go back to my family's home and watch crops grow... and perhaps children, if I am so blessed."

North raised his brows. "Indeed, sir, I did not know you had considered it out so far." He fell silent for several seconds, and then began to nod slowly. "I pray it works out as you hope."

"And what about you, Lieutenant? Any plans for the future?"

Lieutenant North answered quickly, his tone brusque. "Just the next assignment. My only plan is to serve His Majesty, Captain. I would just like to know what that plan is."

"So would I." Nick grunted. "I'm still in the dark about much of what Durham wants me to do, assuming I'm able to get messages through to the French. I just have a rendezvous in case matters go sideways."

"Well, sir. Let us hope they do not. And with all due respect, you should be resting, to prepare for tomorrow. I have first watch."

Nick smiled thinly and gave a half-hearted salute. "Yes, 'sir.' Goodnight."

25

"We'll rendezvous *here*, after I pass on the message," Nick said, pointing at North's map. "And if the plan goes awry, we go *here*, to contact Durham. There's a cottage just south of Buckland—at least, that's what I am told."

"It's there, sir," North confirmed. "I've seen it. There's a gamekeeper and his wife who live there. Supposedly."

"Very well." Nick scanned the faces of his men. All three wore ragged dark cloaks over their uniforms tonight, with coffee grounds rubbed into their faces so they resembled common ruffians. But they could reveal themselves as His Majesty's finest in an instant, if necessary.

"If I should be compromised, you are not to attempt to recover me. I'm a highway-man—a criminal. You are His Majesty's soldiers, with orders to shoot to kill. Are we understood?"

"But sir!" Daniels protested. "I won't shoot my captain."

"You will if the French manage to capture me. I know too much, Sergent, and my own name with a sketch of my likeness is probably already circulating among the militia. It is no stretch to imagine our enemies might also suspect something, and stronger men than I have been tortured into betraying their country. I prefer the mercy of a bullet."

"But that won't happen," North argued. "This is just a short drop, just enough to be sure that we have rounded up that 'monk,' then we'll have him surrounded and captured in a twinkling."

"No. We let him go."

North's teeth clenched and for the first time, he looked as if he might defy his orders. "But Captain! Did not Durham order you to cut the snake in twain?"

"He also ordered me to see that the false message got through. They're using Richards' treachery to their advantage. Our orders are to follow the messenger if we can, learn who he is, and capture him once he passes it off. Keep your distance. Secrecy and the success of the mission is more important than capturing one French spy."

The lieutenant growled under his breath, then saluted. "Yes, sir."

"Right. Take your positions, so you will be well secreted before our jolly monk arrives."

The men dispersed, each in their separate directions. Nick himself would be some two hours behind them, and his arrival would be in keeping with his previous exploits. Velvet coat, laced silk, buttercream breeches, the whole costume.

He took exceptional care in dressing this one last time. *Hopefully,* the last. His boots were polished to a mirror shine, and the moonlight bounced off his sword hilt like the beam from a lantern. Black Bess stood quivering at the ready, and when Nick at last swung into the saddle and swept the folds of his coat over her back, she snorted and half-reared in eagerness.

His path to Buckland tonight was already planned out, as were those of his men. North had been meticulous... and perhaps a touch sentimental in mapping Nick's route, for the five-mile ride took him within a stone's throw of the Bittern. And Bess.

He should stay away. He'd already warned Bess that it was too dangerous for them to be seen together, and he would only frighten her if he turned up without warning. But if his instinct this evening was right—and it nearly always was—he might never see her again. To not steal one last look at her bonny sweet face through the candlelight window... that was too much. And according to North, the militia were three miles away from the Bittern this night.

It was past midnight when he edged up to the clearing surrounding the inn. He had approached from the southeast, where the stables lay on the edge of the courtyard. A breeze whispered through the bare branches, making them creak and groan like the ribs of a ship settling on the waves. Green eyes flashed across the courtyard from a prowling cat, and an owl trilled softly somewhere to the east. But not another soul seemed to be about. Even the horses in their stables had quieted down for the night.

Nick drew behind the veil of the trees to circle the courtyard until he marked the place where Bess's roses grew amid the thorny oaks. Her light footpath, leading straight back to the inn door, drew his eyes inward. All the doors would be barred for the night, and the windows were shuttered and dark—even hers. The only light was the moon's reflection on an uncovered windowpane.

That was as it should be, he consoled himself. Sharp as was his longing to look on her face, nothing of good could come from her watching till sleepless dawn. Let her rest, knowing and fearing nothing until it was over.

But was that…? He drew rein and stepped his horse around for a better angle. And there it was again—a flicker of a candle, glowing through the cracks in Bess's shutters. She was awake, after all.

Longing overpowered his good sense, and he nudged his horse forward. Her hooves rang gently on the cobblestones, and he tensed, certain that someone would hear him. But when no dogs barked at his arrival and no windows flung open, he drew an easier breath.

Nick stopped below her window and paused, just long enough to be sure that *was* the flickering of a candle he'd seen between the slats. He slipped his riding whip from his boot and tapped it gently on the shutter, hoping she alone would hear the sound and understand its meaning. Seconds ticked by, but there was nothing. He probably sounded no different to the wind itself, creaking the shutter on its hinges.

He glanced around, assuring himself that the courtyard was still empty, then cupped his hand to his mouth and whistled the call of a nightingale—a song that an alert person might recognize from the spring of the year, not a windy autumn night.

There was a pause, then he heard the window being unlocked, and a slender hand pushed the shutter aside. He saw only her profile as she searched the trees, her fingers absently twined in her hair at the base of her ear.

"Bess," he whispered.

She started with a gasp and drew close enough to the window for him to see the fullness of her face in the moonlight. "Nick! What are you doing here?"

"I had to see you." He sat back in his saddle, merely drinking her in. It was no simple bedtime plait she'd been twisting into her hair, but an elaborate lover's knot, just as he had begged one day to see—with that rich red ribbon writhing through the thick rosette of her black hair. "Ah, my lass, but you're a sight to rob a man's very soul! How fine it looks against your fair cheek."

She smiled bashfully and took up her candle, then turned her face to let him see it better. "I couldn't sleep. All I could think about was you, and where you might be—if you were safe. Mayhap I even conjured you with this bewitched bit of ribbon."

He shook his head. "Nay, for you need naught but your own sweet voice for that."

Bess set her candle aside and leaned through the casement to stretch her hand to him, the tips of her fingers only just brushing his when he stood in his irons. "I thought you had to stay away."

"And I disobey even my own orders! Aye, I know it, but I had to have one last glimpse of your window. I never expected to see a light through the shutters at this hour. But I am going now. Tonight is the prize—the end, I hope."

"Then it will be over?

"One way or another," he murmured. "Yes, I think tonight shall finish it."

"Promise me, Nick," Bess implored, "Promise me you'll return. Promise that you belong to me, and I to you—they cannot take you from me!"

He shook his head, his gaze still transfixed by her form in the pale warmth of her candle. "Never. Even should a bullet claim me, my spirit will be ever yours."

"Do not say such things! You'll put a curse on yourself."

"Impossible! I swear on my honor, Bess, that I shall return to you. I'll come this very night, if I can, or tomorrow at dawn—all polished and respectable once more in my own uniform to ask for your hand. But..."

"What is it?"

He set his jaw. "It may be more complicated than that. I've been betrayed, and setting matters right might take more than a simple word of explanation. I may not be able to show my face for some days yet."

"But you'll find some way to let me know you're safe, will you not? Have one of your men leave a note for me by the roses. I can go there in the afternoon—"

"No." He shook his head. "I'll not have you venturing to the woods looking for me until I know you'll be safe. I'll come to you in secret, just as I am now. Watch for me by moonlight—you'll see me coming up that road, over the hill. Or keep your shutters closed and listen for the nightingale. I *will* come, my brave one."

She swallowed, sniffing and blinking back tears. "I don't feel very brave."

He shook his head with a low laugh. "Do you not know, Bess? You are the one who gives me courage. You with your saucy tongue and that daring stubbornness about you that makes strong men go weak in the knees. Can you bear up just a little longer?"

Bess dashed a hand across her cheek, then nodded with a fractured smile. "As I must! I'll wait for you, my love. No matter how late it may be—all night if I must—I'll be watching the road to the west."

Nick stood again in his stirrups, aching to graze his gloved hand against her cheek, to caress away a second tear that had followed the first. But he knew the distance would be too great, so he would have to content himself with one more brush of her fingertips. "Would that I could kiss you once before I go!" He sank back down with a broken sigh, reaching for his rein.

"Wait," Bess pleaded. Her fingers ripped into the plait at her ear, tugging free the ribbon and loosing a cascade of sweet glory to spin and tumble out the window. She leaned as far as she could through the casement, and the shimmering lengths of ebony fell over his shoulders, cloaking his chest, and drowning his face in the scent of rosewater perfume.

"Oh, Bess," he groaned, as he gathered and twined her hair through reverent fingers and brought it to his lips. It was like flame licking his bare flesh, the tender agony of losing himself in her—just for a moment. To each curl and ringlet, he pledged his devotion, and his lips memorized the honeyed spice of those rich waves. But all too soon, he had to let those satin tresses slip from his fingers.

"Watch for me, love." he said. She nodded, and her hair drifted from his shoulders as he tugged his rein and turned to the west.

WITH A FINAL, LINGERING look, Nick had turned his horse, the black nightmare carrying him away from the inn and into the frosty night. What waited for him, out there in the silvery darkness? Bess leaned out her window, gazing after his galloping figure until he was out of sight—a hand cupped over her mouth to stifle a sob of fear and excruciating pride. Her Nick would do his duty, and, God willing, would ride back for her with the look of triumph fresh upon him, his hand outstretched for her alone.

But if he did not...

No! She refused even to consider that. Nick *would* return. He simply must! Bess sniffed back the terror that kept clawing at her mind, the icy fingers of doubt and dread that battled with hope. Nothing would stop Nick from coming, so long as she herself kept faith.

Bess reached to pull in the shutters, but a movement across the courtyard caught her eye. Probably a cat, or that infernal rooster, somehow escaped from his coop. She leaned out to see better, and terror stabbed her heart when Tim's accusing glare met her.

He was hiding nothing, but staring freely, his lip curled in disgust. He seemed to *want* her to look on him, for his stare locked with hers for several torturous seconds. And he was laughing. Then, he tugged his cloak over his shoulders, drew a ragged hood over his face, and ambled off, into the woods.

Bess yanked the shutters closed and locked her window with trembling hands. What could he mean by glowering at her like that? And that dreadful laugh, as if he held some power over her at last! Had he seen Nick? He could not possibly have missed him, but... had he seen Nick's face? What did he know?

She scrambled into her bed and tugged the coverlet up to her chin, as if it could ward away the image of that wicked ostler, leering at her in the moonlight. Well, what matter if Tim had seen Nick, or knew who he was? There was nothing one such as Tim could do to harm someone so brave and resourceful as Nick. Surely.

Bess rolled to her side and crushed her pillow to her cheek. She would not sleep this night, but at least she could smother her fears until dawn.

NICK'S HEART THUNDERED IN his chest as he approached the river. His men would be in position by now, but those positions were each nearly a quarter mile away—near enough to discretely follow anyone splitting away from the brook, but not close enough to ride in to his rescue, should this prove to be a trap. Not even close enough to warn him, for that matter.

His horse snorted as the soft loam of the forest floor gave way to the gravel of the riverbed under her hooves. Concealment was impossible now. Anyone within two hundred yards would have heard the ring of iron shoes against stone. But he wasn't dressed like a dandy so he could be concealed. He meant to be noticed. A shiver crawled up his spine, and he fingered the encoded note. A few minutes more, and he could whirl his horse about and be away.

Where was this cursed "monk" tonight? Nick squinted into the darkness, waiting for the sound of footsteps, or the movement of a shadow. But no such figure emerged. Nick hung by the brush at the edge of the stream, unwilling to commit himself to the open until he knew his contact had arrived. But for over a quarter of an hour, all he heard was the babbling of the brook and the occasional hoot of an owl through the trees. Black Bess shifted beneath him, her hooves stirring the wet, rocky bed, and her ears spinning with the wind—listening for something and hearing nothing. Nick growled a silent curse and glanced at the angle of the moon overhead. Where *was* the blackguard?

And then, he heard a boot, splashing in the stream, and a muffled oath. Nick stiffened in the saddle, his eyes sharpening on the stream. The voice had not sounded like the cackle of the old vulture he'd seen before.

His hand tightened on the rein, his senses straining. But before he could make a decision, several figures materialized from the darkness—redcoats closing in with a rush and cries for his head.

There would be no meeting with the French spy tonight. *Bah!* For all he knew, the spy might have been the one to tip off the redcoats! A fine way of neutralizing him. Someone must have blown his cover, but it didn't matter now. The ambush had been sprung, and he was the quarry.

Panic seized his chest, but he fought to regain his composure. Doubtless he knew the terrain better than they, and he was mounted on Fury herself. They couldn't catch him. Not unless their numbers were treble what they appeared to be. He yanked his pistol from his belt and fired a shot in the air, even as he wheeled Black Bess for flight.

"Surround him, you dogs! Leave no escape!" Chesterfield's voice bellowed.

Chesterfield! But he was supposed to be miles away! Nick's mind raced, calculating his chances. He had to get away, without endangering any of the soldiers' lives. With a burst of adrenaline, he dug his heels into his horse's sides, demanding everything she could give him. The chase was on.

The forest seemed to close in around him, trees becoming an intricate maze of shadows. Bullets whizzed past, the deadly hiss of metal slicing the night air. He leaned low over his horse's neck, the icy wind searing at his face and stealing the very air from his lungs. He glanced back, only once. The redcoats had multiplied, and the leaders were going to their whips on fleet, long-legged monsters that gave even Black Bess a hard race.

"Go, Bess!" Nick needed neither whip nor spur. Black Bess stretched out her neck and flattened along the frosty earth until she was gliding like a falcon.

The redcoats thundered behind him through the dense forest, the dark trees blurring into a frenzied haze. The pounding of their hooves reverberated in his ears, matching the galloping of his heart. But Nick's feints through the brush had lent him an edge. The soldiers were starting to lose ground now, and each stride brought him closer to freedom, closer to eluding his pursuers.

"Shoot him down!" Chesterfield raged at his men. "Don't let that vermin escape!"

Nick risked one more glance to gauge the distance. They were in a wash now, with fewer twists and turns to lose the pursuers in. Redcoats were closing in once more, their figures illuminated by shards of moonlight filtering through the leaves. More than still within firing range—he could almost feel the steam from their horses' nostrils at his back.

His mind raced, scanning the terrain ahead. He needed a way out, a path that would lead him to safety. His fingers tightened around the reins, and he made a split-second decision. With a powerful tug, he steered his horse over a rocky ledge, Black Bess's muscles coiling beneath him as she leaped over fallen logs and bounded through thick underbrush.

The redcoats struggled to keep pace, caught off guard by his sudden change of direction. The undergrowth clawed at Nick's clothes, the branches whipping past like accusing fingers. His chest burned, his breaths ragged and desperate.

Sweat trickled down his brow, under his mask, but it chilled by the time it reached his jaw. Even the sweat upon his horse's neck was condensing to white frost in the pale moon. He couldn't ask her to keep up this pace much longer. But their feint had worked, and the redcoats were falling farther behind with every passing second. A few minutes more, and Nick pulled his horse under the shadow of a fallen oak, its great uprooted anchors spanning behind them like a bulwark. He forced his breathing to still, just long enough to be sure that their shouts were carrying them in the wrong direction.

Nick waited another ten minutes before emerging from his shelter. The rendezvous in the neighboring town awaited, and he could only hope his men had already arrived. He rode on through the night, horse and man both quaking in exhaustion, until a welcoming sight came into view—the safe house. Nick reined in his horse, slowing to a halt, and swinging numbly down from the saddle.

Lord Durham was there at once, catching his bridle and expertly feeling down Black Bess's neck and legs for injury. "What happened, Hunt? North says there was an ambush."

Nick nodded, leaning on Black Bess for support. "My men?"

"They stopped long enough to give their report, then North led them back toward Buckland to try to distract the redcoats. Did they make you out?"

Nick's breathing was still short and gasping. "I don't know, but they were waiting for me, blast it! Someone betrayed us. That monk—it had to be him! Or the old hag... *Someone* told the redcoats where I would be."

Durham's eyes narrowed, his voice sharp. "The message! Did the message get through?"

Nick rested a hand on his saddle and shook his head. "No."

Durham hissed under his breath. "And you are compromised. Richards will know by now that we are on his trail. We *must* see that *his* message, at least, is intercepted, or Wellington is exposed."

"But how? We don't even know who he would use to carry such a message."

"Adelaide does."

Nick sucked in a stabbing breath and instantly held a hand to one of his ribs. Was that a bullet wound? Had he been hit, after all, and failed to notice? But it was not the blood of a bullet wound that clung to his fingers when he pulled them away. It was shards of bark. He must have crashed against a tree branch hard enough to crack his rib.

"Are you well, Hunt?"

He swallowed and nodded. "Perfectly, sir. You said that Adelaide knew something?"

"Aye," Durham agreed darkly. "However, I had not intended to risk her. We have already pressed too hard there—I do not like her chances. But I've no choice now." Durham turned with a heavy sigh and braced his hand on the door frame.

"I'll see to her protection."

His lordship turned back. "You're barely standing, Hunt."

"I just need to catch my breath. I was the one who failed, sir. And I'm expendable."

"No, you're angry, and angry men are not wise. Offended that Richards played you for the fool for so long, are you?"

Nick's jaw clenched. "Nevertheless, the thing needs doing, and I'll do it. One way or another."

Chapter Twenty-Five

D AWN CREPT OVER THE horizon like a thief, defying Bess's searching gaze out the westerly window. How dare the pale sun slip over the inn before Nick returned? But there it was—day had come, and he had not.

And now he would not return to her until night fell again; he had said he could not, so she must survive the day, praying against the unseen and unknown until he could ride back to her. Her heart climbed farther into her throat with each hour that passed, and her usual practiced charm was flat and useless today.

By evening, she was a knot of worry and restlessness, more often isolated by her own thoughts than aware of her surroundings. She moved in a fog about the dining room, serving ale to anyone who asked, and to several who did not. But her hands trembled, often sloshing the drinks over the rims of mugs and tables.

One annoyed customer, who had been twice on the receiving end of her clumsiness, grabbed her by the elbow and nearly spilled the rest of the ale pot over his own arm. "Watch where you're going, you sloppy girl! I meant to drink it, not wear it."

Bess jerked away. "I'll thank you to keep your hands to yourself, or I'll do much more than—"

"Bess!" Her father's voice cut through the room. "That's enough."

She snatched a glare of betrayal at her father. "So, I'm to let this bloke rough me up?"

Her father pointed back toward the kitchens. "Leave off. *Now.* Go get the washing in before it rains."

He... he would not stand up for her? Papa had never reprimanded her before a customer! The man was smirking at her in contempt, too—reveling in her apparent fall from grace. Bess fought back tears of humiliation as she retreated to the kitchen with her empty pot.

But the door did not close behind her to block out prying eyes, for her father was close on her heels, his face red with anger. He bolted the door behind himself and whirled upon her.

"Now, what's this?" he snapped. "You're lollygaggin', spillin' drinks, mooning about like some witless daisy. Tell me it's not that Cumberland chap what's got you all a'dither."

"Papa, I wish you would give him a chance," Bess pleaded. "He's a good man."

"You're blinded by your foolish infatuation, Bess. That man is a cad and a bounder. You have no business involving yourself with him!"

Bess's eyes welled up with tears. "But he isn't! What do you think you know of Nick that makes you hate him so?"

Her father's eyes narrowed. "'Nick,' is it? You know him by name, do you, lass?"

"I know more than his name, Papa. I wish you'd let me tell you."

"Aye, I know enough on him. He'll bring naught but harm to such as you."

She took a deep breath, her voice shaking. "You don't understand, Papa. He's not who you think."

"You speak as if you know him better than anyone. Do you not think other lasses have fallen for the same yarn? What can you really know about this man?"

"I know that he loves me. And I'll have no other, Papa. Have I ever been swayed by pretty words from a fool? Why can't you trust my judgment when I do fancy someone?"

"Because your own mother was fooled! How should I expect you to be any better?"

Bess's breath left her in a horrified gasp. "My mother? What does Mama have to do with this?"

But her father heeded her not. He dropped his face into his palms, his body quaking bitterly. "I tried. I tried to do right by you, but ruin came for you, all the same. One day, you'll thank me, lass. I had to do it."

Bess's eyes widened with confusion and fear. "What do you mean, Papa? What have you done?"

"I went to Captain Chesterfield with the militia," he confessed, his voice filled with guilt. "I had suspicions about this young Cumberland. He seemed fair enough, and I thought he'd move on, but then those robberies on the highway... I dismissed it as a coincidence until I heard about those. He's a dead ringer for old Cumberland, what once terrorized those roads."

Bess's breath caught in her throat, her voice barely a whisper. "You think... Nick is the son of that man?"

"He's a villain and a rogue, just as his sire was. I wanted to protect you, Bess. That's all I ever wanted."

"But you went to Chesterfield! Papa, don't you understand, Nick will be killed! He's not who you think, Papa. He's not Cumberland at all!"

Her father checked himself. "What's that?"

Tears streamed down Bess's face as reached for her father's hand. "He's an officer in the Regulars, assigned to track spies, and his name is Captain Nicholas Hunt. He's only carrying on as Cumberland because the old thief was involved with French spies. Nick shot him, Papa, and now he's trying to track down Cumberland's allies. He is working almost directly for His Majesty. And you have set the militia after him!"

"Cumberland shot?" Her father's brow creased in astonishment. "Nay, I don't believe it. He's loaded you with a lie, that's sure."

"He hasn't, Papa. How many rascals come in here trying to pinch me and make me smile for them? Don't I know when a man's lying to my face?"

Her father sighed, nodded reluctantly, and sagged deeper into his chair. "Bessie, lass, you're sure?"

She sniffed. "I've seen him in his uniform. I've even seen his orders myself. They had an official seal from the war office."

"Good heavens." Her father mopped his forehead and scrubbed his face. "Dear God, what have I done?"

She reached out, embracing her father. "Oh, Papa," she sobbed, clinging to him. "You did what you thought was right, but you don't understand. Nick... Captain Hunt... he's not what you fear. He's a good man, Papa. Isn't there some way to call off Captain Chesterfield?"

He shook his head numbly. "It's too late. He'll already have his men out on the highways, and he'll know the man with or without his mask." Her father's voice cracked with emotion. "I'm so sorry. I did it to protect you, Bess," he said, his eyes welling up with tears. "I couldn't bear the thought of losing you, of seeing you hurt. And me never havin' told you the truth and all..."

Bess's breath caught in her throat. "The truth? What truth?"

Her father's voice was barely a whisper. "The truth? Cumberland, the highwayman of old... it was he what gave your mother that rose bush she kept in the wood."

"I don't... I don't understand, Papa. Does that mean...?"

He closed his eyes, his agony raw in the lines of his face. "It means that you and Samuel are not mine."

She tried to gulp for air, but none would come. Stars danced in the blackness of her vision, and her heart felt as if it might burst. "But of course, we are! I have your nose, you always said, and Samuel has your ears, and..."

"Mere coincidences." He smiled weakly. "I never thought of you as anything but my own, you know. It eased your poor mother's heart, because after almost dying giving birth to both of you, she could never have another child. We were content, and that was all that mattered."

Bess shook her head in denial. "No, no, I cannot believe it. Mama was always so proper, so modest. Yes, she teased the customers for tips, but she was never indecent. You know how she disapproved of Hattie and Millie. Why, she would have dismissed them if they were not so popular with the gents. She would never have fallen with child!"

"She was proper and modest because she was brought up the daughter of a country squire," her father insisted. "She disapproved of the other girls because she knew what awaited them. And she was right, was she not? We haven't seen Millie in over six months."

Bess caught her lips between her teeth and bit down until she could taste copper. "How did it happen, then?"

"Bessie, there are some things a man... cannot abide hearing. Not when it concerns the woman he loves. I only bless the day that her father's solicitor came to me with his offer. It was business, at the time. Her settlement built a new stable yard and finished the western wing of the inn, and I gained a help meet to run the place."

Bess' throat constricted and her voice was brittle when she spoke. "He bartered away his own daughter?"

"Many fathers would not have done so much. At least he saw her cared for, and if you can believe it, he even permitted her the choice of whom to marry." A wistful smile touched his lips. "I had met her once before, you know. She ended up here after the cad abandoned her. I helped her... she remembered."

The world spun around her, the revelation hitting her with a force she couldn't comprehend. The ground beneath her feet felt unsteady as her father's words sank in. "You're not my real father?" she whispered, her voice filled with a mix of confusion and pain.

Her father reached out, his hands trembling as he gently cupped her face. "I loved your mother, Bess. And I loved you and Samuel. I married her to protect her—to give you a name, a home. I thought I could shield you from the truth, but it seems I've only made things worse. Is this... Captain Hunt... is he really the man you claim he is?"

She nodded, dashing a tear from her cheek. "He is good, Papa. The very kindest and best man I know."

"Then I've done wrong," he breathed. He stared blankly at the wall. "Bessie, my Bessie, can you ever forgive me?"

She sniffed and clasped her father's hands. "Papa, Nick is brave and clever. He knows how to keep safe, so we must believe that he will be well until the truth can be in the open. We'll see Nick tonight, sure as I'm sitting here, and Chesterfield and his redcoats will still be miles off his scent."

Her father smiled weakly. "You're sure?"

Bess opened her mouth to declare it a certainty, but just then, a thunderous knock reverberated through the inn. The sound of marching boots echoed outside the door, their ominous rhythm sending shivers down their spines.

"Open up, in the name of His Majesty!"

Bess's legs quaked inside her skirts, but she stiffened her spine and stared back at Captain Chesterfield and his men. "What's this, then, Captain? You come all a'blazing as if we were a band of outlaws. Whoever you're looking for is not here."

Chesterfield gestured, and one of his men grabbed Bess by the elbows, pinched them together behind her back, and shoved her forward to face the captain. He removed his gloves, his eyes never leaving Bess's face. "Miss Reynolds. This will be much simpler if you drop the offended princess act, and simply tell us what you know about the highwayman."

Her father, red-faced and sputtering in anger, collided through the barricade of redcoats surrounding Bess. "I tell you, she knows nothing! Leave my daughter be!"

But his pleas were ignored, for one of the soldiers pushed him down hard enough to knock him off his feet. Bess cried out and tried to twist free, to help her father to stand, but the soldier at her back wrenched her arms almost from their sockets and jerked her upright again.

She refused to whimper, though bolts of agony from the cruel way her arms were yanked almost dropped her to her knees.

"She'll fight like a wildcat," Chesterfield said. "No sense in letting her harm herself more. Tie her hands behind her back."

"No!" her father shouted, lurching back to his feet. "Chesterfield, have I not cooperated with everything you could have asked? You won't lay a hand on my daughter!"

Chesterfield's eyes flashed with rage, and he drew his pistol, aiming it at her father. "Silence, innkeeper! You've sheltered that outlaw under your very roof, and knowingly, too. You'll be wise to keep quiet if you wish to see another day."

"He didn't know!" Bess blurted. "Please, leave him be!"

Chesterfield rounded on her, his pistol coming to rest just under her chin. "We will see about what he knows. Right now, it's what *you* know that interests me. And *who* you know."

Rough hands were binding her wrists with ropes now, and Bess reeled, twisting her hands behind her, and stomping on the redcoat's boots in a last bid for freedom. "I don't know *what* you're talking about!" she snarled.

"Don't you?" Chesterfield snapped his pistol up to his shoulder with a sneer. "Oh, faithless wretch, thy name is woman. Ostler! Come in here."

Bess's stomach curdled, and she jerked her head around to lock eyes with her father. He was pale, his head shaking vaguely. "Can't be," he whispered.

But the inn door swung open then, just wide enough for a figure to creep through. And Bess's world tilted upside down when Tim's withering gaze met hers.

"*You!*" she spat, her voice filled with venom. "You betrayed us!"

"I says, do I not, that the lassie's bound for naught but meself."

Molten outrage flared in her breast. She would see Tim hang by his innards! "Captain Chesterfield, you'd listen to the lies of a drunken boor? He's naught but a dog what bites the hand that feeds him. You're on the wrong trail!"

The captain rushed upon her, his face only inches from hers. "And what trail *should* I be on? Hmm? Shall I show you my orders and see what you make of them? Perhaps you know where our friend is to be found?"

Bess's nostrils flared, and she set her teeth. "I won't tell you anything." she hissed.

Chesterfield's eyes narrowed. "How sad. But happily for me, I don't need you to tell me anything. Corporal, take her up to her room. We'll just let her keep watch, shall we?"

"No!" her father cried, trying to leap over the man restraining him. "Take me! Leave my daughter—" But his protests were cut short when the soldier shot his elbow into the innkeeper's face.

"Papa!" Bess watched in horror as her father toppled backward, blood gushing from his nose. Was he unconscious? Dead? She was too numb to even struggle against their grip. It wouldn't have mattered, anyway. There was a soldier at each of her elbows, dragging her to the stair with her feet barely supporting her weight.

They never had to ask—they knew which room was hers. And once inside, they wasted no time about searching it, for anything they could find to incriminate her, or to amuse themselves.

"Look, sir!" One of the men held up her scarlet ribbon. "It's as the ostler said."

"Aye, and look here!" crowed another, as he tugged Bess's hidden money box from beneath her bed.

Chesterfield rounded on her, his lips pulled into a smirk. "All this time, we thought her a respectable lass, but she's been entertaining all comers. Lads, we were fooled!"

Bess surged forward until the soldier at her elbows jerked her back. "You'll take that back, you mongrel!"

"And a wicked tongue on that one. Gag her and be sure the knots are fast." Chesterfield stepped toward her and drew a finger down her cheek, even as she tossed her head and tried to spit on him. He only chuckled and whispered low in her ear. "We cannot have that mouth of yours warning Captain Hunt, now, can we?"

Hunt! So, Chesterfield *knew* it was Nick, and he still meant to capture him as a criminal? "You're wrong about everything!" she raged, jerking and scrambling against the soldiers holding her. "There's a plain answer, but you won't hear it, you arrogant, w—"

They shoved the gag in her mouth—a wad of soiled handkerchiefs and a neckcloth that reeked of sweat. Bess's jaw was pried open with the force of the knot, and tears poured involuntarily from her eyes. The only sound she could make at all was a garbled moan, and her throat tried to rebel with useless heaves until she buckled to her knees.

"There, that's better. But keep a watch on her! No—better still, tie her to the bedpost so she can make no trouble. And someone, go fetch us some ale! We've a long night ahead."

There was nothing she could do. They dragged her to the post of her bed and began to make her fast, but Chesterfield stopped them.

"No, not that post. Over here, so she can watch out the window."

Bess was jerked to the other side of her bed, and one of the soldiers produced a long rope. They lashed her tight, from her neck to her feet, with the bed post pressing sharply into her shoulders and a musket bound beneath her breast, forcing her to stand at attention.

Tears slipped freely down her cheek, and she was gasping, seething around the gag. Mangled protests were all she could manage—nothing intelligible or useful. She felt as if the force of her rage and indignation must tear her apart, or at least give the soldiers pause enough to consider the monstrosity of their actions.

But they only laughed. Rough hands made free with her body, strange mouths pressed against her gag, fingers pointed mockery and shame at her until her lungs racked with sobs.

"That's enough," Chesterfield declared after one of the soldiers arrived with a cask of ale under his arm. "Set watches at each window."

He came to Bess himself, then, his breath laden with ale stolen from her father's cellar, and leaned down to kiss her neck. Nay, it was more than a kiss. He was drinking of her, dragging his mouth over her skin, and savoring the taste of her as if she were a flagon of wine.

Bess shuddered at the feel of his lips, claiming liberties that were not his to take. She would have kicked him, shredded him with her tongue or her fingernails, but she was too helpless to do more than moan in rage.

Chesterfield chuckled and brushed a tear from her cheek with the back of his knuckle. "Fear not, lass. I'm sure this will be over soon enough, and then we shall have some real sport. Keep good watch, now. You will not want to miss this."

She was trembling, her throat quivering with outraged tears. They were going to kill Nick, and they meant to force her to watch.

And she could not even warn him.

Chapter Twenty-Six

NICK MAINTAINED A DISCREET distance, a phantom shadow stalking the night, as Adelaide's carriage trundled through the deserted streets. If he was seen tailing the coach, the game was up. But if he was too far away to save her if matters went awry, the entire mission was in jeopardy.

The carriage halted, its wheels grinding against the cobblestones, outside the cottage of a washerwoman. Nick pulled his horse back behind a building, his senses straining to pick up every sound. The flickering lamplight cast eerie shadows, playing tricks on his eyes, so he closed them and relied on his ears.

Adelaide exchanged words with someone who came to the window, then all was silent for some minutes. Another voice was now at the door—a lower voice, bidding her leave her driver outside and come alone. Nick heard her speaking to Duncan, then her carriage opened and her shadow filled the frame of the cottage door for the briefest flash.

Nick leaned a little around the corner, but he was unable to see the face of the one who summoned her. All he caught were snippets of their conversation—fragments of words carried on the faintest whispers of the wind. And then the cottage door was closed, and he heard no more.

Minutes vanished... a quarter of an hour. What was she doing in there? Nick did not want to imagine how a woman could have come to such employment. Imagine Bess, his own sweet love, saving her country and the people she cared for, but betraying her own body and soul? *But that would not come to pass,* he comforted himself. Bess would spared from such ethical quandaries.

And Adelaide was not Bess. She was seasoned, well-trained, and from what he could see of her, she was skilled at her craft. Her objective had been to somehow relieve the operative of the secret missive from Richards—the one that could betray Wellington if it got out of England. Even better if she could plant another message in its place—but Durham had not specified the means. All he said was that the Crown could not be implicated. No uniforms, no rules.

Nick tugged down his mask, cursing the stupid thing in the same breath with which he gave thanks for it. When this was over, the last thing he wanted was to have his name and reputation attached to this affair. Even Black Bess seemed insulted by lurking in the shadows outside. Her ears turned down flat, and her nostrils wrinkled in annoyance. She didn't even seem inclined to paw or snort with her usual impatience.

The tension in the air grew palpable, a wire pulled taut, as the sound of shattering glass erupted from within the house. Nick vaulted from his horse, the seconds ticking by as he sprinted to the cottage door. The driver, Duncan was already there, slamming his shoulder into the barred door and shouting, "Milady!" At Nick's arrival, he held back just long enough for them to join their efforts.

It took three hard hits before they breached the threshold, and Nick's heart was slamming into his ribcage when they at last tumbled into the room. Adelaide could be dead already, or carried off where she might be tortured, made to talk. But as Nick lifted his head and picked himself up off the floor, he heard a woman's scream from the next room, followed by a crash and a curse. Nick was on his feet before the old Scot, and he flew through the door of the second room as if it were cheesecloth.

Adelaide was on her back, her face bloodied and her bodice torn, kicking desperately at a man who sat on her stomach, his hands squeezing her neck. Another man had her arms pinned over her head, with a pistol stuck at his belt. Adelaide's eyes were beginning to glaze, and her cries for help gasped to nothing in her throat.

Nick dove into the fray first, kicking the armed man in the teeth, and ploughing through him until he was wrestling him backward. Duncan followed with a bellow of rage, and from the corner of his eye, Nick saw the flash of a Scottish dirk. But Duncan was not falling on a helpless foe, any more than Nick was. Fists collided with bone, no one gaining the upper hand for some minutes.

Nick's adversary was a brute of a man who smelled of sweat and raw fish, with a fist the size of a dinner plate. That fist hammered into Nick's jaw, then descended like a mallet into his gut, and finally crashed into his already wounded ribs. Each punch threatened to drown Nick in pain and darkness, but he gritted his teeth, and the metallic taste of blood, more than anything, kept him alert. Until he got one hand around Nick's throat and threw him up against the wall.

As the assailant tried to gain the upper hand, pinning Nick with his thick arms, a glimmer of steel caught Nick's eye—the man's pistol, momentarily forgotten in the heat of the brawl. A haze darkened his eyes—it was now or never. Nick made a desperate lunge and surprised even himself when he managed to grasp the pistol's handle, even as the world dimmed. With a heart pounding louder than any gunshot, Nick fired at point-blank range. The giant's grip loosened, his body going slack, and he crashed backward.

The silence that followed was punctuated only by the steady dripping of blood onto the wooden floor.

Nick stashed the pistol in his own belt and straightened, surveying the wreckage of the room. Duncan had subdued his opponent and was at his lady's side, trying to help her to sit up, but the air had been knocked from her lungs and all her desperate heaving for breath was in vain.

"Put her arms up," Nick commanded. "Open her airways."

He was striding quickly to her side to help, but a shriek pierced his ear behind him, and a figure leaped onto his back and began tearing at his throat, his mouth, his mask. "'E's a rare one, 'e is, Captain Bennick! Kilt my lad, 'e 'as!"

Nick froze. *Could it be...?* The crazy old hag from the ribbon shop? But he had no time to hesitate now, for sharp fingers tried to gouge out his eyes, clawing and stabbing with weathered nails. She was not strong, but she was frantic, and he could scarcely even shield his face, let alone fight her off. At last, he was able to dislodge her by rearing backward and slamming her head into the door frame.

She crumpled at his boots, dazed but not dead. He yanked her to her feet. "Who are you? How did you get here?"

But before she could make a sound, a pistol cracked, and she slumped in Nick's arms. Dead. A pool of blood was slowly spreading on the floor... on his hands. He released her in shock, letting her crumple to the floor.

He pivoted, eyes zeroing in on the man clutching the still-smoking pistol. With a guttural roar, Nick lunged at the man, intent on meting out swift vengeance. But Duncan, driven by the same fervor, beat him to it, wrapping his arm tightly around the shooter's throat, choking off any chance of escape or mercy. "Ye daft eejit! Thought ye could get one over on us, did ye?"

Nick drew the pistol he had just picked up and pointed it at the man's head with a snarl. "Why did you shoot her?"

"It were *ye* he were aimin' for," Duncan growled. "Milady gave him a kick and a shove at the very last tick."

"Who was she?" Nick demanded. "Do you know?"

Adelaide was sitting up now, and she looked quizzically at him. "Have you seen her before?"

He nodded. "She knew my contact, the one who betrayed me to Chesterfield. Blast, I needed to know who she was!"

"I never knew her name. Only 'the washerwoman.' This was her... establishment, and she claimed that man there—" Adelaide sneered at the man Nick had shot— "was her son. But I never believed that. Perhaps it was true."

"Aye, but this one's no'. I'm meanin' to bloody the bugger," Duncan spat, pressing his knee into the throat of the man who had tried to shoot Nick.

"Not just yet. We need him to talk first." Nick wiped a trickle of blood from his lip, then gave his hand to Adelaide. She took it and struggled to her feet, then wrapped the remains of her cloak about herself. "Are you well?" he asked.

She nodded, but her eyes never left her foe—not in fear, but in thought. She was bloodied and battered, no less than he was, himself. Yet somehow, she held herself erect. A soldier, if he ever saw one.

That was more than he could do. Nick leaned against the wall for support, his body aching from the toll of the fight. His rib must truly be cracked through by now. Beads of sweat trickled from under his mask and mingled with the blood and grime on his jaw, and something was piercing sharply against his lungs when he drew breath.

"Is the other one dead?" Adelaide's voice cut through the haze in his mind, her tone eerily calm.

Nick, still catching his breath, merely nodded in affirmation.

"Search him thoroughly."

Holding his ribs, Nick bent to rummage through the man's pockets. They seemed strangely bare, as if he had deliberately traveled light. Adelaide's voice, softer now, but no less authoritative, came again, "Look inside his boots."

Casting a curious look her way, Nick caught the gleam in Adelaide's eye. Was that a note of intrigue in her voice? She responded by delicately dabbing away a smudge of blood from her alabaster cheek with a pristine satin handkerchief. "This is not my first encounter with that fellow, Captain."

His curiosity piqued, Nick obliged. The first boot revealed only a grimy stocking. However, as he tugged at the second, a neatly folded slip of paper made its unexpected appearance, drifting lazily before settling on the cold floor.

And there it was—the unmistakable script of General Richards, encoded, but it was a message Nick had seen before. He scanned it quickly, and within a few seconds, was able to make out the name "Wellington."

"This is it. We've stopped it." He passed the message to the lady, then bent to question the surviving attacker who was even now groaning at Duncan's feet. He rolled the man over on the floor and brought his own pistol up under his chin.

"Now, then," he began, "who do you work for?"

The man glanced towards the lifeless form across the room. "That one there. Ye've done him in. Now I work for nobody."

Nick's voice dropped to a dangerous whisper, "And you'll still tell me what you know. I've spilled blood in defense before, and if need be, I won't blink to do it again. But play this right, and you might walk out with a breath left in you. So, where were you off to next? Who's waiting for your report?"

Fear flickered in the man's eyes as he hesitated. In response, Nick's grip tightened on the pistol, priming it with an ominous click.

"Buckland," he growled.

Buckland? Nick fought a tremor of his hand. "And whom were you to meet?"

The man said no more. He only glared back, as if daring Nick to pull the trigger. Nick studied him for a moment—the way his breathing was growing weaker, the faint rattle in his chest. Surely, his lung was punctured, and it made Nick grow cold to listen. One more hard hit in the sternum, and that could be him.

"Look here, you haven't much time, unless I send Duncan here in search of a physician. Do you want to live? Or do you prefer to gasp your last with my knee on your chest and your own pistol held to your head? *Whom* were you to meet?"

The man's face had taken on a yellowish tinge, and he closed his eyes and coughed. "Enough, you bastard," he muttered. "'Twere the ostler." Another cough. "Bittern Hollow."

Nick's grip loosened on the pistol. Tim! *Tim?* The most useless bag of flesh in the whole south of England? *That* ostler?

He sat back, his expression dazed. Dimly, he was aware of Adelaide motioning for Duncan to find a doctor for their captive, so they might keep him alive long enough to bring him to justice. Much good it would do them. But Nick's mind was already miles away, stumbling for reason and sense where there seemed to be none.

Was it possible that the old ostler had made him from the beginning? That he... *oh*.

Nick scrambled to his feet. "I've got to get back to Buckland," he was muttering. "Back to the Bittern, at once! Milady, will you be well? I must go!"

Adelaide caught his arm as he strode past. "Captain, whatever it is must wait. You have to get word to Durham, to let him know we have intercepted the message."

He jerked his arm away with a hiss. "We've succeeded. That is enough for now!"

"Captain, you must—"

"No! I *never* wanted to be part of this, and I've done my duty. Now, I need to make sure I haven't put others at risk."

Chapter Twenty-Seven

BESS'S WRISTS WERE BOUND so tightly that she had almost no room to even wriggle them, and her hands grew increasingly sore and raw. Beads of sweat mingled with the blood trickling down her hands as she fought desperately to free herself. Her arms had long since grown numb, but not the painless sort of numb. Every clumsy twist of her hand shot jolts of fire up her arm, straight to the nerves of her neck. But it was just rope... and rope could stretch. Knots could be pulled at, and sweat-streaked wrists could slip free.

Moonlight streamed through the window, casting silvery rays upon the room and all the faces within. Over the heads of the soldiers keeping watch, Bess could see the road stretching westward. Every now and then, her eyes darted to the wind-stirred woods from the other window. Nick *might* come from there, but she dared not let her gaze linger there. She must not betray any hint of that possibility to the soldiers.

Oh, but would it matter? Even if he did not come by the road, the moment the soldiers heard the call of the nightingale, he would be exposed.

Eight o'clock. Had it only been half an hour since the soldiers stormed her home and dragged her upstairs? Each tick of the wooden clock on the mantel grated like a rusty hinge, shooting bolts of fury and despair through her veins. Bess wrestled and strained against the bedpost, desperate for just an inch of slack in the ropes.

With each effort, her fingers, coated in a grim mix of blood and sweat, fumbled over the cruelly knotted binds. Why the deuce wouldn't they give? The persistent strain on her wrists was maddening, made worse by the agonizing twist of her arms yanked mercilessly behind her. Every new angle of pull, every fruitless tug seemed to scream one word back at her: *trapped*.

There *had* to be a way. She took a deep breath, attempting to block out the pain, to clear the panic from her mind. But as the minutes dragged on, the daunting reality loomed larger: she might truly be out of options. Oh, where was her father? Where had all the customers gone, and Sarah and Hattie? Would *nobody* come to her door to plead for her release? Bess clenched her eyes and choked back the sobs—they only made the gag more odious and drew the attention of the soldiers to the quakings of her breast when she cried.

Nine o'clock. One of the soldiers went back downstairs for more ale, and when he returned, he was laughing about "that dodgy innkeeper weeping like a woman in the straw." Bess stopped straining at her binds long enough to pay attention, and it sounded as if her father was just as much a prisoner as she. He could do nothing to help her... and it seemed there was little she could do to help herself.

What if she *did* manage to free one hand? Her body was cinched tight to the bedpost with more ropes. She could not possibly loosen all of them—not without the soldiers noticing. And even then, did she really think she could tear off her gag and make it across the floor before they overpowered her? Rip open the window and shout a warning at Nick before he came into range?

Her heart thudded as a chill crept through her bones. Shouting out the window at Nick would be the very *worst* thing she could do. If he heard her voice and thought she sounded as if she were in peril, he would try to race to her rescue. No! Even if she could get to the window, it would only doom him. But there must be *something* that remained in her power!

Ten o'clock. The soldiers traded the watch at the window, and the new guard levered into position, their muskets at the ready. The ones who were relieved exchanged looks and jeers, elbowing each other, whispering, and, worst of all, pointing at her. Bess tried to slouch, to hide from their stares, but it was as if they had purposely forced her into a posture where her figure was on full display. Their lecherous stares were a different kind of torment, their implications clear and revolting. She felt exposed, violated by their gazes. And the gag in her mouth prevented her from voicing her disgust as she had always done in the past.

Chesterfield was the worst. He did not keep watch with the men at the window, but sat idly behind her upon her bed, his feet propped out before him as he stared at her back. Occasionally, he would lean forward and catch a lock of her hair to wrap it around his fingers, and chuckle to himself when she tried—unsuccessfully—to jerk her head away. No doubt he had seen how her hands were plying at her binds and had not bothered to stop her. Why would he? He knew she could do nothing about it. But sometime after the clock struck ten, he got up to relieve himself in the chamber pot. She closed her eyes and heard him laugh.

"Maiden, indeed," he scoffed as he turned back to her. "We shall see, Miss Reynolds."

Bess opened her eyes to glare at him, but the gag made her heave when she tried to growl her outrage. Chesterfield only snorted and went to join his men with their ale.

But he was no longer sitting behind her. Inspired, Bess began her struggles afresh. Her hands had cooled and grown sticky in the darkened room, and they felt thick and swollen. Like lead—too weak to hold their shape, but too heavy and awkward to move readily. But her desperation was stronger still than the numb pain that lanced through her hands.

Eleven o'clock. A mad plan had begun to take shape in her mind. Even if she *could* cry out the alarm, Nick would only be drawn to her voice. But if he heard a shot… if he thought someone was shooting at *him*, he would turn and flee. He would do it to draw the shooter away from her, and to keep from harming any honest soldiers who were only following orders. He would ride away on that black devil of his and would not return until long after the danger was gone.

The musket beside her beckoned. The long shaft of the barrel crushed against the left side of her ribs until she was bruised, but if she twisted just a bit, and writhed both hands together, she could almost reach the cold steel in the moonlight. If she could not free herself, she might at least change the ending of this nightmare.

But oh, what it would mean! The muzzle pressed under her heart, the shot would certainly tear through flesh and bone. Her very life! Could she do it?

Could she *not*?

Chesterfield had made his intentions for her plain. He would make her watch as he shot down her love, taking her spirit and the light of her life… and then he would take the rest at his pleasure. And what then? Would he merely cast her off? Find some excuse to kill her? Or hand her over to his dogs to pick at her bones?

Fear had long since given way to hatred and revulsion. How *dare* that measly grub of a human, that miserable excuse for a man, plot to take everything from her? The only way she could think of for Chesterfield to be robbed of his victory and Nick to be spared was for her to find the courage to do the unthinkable.

Bile filled her throat, and she gagged against the neck cloth in her mouth. The sobs were too much to keep at bay now, but half the men were drunk enough that they did not notice how she trembled. Bess squeezed her eyes shut, and a flood of tears splashed down her cheeks.

She wept and raged and prayed against fate, for the hand of God to intervene, but another half an hour slipped away, and no earthquake shook the inn. No holy gale swept through the window to strike down her foes, and no urgent message was brought to the soldiers, declaring their warrant to arrest a good and worthy man all a misunderstanding. Denial was no help, and tears availed her nothing.

And so, she embraced icy determination, stretching her nearly useless fingers until she was sure her hand must be severed from her wrist. She had to be close... the trigger guard was withing reach. A hair's breadth farther!

And then, just as she thought she could strain no more, the clock began its solemn midnight chime. As the first stroke resonated through the room, Bess's fingertip brushed the cold metal of the musket's trigger. She sucked in a sharp breath. Was that truly it? Such a small thing! Gently, she swept her throbbing finger over the curve of the metal to be sure of it. And, indeed, it was hers.

She dared not move more. Chesterfield could come sit behind her at any moment, and any sound heightened her chances of being discovered. What she had was enough, and it could not be long now. Nick would not want her to watch until the small hours of the morning. He would come as soon as he felt sure of his way, and as soon as he knew that even the boors at the tap would be long gone from the inn. Surely, the next hour would see him riding to her.

Bess's breaths had grown steady now. The life she had hoped for, the love she had cherished—all hope of those was lost. But for Nick, for the man who saw *her*, and gave up his own chance of happiness to serve others, she would do this one last thing. The soldiers meant to use her to kill him, but she had the means to save him.

The first hint of distant hoofbeats was barely more than a whisper, but it was enough to jerk Bess's senses taut. It was as if every fiber of her being zeroed in on that distant *clip-clop*.

The regular rhythm cut through the stillness, growing louder and clearer with each passing second, the anticipation winding her tighter. Would the others hear it? The weight of the moment pressed down on her, dread and hope colliding. It became an incessant drumbeat in her ears, drowning out everything but the knowledge of what was to come. Was that Nick?

The sound grew even louder and clearer, and there was now almost no doubt in her mind that it *must* be him. He approached by the western road, and was it her imagination? Or did she hear a shrill whistle on the wind, the call of that black nightmare he rode as she drew close?

Bess cast anxious glances at the soldiers. Why weren't they reacting? Were they so drunk on her father's ale that they failed to notice? From her constrained vantage point, a moonlit path stretched over the hill, and soon, a silhouette galloped into view. It *was* Nick, with his scarlet cape and his buckskin breeches, and a billowing black mane before him.

Realization finally dawned on the soldiers. Once languid, they were now propelled into a sudden frenzy, their hands scrambling over muskets, their voices muted to harsh whispers. They lined up at the window, one man almost stacked atop another until Bess could no longer see him. But she had never needed to see Nick to know he was there. Her heart felt like a trapped bird, battering against the cage of her ribs. The room fell deathly quiet now, each man waiting for the horseman to come into range of his musket.

Bess closed her eyes and her nostrils flared in one last breath. The world seemed to narrow, her focus purely on the man out there on the highway and the trigger at her fingertips. He would never again hear her voice, saying that she loved him, but she prayed he would live knowing that she had loved with the last breath in her body.

In that suspended moment, her finger grazed the trigger, and she opened her eyes for one last act of defiance. It was Captain Chesterfield himself who happened to glance round, and when she flashed that final look of contempt, his jaw fell suddenly slack with a mix of alarm and realization. His reflexes surged to life, and he lurched across the room, shouting her name. With lightning speed, he jerked the musket just as she gave a vengeful press of the trigger. And the shot that should have shattered her, instead blew through the windowpane, blasting shards of glass and wood splinters about the room.

The soldiers erupted into a flurry of shouts and curses, their actions a blur of motion. The acrid scent of gunpowder hung in the air, shrouded by a fog of smoke and dust. Bess was dazed, her ears ringing, and she shook her head. How was she still breathing? She should be dead.

"Fire, lads, fire!" Chesterfield shouted. "Bring him down!" Muskets blazed from the window, but when they all fell silent, there were no cries of triumph, and no one was bothering to reload.

"Damn you, whore! You've ruined it!" Captain Chesterfield roared at her. "The blackguard has flown back to the hell he came from!"

Bess only blinked in the face of his fury. Why was he yelling at her? *Oh!* The blur of confusion passed nearly as quickly as it had struck, and she almost laughed in his face despite the gag. She had won! Chesterfield had lost his prey, and Nick was safe.

But the same could not be said for her.

Chesterfield's fist lashed out, striking her with a force that would have sent her sprawling, if she had not been trussed to the bed. Pain exploded across her face, down her neck, and across the back of her head where it slammed into the bedpost. Her nose and her forehead gushed blood, crimson droplets staining the floor beneath her. Dazed and disoriented, she struggled to focus her gaze, her vision blurred by an instant swelling of her cheekbone and a bleeding gash just above her eye.

"Get her out of here!" Chesterfield barked at his men. But then, as they were beginning to untie her wrists, a different thought flashed across his face—a cruel satisfaction in denying her a dignified end. "No, wait! Take the gun away from her. Let them think she carried it off." A twist played at his mouth. "And go untie the innkeeper, long enough for him to hear and spread the word. Tell him that his daughter loved a villain more than her own life."

Bess's head rolled; her eyes crossed. She would have spat the blood from her mouth right into his face, if she could... just...

But the blackness rolled over her, and she knew no more.

Chapter Twenty-Eight

H IS PULSE RACED, MATCHING the mad thunder of his horse's hooves. The evening's chill seeped through his cloak, but the cold he felt was more from dread than the biting air. That wretched ostler had burned both ends—first betraying his country to the French, and then using the militia to set a trap for anyone who might be able to finger him.

How much did Tim know? He used to watch Bess everywhere she went with a lecherous eye. Had Tim ever seen Bess go into the woods? Could he have learned that she was keeping watch for Nick himself? If so, she was not safe at the inn any longer.

As the distance shortened and the inn drew closer, his sense of urgency only heightened. Every second felt crucial. He knew the path ahead well, and he strained his eyes, trying to catch a glimpse of that familiar casement—*her* window. Had she drawn the shutters like he'd told her to? Or was she sitting there with her candle burning bright, waiting for him to gallop up with a whistle?

He spurred his horse faster as the Bittern Hollow Inn began to take form against the horizon. Every thud of hooves against the cold, hard ground echoed the beat of his heart. Memories of late-night conversations held under hushed breaths, secret embraces shared over her roses, and of course, those last few moments beneath the window, when he had reveled in the luxury of her hair, played before him. A few moments more—that was all, and she would be in his arms once more, and he could know that she was safe. He'd ask her to climb out, if he had to, and he'd put her on his saddle and carry her off until he knew all would be well.

The biting October wind lashed against his face, numbing his cheeks, and blurring his vision. Yet, even through the sting of the wind, he could see that the comforting light was missing. The shutters were flung wide, but the window, through which he had worshiped her warm presence so many times, was dark tonight.

A cold weight settled in his chest, heavier than the wind's chill. Something wasn't right. Alarm bells screamed in his mind, clashing with the distant memories of warmth and safety. The absence of that guiding light, he feared, might indicate an absence of something even more crucial: Bess's safety.

The mare's ears twitched, and she tugged on the bit as she recognized the familiar scent of the Bittern Hollow Inn. Then, without warning, she lifted her head and released a sharp, piercing whinny that shattered the stillness of the night.

Oh, blast! If something *was* amiss, he had no hope now of a discreet approach. "Steady, girl," he whispered, his voice tight. "No more of that!" Perhaps if she made no more sound, it could be overlooked as the screech of an owl.

But as the final notes of her cry faded, a louder, more ominous sound filled the night air—the unmistakable crack of a musket. Time seemed to slow for a fraction of a moment, and in that tiny window, all his fears for Bess surged forward, compounding with the immediate threat to his own life. Panic, visceral and potent, clenched his gut. Whoever was shooting at him, he had to draw them away!

Instinctively, Nick wheeled Black Bess about and spurred back to the west—back toward Buckland, where the Redcoats had first set upon him. With any luck, he might even meet up with his own men again. He risked only one glance over his shoulder, to see if he was being followed, but all his senses discovered was the cold wind screaming past him. Trees became blurred streaks as they dashed westward.

Seconds after the first shot, a chaotic volley of musket fire followed. It was a sound he knew well—a disorganized, panicked melee. Each shot echoed in the distance, none close enough to pose a real threat. Still, their speed and intensity told him all he needed to know. This wasn't just one or two stray soldiers; it was a coordinated effort, and something had gone wrong. The shots sounded desperate, as if the redcoats had misjudged their range or had been startled. Either way, their blunder gave him a critical edge.

As trees closed in around him, their dark branches obscuring the path, he turned and caught a last glimpse of the inn. From this distance, Bess's window was but a dark speck… but there were no other windows with such a clear view of the road. And a sudden realization pierced him—the shots *must* have been fired from her very window!

So, where was she? Had they moved her? Or... His heart stopped dead in his chest. Was it possible that they were using her as bait?

His immediate impulse was to circle back, to ensure her safety, but reason restrained him. Engaging now would jeopardize them both. He couldn't help her if he was captured or worse.

Lord Durham was his best chance. The safe house was not just a refuge but a beacon—his sole hope of clearing his name. Only then could he return for Bess, armed with a plan and the means to ensure her safety.

THE FIRST LIGHT OF dawn hadn't yet crept over the horizon as Nick galloped up to the woodsman's cottage where Durham was waiting or him. The long detour, throwing any potential pursuers off his scent, had cost him precious time. Fatigue weighed heavily on his eyelids, but adrenaline and determination kept them open. His mare's breathing was laboured, her flanks slick with sweat, but she had refused to break her gait, even when he had tried to let her catch her air.

The door of the cottage burst open before Nick had fully dismounted, and Lieutenant North rushed toward him, followed closely by Sergeants Daniels and Wesson.

"Captain!" North greeted with a sharp salute, though concern creased his brow. "We were growing worried. Are you injured?"

Nick braced a hand against his injured side and leaned on his horse. "The inn," he began, his voice cracking, "Bess's window... shots fired. Tell me what you know."

The men exchanged confused glances. "*Shots* fired?" North repeated.

Nick nodded. "What happened? Was it Chesterfield?"

Durham stepped forward from the shadows of the doorway. "Hunt, we've heard nothing of this. Where is Adelaide? Is she safe? Did you intercept—"

Nick ripped the intercepted message from his breast pocket and shoved it at Durham. "She stayed behind. The inn, Durham! Where are the militia?"

Durham's eyes scanned the message, and his chest rose in a sharp sigh of relief. "You've done well, Hunt. But as to the militia, the last we saw them was... North? Did you not say they lost your trail five miles south of Buckland? And that was a full day ago. We've heard nothing more."

Nick's heart plummeted. The uncertainty, the not knowing, was perhaps worse than any news could have been. "Who holds Chesterfield's leash? Colonel Stanwick? I need Chesterfield called off immediately, so he stops trying to shoot me!"

"All in good time, Hunt," Durham soothed. "I have no authority over the colonel, but I have good contacts who—"

"Oh, to hell your contacts! I need to know what's happening at the inn!"

Durham closed his mouth and shook his head. "I can't help you with that, Captain."

North stepped forward, his jaw tight and his stare steely. "I can, though. Chesterfield doesn't know me. Even if he is still there, waiting for you to return, I can get to the village and ask questions without raising his suspicions."

Nick yanked his gloves off and slapped them on his thigh in frustration. "Would that I had my uniform, but it's ten miles away! 'Twould be nothing if I were to present myself as a captain. They might arrest me, but they would not shoot me."

"With all due respect... *Captain*..." Durham put in, "I doubt that. Richards had no intention of letting you be brought to court martial on those charges. You know too much, and he wanted you silenced."

Nick tore off his tricorn and snagged his hands through his sweat-soaked hair. "Then what do you suggest, my lord? And make haste to speak, for I am mere seconds away from galloping back there myself!"

Durham scoffed. "Be reasonable, Hunt. Your horse is done in, and you're barely standing yourself. Your lieutenant here has a capital suggestion. Were you not so frantic and exhausted, you would see the sense in it."

Nick blew out a sigh and felt his rib scream in protest. "Very well," he mumbled, sliding his gaze to North. "Bring me word as soon as you can."

North gave him his hand—firm, reassuring, and confident. "I'll not fail you, sir."

THE COTTAGE INTERIOR, SUFFUSED with the scent of old timber and cold stone, felt narrow and stifled when Nick ducked inside. As his eyes adjusted to the darkness, he let Wesson take his coat and carefully loosened the buttons of his shirt to inspect his side. As he peeled back the silk shirt, a sinister shade of purple revealed itself. Each inhalation caused the injured rib to shift and the bruise to pulse with fresh agony—each exhalation a momentary relief before the cycle began again.

Sergeant Wesson noticed his captain's grimace and change in posture and was at Nick's side in a moment. "Sir," Wesson asked, "may I?"

Without waiting for a response, Wesson gently probed Nick's side, causing him to wince. "You've likely got a broken rib there, Captain. Best to lie down, keep quiet for a bit. Movement will only aggravate it. I'll ask Daniels to fetch you something to wrap your ribs."

"I don't need to rest," Nick argued, trying to pull away from Wesson's probing fingers. "I'll wait for North to report back."

Wesson met his gaze, unyielding. "Sir, with all due respect, Lieutenant North won't be back for hours. You killing yourself with worry won't make him return any faster."

Nick absorbed his sergeant's words, then hissed a sigh and nodded. With Wesson's help, he slowly made his way to a makeshift cot in the corner. Lord Durham was at his side in a moment, helping Nick to ease down to the cot. "You did well, Hunt," he murmured, his hand resting on Nick's shoulder. "Lord Aston would be proud to hear of it."

Nick grunted, his eyelids already weighing heavily. "You'll clear my name?"

Durham glanced over his shoulder to be certain that Wesson had gone back outside. "I will speak with no less a figure than His Majesty," he whispered. "King George has taken a special interest in the affair. Rest assured, with the evidence we've gathered, Richards won't see another sunrise as a free man. And I promise you, within two days, the truth will be known and you will be a hero rather than a wanted criminal."

Nick nodded, his voice barely a whisper. "Thank you, my lord."

With a final nod, Durham turned on his heel, his boots echoing against the wooden floor. From his prone position, Nick could hear the distant creaking of carriage wheels and the faint clop of horse hooves as Durham made his departure. And that was the last thing he remembered for hours.

THE DISTANT THUD OF hooves, initially a backdrop to Nick's fitful dreams of Bess, grew louder and more pressing. Their beat resonated, piercing his hazy consciousness, pulling him back to reality. As clarity returned, Nick opened his eyes just as Lieutenant North burst in the doorway, face contorted with sheer terror.

Nick shot upright, despite the screaming protest of his ribs. "North! What is it?"

Lieutenant North's gaze darted to Daniels and Wesson, then back to Nick. His hesitation did nothing to relieve Nick's fears.

"Speak, man!" Nick demanded.

"It's... It's about Bess, Captain," North began hesitantly. "I spoke with the village blacksmith. He... he said that the redcoats... the innkeeper's daughter... she..." He took a deep, shuddering breath.

"What? Tell me!"

North swallowed. "It was Chesterfield, sir. They said he marched on the inn at dusk and sent all the customers away. The old innkeeper he trussed up in the cellar, and his daughter, they dragged to her room and... sir, please do not stand!"

Nick was already struggling to his feet, his face hot with rage, but Sergent Daniels, with his great bulk, pushed Nick back to his cot. Nick shot his sergeant a glare for his insubordination, but then his attention was all for North again. "And what? Did he harm her? Out with it!"

North screwed his mouth shut and looked at the floor. "The redcoats had her tied and gagged. They, uh... the villagers say she was watching for her lover through the window. She shot herself to warn him off."

The room seemed to tilt and spin, and his face felt cold as ash. Nick staggered to his feet once more and, mindless of protocol, shook his lieutenant by the lapels. "No, no, you must have heard wrong. It can't be true!"

North grabbed his captain's fist and twisted it until he could grasp Nick by the hand, and stared gravely into his eyes. "I thought the same, sir. No one can believe it. But... I confirmed the report with a woman from the ribbon shop and a serving girl at the inn. They all said the same."

Nick's world crumbled. The walls of the cottage seemed to close in on him, and he felt the crushing weight of grief, guilt, and regret pressing down on him. Tears streaked down his face as he collapsed to his knees, a guttural cry of anguish tearing from his throat—raw, primal agony such as no man should bear.

The sobs wracked his frame, the sheer intensity of them threatening to consume him entirely. Time seemed to stretch and distort, every second weighed down with the gravity of his loss. But as the waves of grief washed over him, something began to change. Deep within, a spark ignited, transforming the raw edges of his pain. The crushing sorrow started to give way, replaced by a heat, a burning, building anger.

He lifted his head, his teeth clenched and his eyes glittering with pure, unbridled fury. "Chesterfield," he spat. "I swear on everything holy, I will make him pay!"

Daniels stepped forward, blocking Nick's shoulder with a firm hand. "Captain, we need to think this through."

Nick whirled to face him, eyes blazing. "*Think?* There's no more time for thinking!"

Wesson, his brow furrowed with worry, chimed in, "Sir, you're injured, you cannot—"

But Nick cut him off, pushing past both sergeants. "Chesterfield will die for this."

He thrust the safe house door open with a violent crash, the wood slamming against the outer wall. His men followed close behind him, but Nick heeded them not. Instead, he dashed to the bush behind the cottage, where the horses were hidden. Finding his black mare, he approached her, tenderly stroking her muzzle.

"Forgive me, girl," he whispered, his voice thick with emotion, "for asking this of you." Then with one fluid motion, he swung aboard, and gathered his rein for one last ride.

Chapter Twenty-Nine

BESS'S SENSES RETURNED TO her slowly. First, the musty scent of straw and old wood greeted her nose. A dull, throbbing pain pulsed at her temple, making her wince. She tried to move, but her limbs felt heavy, her hands and feet bound with a weathered rope that chafed against her skin. Confusion clouded her mind, memories jumbled.

She blinked several times, allowing her eyes to adjust to the dim light. The room looked vaguely familiar, but she wasn't in her own bedchamber. There were no decorative curtains, no soft rugs. This place was much more spartan. She tried to sit up, but the binding on her wrists hindered her, pulling at her skin and sending a fresh wave of pain down her arm.

A golden ray of sunlight peeked through a crack in the window, casting a narrow beam across the wooden floor. Outside, the distant crowing of a rooster confirmed it was morning.

Realization washed over her like a tidal wave. She was in the lower room of the inn—the very room where Nick had stayed on his first night. Panic rose in her chest. Why was she here? Where were the soldiers? And what had happened after that fateful shot?

She wriggled her wrists, testing the ropes, but they held firm. With every passing second, the memories of the previous night came crashing back—her intended sacrifice, the thundering hooves, Nick's shout. She needed to break free, to find out what had happened and, most importantly, to find Nick.

Light from the lone window cut across the room, drawing sharp contrasts between shadow and illumination. The dust in the room seemed to dance to an invisible tune, swirling and glinting as they caught fragments of sunlight. The ropes bit into her flesh; her wrists were chafed and raw, the dried blood making the bonds even more unyielding.

Yet, the memories of her earlier struggle had sharpened her resolve. Every pull, every tug at the rope that had previously seemed futile, was now her weapon. She'd studied this trap. Now, with no one to actively stop her, she would find a way out.

Carefully, she shifted her weight, biting back the pain as her stiff muscles screamed in protest. She managed to tuck her feet through the loop of her bound arms, and gradually, inch by inch, her hands moved from her back to the front.

The relief was immediate yet fleeting. Her hands, now in front of her, were still bound, but this slight change in position awarded her a vantage she hadn't had before. Bess's gaze now flicked over the knots, learning their structure, understanding their make. She might not have the use of her fingers, but her teeth could serve.

Her heart raced as each second ticked by. The absence of guards might have granted her some time, but she was under no illusion that her window of opportunity would remain open for long. If they were truly gone from the inn, someone would have already freed her. No, they must still be upstairs. And that must mean they had not yet captured Nick.

The taste of iron hit Bess as she bit at the stiffened knots around her wrists. The dried blood had stiffened the ropes, made them impossible to work upon with what little she had available to her.

Her eyes darted around the room, searching for an alternate escape route. They landed on her ankles—still bound, but easier to manage than the rope at her wrists.

With renewed hope, she lifted her ankles close to her fingertips. The knots there were tight and complex, but without the hindrance of dried blood, they were somewhat more pliable. With gentle tugs and strategic twists, she felt them give way little by little. The sensation of the rope loosening around her ankles was like a breath of air, nearly the same as when she went swimming with Samuel as a child and would rise to the surface after being underwater for too long.

The last loop of the rope fell away, and for the first time in what felt like an eternity, Bess could move her legs freely. She flexed her ankles, relishing the fleeting sense of victory. But there was no time to dwell.

Bess moved cautiously around the room. Each step was deliberate, each creak of the wooden floor beneath her a potential alarm. She tiptoed softly to the door and, without touching it with her hands, put her ear close to it for a moment. There was no sound.

Cautiously, she pressed against it, and the heavy thump of a wooden bar from the other side confirmed her suspicion. They had locked her in.

But the door wasn't the only way out.

There was still the window—assuming the soldiers had not found some way to lock it, too. It looked like it was frozen with rust, so they may have left it alone. But she had slipped through it once herself. At the time, she had been little concerned with the noise from the hinges. She could not possibly afford a sound now.

Nick had been able to slip out that window almost soundlessly. Perhaps if she were more patient this time, more deliberate... unless the redcoats had somehow locked it, too.

She approached it, her heart hammering in her chest, hoping against hope that the redcoats had overlooked it in their haste. But even if they had, would Chesterfield truly have left her unattended? Surely, a guard lurked just outside, waiting for her to attempt this very thing. Bess crept toward the window, edging into the corners of the room to keep out of sight in case there was a redcoat waiting outside. Carefully, she stepped round each angle, peering through the funnel of the window from corner to wall and back again.

She allowed herself a breath of relief. No guards stationed outside, no sound of approaching footsteps. It was as if, for a moment, fate was on her side.

With trembling fingers, she began working on the window. The initial tug yielded little movement, but she was using as little force as possible. Perhaps... just a bit more... With a combination of gentle nudges and firm pulls, she felt the first hint of give in the window. And wonder of wonders! A tiny crack of light shone through the edge. The cool morning air wafted in, bringing with it the promise of freedom.

Slowly, now... she could not let that tiny success make her sloppy. Carefully, she turned the hasp a little further, pushing the frame outward, and felt a rush of fresh air. With every inch she moved, she listened, ready to retreat at the slightest hint of danger.

The yard, eerily devoid of activity, held no guards or sentries. But occasional bursts of laughter, originating from directly above her, served as a chilling reminder of the ever-present danger. Glancing upwards, her pulse thundered in her ears. The glint of the musket's barrel peeked from her own bedroom window.

Drawing a silent breath, she took a moment to consider her situation. Her hands, still tightly bound, limited her movements, but her feet remained her asset. The room's sunken design, coupled with the ground's proximity to the window, played to her advantage. Gritting her teeth, Bess anchored her feet against the window's ledge.

With all the grace and discretion she could muster, she hoisted herself, her legs straining with the effort. The window, though wide enough, proved a tight squeeze given her restrained hands. Clumsily, she managed to roll out of the room and onto the ground outside.

Instantly, she was on her feet, hugging the building's exterior to shield herself from the watchful eyes above. Punctuated conversations and easy laughter continued to echo from her room, giving Bess the brief window of distraction, she needed. She would have to move fast.

Just then, that cursed rooster, with its bright red comb and gleaming eyes, spotted her and tilted its head. He was probably looking for his corn, and he followed her movements expectantly. Bess turned sharply away, hoping he wouldn't think she was coming toward him. But the wretched thing started strutting after her, let out a sharp cluck, followed by a resonant crow.

Heart hammering against her chest, Bess froze in place, every instinct screaming at her to run, yet fearful that any sudden movement would bring those guards to the window. "Shh," she whispered desperately, her eyes darting towards the bird. "Quiet, now!"

She dared to lift her gaze upwards, half expecting to meet the eyes of a curious soldier. But the laughter continued, unabated, and no shadow darkened the window. It seemed, miraculously, that the rooster's call had gone unnoticed, or perhaps the soldiers had grown so weary of hearing it all morning that they now knew to ignore it.

Bess didn't hesitate another instant. With light, rapid footsteps, she skirted the edge of the building, keenly aware of every sound, every rustle. The eastern corner of the inn beckoned, and she willed herself to move faster, every ounce of her being focused on reaching cover. As she rounded the corner, and the distance between her and her captors grew, her breathing lightened, and her feet flew ever faster.

What time was it? Surely, there should be people about. Bess cast a desperate look to the sky and found the sun almost at its zenith. The London coach should be due at almost any minute. And with its departure, the prospect of escape.

But that thought would have to wait. Before she could think of saving herself, she must first see to her father, and learn what had become of Nick.

T HE MISTS HAD BURNED off the moors; the fog lifting to reveal a bleached road, its ruts and grooves withered by the winds of the night before. Hardly a soul stirred on the highway east from Buckland, but of those who did, not one dared to pause or stare at the raving maniac in the blood-red velvet coat, who dashed round bends and bore down upon hapless travelers as if the very devil were at his heels.

Nick's voice split the heavens and echoed over the rolling moor—a raw, inarticulate shriek of rage and grief that seemed insufficient to his agony. The earth itself would pay! Every ounce of his being demanded vengeance for the injustice dealt to him and to his beloved Bess. And if the price for her death should be his own blood—he, who had brought the monster to her door—then so be it. His life in payment of hers.

"Bess!" Nick's cry shattered the silence shrouding the heaths. "*Why you?* It should have been me!" He broke down, shuddering with sobs even as he screamed curses and revenge. He would put his blade to Chesterfield's throat, if Fate should give him that chance. He would make the man plead for his life, and then he would exact the price that was owed. No more, no less.

Black Bess was foaming at the mouth, with droplets of red spraying from her nostrils, but she wanted no whip or spur. The moment he'd touched the saddle, she'd sensed his wrath. Now, her blood was up, her hooves pounding the dirt road with frenzied courage. For five miles, she galloped thus, never slackening her pace—not even when Nick's spine stiffened as the blackened roof of the inn came into view.

And there was the fated window—the very casement through which he had last kissed her. The glass through which she had waved that last farewell. Now, it was not Bess leaning out to greet him, with her hair tumbling in sweet waves for him to lose himself in.

Now, it was a cluster of muskets.

Nick drew his rapier and pierced the golden sky, its edge menacing and defiant. "*Chesterfield!*" he thundered. This time, his cry took on a different timbre. It was darker, fueled by a pure, fulminating rage. "I swear on her life, Chesterfield, you'll pay for taking her!"

Red-coated soldiers lined the inn's windows, muskets at the ready, their eyes trained on him. Every man among them knew the exact distance for a clear shot. Every man, including Nick.

But Nick didn't care. He spurred his mare forward, driving her faster and harder towards the looming danger. With every stride, the inn grew larger, the soldiers more distinct, and their muskets more menacing. Whispering an apology to his loyal mare, he gritted his teeth, eyes locked on the prize—Captain Chesterfield.

"Chesterfield!" It would be the last word he would utter—the name of his enemy, the one who had taken the light from his life. At the last second, Nick tossed his rein to the wind and drew his pistol as he plunged into range of the soldier's guns.

Then came the thundering of muskets. The world erupted in a cacophony of smoke, fire, and lead. Two bullets found their mark, slamming into Nick's shoulder with searing intensity. Pain radiated through him, his vision blurring with a mix of rage and agony. The force of the shots jolted him, toppled his mare, and the sky spun round his head as his boot slipped from the stirrup.

The ground met him with a cruel thud. Blood filled his mouth, and breathing was an impossible torment. And as darkness crept into the edges of his vision, the delicate fabric of his lace cravat floated down, settling gently across his face as the world went silent.

THE SLANTING SUNLIGHT BARELY lit the ale cellar, casting a muted glow on the aging oak barrels and the cobwebbed corners of the room. Bess eased the door open, the rusty hinges creaking softly. As her eyes adjusted to the dimness, she took in a heartbreaking sight: her father, bound to one of his own barrels, his dear, familiar face marred by a bloody gash on his forehead. Was he breathing? He did not lift his head at her entry, and her stomach squeezed in panic.

"Papa?" she whispered, tears forming in her eyes.

His head jerked up, a look of utter shock and disbelief on his face. "Bess?" he rasped. "Oh, my Bess!" Tears streamed from his eyes, glistening trails down his dirt-smudged face. "I thought you...Chesterfield told me you'd taken your own life."

Bess swallowed hard, her throat tight. "I meant to." She sniffed, then nodded. "But now, I mean to live. Come! We must go before they discover I am missing!"

He was still shaking his head, his jaw slack and his misty eyes caressing her face. "Oh, my child! Can you ever forgive me?" His face crumpled and his body trembled with sobs. "Had I not pressed you! Only had a little faith—"

"Shh, Papa." Her hands were still bound, but she lifted them together and cupped his face. "You were only trying to protect me. Now it is my turn."

She stood and fumbled around in the dark, searching for the old sharpened wedge he kept there for prying lids and mending staves. Surely, it must be... *there*. Her fingers closed around cold iron. It was not very sharp, but it would be enough. Awkwardly, with her tied hands, she began sawing at the ropes binding her father.

Once he felt the ropes loosen, he began to jerk and tug frantically at the loops until they fell away. His first act as a free man was to cradle her cheeks with both hands, his fingers rough from years of hard work but tender with love for her. He sobbed openly, pulling her into a tight embrace.

"Oh, my child," he wept, his voice thick. "I thought I'd lost you forever!"

She sniffed and shook her head. "Never for a moment."

His fingers traced her quavering smile. "We are a fine sort, are we not? Here, let me cut your hands free."

Bess lifted her wrists, and her father touched them with a gasp. "My child! Your hands—that brute!" He shook anew. "What have they done, Bess? Did they..."

She shook her head. "I was used badly, but not what you fear. Quickly, Papa!" She thrust the ropes into his blade, and he hacked his way through.

"We need to find somewhere to hide, at least until those soldiers are gone," he whispered.

Bess nodded, her eyes darting around the cellar. "Have you heard anything about Nick? Do you know if he's safe?"

He shook his head. "No word. All I know is they're looking for him, and Captain Chesterfield refuses to admit defeat."

Before Bess could respond, a sudden scream pierced the air, echoing through the cellar's stone walls. *"Chesterfield!"*

Bess's heart leaped into her throat, her pulse pounding loudly in her ears. That was *him!* She held her breath, both hopeful and fearful of what would come next.

"I swear on her life, Chesterfield, you'll pay for taking her!" The voice, unmistakably Nick's, reverberated with a mix of rage and desperation.

"Dear God," her father breathed. But Bess was already on her feet, her skirt gathered in her fist as she punched open the door of the cellar in a headlong dash to find her love.

And then, a chilling succession of gunshots sounded, splitting the tense silence. They were merciless—round after round, no doubt tearing flesh and bone. The gunfire's rapid staccato left a deafening silence in its wake.

The color drained from Bess's face, and her legs buckled beneath her. "Nick!" she gasped, her voice barely audible, trembling hands gripping her father's arm for support.

Chapter Thirty

WITH A WILDNESS BORN of raw terror, Bess's feet pounded against the cobblestones as she rounded the inn's corner. The world seemed to narrow to a singular point, everything else fading into a blur: the soldiers, their attention having been so singularly focused on the fallen man, now turned their gazes upon her. The realization of her escape rippled through their ranks, with shouts of "She's out!" and "The girl's escaped!"

Captain Chesterfield, in the midst of barking orders to his men, paused as his cold eyes locked onto Bess from the window above. Their gazes clashed, his filled with surprise and a hint of fury, hers blazing with a mix of anguish and hatred.

With a haughty lift of her chin, Bess turned away from Chesterfield and ran, but Chesterfield's voice raged behind her. "Bring the whore back!" he snarled to his men. "Who was posted guard? Have him flogged!"

But Bess cared nothing for his threats. What matter if he sent his soldiers to recapture her? They could do no worse to her than they had just done! Her arms pumped, her feet flew light and fast, and she raced toward Nick.

His motionless form lay crumpled on the road. His horse was downed in the ditch, her sides heaving with shallow breaths. Every step Bess took felt like an eternity, her breaths coming in short, sharp gasps, not just from the exertion but from the rising tide of dread threatening to engulf her.

But she was not alone, for the rapid footsteps of the soldiers thundered behind her. She had the earlier start, but they had the advantage in every other way. Every fiber of her being strained towards Nick, his prone form drawing her closer with a pull stronger than the tide for the shore. She was so close! Just a few steps more, and she could cradle his head, see to his wounds, offer whatever solace she could.

But then a vise-like grip clamped around her upper arm, yanking her backward. The world spun as she was whipped around to face her captor. The momentum nearly made her lose her balance, but her assailant's grasp kept her upright, albeit barely. She blinked against the disorientation, her eyes soon locking with the steely gaze of one of Chesterfield's men.

"You thought you could escape us?" he sneered, his breath foul with ale as it washed over her face.

Bess, panting and desperate, slammed the heel of her shoe into the soldier's instep. Ladylike, it was not, but she needed to get to Nick, and every second mattered. "Let. Me. Go," she hissed, trying to wrench her arm free.

He laughed. Why should he not? He was only the first of half a dozen redcoats to swarm her, and there was no reason for him to fear her. As more soldiers approached, ready to seize her, a deep, guttural sound resonated in the silence, followed by the unmistakable clatter of hooves against cobblestones. At first, the soldiers paid little heed to the noise, dismissing it as the death throes of a wounded animal. But then chaos ensued.

From behind, a seething mass of black muscle and rage burst forth. Black Bess, her eyes savage with fear and pain, bore down upon the soldiers, her powerful body cutting through their ranks like a storm. Soldiers scattered, taken off guard by the mare's sheer ferocity and speed. She was a beast unhinged, squealing and whistling as she struck with hooves and teeth. With no further thought for Bess, their company exploded apart; some reaching for pistols that proved to be already discharged. Not one of them dared take hold of the mare's bridle.

As the mare surged closer to Bess, her ears were pinned flat against her head, her teeth bared in a threat that promised disaster to anyone who dared approach. Bess trembled. Nick had said that his horse could be fearsome, but she had never seen *this!*

But just before the bared teeth lashed out to strike, Bess put up a hand and murmured her name. "Easy, my lady," she crooned. "There, there, you have won. See? You have set them to flight, but I am not come to harm you. Do you remember me?"

The mare paused as a candle snuffed out—the fierce ripple above her nostrils smoothing as the fire faded from her eyes. Her ears swiveled, and she cast one more threatening sneer at a soldier who looked as if he might dare to do something foolish. Then she licked her lips, blew out a sigh, and took a step toward Bess. A lame step.

Bess darted in, her fingers exploring the mare's black flesh until she discovered the dark, wet stain on her shoulder, and the unnatural angle at which she held her leg. It looked grave. She cupped her hand over the bullet wound to try to stanch the flow of blood, but she had neither the tools nor the knowledge to truly help.

"I promise, Black Bess," she whispered, her voice thick with tears, "once I look after Nick, I'll see to you. Hold on just a little longer."

She gave the mare one last caress, then turned back to Nick, ready to fight for him with all she had. As she reached him, she collapsed to her knees, her hands trembling as they brushed the strands of hair from his bloodied face. His chest rose and fell, each breath ragged and shallow, but it was a sign that life still lingered within him. Tears of relief and despair mingled on her cheeks.

"Nick," she choked, pressing her palm against his cheek, willing him to wake, to give her any sign he heard her. The soldiers, disarrayed and on edge, kept their distance. The horse's savagery would not keep them at bay for long, but in that moment, Bess's entire life was bound up in the fragile rattle of Nick's chest and the thready pulse at his throat.

But one last set of footsteps sounded behind Bess, and these were not the boots of cowed men. "What in the devil's name is going on?" Chesterfield thundered. "Why are you men just standing there?"

One of the soldiers, a younger man with a wavering voice, pointed to the horse. "She's a devil, sir. A real beast! She went for us, she did. No horse acts like that."

Chesterfield scowled, his eyes locking onto the injured horse. "Then put the outlaw beast down. It's crippled anyway."

Eyes darted among the soldiers; none had a loaded weapon ready. Growling with impatience, Chesterfield drew his own pistol and stalked toward the horse, angling for her forehead.

"No!" Bess cried. Nick's head was still in her lap, but she held a hand out in entreaty. "Captain, the horse belongs to me! You will not destroy her."

Chesterfield cocked her a cynical glare and laughed. "You are full of false tales, Miss Reynolds."

"I will prove it!" Gently, Bess lowered Nick's head to the ground and rose to her feet, dusting the road from her skirt. Then she walked to Black Bess and gathered her rein. The mare draped her head round Bess's shoulder, sniffing her clothing and emitting a low chuckle in her throat.

"There. I dare you or any of your men to do the same," Bess said, leveling a challenging stare at Chesterfield.

He scoffed. "Anyone can walk up to a horse when it's calm and wounded." He marched closer to prove his point... but he made only three paces before the whites of the mare's eyes showed and she made a lunge for his throat.

"Egad!" he yelped. But with a jerk of his red coat, he squared his shoulders and tried to recover his dignity. "It's a trick. You've been feeding it, or you're a witch."

Bess shook her head. "No. I'm the natural daughter of her first master—the highwayman named Cumberland. And apparently, I must call one or the other of her masters to her mind."

Chesterfield swiped a gloved hand across his mouth. "Enough of this nonsense. Mystical highwaymen and murderous horses? Stand aside, or the first bullet goes into you." He raised his pistol again, closing one eye.

But Bess would not move. She lifted her chin, her eyes streaming, and prayed with everything she had for a miracle. What was to stop Chesterfield from shooting Nick, his rival, next? Only mercy, and the captain seemed to possess none.

"Hold your fire, Chesterfield!"

Bess, still sheltering in the bend of the mare's neck, peered with desperate curiosity at the new arrival. It was Colonel Stanwick! Even in her fraught state, she recognized the insignias, and recalled the name of the regiment's commander. Flanking him were men she didn't recognize, but from their grim expressions and the way they seemed to rally around Nick's fallen form, she deduced they were his loyalists.

"Captain Chesterfield," Colonel Stanwick growled, "I told you to bring down Captain Nicholas Hunt, not engage in a massacre at Bittern Hollow Inn."

Chesterfield gritted his teeth. "I was merely putting down a wounded animal, sir."

Cold fury flared in Stanwick's eyes. "You kidnapped innocents! Captain, your reckless actions have endangered the populace and brought dishonor to this regiment. Arrest him," he ordered, pointing at Chesterfield.

Two soldiers stepped forward hesitantly, exchanging glances, but they did as commanded, securing Chesterfield's hands behind his back.

"Lieutenant North—" the Colonel then directed his attention to a younger officer who had been standing in the backdrop. "Please confirm the identity of Captain Nicholas Hunt and attend to him immediately. And one of you see to the beast's wounds. Perhaps it can be saved."

Lieutenant North approached Nick's prone form, nodding. "It's Captain Hunt, sir." He then started barking orders for medics and supplies, doing all he could to save his captain.

Another of Nick's men quietly approached Bess and eased the horse's rein from her hand. "It's all right, Miss," he promised. "She may not like me much, but she doesn't bite me anymore. I'll try to clean her wound." He tugged on the bridle, and after a few seconds of hesitation, Black Bess limped after the sergeant.

Meanwhile, a cluster of men were gathered around Nick, and their voices, the words they exchanged, gave her hope. "Bullet in the shoulder," she heard. "Broken rib... Bullet in the thigh..." But no one said he was dead. Yet.

Bess watched in detached amazement, her heart surging with real hope for the first time in days. Nick and his horse were now captives, it was true... but they were safe. As the blur of uniforms and shouted instructions surrounded her, a hand touched her elbow and a kind voice spoke at her side.

"Am I to understand that you are the woman that Captain Chesterfield bound to her bed as a prisoner?" Colonel Stanwick asked.

Bess nodded numbly.

"Then I am pleased to discover you are somewhat more alive than the reports I heard. I hope you will be so good as to give me a full account of the affair, for I shall collect the evidence to use in Captain Chesterfield's Court Martial."

She blinked and swallowed, her voice trembling. "Y-yes. But first... please, may I go to Captain Hunt?"

The colonel looked hesitant, then relented. "As you wish, madam."

NICK SLOWLY DRIFTED TO consciousness, the weight of pain pressing him back into a hazy delirium. Pain... why was there still pain in death?

But it was inescapable. The first sensation that struck him was the dull throb in his shoulder, a pulsing torment that echoed the beat of his heart. His thigh and upper arm ached too, sending sharp reminders of the ghastly things of yesterday. However, overshadowing these, a leaden weight around his chest cracked fire through him with each breath.

His eyelids felt impossibly heavy, but he worked them open. All he could see was a stream of red-gold light cutting across the room from a window he didn't recognize. The unfamiliarity of the place combined with the setting glow of the sun made him consider for a brief moment that he must have crossed over to another world—that this was what lay beyond life.

But then he felt it: a warmth encircling his hand, anchoring him to the tangible world. Nick mustered enough strength to lift his head ever so slightly and was met with a cascade of black hair spilling over the side of the bed. *Bess.*

His heart gave a great flip, and the wound in his shoulder swelled in tandem until he dropped his head back again. Was that truly Bess? Then, either he truly *was* dead, and they had somehow found one another in the hereafter...

Or she was alive. And that would mean that he was, too.

He moved his hand in hers, testing the softness of her skin and the living warmth of her grip. Sweet glory, she *was* alive!

More cautiously this time, he raised his head off the pillow to look at her. Her forehead rested on the mattress near his hand, her black lashes twitching ever so slightly over her cheeks in dreams. A wisp of hair had slipped over her face, and it drifted gently in and out, with the rhythmic rise and fall of her breath.

Nick's gaze shifted, and he caught sight of a soldier, standing at attention, his expression stoic yet watchful, guarding the room. The scene slowly pieced itself together in his mind. He wasn't dead, not yet, but he wasn't out of danger either.

"Bess," Nick rasped, the name slipping weakly from his parched lips.

Her response was immediate. Her head jerked up, and her wide, tear-swelled eyes met his. Recognition and relief painted her face in quick succession.

"Nick!" She brought both her hands up to cup his stubbled cheeks. "Oh, Nick, please tell me you are well!"

He managed a feeble smile, letting his hand tangle in a ripple of her hair. "Considering I just woke up to your face, I should say that I'm doing better than expected."

Bess let out a fragile laugh, but her eyes were still shadowed with worry. "You gave us quite the scare," she whispered, leaning in to press her forehead against his. "Lieutenant North has been here almost every moment, and he only left half an hour ago because Colonel Stanwick ordered him to."

Nick's cheek flinched. "Stanwick? What happened to Chesterfield?"

"Arrested," she retorted, with almost savage satisfaction.

"And I assume I'm under arrest, too?"

"You *did* brandish your weapons at a troop of His Majesty's soldiers. What the devil were you *thinking?*"

He let out a short laugh and immediately regretted it. "I was thinking I'd lost everything that mattered to me," he wheezed. "I think Heaven must have broken the chains of Fate, for I cannot think of a single earthly reason that neither of us managed to die."

She brought the back of his hand to her lips and kissed it, then rested her cheek against it. "What do you mean by that?"

He lifted his head. "If any of *my* men were such terrible shots, I'd have them horse-whipped."

Bess sputtered a laugh, then dashed a tear from her cheek. "I should say that lot deserved it."

He let his head fall back to the pillow, a weary smile warming his face, but then a look of horror dawned. "Black Bess... I felt her fall. Is she...?"

"Sergeants Daniels and Wesson are tending to her. They've been sending word to me, because they knew you would ask the moment you awoke. They said to tell you it is the same as with Rob Roy, whatever that means."

His chest fell in relief. "Then she will live, God willing." He snagged his fingers through the thick of her hair and allowed a whimsical smile. "She may never terrorize the night highways again, but I plan to hang up the velvet coat. She's earned her retirement."

"I doubt you will be able to convince *her* of that." Bess smiled down into his eyes, then leaned in to press a soft kiss to his chapped lips. "I will bring you some ale," she whispered. "Or would you rather have tea?"

He caught her sleeve and shook his head. "I just want you."

She let him draw her back and settled again at his side. Nick wrapped her hand up in his and kneaded her fingers as his eyes drifted closed. "How did you convince your father to let you stay with me?"

Bess traced the lines of his face with her free hand. "I told him who you were. And he told me who I was."

Nick opened his eyes. "What does that mean?"

Bess glanced at the soldier standing guard, whose eyes had been fixed to the wall through the entire exchange. Then she leaned to whisper in his ear. "It seems that your Mr. Cumberland was my natural father. That was his objection to you—he thought you were a son, and therefore, my brother."

Nick's eyes rounded in awe, then he chuckled weakly. "Well. I have heard many things that were more unbelievable than that. Perhaps the truth will smooth my way when I ask for your hand."

Bess kissed his forehead. "Get to your feet first, soldier. That's all I want for now."

He smiled as his eyes drifted closed again. "Yes, ma'am."

T HE SUN HAD RISEN to a brilliant golden hue, casting warm glows throughout the inn. The low hum of conversation and the clinking of dishes and mugs permeated the air. Bess moved lightly through the room, the tray she carried filled with a steaming pot of broth, fresh bread, and a cup of tea—all for Nick.

"Oi, Bess! Any chance for a cuppa over here?" shouted Mr. Watson, one of the regulars, as he waved her over.

Bess flashed a radiant smile. "Sorry, Mr. Watson, not this morning! This is a special delivery."

Her father, emerging from behind the counter, met her gaze with an enigmatic expression. "Bess," he began, stopping her with a gentle hand on her arm, "it's poor form to be neglecting our good customers."

"But, Papa, I..."

He interrupted her with a chuckle. "I am only teasing, lass. It warms my heart to see you so happy. I never thought I'd see the day my child would let her head be turned by *anyone*, but I see it's gone far beyond mere fancy. You look like a girl swept off her feet."

"Swept off my feet—nonsense. Everyone knows it was I that chose him."

Her father laughed. "And a lucky bloke he is." He clapped his hands, bringing the room's attention to him. "Sarah! The patrons need their coffee. Bess's serving days are officially over, and I'll thank you all to congratulate her on her betrothal."

A smattering of applause erupted, with a few cheeky cheers. As the noise settled, the inn's front door swung open, admitting a gust of fresh morning air and the imposing figure of Colonel Stanwick. His sharp eyes found Bess, noting her tray, and his lips thinned in obvious approval. Approaching with measured steps, he removed his hat.

"Miss Bess," he greeted with a nod. "I assume by your tray that Captain Hunt is mending?"

"He is somewhat better this morning," she replied. "Sergent Wesson tended his wounds and believes that he will heal in time."

"Very good. Would you be so kind as to take me to him?"

Bess inclined her head. "Of course, Colonel. Right this way."

She led the way, the weight of the tray in her hands now seemingly lighter than before. With practiced ease, she shifted the tray to one hand and turned the latch on the door of his room. "After you, Colonel."

"No, I insist. I'll not keep an injured man waiting for his breakfast, or make a lady wait in the hall." He caught the door and held it for her.

This was a new thing. Was *this* the way gentlemen treated ladies? And was she considered such a creature now? Her cheeks unaccountably warm, Bess waltzed into the room with the tray, and the colonel helped her to settle it on the foot of the bed.

Nick tried to sit up to attention, but the colonel stopped him. "At ease, Captain. I shall make this brief, given your present condition." He withdrew a letter from his pocket, the seal broken, and held it out.

Nick took it, and his eyes widened when he examined the wax. It was the seal of King George himself! "Durham," he murmured.

"I'd imagine you will comprehend what a singular honor you have received," the colonel replied. "That came by express rider only this morning. Whatever this business was—and I was not told the whole of it—the king has granted you a full pardon. You are no longer under arrest, Captain."

Relief etched in Nick's face, and he folded the letter to clasp it tight. "Thank you, Colonel."

Colonel Stanwick chuckled. "You ought to read the rest, Captain."

Nick's brow clouded, and he opened the royal letter again. And all the color drained from his cheeks. "*Knighted?*"

The colonel offered a tight smile. "As it pleases His Majesty. It seems that you have some powerful allies, Hunt."

Nick's eyes found Bess, a dazed smile growing. "I am gladder simply to be a free man, with my own name again."

"Indeed. Captain, I would like to apologize on behalf of all my men. Chesterfield stepped outside his orders for personal reasons, and that is a thing I do not take lightly. You may be assured that he will be tried for his offenses."

Nick nodded, his gaze once more wandering to Bess. "Thank you, Colonel."

"I have assigned three men to assist your Lieutenant North with anything you should require. The lieutenant has accepted the innkeeper's offer of lodging for your men for now. I imagine it will be some days before the War Office gets round to communicating your new orders. You take my meaning, I expect?"

Nick's smile widened. "Understood, sir."

Stanwick dipped his head quickly. "Then, I shall take my leave. Rest well, Hunt." He bowed to Bess, then turned and closed the door behind him.

Bess eased up to his side, drawing a chair so she could help him with his tray. "What did he mean when he said it would take time for your new orders?"

Nick accepted the teacup from her and sipped. "It means we are on informal leave for now. But that doesn't matter to me, anyway. I'm selling my commission and going back to Lincolnshire. What do you think, my love? Should you care to be a lady of the manor, wife of a knight of the realm? Lady Hunt. How well that sounds!"

"Better even than... what was it you said they called me? 'Duchess of Surrey' or some nonsense?" She took his empty cup away and leaned in to kiss him—this time, with the heat of promise and desire. "I just want to belong to you. That's enough for me."

He brushed the hair from her cheek and twined it around her fingers. "Me too, my black-eyed, bonny Miss Bess. Me too."

Epilogue

18 December 1810

T HE SNOW-COVERED FIELDS OF Lincolnshire stretched before them—broad, open, and less wild than the heaths of Surrey. Nick rested his head on the squabs and simply gazed adoringly at his wife as she took it all in for the first time. As they approached the tiny village, the fields gave way to naked groves and tidy garden fences, and the streets were soon lined with neat little cottages.

"Not much farther now," he said. "Just through the village and half a mile beyond."

Bess nodded. Her gaze never left the window, but her hand strayed to his, their fingers tangling. As the carriage drew past the last house in the village, he sat up and pointed to the left. "There it is. Modest like I said."

Bess's breath caught, and she snatched a look at him that spoke of hope and pleasure. "It is just right." But then she clamped her teeth into her lip. "And your father... you *did* tell him about me? *All* of it?"

"Everything. We've no shame to hide, love. If he still bears any resentment, it will be for me alone. I have not always been the son I ought to have been."

She squeezed his hand. "It's all new, now. A fresh start for all of us. Even for the two of you."

"I hope so." He peered around her shoulder at his father's estate and let go a tight breath.

Indeed, he *had* written to his family that he was coming home, and that he was bringing a bride. He'd owned his mistakes to his father, spoken warmly of his mother and expressed his longing to see his sisters and Alex.

But his letter was met with only a short reply, carried by an express rider. *"Alex is gone. You are my only son now."*

Nick had spent hours in grief over that news. So much time lost! To never again see his brother? It was a wound he would carry the rest of his life, knowing that he had been a month—nay, a week too late. But what more must his family have suffered? And he had not been there for them through it. He was a faithless sort of son, to leave his family to mourn his brother alone. That it had been in the service of king and country was paltry consolation when Nick thought of his grieving parents.

What sort of reception awaited them now? Had he been forgiven, or did the bitterness of Nick's absence still linger in his father's heart?

He prayed not. He prayed for peace, and for a home and family he could happily lay down his life for. It *could* be a good future for him and for Bess here. He had not yet resigned his commission, but he would, soon. After he could be sure that his men would be properly reassigned, and promoted as they ought to be. Once that was settled, all his thoughts would be for his home—his wife, his family, and aye, even his two favorite horses.

The carriage grew closer and he could see the full face of the house now, its stone face warmed by the late afternoon sun. He sketched it again in his mind, recalling details long forgotten.

He had lived here only a few years before going away to school, then enlisting in the militia, and had only seen the house a handful of times in all the years between. But the peacefulness of the country had always appealed to him, and he felt sure that Bess would be at home here.

The wheels of the carriage crunched against the gravel as it rolled to a stop in front of the main entrance. The horse-drawn van carrying Black Bess followed closely behind, its sides heaving and rattling as its precious cargo stomped her impatience to be freed. She would live out her retirement as a pampered queen, as she deserved.

A dog rose to his feet and barked, and the manor door flew open. Nick's mother dashed toward the carriage, her eyes, undimmed by age, locked onto him. Bess gripped Nick's arm, helping him alight. Before his feet touched the ground, his mother swept him into her arms, tears cascading down her cheeks.

"Oh, my dear Nicholas," she choked, her voice thick with emotion. "To see you again, after fearing the worst..."

Nick gently pulled back, his eyes cloudy. "I'm home, Mother. And I've brought someone special."

His mother's gaze shifted to Bess, who stood beside him biting her lip, with her dark eyes wide in apprehension. "This," Nick began, offering Bess his arm, "is my wife, Bess."

The older woman reached out, taking Bess's hands in her own. "Welcome to our family, my dear. We've heard so much about you. I feel like you're my own daughter!"

Before more could be said, two younger figures, their dresses fluttering, sidled up beside Nick's mother. Both clasped their hands over their skirts and held back with shy smiles.

Nick's eyes stung with tears. He would hardly have recognized his own sisters! He extended a hand, and Isabelle and Theresa threw themselves into his arms.

"Oh, my dears!" he rasped, taking each of their faces in his hands by turn. "Look how tall you both are! How I've missed you both. Look here!" He stepped back and wrapped an arm protectively around his bride's waist. "This is Bess," Nick introduced again, wrapping an arm protectively around her waist. "Your new sister."

Isabelle, ever the bolder of the two, stepped forward, extending her hand with a warm smile. "It's a pleasure to finally meet you. Nick's letter was full of nothing but you."

Bess laughed and took Isabelle's hands. "And to me, he has done nothing but praise you."

As Nick adjusted to the familiar faces around him, the manor door opened once more, and his gaze fastened on the man who emerged. *Father.* His approach was deliberate, but his eyes gleamed with newfound warmth and anticipation. Nick, taking a deep breath, stepped forward to bridge the gap that had once separated them.

"Father," Nick acknowledged, voice thick with all the respect he ought to have tendered long ago.

The older man paused for a moment, studying his son, as if taking in the years and battles that had molded him. "You've grown," he remarked, a hint of pride shining in his voice.

Nick gave a small smile. "It's been a long journey."

His father's eyes softened, and the corners of his mouth curled into a genuine smile. "Too long," he murmured. "But right now, all that matters is you're back. Welcome home, soldier."

W OULD YOU LIKE TO read more sigh-worthy romance? I have a swoony, second chance tale of love and adventure for you to try next! Reserve your copy of _The Shepherdess and the Soldier,_ and find out what secrets haunt Lieutenant North. Who is the mysterious lady who owns his heart, and will she ever forgive him for the mistakes of his past?

From Nicole Clarkston

T HANK YOU FOR INDULGING with me and spending a little time with this sweet couple. I hope you've had a delightful adventure! I would love it if you would share this book with your family and friends. As with all my books, I have enabled lending to make it easier to share.

If you leave a review for **_Bess and the Highwayman_** on **Amazon, Goodreads, BookBub**
or your own blog, I would love to read it! Email me the link at **Author@NicoleClark ston.com**

Would you like to read more sigh-worthy romance? I have a swoony, second chance tale of love and adventure for you to try next! Reserve your copy of **_The Shepherdess and the Soldier,_** and find out what secrets haunt Lieutenant North. Who is the mysterious lady who owns his heart, and will she ever forgive him for the mistakes of his past?

And if you're hungry for more, including a gift ebook of **_The Ruin of Lord Aston's Daughter_**,
stay up to date on upcoming releases and sales by **joining my newsletter: https://su bscribepage.io/V5dPFd**

Keep reading for a sneak peek at ***The Shepherdess and the Soldier!***

www.ingramcontent.com/pod-product-compliance
Lightning Source LLC
Chambersburg PA
CBHW020054180626
46812CB00006B/2323